EARL'S HELMSMAN

THE WARRIORS OF TIR NAN OG

BY ALISON SCOTT

Icy blackness swallowed Gil. His back scraped the stone of the Indian Kettle. The surge of water sucked him downwards. Ride it out! It ends soon! But it didn't end. Panic broke over him like a sea wave. I'm drowning. There's no doorway. No Underwater Bridge. No land of Northmen and knights. No Janetta . . .

Then suddenly the pummelling stopped and the roar of the whirlpool stilled. The white stone tumbled from his fingers and landed with a little thud. He was lying on his back, his arms outstretched. He opened his eyes and stared at a blue summer sky.

His shield lay on the grass beside him. Adjusting his sword belt, he stood up. Ten feet away, a rough grey slab of stone loomed upright amid flowering heather. Beyond was another and another forming a great ring in which he stood beside a glistening disc of water, blue as the sky above. Something white shone in the grass at the pool's rim. Gil snatched it up. Aidan's seeing stone that Feannag had carried to him across a thousand years of time.

In the Wood of White Trees, the path was worn and familiar, but when he looked down at Cille Aidan he recognised nothing. Seeking the church, he found only fire-scorched walls. The cells were roofless circles, the longhouse a ruin of charred timbers and blackened stone. Every building had been set ablaze. 'Like Camelot,' Gil whispered. He knew at once who had been here.

His foot clattered against something white that rolled over, revealing empty eyes. A skull with four small horns. "Why?" he cried aloud. "Why kill his little sheep?" Drawing his sword he ran down the hill into Aidan's desecrated hermitage, swinging the blade in vain fury. Then slowly, wearily, he lowered the sword. The weathered bone and the height of the meadow grass told him the burning of Cille Aidan was long past. Nothing moved here; not friend, foe, bird or animal.

He looked up. Feannag had come for him. Why, if there was no one left? Returning the sword to its scabbard he set out onto the wild hill, walking alone to the one refuge he knew: Magnus Redbeard's Einar's Holm. When he reached the last ridge, the sun had vanished. Rain splashed down. Legs shaking with hunger and weariness, he went on, drawn by the hope of fire and food and his friends, safely guarded by Magnus and Floki and sixty Viking warriors.

But as he climbed the final feet he was filled with a strange unease. Where was the smoke of the great longhouse hearth? Where the farmyard chatter of Einar's Holm? Cresting the ridge he stumbled to a disbelieving halt . . .

Pro Christo Domino

A cold winter, Odin's Maidens dance,
My household sleeps in snow.
Ravens claim my father's roofless hall.
Plough, seed and hairst
I bear a sea-king's scorn.
My longhouse sails a sea of bere;
My patience bears its fruit:
Seven swans and a farmer's silver
Avenge my love in chains.
Boldly, a sister pleads in vain:
I harry Frigga's Spindle south.
To merchant earl and Frankish hall,
I sail with the sons of kings.

from *The Saga of Floki Magnusson*
circa 900 (?) AD

Vast floods cannot quench love,
Nor rivers drown it.

Kethuvim

CHAPTER ONE

The day the Stonepecker came back, Gil Lake was fourteen years, five months, and twenty-three days old, according to his birth certificate; and fourteen years, ten months, and seventeen days old, according to Gil. It wasn't a big difference, really, less than half a year, but enough to keep him locked up in Safe Haven, probably forever.

"Lie!" Benita said. "Tell them what they want to hear!" It was free time and all the kids from both the boys' and the girls' wards were lying around on the grass under the big oak trees. It was the third week in September, already, but still hot. Benita gave Gil her 'look at me' grin and waved her cell phone. Gil stared at it hungrily. Say the right words and he'd get privileges, too. Even, maybe, go home at weekends, like Benita.

But Gil couldn't lie. Because what they wanted him to say was that his father was dead. And there was no way he was going to say that, even if he had to stay in Dr. Fairchild's clinic to the end of time. He shook his head. Benita shrugged; then flopped back onto the lawn. Her dark hair spread out across the grass and for a moment Gil saw another girl in another far place.

"It's not like you're that dedicated to the truth, Gil; is it?" Benita said, looking up at the trees. She turned and smiled wryly. Benita liked his stories about his Other Place; the knights and the horses, the Northmen and their great ships; but she didn't believe a word.

"It's all true," Gil whispered. But Benita wasn't listening. Her gaze was fixed on a branch above her head.

"Hey, look at that funny bird," she said. She propped herself on her elbow and stared. Aaron, Gil's roommate, who was curled up silently beside Gil, uncurled and squinted, and then Gil looked up and saw it, too.

The bird was huge; a crow, grey and black, with a fierce black beak and yellow glittering eyes. It flapped its black wings and made a hoarse, croaking cry. Benita shouted and Aaron covered his ears and buried his face against his elbow. Gil patted his back gently.

"It's okay," he said, trying to keep the joy from surging into his voice. "It's *Feannag*," he whispered wonderingly. "Now *everything's* okay." He stood up, never taking his eyes from the bird. Aaron crouched fearfully.

Benita stood, too. She tugged at Gil's sleeve and pointed, "It's got something in its mouth."

The bird made its raucous cry again; then raised its wings, swept from the branch, and flew straight at them. Benita and Aaron both shouted and ducked, but Gil stood there, still and sure, reaching out already for the treasure clamped in the huge bird's beak.

It fell, smooth and cool, onto his palm. His fingers found the hollow center and he closed his hand in triumph as the bird wheeled and soared away. "Thank you," he whispered, and shut his eyes.

Then suddenly he opened them again and stared at the sky. The bird was already a black speck against a puffy white cloud. "Wait!" Gil shouted. "How do I use it? I'm a hundred miles from the river and I'm locked up ...." His voice trailed away. The bird was gone and Aaron and Benita were staring at him as if he was crazy, even for here.

"What are you holding?" Benita asked warily.

Gil shrugged and opened his hand. "Just a rock. I picked it up to chase that monster." He shrugged again, amazed as usual how well he could lie when he wanted to. He closed his fist quickly around the stone and waved it at the vanished crow.

"It's got a hole in it," Aaron said and Benita reached her hand out.

"Let me see it."

Gil opened his hand. The stone was round and flat and

white, worn by river or sea; and in its center was a perfect round hole. "Hey, cool," he said as if he'd just noticed it. He shoved the stone casually into his pocket, his heart thudding. He could not tell them, even if they would believe him. *Home. This will get me home.* With a strange excitement he realized 'home' no longer meant his mother's house in Greene Mountain Falls, but another place, greener and more beautiful and far more dangerous than anyone in this world had ever known. And the stone would take him there ... but not from here.

He pictured the river at Greene Mountain Falls and the black eye of the whirlpool of the Indian Kettle Pool. Then he squinted up at the sun. September twenty-first. Saint Matthew's Feast. The equinox! Of course! The door would be open, so Feannag brought him the key.

But there was no time to spare – three days only at each Crossing time, Aidan had said. Then the door would close again until the Nativity. Gil groaned. Christmas. Three more months at Safe Haven was bad enough. But what of *there*, where time ran like the river in high water, and days turned into months and months to years?

Gil's eyes swept the empty sky as if Feannag would somehow return with the key to the clinic's black iron gates, as well. Then his gaze fell to the high stucco wall, featureless and impossible to climb, unless you were a cat. Unless. A hopeless yearning filled him and he seemed to feel the twitch of phantom paws and the flick of a phantom tail.

Maybe it would work here just once! he thought wildly. But he knew it wouldn't. He had tried. He had found circles and said the blessing and tried and tried until he felt silly and even doubted Cat had ever existed. *Change-things are gone from that world.* He heard Aidan's voice, a whisper of wind in the trees. His fingers tightened on the stone and he stared bitterly at the wall. A hundred miles. Just a couple of hours in a car. He needed help, adult help. But who?

Not his mother. Even if she sometimes almost believed him, she trusted Dr. Fairchild far too much. Not Danni's father, Brian; he didn't break rules. Nor her mother either: even flaky

Sophia thought he was "better off in here." Then his fingers gripped the stone hard. *Ivan.* Dad's weird friend on the river, with his ponytail and the eagle feather in his headband. Ivan. Crazy Ivan. Gil grimaced. The name said it all. Only Crazy Ivan thought Gil was sane.

He eased his grip on the stone and turned back to the others. They still watched him uncertainly. "Benita?" He smiled. She smiled back and flicked her long lashes, looking quickly away. Benita was sixteen and really pretty, but, kind of miraculously, she had a thing about Gil. And he certainly could have felt the same about her, in some other life where he'd never found Janetta.

He smiled again, uncomfortably. "Let me use your cell." She shook her head. He touched her arm softly. "Please."

She shook her head again. "I'll get in trouble," she whispered. But she handed him the cell phone anyhow. Turning his back, he hastily punched in Ivan's number and tapped:

Got2go.Plshlp.Gil.

He hit send, praying Ivan wasn't on the river or belayed halfway up a cliff.

A bell rang from the white clapboard clinic; not a jangling, buzzing bell, like at school, but a sweet bell, like a church bell. It was meant to be soothing, for kids like Aaron who freaked at loud noises. But for Gil it aroused, as always, a misery of longing for a low stone building beside an unreachable sea.

Benita held her hand out for her phone.

"Please," Gil begged, as much to Ivan as to the girl, clutching it a desperate moment longer. Then, as he turned to surrender it, the answer came:

2niteDude4AM.I.

Gil's face broke into a gleeful grin, as he hit delete.

"What's made you so happy?" Benita stuffed the phone back into her pocket.

Gil looked straight into her eyes. "My dog just had puppies," he said. "*Eight* of them." He didn't even blink.

That night, he dreamt of the Forest of Pentecost. Maybe it was the lie about the dog that started it. He'd gone to bed early and set his alarm for three-thirty, so, however Ivan planned on rescuing him, he'd be ready.

But then the next thing he knew, he was Cat, running through the night on velvet paws, low and long, tail stretched behind, a striped, orange streak through the dim snowy trees:

There was something round and small clutched between the toes of his right forepaw, but it did not slow him. Behind, he heard the baying of the hounds, the rough, low bark of the lymer, and then a high, sharp yapping. Terriers! They'd root him out, tear him to pieces. Ears flattened, he leapt frantically for a clump of tangled briar. Then something closed around his leg, like a jaw, bringing him down to the forest floor.

Then he was Cat no longer, but boy, lying helpless, looking up at a tall, grim figure, a knight in armor of glittering gold. Shadowed beneath his helm, the knight's eyes burned pitilessly blue, and then his handsome face broke into a smile as he raised his gleaming sword.

"No!" Gil shouted. "No!" He struggled to turn, flailing in the darkness. *Light flashed from the sword all around him* …. And then he was back in his room, tangled up in blankets, with Aaron staring wildly from his own bed. But the tall figure was still there, the blue eyes as piercing, the smile as broad.

"Get away!" Gil flailed again.

"Of course, Gil." Dr. Fairchild stepped courteously back. He pulled out a chair and sat down. "Is this better?" The psychiatrist smiled again. "You were shouting." He turned toward Aaron. "Your buddy here got a little worried."

Gil saw that Aaron was still clutching the red alarm cord by his bed. Aaron ducked his head. "Sorry, Gil."

"I think you had a little nightmare," said the psychiatrist. "I can give you something to help you sleep."

"No!" Gil cried, too loudly. He stole a glance at his watch. Midnight. In four hours, Ivan would be here.

"Alright, Gil," the doctor smiled soothingly. "But it would be best."

Yeah, right. Until Benita had taught him to spit pills out when the nurses left, Gil had slept twelve hours a night and the days were pretty foggy, too. "I'll be fine, now." He grinned wildly. "Too much cheese at supper or something."

Dr. Fairchild rocked his chair back and studied him thoughtfully. "I know you're not happy here, Gil." He spoke gently but his eyes peered fiercely into Gil's.

He knows. Gil clutched the stone in his right hand and pulled the covers up higher with his left. He had gone to sleep holding it, afraid if the nurses saw it they'd take it away – like they took away his laptop and his cell phone – even though they didn't know what it was. But Dr. Fairchild would know. Gil saw again the blue eyes beneath the knight's helm.

"Want to tell me about this dream?"

Gil looked up and met the same piercing gaze. "Sure," he said. He looked boldly into the psychiatrist's eyes. "I dreamt I was Cat in the Forest of Pentecost."

Dr. Fairchild was silent. Then he smiled again. "That must be fun, Gil, pretending to be a cat."

"I'm not pretending, and it wasn't fun with your hounds chasing me."

Fairchild leaned back in his chair and closed his eyes. He put his palms together like he was praying and rested his chin on his fingertips. "Gil," he said evenly, "Do you *perceive* why your mind casts me as the villain of the piece? Why *I* am always your enemy, the Golden Knight?"

"Because you are."

"Yes, that's true, Gil," Fairchild said mildly. Gil gripped the stone beneath the blankets. *Was he really admitting it?* But then the psychiatrist shook his head and added, "In a way." He leaned forward again and his eyes bored into Gil's.

"This is how I'm your enemy, Gil: you have walled yourself into a world of your own – a castle. Within it, all you want to happen; does happen. This wonderful fantasy place where you live this other life with the Vikings and the knights and the talking horses …."

"He's not a 'talking horse.' Lionheart's a normal horse, and I can hear him, that's all."

"And your father," Fairchild continued as if Gil had not spoken. "The best part of your fantasy world, your castle, the most important part, is that *there*, your father is not dead. In spite of all the evidence."

"No evidence. They never found his body. Still!"

"But he *is* dead, Gil," the psychiatrist continued smoothly.

"Your mother knows. His friends know. I know. And, yes, *you* know." He leaned forward. "You see, Gil, even a part of yourself is outside the castle, trying to get in. The real part of yourself that accepts rational evidence. That part knows your father is dead."

"He's not!" Gil raised a fist and dropped it. He saw Aaron watching with the frightened eyes he got when people shouted. Gil dropped his voice. "He's not dead. He's older, a whole lot older, and he's different, but he's not dead."

"Of course you cling to this," Fairchild smiled gently. "It's comforting ... but you *will* let it go. And then we can let *you* go."

"It's not comforting," Gil murmured. "It's really, really scary. But it's true. *That's* why I cling to it. Because it's true." He glanced again at Aaron who suddenly smiled.

Gil looked back at Fairchild. The psychiatrist's face was calm and remote. "Our minds are wonderful things. They think in pictures, don't they?"

Gil nodded uncertainly.

"Symbols," said Fairchild. "Metaphors. And what could be a better metaphor for a person attacking your 'castle' of fantasy, to wrest from you the 'treasure' of your false belief that your father is still alive, then a knight?" He smiled. "A Golden Knight, at that?"

"He's real. You know he's real. Because he's you. And you know my father's real, because you fought him. And *lost.*"

Something humorless flashed momentarily behind the calm. Fairchild suddenly reached inside his jacket, and Gil flinched. The psychiatrist laughed. "They don't allow guns in here, Gil," he said. He opened his hand.

"An iPhone?" Gil said. He felt sleepy suddenly and confused. "Why?"

"Show you something." The psychiatrist's fingers played across the little screen. Then he smiled and held it up for Gil to see.

"'Palamedes'" Gil read. "'Knight of the Round Table. In the Arthurian cycle ....'" He felt a surge of delight. "See!" he cried. "He's real. Sir Palamedes. He's a real person from history ...."

"He's a character from a tradition of Arthurian legend. And

you're reading about him on the internet." He flicked his fingers again. "Just like you read all the rest."

"No!" Gil protested.

Fairchild held the iPhone up again. "See. Here's Tir nan Og. The Gaelic Heaven, according to Wikipedia – oh, but that's wrong – *this* is Tir nan Og, right. It's us, isn't it?"

"They mean the future. People back there don't understand about the time thing," Gil said. "Look, I couldn't make it up. I never heard of any of it. The Northmen and the ships and the Standing Stones and Aidan's church – I've never been in *any* church before!"

"And it's all here, Gil. There's nothing you've told me I couldn't find right here. Which is where you found it all. Just like you found your Viking costume. And now you've walled it all up in your fantasy castle, so well, that even you can't get in to defeat it."

Gil buried his face in his hands. He was so tired. And Ivan was coming. Soon. "Okay," he said. "Whatever you say."

He heard the chair creak. Looking up, he saw Fairchild standing at the door, his hand on the light switch. "If you were me, Gil," he said quietly. "Which would you believe? That your father drowned in a kayak accident in white water? Or that he travelled through a hole in the river to King Arthur's Court and turned into Lancelot?"

He smiled and went out and turned off the light.

After a moment, Gil heard Aaron whimper. Aaron was kind of old for being scared of the dark, but Gil guessed he had reasons. Sometimes, with his curly dark hair, Aaron reminded Gil of Ismail who had travelled and fought beside him from Cille Aidan to Camelot. Ismail was African and an orphan, and Aaron was American with rich parents, but they had the same look in their eyes, like they expected to see bad things.

"It's cool, Aaron," Gil said. For some dumb reason, they weren't allowed lights after bedtime.

"Can I have the angel?"

"Sure." Gil reached under his bed for the drawer where he kept whatever books and games they allowed him, and found the angel hidden inside an old sock. Sophia had given it to him on her first visit. It was white plastic with sparkly stuff on the wings and a crystal in its halo. There was a battery inside to make it light up. Gil pushed the switch and grimaced. Sophia sure knew how to pick them.

But Aaron grinned happily when Gil put it on his bedside table. Then he put on a serious face. He put his hands together and rested his chin on his fingertips, exactly as Dr. Fairchild had done. "Do you *perceive* why I am such an idiot, Gil?" he declared in Dr. Fairchild's voice.

Gil curled gleefully on his bed and stuffed his blanket in his mouth to muffle his laughter. "You are an *ace* mimic, Aaron," he giggled. "Like *parrot extraordinaire!*"

Aaron grinned again. Then he put his hand out and held the angel. "Can I have a story?" he said.

Gil got up and went to the window. He pressed his face against the glass. The grounds were pitch-black. Beyond the wall, one streetlight flickered as the wind stirred branches in front of it. Nothing else moved. He looked at his watch, again, and tried to imagine how Ivan was going to get him out of here.

"Tell me about the dragon," Aaron said, from the safety of his angel light.

"You sure? It's pretty scary."

Aaron squeezed his eyes shut and then opened them. "But it can't get *here*, right?"

Gil thought quickly. Animals could cross at any time. Aidan said so. And a dragon was just an animal, like Floki told Bjorn. He imagined squashing it through the Indian Kettle and shook his head. "Wouldn't fit."

Aaron nodded in relief and clutched the angel like a stuffed toy, waiting for his story. So Gil told him again how the dragon had glided out of the mist on Alba's Great Loch and attacked their longship. And how Floki had fought it and nearly been killed by it, and then how Danni, who was just a fourteen-year-old Greene Mountain Falls kid, like himself, faced it with Floki's sword, and drove it away.

"And then we sailed on, to the Falls of the Fugitive, and the road to Camelot," Gil finished. "Okay?"

Aaron snored gently. Gil grinned. *Not my idea of a great bedtime story, but whatever makes you happy.* He got up and carefully took the angel out of Aaron's hand and switched it off. Then he sat down on a chair by the window, leaning against the glass, until, in spite of himself, he drifted toward sleep.

Something rattled against the window, shaking the pane pressed against his cheek. Gil started into bleary consciousness. Feannag again? Why? He had the stone already, still clutched in his sleep-damp palm.

He shaded his forehead with his hand and peered uncertainly through the glass. A lean figure, pale and ghost-like, moved on the lawn, its upturned face a smudge of white, pale hair haloing it. Gil's befuddled mind leapt to the Golden Knight's prison in Merlin's bone-strewn tower, and his miraculous rescue by the Viking, Floki Magnusson.

Then a light flashed below and Gil sprang to his feet. "Ivan!" he shouted; then clamped his hand over his mouth as Aaron stirred in his bed.

The light switched off again. Gil struggled to open the window. Locked. Of course. And alarmed. He waved frantically. Below, Ivan nodded. Gil could see the climbing rope over his shoulder, and the eagle feather tucked into the strap of his headlamp.

Ivan raised his left arm and pointed carefully to the far end of the dormitory. Gil's heart sank. The fire escape. Sure. But the door was alarmed, too. He shook his head, but Ivan only pointed more emphatically and then turned and strode away to where the metal staircase descended to the grass.

"Great, Ivan," Gil muttered, remembering that was always Ivan's way; teaching kayaking, or skiing, or climbing. Work it out yourself or die trying.

Thinking wildly, Gil scrambled around the dark room, pulling on his jeans and fleece over his pajamas, feeling for his socks and sneakers under the bed. Dressed, he slipped Feannag's stone into his pocket and stepped cautiously to the door. Opening it a crack, he peered down the corridor at the fire escape.

He turned and looked the other way at the stairwell at the far end of the hall. At its foot was the nurses' station. It would take the duty nurse about three seconds to climb the stairs once the alarm rang. Before he was halfway down the fire escape, the security lights would be blazing and the whole place crawling with staff.

He stepped back into the room, where his empty bed would proclaim his guilt, even if Aaron didn't pull the red cord in panic. He smiled wryly, remembering Aaron's Dr. Fairchild impression. Maybe Aaron could pretend to be Gil. *No,* he thought suddenly. Not him. Someone much better. Much, much better. Eagerly, he reached out and shook Aaron's shoulder.

Aaron sat up like a shot, mouth open to scream. "It's cool, it's cool," Gil whispered. "Just me." He reached to the bedside table and switched on the angel light. "See?"

Aaron looked around, blinking. "It's night. What are you dressed for?"

"I'm going away, Aaron," Gil said quickly. Aaron looked stricken. "And I need your help."

"*My* help?" The idea seemed to cheer him, so Gil nodded vigorously.

"Can't do it without your help." He paused. "Aaron, remember that kid, Tommy, who had the fits when they got his meds wrong?" Aaron nodded.

"Little Tommy?" He held his hand out, at Gil's shoulder height.

Gil nodded. "Can you do him? Like you did ...."

Aaron grinned hugely. Then he flopped backwards on the bed, rolled his eyes up so the whites showed and thrashed his arms and legs so the bed shook.

"Oh, *yeah*," Gil murmured.

"Look, I can drool, too!" Aaron demonstrated gleefully.

Gil winced. "Right. Perfect. You can stop now."

"I think I can fart ...."

"It's *fine*, Aaron. You've got the Oscar." Gil reached out and grabbed the red alarm cord. "Now, listen. As soon as I've gone, count to ten, and pull the cord. The moment they come in, do Tommy. You'll hear the fire door alarm, and the security lights will come on, but don't stop."

Aaron nodded solemnly. "You're going to your place, aren't you?"

"That's right."

Aaron's eyes got their sad, scared look. "Will you come back?"

Gil crouched down beside the bed. "Aaron, this place I'm going to, it's, like, kind of dangerous?"

"Dragons?"

"Yeah. Dragons." *If only that were all.* "But if I *can*, I'll come back. Okay?" Aaron shook his head. "Look," Gil grabbed Sophia's weird gift and stuffed it back in its sock. "You can keep the angel. Hide it before they come. But it's yours." He placed it in Aaron's hands, and Aaron made a small, brave smile.

Gil rose and stood at the door. Aaron's smile broadened. "Fight a dragon for me!" he called as Gil slipped silently into the hall.

Beneath the white exit light, Gil rested his hand on the steel latch of the fire escape door and drew a deep breath. Then he banged the door open and leapt out onto the iron grid-work. The alarm exploded into buzzing, jangling life. "Hang in there, Aaron," he whispered. "Pull the cord. Pull the cord!" Then, as fierce white lights flashed on all over the building, he clattered down the stairs.

"Ivan! I'm here!"

"Tell the world, Dude," Ivan laughed from the shadows. He caught Gil's shoulders in a friendly hug. "Right. Now, run!" He shoved Gil forward onto the light flooded lawn. "The trees!" Ivan shouted, and Gil lengthened his stride and sprinted for their shelter.

Ducking and dodging through the shadows of the tall oaks, they reached the wall. "Now, where?" Gil cried.

"Over it."

Gil stared up at the featureless barrier. His shadow loomed, huge and black. Behind, the lights yet blazed and shouts sounded over the jangling alarm. "It's twelve feet high!" he protested.

Ivan crouched down. "On my shoulders." He ducked his head and Gil straddled his neck, gripping the sheepskin collar of his leather jacket, as Ivan got to his feet. "Now stand and pull yourself up." Gil carefully got up on his knees on Ivan's shoulders, braced himself against the wall, and stood. "Watch the broken glass on the top," Ivan warned, adding in a growl, "Safe Haven, my ass."

Gil set his hands on the top of the barrier, just short of its jagged defenses, and pulled himself up. Below, Ivan dusted his hands with chalk from a pouch at his waist and leapt at the wall. Fingers and feet finding invisible cracks and lumps, he scampered up it like a spider.

A voice shouted close behind them. Ivan glanced over his shoulder. "Jump!" Together they launched themselves from the wall. Gil hit the soft ground, rolled over on his shoulder, and leapt to his feet.

Something gleamed in the streetlight, half hidden behind a fir tree. Gil peered at it and then shouted in glee, "Wow! You brought the Norton!"

"Well," Ivan wheeled his classic motorbike out of its shelter, "You said you wanted a ride on her." He plonked his helmet on Gil's head and tightened the chinstrap.

"What about you?" Gil said, mounting the bike behind Ivan.

"Not planning on coming off. Hang on!"

"Neither am I!" Gil shouted, but the wind tore the words away as the Norton roared out into the night. Dimly lit houses whipped past as Ivan threaded a route through quiet streets.

"That'll wake 'em up," he grinned over his shoulder. "Okay back there?" Gil nodded. "Well, hold tight." Ivan hunched forward and opened the throttle, "Now we're going to move."

"I thought ...." Gil shut his mouth and buried his face against Ivan's sheepskin collar as they pulled out onto the highway. The wind clawed at his hair, beneath the helmet, and the signs flashed by quicker than he could read. But Gil knew in his joyful heart, they were headed north.

Lulled by the ceaseless battering of the wind and numb with cold, he struggled against sleep; his mind drifting until he was on the back of a great white horse, clinging on for his life as Floki Magnusson drove it through the Forest of Caledon ....

"Whoa! Wake up, Gil!" Ivan's hand clamped over his arm. "You were half off there."

"Awake now," Gil mumbled. A cold splash of rain revived him as the sign for Greene Mountain Falls caught the headlight. Then, up ahead, he saw a white blur in the darkness; his mother's house. A window glowed downstairs, and at the gate sat a four-by-four with a blue light turning on its roof.

"Police!" Gil cried.

"Yup." Ivan leaned hard to the right and swung the bike off the road. They hit the bank with a bone-jarring thud and jounced out over the lawn. "Head down!" Ivan shouted as they reached the big pine.

"You're not going …." Gil cried, horrified, but the Norton's wheels tore into the steep, narrow river path, branches whacking on either side. Slithering over roots and launching off boulders, they rode wildly down toward the rushing water below. Tearing through a last tangle of branches, Ivan skidded the bike sideways to a halt on the Lookout Rock itself.

Gil slid shakily to the ground. "Didn't think that was possible," he murmured weakly.

"Wasn't sure myself," Ivan grinned. Then his face grew serious. "Got some stuff for you." He scrambled down the rocks and disappeared into the shadows of the trees.

Gil stood staring down at the black, silken surface of the Indian Kettle Pool, glimmering in the first light of dawn. The whirlpool of the Underwater Bridge churned its white foam. He closed his fingers around the white stone in his pocket.

Ivan climbed back up to the Rock with a cylindrical dry-sack, like he used for his kayak gear, under his arm, and something that glinted in the dim light, slung over his shoulder. He unrolled the top of the sack and turned the waterproof bag upside down. A neat roll of cloth tumbled out.

"Oh, ace!" Gil cried, unrolling the cloth and releasing its contents. "You kept my gear for me!" He clutched up the thick grey woolen trousers and fur-lined boots, and the beautiful, braid-trimmed red tunic. But the best thing was the cloth that had wrapped it all; his cloak of sky-blue wool that Danni had woven for him, her long winter alone at Cille Aidan.

"Might be a bit moldy," Ivan said. "I hid it in that hollow tree you kids used to crawl through. *Thought* you might need it some time, in a hurry."

He leaned forward then, slipping from his shoulder a round wooden shield, bound with iron and adorned with a painted cat, and a silver-trimmed wooden scabbard, from which glinted the hilt of a Viking sword. Gil grasped the sword with a cry of joy.

"I came out and oiled it, once a week," Ivan said. "So it wouldn't rust."

Gil raised his eyes from the sword and shook his head wonderingly. "Dad always said to me, if I was ever in big trouble; find Ivan. Now I know why."

"Bullshit," Ivan said, but he smiled.

Gil drew the sword from the scabbard, sighted down its length, tested the edge of the blade with his finger, and then swung it in two slicing arcs through the grey air.

"Well, you didn't learn that on the internet," Ivan murmured. Then he said, "I left that cup you were carrying with Sophia. Kind of valuable for hollow logs."

"Has she hidden it?" Gil asked urgently.

"In plain sight. It's up on that shelf of hers with the angels and crystals and that picture of Elvis with wings. Looks right at home." Ivan grinned. "She tells everyone it's the Holy Grail."

"It's not," Gil said. "It's just a reliquary!"

Ivan grinned again. "Do you think anyone believes her?"

Gil shook his head uneasily. "I don't want Sophia to get hurt."

Ivan's expression hardened. "She won't while I'm around," he said quietly. "You go and look after Danni and little Percy. I'll take care of Sophia." He looked up suddenly. Beyond the river woods, headlights flashed and a car door slammed. "Move, Gil," he said.

Hastily, Gil changed from his jeans and fleece into the garments from the dry-sack. Wrapping the cloak around himself, he fastened it with its silver pin. Then he strapped the sword belt around his waist, slung the shield around his neck, and grasped the white stone in his hand.

Ivan stuffed Gil's discarded clothing into the vinyl dry-sack and held it out. "Take it with you. Useful."

Gil shook his head. "It won't cross." He smiled gamely, "Back to wool and sheepskin and privies-from-hell." Then he turned to face the dark whirlpool and fell silent.

"Scared?" Ivan asked, over his shoulder.

Gil nodded.

"Don't blame you."

Gil turned, meeting Ivan's troubled gaze. "You really believe me, don't you?" he whispered.

Ivan laughed and waved an arm at the waiting whirlpool. "Do you think I'd let you jump in there, like that, if I didn't?"

Gil smiled. "Thanks, Ivan," he said.

He turned, adjusted his sword belt, tightened his fingers around the white stone and leapt, feet first, into the black pool. Plunging under the freezing water, he bobbed back up again just long enough to hear Ivan shout, "Tell your father he owes me a beer!"

Then the dark water closed over his head and the whirlpool grabbed him and drew him down into its fierce, pummeling core.

CHAPTER TWO

Icy blackness swallowed Gil. His back scraped the smooth stone of the Indian Kettle, his feet, reaching for grounding, found nothing. The surge of the water sucked him downward, deeper and deeper, twisting his limbs as if to wrench bones from sockets. He clenched his fist around the white stone and fought to hold his breath. *Ride it out! It ends soon!*

But it didn't end. It went on and on, battering his body, dragging him ever downward. *Too far. Too long.* Panic broke over him like a sea wave. *I'm drowning. It's just a hole in the river. There's no doorway. No Underwater Bridge. No land of Northmen and knights. No Janetta ...* He was insane, like Dr. Fairchild said. He and Crazy Ivan. *Ivan!* he thought wildly. *Ivan on the Lookout Rock above.* Gil strove to cry out to Ivan for help, but the power of the water closed its icy hand on his lips. *Too late.*

Then, sweetly and suddenly, the cold left him. The pummeling stopped and the roar of the whirlpool stilled. Warmth flooded his body, flowing pleasantly into each of his limbs. *Dying doesn't hurt. Everyone says that.* He let go of the white stone and it tumbled lightly from his fingers and landed with a little thud.

"But I don't want to die," he whispered. He heard his own voice, clear in the still air that, with no difficulty at all, he was breathing. Startled, he pressed down with his hands and felt solid ground beneath him. He was lying on his back, his arms outstretched as if flung there by the force of the water. He patted the ground, fingers tugging at warm, dry grass.

Tentatively, he drew one arm in and touched the edge of his cloak, spread out beneath him, and then the hem of his tunic.

Both were dry and warmed already by the sun that glowed red-gold behind his closed lids. He opened his eyes and stared up in amazement at a perfect blue summer sky.

His shield lay on the grass beside him. He pulled it closer and slung it over his shoulder. Then, adjusting his sword belt, he stood up. All around him stretched sunlit green meadow grass, dotted with white and yellow flowers. Ten feet away, a rough grey slab of stone loomed upright amidst a clump of flowering heather. Beyond was another and another, marching in a curving line against a backdrop of sunlit sea.

Gil whirled joyfully. The line of stones continued behind him, forming a great ring, and he himself stood exactly in its center, beside a little glistening disc of water, blue as the sky above: the Wandering Pool, this world's gateway to the Underwater Bridge.

He crouched and trailed his fingers at the pool's sun-warmed edge, barely able to believe the dark ferocious journey he had endured just beyond its placid surface. Something white shone in the grass at the pool's rim. Gil snatched it up: Aidan's Seeing Stone that Feannag had carried to him across a thousand years of time.

He stroked the smooth surface, remembering Benita and Aaron in the grounds of Safe Haven. Yesterday. Less than a full day past, and a millennium in the future. He stared at the deceptive blue mirror of the pool. All his world lay beyond it. But there was no going back, not even with the key in his hand. The bright bell heather and the brief midday shadows told him it was neither solstice, nor equinox, but high summer, here. The door to The Bridge was closed.

Gil slipped the white stone in his pocket. Then, raising his head, he looked all around the stone circle enclosing him in its ancient protective ring. His eyes returned to the Wandering Pool. He was used to it moving around. He had seen it beyond the ridge. He had seen it inside the Turnip Head Tomb. He had seen it at the door of the church. But only once before had he seen it here, centering the Great Stones like the shining boss of a shield: the day he had drawn from its depths the talisman of his feline Other.

His hand flew to his throat, his fingers closing on the knotted thong. It was still there! And, safely suspended from it, the little leather pouch with his single cat's whisker tucked inside. *Keep it with you. Always. Always. Always.*

"I've got it, Aidan," Gil grinned. "And it hasn't been easy." He reached up and untied the thong, slipping it from his neck. The leather pouch was hidden entirely by a larger, brighter pendant. Sophia had given it to him, the day they took him to Safe Haven. Unsurprisingly, it was an angel, made of silver this time, and with outstretched wings.

Carefully, Gil slid it from the thong. It had served its purpose. Dr. Fairchild had smiled his indulgent, "you'll grow up soon," smile, and left it, and his precious talisman, alone. *Hidden in plain sight.* Gil regarded the angel ruefully. Jewelry was kind of okay, here. *Floki* wore bracelets. But this was definitely a girl thing. He slid it into his pocket, beside the Seeing Stone. As it happened, he knew a girl.

The thought that she was here, maybe just a few hundred feet away, made him suddenly giddy with joy. He hastily retied the thong around his neck and swept the horizon with his gaze. Beyond, in the next little hollow, was the rowan bordered stream. And then the land rose gently to the Wood of White Trees, and beyond that lay Cille Aidan with its turf-roofed church and the seven round cells.

Dreamily, he imagined Janetta maybe sharing a cell with Danni or Rachel. Or, even better, surely they would have given her his, since he was gone, far away to Tir nan Og. He pictured himself surprising her there, and then honorably retreating to sleep in the longhouse among Aidan's little four-horned sheep. After all, she was just thirteen.

Or was she? The thought chilled him as if a cloud had shadowed the summer sun. Fearfully, he studied his surroundings anew. How much time had passed? In his mind he saw Aidan in the church, holding his jeweled chalice to the light and casting a shifting rainbow on the floor. *Time bends like the light. It passes faster here.*

He had been in Safe Haven for three months. How much time had passed here? He thought of the months and years stretching out like the shadows of the Great Stones at evening. What if she was older than him, now? What if she was older than Benita? Maybe eighteen; looking down on him with scorn; or worse, that sweetness girls got when you were just a little kid in their eyes. But it could be worse, even than that. She could be grown up. A woman. Even old. Even ....

"No!" he shouted. His eyes swept over the Stones, the low hills, the shining sea beyond. Nothing had changed. But nothing would change. The hills and sea would be the same almost forever. And the Stones hadn't changed in a thousand years. Rachel had seen them in their own world and known them here, at once.

Slinging his shield behind him, Gil flung back his cloak and ran toward Cille Aidan as if he could outrun the lengthening shadows of time. *Let her be young,* he murmured. *Please, please, . let her be young ....*

In the Wood of White Trees, he slowed to a panting halt. Beneath his feet, the path was worn and familiar. Familiar, too, the small, gnarled birch trees on either side. His spirits rose, cheered by the sight of one and another he was sure he recognized. Trees grew slowly in the Northlands' salt winds, but they did grow, and change, and even die. And all that seemed different were a few fresh, green branches hanging lower over his head than he remembered.

Then, ahead, he spotted a tree he knew almost too well; its leaning divided trunk marking the spot where Magnus Redbeard had dragged him at sword point from the path. Gil patted the tree solemnly as he passed, remembering Aidan's gentle, unarmed hand turning away the old Viking's sword.

I would be a slave in Norway, now, he thought, *if it weren't for Aidan.* He looked down then as he left the tree behind, and something pale at the edge of the path caught his eye. Buff colored and shabby, it barely showed beneath a heap of dead leaves. "Just litter," he murmured, "Old newspaper."

But his mind was already protesting: *No. There are no newspapers here. There's no litter here.* Nothing manmade was ever thrown away. Not cloth, or metal, or carved wood or stone. Everything was too precious. Everything was used again.

Gil knelt down on the sun-dappled ground and brushed the leaves aside. It wasn't paper. It was vellum, the fine smooth animal skin on which Aidan wrote his beautiful red and black script. Gil lifted the pale thing and the pages fell open like pleading hands. Lying abandoned in the leaf mold and grass was the most precious of all objects at Cille Aidan: a book.

With trembling fingers, Gil turned a page, and then another. Water-stained and smeared with dirt, it was yet stubbornly legible. He traced the lines with a finger, hearing in his head Aidan singing his soft Latin chant.

"Maybe he dropped it in the dark or something and couldn't find it," Gil whispered. But his mind rejected the absurd lie as fast as he made it up. The wooden cover of the book was splintered at the edges where the hinges and clasp had been roughly torn free. Shorn of its gold and silver, the wonderful book itself was just thrown away.

Sadly, Gil brushed as much dirt from the vellum as he could and gently closed the pages. He unpinned his cloak and wrapped it in a long roll around the book, and then slung it over his shoulder and tied the ends in a knot. Then, with his hand on his sword hilt, he crept silently to the edge of the trees. Hidden yet in their shadows, he braced himself and looked down on Cille Aidan.

For a moment, he recognized nothing. His eyes sought the green turf roof of the church, and found only fire-scorched walls; the stone cross forlorn against an empty sky. The cells were roofless circles, the longhouse a ruin of charred timbers and blackened stone. Every building, no matter how small, had been set ablaze. "Like Camelot," Gil whispered. And he knew at once who had been here.

His hand firm on his sword hilt, he crept from the trees. Nothing moved below and there was no sound but the sweep of a gentle sea on the white sand. Nettles grew tall in Aidan's garden and the apples hung, bright and abandoned, on his little tree. Gil turned in a full circle, and, certain he was alone, stepped out again on the path.

His feet clattered against something smooth and white that rolled over, revealing black empty eyes. A skull, small and delicate, with four small horns, bleached pale as the bone, lay half-buried in the grass. Beneath it, he glimpsed a white curve of rib, a broken column of vertebrae. A ragged patch of brown fleece yet clung to the scattered bones.

Suddenly, he was shaking with fury. "*Why?*" he cried aloud. "Why kill his little sheep?" Drawing his sword, he ran down the hill into the center of Aidan's desecrated hermitage, swinging the blade in the vain, stupid hope that the destroyers were yet within reach.

Then, slowly, wearily, he lowered the sword. The weathered bones of the sheep and the height of the meadow grass growing all around the roofless cells told him the burning of Cille Aidan was long in the past. Nothing moved here, not friend, foe, bird, or animal.

Numbly, he went from cell to cell. He hardly recognized his own, with sunlight pouring down on its soot-stained walls and the charred ruins of his desk and bed. He turned away quickly and went to the church.

The bell was gone from the frame outside the entrance, and the wicker door was gone, too. Rainwater filled the hollow stone cup inside the doorway. Gil dipped his fingers and blessed himself the way Aidan had taught him, anyhow.

The little rectangle of stone walls seemed smaller than ever without its roof. The table where Aidan had read prayers and the altar where he sang the mass were charred ruins. The oil lamp that had burned above them, night and day, lay cold on the floor.

Something stirred at one of the two narrow windows, and Gil turned, imagining for a joyful moment he would see the Noble Cat looking down at him. But it was only a tuft of weed, rooted in the fire cracked stone, swaying in the sea wind. He raised his eyes to the three bare stone niches in the wall above the altar. The treasures of Lindisfarne were gone. What came here was too strong, even for a tiger.

He looked up then, through the burnt and broken roof beams at the wide sky. *Feannag.* Feannag had come for him. Why, if there was no one left? But the sky remained empty and with a last sad glance at the ruined altar, Gil turned and left the church.

In the roofless longhouse, the wooden kists were burnt to

ash and the loom on which Danni had woven his sky-blue cloak was a mound of blackened timbers overgrown with weeds. Beneath the pot-chain, still hanging from the charred roof beams, Gil found the cooking pot, turned on its side. When he lifted it, a fat mouse ran from its shelter.

Feline excitement twitched at his hands and the sides of his mouth. His stomach growled and he realized suddenly how hungry he was. He had not eaten since the usual dreary supper at Safe Haven and stupidly, he'd eaten only half of that. And, he thought, staring sadly at the abandoned hearth, there would be no welcome feast for him here.

Something caught his eye then, at the back of the room; a small, familiar triangular shape. He clambered over a heap of burnt thatch, crouched, and brushed the ash and dirt away from the frame of Danni's little harp. Broken in half by the stroke of an axe, it made a small, sad twang as he lifted it from the rubble and held it in his arms. "Why?" he whispered, as he had over the slaughtered sheep. "Can you murder music?"

Then, all the nights of song and story and firelight came rushing in upon him and his eyes filled with tears. Savagely, he brushed them away with his sleeve. Setting the harp down again in the ashes, he stood and strode from the longhouse, burying his grief in purpose.

Methodically, he hunted now for clues to the fate of all who had been here when the Golden Knight struck. He climbed to the pony field and searched for bones until he was certain the ponies, at least, has been spared the sword. But ponies were valuable and could be taken away and sold. He closed his mind to the thought of Lionheart lost and frightened in some far place and went back to the shore.

Beneath the bell frame, the hollow in the sand where Aidan beached his fishing boat was empty. Gil searched the white strand in both directions, but found neither hull, nor mast, nor oar. With rising hope, he looked back at the empty pony field. By either sea or land, they could have fled to refuge. His heart lifted, picturing the little fishing boat flitting across the waves, and the ponies, hastily loaded and bearing his friends away from the swords and the flames.

But away from him, too.

He looked back to the shell of the longhouse. Once, he had imagined Cille Aidan ravaged like this, and Danni returning on her wild goose wings, and finding everyone gone. Now, it had all happened, exactly as he had pictured it, only not to Danni, but to him.

His eyes flew to the roofless scriptorium. He had written her a message, so she might follow them. Could she have done the same for him? He started up the hill and then broke into a run. Reaching the round cell where Aidan had worked, he wrenched open the sagging wickerwork door and then drew back in dismay.

Even with all he had seen already, he was stunned by the destruction within. Light flooded brutally down on smashed shelves of inks, on Aidan's desk, stained by soot and rain, and on his books, torn and scattered on the floor, burnt and rain sodden; all utterly ruined for the sake of silver and gold. "And vengeance," Gil murmured.

The desire for vengeance sparked and flared in his own heart then, and he turned away with a trembling hand on the hilt of his sword. But his feet, scraping disconsolately in the ashes, suddenly turned up a scorched ragged page, and he saw writing in a familiar hand. Eagerly, he snatched it up, and then he laughed quietly as he read: "And all will be well ...." There was the message; Rachel's message to her father, across a thousand years.

"No," he whispered. "All will *not* be well." But he unrolled his cloak and took out the surviving book and laid Rachel's scrap of vellum within its pages. Then he wrapped it again, slung the cloak across his shoulder, and left the scriptorium. Loosening his sword in its scabbard, he set out, onto the wild hill, walking alone to the only refuge he knew: Magnus Redbeard's Einar's Holm.

The walk seemed far harder than he remembered. But he'd never before been so tired or so hungry. When he reached the last ridge, the sun had vanished. Grey clouds scudded in off the sea and the leaves of the little scattered trees flicked in the wind. *Storm coming*, he thought dully.

Rain splashed down, damping the shoulders of his tunic and plastering his hair against his forehead. Stubbornly, he refused to unroll the cloak protecting Aidan's last book, but plodded on up the hill, legs shaking with hunger and weariness. Only the thought of food and a fire kept him putting one leaden foot after the other. That and the certainty that his friends would have sought the same refuge, and the hope that he would find all here, safely guarded by Magnus and Floki, and sixty Viking warriors.

And then, as he climbed the final few feet, he was filled with a strange unease, a conviction that something was wrong. He stopped and listened but heard nothing. He turned and looked all around but the pastures were empty of threat, the tall grass rippling in the rising wind. Instinctively, he sniffed the air, as Cat would. But he smelled nothing. And that, he realized suddenly, was what was wrong.

Where was the smoke of the great longhouse fire? Where was the farmyard chatter of Einar's Holm? The cattle lowing, the geese and hens and sheep; the ponies whinnying on the hill?

Weariness vanquished by desperation, Gil trotted and then ran until he crested the ridge, and there, stumbled to a disbelieving halt. Below him, amid unsown fields stretching to the sea, Magnus Redbeard's mighty longhouse stood roofless and empty beside its blackened byres. Nothing moved but the grass in the wind, and the only sound was the crying of seabirds riding inland from the storm.

Gil stood in silence, his mind filling with images of Magnus, wielding a battle axe with his tree trunk arms, of Shony, his fierce, beautiful selkie wife, and of Floki with his playful grace and his deadly sword. He could not imagine them defeated. And yet, the Golden Knight had swept down upon the island like a hawk on a dovecote and carried everything away.

Slowly, Gil sank to the ground and sat, cross-legged, head in hands, the enormity of what had happened here pervading his mind like the rain soaking his clothes. Cille Aidan, unarmed and innocent, was easy prey. But Einar's Holm could not have fallen without a fight. Who had survived it? And where were they? Was there anyone he knew left in this world?

Hungry, cold, and alone, he fought the urge to be a kid and cry. *We're not children here.* Danni had told him on the day he arrived. Like in Ismail's African home, childhood was a luxury here. He raised his head and watched the gulls above the white strand where once Floki's *Silver Dragon* sailed grandly to her beaching. Peering into the mist as if he could will a sail into being, he whispered, "Come. Come for me." But then he remembered that this was a battlefield, and its victors had also come by sea.

Wearily, he got to his feet. Brushing his drenched hair from his eyes, he drew his sword from its scabbard and, in the wind and rain, trudged down the hill.

At its foot, he set out across the farmyard, checking each of its outbuildings, as he had at Cille Aidan. As at Cille Aidan, every one was roofless. He searched the furthest, the grain store, first, finding only a miniature barley field, sprouted from fallen seeds. The byre was silent, bereft of Shony's milk cows, and the cool, shadowy dairy, where the great wheels of cheese and the casks of ale had rested, was bright with unaccustomed daylight. The pony pen was empty and the wood-store a collapsed ruin.

Memories met him everywhere; the wall of the longhouse where he and Ismail had flopped exhausted after hours of sword practice. The courtyard where he had first ridden Lionheart. And the open field where Sir Palamedes, Master of Lances, had held his jousting school. Gil left the longhouse until last, reluctant to surrender the past of feasting and song for the present of desolation.

Within its bare walls, stripped of their swords and shields, lay a rubble of turf and burnt beams, so overgrown with weeds that the long hearth had simply vanished. Of Magnus' great feasting board there was no trace; nor could Gil find Shony's loom beneath the ruins of the fallen sleeping loft. The driftwood tree-ladder, where Floki had mocked his parents' gods, reached up now to empty sky.

Do not bring the curse of Odin on this house.

Gil crouched down by the scorched remains of a barley kist and ran his hands through the ash.

The rain, pelting steadily on his soaked shoulders, warned
him that he had little time to mourn. He still had to find shelter.
He had to find food. He had to make a fire. His hand sought the
pouch at his belt that held his steel fire-striker and closed on its
reassuring shape. Cheered that the helmsman, Erling's, precious
gift was safe, he stood up and began diligently searching the
ruined hall for anything of use.

A bit of horsehair rope, at the bottom of a half-burned kist,
would make a snare. And he'd seen an old fishing net behind
the byre. The byre itself could serve as a shelter, if he roofed it
with rescued beams and cut heather for a thatch. And, in spite
of the storm, it *was* summer. There'd be berries to gather, and
light half the night … for now.

But summer would end. And without stores and provisions,
he could not survive winter, here, alone.

Bleakly, Gil sank down again beside the barley kist.
Something moved, at the corner of his eye. Whipping around,
he saw, as at Cille Aidan, a fat brown mouse, enjoying an
unexpected bounty. "Okay for somebody," he murmured wryly.

He felt the familiar paw twitch of Cat and again his stomach
growled. *Cat* didn't have a problem, he thought suddenly. Cat
could live all winter, feasting on mice and curling snug in a bed
of fallen thatch. He felt an excited swish of a phantom tail.

No. Aidan had warned him, the longer he stayed Other; the
harder it would be to return. A whole winter of stalking prey
under the stars, of curling replete in beds of fern and straw,
secure in his feline grace, aloof in Cat-ly arrogance? There
would *be* no return. There would be no boy, Gil, left, to seek his
lost friends.

He had to leave, now. He had to find help. But the nearest
friendly landfall was the island *muinntir* of Hy, and the Golden
Knight's fires had burned there first. He would have to go
further, all the way to Alba, and seek his father. His mind filled
with the battle beneath the Rainbow Bridge: Lance'lot grappling
with the Golden Knight, the knight's sword flung by Gil's own
hand into the pool, the yelps and shouts of pursuing hounds
and horsemen.

Jocelyn Guidbairn's survival was written in the ashes

around him. But what of Lance'lot? *'No one ever saw the place he came from, or the place he made his home.'* And no one knew the Forest like Lance'lot. A surge of hope warmed Gil's heart, as if he already sat at Lance'lot's welcoming hearth in the hidden valley of Caledon. But how would he get there, without a map or a boat?

Not by sitting here on my butt; that's for sure. Ignoring the mouse, Gil jumped to his feet, feeling Cat's resentment of the waste of a perfectly good meal. "*I* can't live on mice," he said, aloud, to his Other. He brushed ash from his hands, and then he heard a sound, quite clearly, as if Cat had answered in a distant human voice.

"Who's there?" he cried, torn between fear and joy. There was silence. And then the sound came again, a soft murmur of indistinguishable words. He turned his head. It was there, behind the wall, or .... "Magnus?" he called softly. Or *there*, up near the broken roof. "Floki?" his voice was trembling, his mind filled with ghosts.

A stone clattered against the wall. Gil spun around. A shadowy figure loomed in the doorway. Gil glimpsed a bearded face, a wind-whipped blue tunic, a wolf skin serving as a cloak. *Northman*, he thought with relief. Then the man lunged across the floor and slammed a fist into his chest.

Gil sat down hard in the ashes, gasping for breath. The man strode closer. "Wait," Gil cried, raising a hand to shield his face. "I'm Gil. I'm a friend."

Then something wet and stinking fell from the wall behind him, a net, enshrouding his face with slime and seaweed. A second man jumped down beside the first and together they tightened the net around him like a noose. Salty rope lashed across his face. He gagged and struggled to free himself. A boot thudded into his side, laying him out on the floor.

Looking up through a screen of fishing net, Gil saw two lean, weathered strangers' faces, staring down with that cold, grim look Northmen carried into battle. "Wait!" he cried again. "I'm not a Raider. I'm a friend. Northmen's friend."

They stared down at him blankly. No English. As Gil searched frantically for words in the Northmen's tongue, the first man gripped two handfuls of net and hauled him to his feet. A shove from behind sent him stumbling over the turf-strewn floor and out into the gale. Another shove and he was staggering ahead of his captors, toward the white strand.

When he saw the beached skiff, lying on the shore, he knew they weren't going to kill him. Nothing was wasted here: young and strong, he was worth good silver. They would take him to Norway and sell him as a slave.

Gil looked back in desperation at the ruin of Magnus' longhouse, as if someone might yet come from it to save him. Then suddenly he knew who could. He staggered to a halt, turned boldly to face his captors, and shouted the one name sure to cast fear into their hearts. "Floki Magnusson! *Vinr!*" He nodded his head vigorously and with one netted hand pointed inwards at himself. "Floki Magnusson's friend!"

They understood that well enough. There was a snort of laughter and the fist thudded harder into his battered ribs. Then, lifting both sides of the net, they flung him into the boat.

CHAPTER THREE

Grunting with effort, the two Northmen dragged the skiff seaward. Gravel scraped the keel beneath Gil's face. Salt water roiled in the bilges, stinging his eyes. With a splash, the little boat floated free; then lurched to one side and the other as Gil's captors clambered aboard.

Oars creaked against wood and the skiff slapped against the incoming waves, jouncing Gil's chin on the wooden strakes. He struggled to turn his head enough to see where they were taking him and managed only a grey glimpse of sky. But a low rumble of surf to his right told him they were heading west.

The skiff began to roll, slowly and sickeningly, as they left the lee of the shore and the helmsman turned the prow north. Gil heard the Northmen ship their oars, and then the familiar creak of rope and spar as a sail was hoisted up the mast.

The wind took it at once and the skiff heeled hard on her steering board. The bilge water pooled under Gil's head, rising to cover his mouth and nose. Jerking back, he coughed and spluttered. The Northmen laughed. With each roll of the skiff, Gil's face ducked under water. He struggled in the net and gasped for breath.

"Hey! Selkie!" one man shouted, as Gil wriggled, seal-like, in his bonds. He gritted his teeth then, refusing to move, holding his breath with each wave of water. When he'd ridden out a dozen rolls of the hull, a hand grabbed the net at the nape of his neck and pulled him upright.

Warily, Gil raised his dripping face to his captors. The one in the wolf skin crouched beside him, while the other, who wore his hair in a long ponytail, clung to the steering oar and tugged nervously at his beard.

Wolfskin drew a long-bladed knife from his belt, and holding it right in front of Gil's eyes, he shouted something, waving the blade back and forth for emphasis. Then he lowered the knife, and with his gaze never leaving Gil's face, began hacking away at the rotten hemp of the net. The fibers shredded and fell apart, freeing Gil's head and shoulders. Relieved, Gil moved to stretch his cramped arms, but in an instant the knife was at his throat.

"Okay," he muttered, racking his brain again for words that belonged here. *In nomine patris* …. Oh, great. Aidan's church Latin. He doubted either of this pair spent a lot of time in churches. Except maybe burning them. Like Cille Aidan.

Then he saw the sheepskin. Lacking a proper cloak, the man at the steering oar had belted a rough jerkin of brown fleece over his tunic. Gil's mind leapt to the white bones on the hillside. Uneasily, he surveyed his captors. They were dirty and roughly dressed and looked poor, even hungry: Men like Sir Owain in the Forest of Caledon. Men who might sell themselves to anyone, even the Golden Knight.

Gil raised both hands, empty palms upward, and looking as innocent as he could, forced himself to smile. "Vinr?" he said hopefully.

Wolfskin caught his wrist and wrenched his arm behind his back, twisting it until Gil cried out in pain. Then he caught the other and swiftly bound them together with a severed piece of the net. He gave his knife to the helmsman, who held it menacingly while Wolfskin cautiously unbuckled Gil's sword belt and tossed it into the stern. Jerking the strap of his shield over his head, he threw that after it, and even took the little hunting knife Gil had from his father, more tool than weapon.

Then, shoving Gil back against the curved strakes of the prow, he scuttled quickly out of reach. Whoever they were, and whoever they worked for, they seemed as afraid of him as he was of them.

Relieved to be upright and breathing fresh air, he nodded his gratitude. As he leaned awkwardly against the wooden planks, he felt the comforting lump of Aidan's cloak-wrapped book between his shoulder blades and braced his bound arms protectively around it. At least he'd kept that.

His captors still watched him warily. Gil forced another smile. They relaxed a little, then, and began talking quietly together, their eyes on the sail and the sea. Cautiously, Gil looked around the little boat.

Narrow and graceful, with a stepped mast of rough-hewn pine and a square woolen sail, reefed against the storm, it looked like a miniature *Silver Dragon*. But it was small; it lacked any decking and the two Northmen perched on bare crossbeams, their feet on the ribs of the hull. There were oar-holes for just two sets of oars, like on the little fishing skiff Floki took out from Einar's Holm. But even Floki wouldn't sail that to Norway. They must have friends waiting for them, with a longship. Or maybe a Vikings' lair somewhere along this wild shore. Gil raised his eyes, searching the breaker-rimmed coast.

Stark headlands guarded white sand beaches. Seabirds wheeled over bleak rock cliffs, cut here and there by deep mysterious gullies. Beyond were hills, bright green or heather dark. Gil had sailed south from Einar's Holm to Pentland and the Southern Isles and Hy. But the land to the North was unknown to him. He could be anywhere.

They sailed for hours, always with the land to the right, off the steering board. The storm blew over. The rain stopped and the sea wind dried Gil's clothes. His bound arms grew numb. He was starving, too, but even imagining his captors willing to feed him, he could see they had nothing with them. They were probably as hungry as he was. And in their ragged clothes, they looked as uncomfortable as he felt.

He stared at the shore, almost hoping to spot some slave trader's camp. At least there'd be food and a fire. But the skiff sailed on, fast and steady in the calming sea, ever northward.

The long summer daylight had faded finally into a luminous silvery dusk, when at last the helmsman changed course. Twisting to look over his shoulder, Gil saw they were following the curve of a dim headland; eastward, he guessed.

He thought of the little metal compass he had given to Floki Magnusson, wishing he could have it for a moment, in his hand.

But if he needed it, Wolfskin and Sheep, like all Northmen, sailed blithely without. Gil turned his head the other way and saw, across an open stretch of water, more land, another island, hilly and dark against the dimming sky.

And then, even as the sea around them calmed to gentle ripples, he heard a new sound, a distant roar, like fierce breakers on an unseen shore. It grew louder and steadier, without the rhythm of surf; a roar like white-water on the river at home. Curiously, he looked to either side and then saw his captors nod to each other uneasily. Wolfskin tightened his grip on the steering oar. Sheep adjusted the sail. Gil turned over his shoulder, again, and saw two things that before he had missed.

Between the new island and their own, the waters were broken by a third; a low, green land, glimmering on the twilit sea. And, on either side, stretching from shore to shore, a white line of churning water cast up a wall of spray. Roaring now like the great Linn of the Rainbow Bridge, it stood directly ahead of the skiff's little prow, and the helmsman was holding his course.

Around them, the water raced like a river, swirling against their high stern, spinning foaming eddies from the steering oar. Gil felt the little craft pick up speed. The sail flapped, wrapping itself around the mast. They were outrunning the wind. White foam rimmed the shore to their left, and spray enveloped the green island to their right.

Something nudged Gil's shoulder. He tore his eyes from the racing waters and turned to see Sheep crouched over him, with his knife. The Northman shouted an order Gil couldn't understand, and then shoved him sideways, until his rough hand found the cord binding Gil's wrists. A quick jerk of the blade slashed the net and Gil's numb hands fell free. Sheep waved the knife again in warning and stumbled away to the stern.

Gil rubbed his wrists and nodded gratefully. Poor and rough his captors might be, but not so merciless as to see anyone cast, arms bound, into that sea. If the skiff foundered, he'd have as much chance as they.

He thought suddenly of his father, taken also by the Northmen, long before he came to Camelot and surviving a shipwreck alone. Then his eyes fell again on the wall of wild water looming directly ahead and he realized no one would survive long in that.

A second later, they hit the wave. The slender prow sliced into it, parting green water on either side. Spray exploded over the skiff, drenching Gil in an instant. The hull shivered and twisted, plunging down and then up again. The bow rose up clear of the water, then the whole craft skidded sideways, down the back of the wave, tipping the low rail of the loading board into the swirling foam.

Water flowed in, tipping the skiff further. Gil scrambled for the steering board, throwing his weight onto its rising rail. He heard a faint shout over the roar of the clashing seas and saw Wolfskin struggling to hold his course and pointing at a leather bailing bucket floating at Gil's feet. Snatching it up, Gil furiously scooped water from the flooded bilge, while Sheep hauled on the sheets of the sail, bringing the wind to their rescue.

Trailing eddies of foam; the half-drowned skiff surfed valiantly down a cascade of swirling currents. And then, quite suddenly, they were free. The roaring died away and the waters around them grew calm. The great wave stood now, a luminescent barrier between their little ship and the open sea. And ahead, glowing like ruddy eyes on the shore of the dark island, were two red pinpoints of fire.

The sail sagged in the lee of the island. Sheep loosed the halyard and lowered the yard, bunching the heavy cloth around it. Then he settled on a cross beam and readied his oars. Wolfskin took the bailing bucket from Gil with a curt nod of appreciation. But any comradeship he felt ended there. Quickly, he rebound Gil's wrists, and Sheep once more waved his knife. Then, with Gil helpless again, they rowed toward land.

The red points of light grew, as they approached, into great flaming beacons planted either side of an enormous dark longhouse. In the shadows cast by the flaring pitch of the torches, Gil saw the dark silhouettes of three longships drawn up on the strand. Nearer, clusters of figures moved in and out of the firelight. If this were a Vikings' stronghold, then they were Vikings who had no fear of being seen.

The moment the skiff's prow nudged into the sand, Sheep hauled Gil to his feet and marched him ashore at knife point. With Wolfskin at his other side, Gil stumbled up the darkened strand, half blinded by the glare of the great beacons.

Up close, the longhouse was like nothing he had seen before. Its walls were huge and dark, built neither of stone nor wood, but of thick layers of cut turfs, still sprouting grass at their edges. Above, the mighty timbers carried a roof of cloth, the same lengths of woven wool that formed the Northmen's sails. Half cave and half longship, it was fronted by two huge doors, painted and carved and, Gil had little doubt, stolen from some other ravaged house.

On either side, the torches flared and flickered, and beneath them; their shadows dancing grotesquely in the light; stood two enormous Northmen, swords in hands. Sheep hung back warily, his knife yet at Gil's back, while Wolfskin entered the circle of light and spoke to the guards. Pointing back at Gil, he waved both hands, as if re-enacting his capture, until one of the Northmen beckoned Gil closer.

Sheathing his sword, he roughly searched Gil's clothes and boots for arms; then spun him around and searched his back. Gil flinched as his hands closed on the bulge in the rolled cloak. With a growl, the guard wrenched the knot apart and flung the garment on the ground.

Wolfskin drew in a sharp breath and Sheep sidled further away. The guard kicked the folds of the cloth aside, crouched, and then lifted out the battered book. His face relaxed and he laughed quietly, showing the worn vellum pages to his companion. The second guard put his hands together as in prayer and nodded at Gil. They both shrugged and laughed together. Then the first man rolled the book again in the cloak and retied it over Gil's shoulder. With a nod of apology, he joined his companion, dragging open the mighty longhouse doors.

Fire and light blazed out into the dusk, carrying with it a rush of sound: the murmur of conversation, shouts and laughter, a dog barking, the sweet notes of a harp. Sheep thrust Gil forward and he stumbled over the threshold and stopped in amazement.

Within, the longhouse was as beautiful as its exterior was ugly. The turf walls were hidden by panels of wood which bore the same painted designs as the great doors. A glowing fire burned in a central hearth that stretched half the length of the enormous room. Smoke rose up through dark beams to holes in the tented roof.

There was no sleeping loft, but broad benches, spread with furs, lined both walls. On them, men sat talking in groups or bent over board games, while young women set out food on long tables either side of the hearth.

Between the tables, a mass of people of all ages jostled for space. Some were dressed finely in bright tunics and cloaks, others in the dull browns and greys of un-dyed cloth. Children played at the edges of the fire. Old men leaned on sticks. A white-haired couple, dressed in faded rags, sat patiently on the floor. Beside them knelt a man in grey, his head covered by a shabby hood, his back to Gil. A bony dog leaned comfortably against his shoulder.

Wolfskin and Sheep hustled Gil through the crowd to the edge of the hearth, where two girls turned roasting meat on a spit. Gil's head spun sickeningly with hunger at the smell of it and his legs buckled under him as Sheep pushed him to the floor. Wolfskin pointed to the front of the room, to the clusters of waiting people, and then to Gil. Overcome with exhaustion, Gil nodded dully, understanding nothing. Sheep sheathed his knife and the two stepped back, like men whose work was done.

Slowly, Gil's head cleared. Bracing himself against his bound hands, he levered his back upright and sat dully looking around. Through the crowd, he glimpsed a third table at the front of the room, where Wolfskin had pointed. Set across the ends of the other two, it was provided with chairs, rather than benches, and silver goblets stood waiting at each of seven places. Three chairs, on either side, flanked a central seat, higher than the rest, with a carved and painted back, surmounted by spiral pillars.

The wall behind the table was wood paneled, like the others, but in the central panel was set a door beneath a carved and painted lintel. Were it not for the cloth roof above, all could have been in a palace, and the throne-like high seat, awaiting a king.

Two low stools were placed by the hearth, before the table. One was empty, like the row of chairs. On the other sat the harp player, a handsome, black-haired man who played and sang with closed eyes, as if he was alone in the room.

At the far edge of the table, stood two burly warriors, as forbidding as the guards at the longhouse door. One had a flame-red beard, as bushy as it was long. The other's face was scarred from one eyebrow to the opposite ear. Both surveyed the room with hands on the hilts of their swords. Then suddenly the scarred man stepped forward and pounded his fist on the table.

Instantly, all talk and laughter ceased. Board games were set aside and the harper stopped in the middle of his song. But when the door in the wall panel opened, and four men filed into the room, he alone did not look up, but remained facing blankly toward the fire.

Gil peered at the newcomers through the watching crowd. They were dressed as warriors, in braid-trimmed, long-sleeved tunics over tight fitting trousers, and each wore a handsome sword belt, decorated with silver. But none were young men. Two were bald, with weather-lined faces, and even the younger pair had grey in their beards. All carried themselves with dignity and took their seats at the table with assurance, though carefully leaving the high seat and the two nearest chairs unclaimed.

Then the door opened again and a tall man and a boy carrying a jug came into the hall. The man leaned over his companion, his hand on his shoulder and his face turned toward him. With his other hand, he gestured toward the table, as if giving some instruction. Gil craned his neck, but still could see neither's face. But by their postures and the similarity of their costumes, far richer than any in the room, he guessed they were related, maybe father and son.

Both wore blood-red tunics, lavishly trimmed with bright-colored braid, and cloaks lined with black fur. A shirt of crisp white linen showed beneath the man's tunic, and his upper arms were adorned with heavy gold bracelets. His yellow hair was elaborately braided at the sides and tied back with ribbons, like a girl's. But there was nothing girlish about his lean, powerful body, nor the sword in its silver-trimmed scabbard, at his waist.

With a gentle gesture, he sent the child and his jug to the table. Then he took his own place on the pillared high seat, and turned a handsome, unsmiling face to the hall. Older, more heavily bearded, and bearing a new white scar across one cheekbone, he was still unmistakable. "Floki!" Gil shouted. Struggling with his bound hands, he scrambled joyfully to his knees. "Floki! It's me!"

Sheep's fist thudded into his ribs. Gil hardly noticed. "I'm back, Floki!" he cried triumphantly. Sheep's foot followed his fist, and then his two big hands clamped on Gil's shoulders, forcing him back down onto the floor.

Floki never moved. His cold, grey eyes, sweeping the room, fell for an instant on Gil's face, and then, without a flicker of recognition, passed on. Turning back to the table, he signaled to the boy with the jug. With his back yet to the hall, the child stepped carefully from place to place, filling the silver goblets with ale. Finished, he looked up to Floki, who, for the first time, smiled. The boy turned then, and with his round, happy face beaming, his slanted eyes squeezed half-closed, yet, with concentration, took his own seat, on the low stool beside the harper.

Gil stared, shaking his head in disbelief. "Percy?" he whispered. He flinched away at once from Sheep's ready fist and slumped against his painfully bound wrists. His head swirled with confusion, as if he had entered a dream world, utterly without logic, where everything was other than what it was meant to be.

Floki looked out into the hall and beckoned graciously to two members of the gathering. The first, a hulking warrior, stepped from the shadows beneath the eaves and strode to the high table. His long red hair bouncing on his shoulders, his scabbard slapping against his thigh, he took the place at Floki's left. Gil's face broke, unwillingly, into a smile. From the belligerent walk alone, he would have recognized him: Einar's Holm was a ruin, but Magnus Einarsson lived.

The second man rose from where he knelt on the floor and

lowered the hood of his robe, revealing a lean, weathered face, and a tonsured head. Men, women, and children all stepped courteously aside and Gil's heart leapt. Aidan. Aidan here and safe. Eagerly he watched as the Ab walked quietly through the company, laying a hand on the harper's shoulder as he passed, and again on Percy's head, and took his place at Floki's right. His eyes searched the crowd, and fell at once on Gil, and Gil saw the recognition in them. But Aidan's face remained expressionless as, almost imperceptibly, he shook his head.

Then, sitting solemnly between his father and the priest, Floki addressed the hall, first in the Northmen's tongue, and then in the Irish of Hy, and two men were brought forward by the guards. Heads bowed, they stood before the young Northman as before a judge.

Floki folded his arms and studied them sternly. Then he leaned forward and spoke softly to each. One man held up a hand with two fingers missing. The other hung his head and shuffled his feet while Floki examined the damaged hand.

A sword was produced and the injured man grasped it clumsily. One of the four warriors leaned over the table, gripped the maimed hand in his own, and briefly arm-wrestled the young man over the board.

Floki sat back then, and conferred with his council of warriors, then with his father, and lastly with Aidan. Then he called the two forward again and spoke quietly to one and then the other. Gil was startled by the kindness in his face as he demonstrated with his own hand what a loss the victim had suffered. Turning then to the guilty man, he spoke what Gil knew must be his verdict.

His eyes still downcast, the assailant untied a leather purse from his belt, and, opening it, spilled a heap of silver onto the table: coins, broken bits of jewelry, raw lumps of metal. Floki measured out several pieces and laid them before his counsellors, who nodded agreement. The silver changed hands; the two young men formally embraced, and then returned to their places in the hall and sat down together, like friends. The guards stepped forward and two more names were called.

Drawn into the proceedings despite his hunger and

confusion, Gil turned curiously to watch. The new complainants were neither young, nor injured. Two grey-bearded farmers arose; men who wore swords only out of old, Viking habit. Their hands were rough from heavy labor, their faces red from sun and wind. Casting each other looks of suppressed fury, they stumped up the hall to stand before the quiet young Northman. Floki looked them over and, with the trace of a smile, spoke to the nearest guard. Gil watched, intrigued, as the red-bearded warrior strode back down the hall and out the great doors, into the night.

There was a scuffle outside, shouts, and then a noise that brought Gil instantly back to Cille Aidan: the baaing of a sheep, entering the longhouse, and the clatter of hooves on the beaten earth floor. Laughter swept the hall, silenced at once by a barked word from the second guard. The first staggered back into the gathering, dragging a huge ram by one curling horn. The beast bucked and kicked, scattering squealing children, as it was hauled right up to the high table and held, baaing furiously, between the two farmers.

Gil looked up and saw Floki struggling to suppress a smile. For a moment, he looked again like the man he remembered, as quick to play as to fight. But regaining his composure, he sat back and spoke as solemnly to the farmers as he had to the young warriors before them.

Both clearly claimed ownership of the ram; each arguing his case and pointing out features of the beast. Floki left his place and came from behind the table and crouched down, studying the branded markings on a horn. Then, returning, he again consulted his council and made his ruling. The ram was handed over to one farmer, and Floki took silver from his own purse and handed it to the other. The council nodded approval and the farmers and the ram left the hall.

It's a court, Gil thought. *Not a law court. A king's court.* Only, there was no king, only the Viking, Floki Magnusson.

The third dispute was between two fierce-looking warriors who stood before Floki and the council with ill-grace. Each made a speech and cast baleful looks at the other. Both responded to Floki's counsel with an angry retort. The guards stepped closer, but Floki waved them away. Leaning forward, he spoke softly to each man, but Gil could see he was getting nowhere. He turned then to his counsellors and two of the four also spoke and were equally rebuffed. Magnus glowered and half rose, but Floki restrained him with a quiet hand.

Gil was surprised again, at his patience, matched only by Aidan's. Eventually, when everyone had spoken again and no one agreed, Northman and priest exchanged a wry smile and a shrug. Floki gestured toward the hall and Aidan spoke to the guard, who called two new names.

The ragged white-haired couple got up and hobbled forward. Floki acknowledged them with a gentle nod, and then looked up at the two complainants and spoke a few sharp words. First one, and then the other, untied his purse, and threw silver down on the table. The two stared at each other, baffled, and then glowered at Floki who gave them his sweetest smile.

Calling the old couple forward, he swept both of the caches of silver off the table and into the woman's hands. Dumbfounded by their good fortune, the two smiled and bowed and stumbled back to their place by the fire.

One of the warriors scratched his head and shrugged ruefully. But the other growled something under his breath and raised an angry fist. Floki's patience and his kindness vanished. In an instant, he was on his feet with his hand on the hilt of his sword.

Every sound in the great hall was stilled. Even the children held their breath. Then, very slowly, like a cat that had strayed into another cat's territory, the man lowered his fist and turned away. Head down, face flaming with fury, he strode past the long tables and out the door. Floki's guards made to follow, but he called them back and shook his head with a light, untroubled smile.

A burst of relieved laughter swept the longhouse, almost drowning out the summons of the next complainant. Gil sat up straight. It was not the guard's voice; it was Floki's. And the name he called, again, in his clear, accented English, was Gil Lake of Tir nan Og.

Gil sat stunned. Not only had Floki recognized him and

deliberately chosen to ignore him; now he was calling him to some kind of trial. He shook his head in bewilderment. But then Wolfskin and Sheep were both beside him, hauling him to his feet. With a shove from behind, Gil stumbled through the gathering, aware of a blur of curious faces turned to watch.

Then suddenly one face stood out vividly among them; a face he had last seen far away, on the beleaguered strand of Hy. "Ciarnan!" he cried.

The boy-monk's freckled cheeks were just the same, though a youthful beard bristled on his chin. But his sandy hair was no longer tonsured but tied back with a hank of wool. And he was dressed not in the grey habit of Hy but in the trousers and tunic of a Northman, with a Northman's sword at his side. Gil took it all in in the moment before Sheep hurried him by, and turning, called "Ciarnan! What's happened?" But the Irish boy ducked his head and would not meet his eyes.

Then Gil was at the front of the room, before the forbidding high table, standing rigidly upright with Wolfskin and Sheep blocking him in at both sides, and the guards watching with slitted eyes and hands ready at sword hilts.

As if I was some kind of threat! It was so absurd it was almost funny. Unarmed and bound, starving, and so tired he was sure he would fall without his two rough guardians propping him up; he couldn't threaten a mouse.

"Gil Lake?" Floki said again, as if he didn't know exactly who Gil was. Gil raised his head angrily but suddenly there was a shriek from the side where Percy sat on his little stool beside the harper.

"Gil! Gil!" he squealed, waving a chubby hand in excitement. Gil turned to answer, but Sheep shoved his chin around again to face the table. Floki smiled at Percy and held his finger up to his lips. Squinting sideways, Gil saw Percy do the same, nodding in happy obedience.

Then Floki turned to face him, and the smile vanished. Gil struggled to hold his composure, but the icy gaze froze his courage and he looked down at his feet.

"How long," Floki said amiably, "Does a man sail from Alba to the North Isles?" He leaned his head to the side and the yellow braids tumbled onto his shoulder.

Gil shook his head. "I don't know," he mumbled.

"Two winters and two summers?" Floki asked innocently.

Gil shrugged and shook his head.

"Were the winds that favored others that contrary to you?"

Gil shook his head again. "Floki, I didn't ...."

"*Silence!*"

"You asked," Gil protested, but Sheep thudded his back with the too familiar fist.

"Let him go," Floki said. Sheep and Wolfskin instantly released him. Gil staggered, and then, finding his balance, looked up, faintly hoping to see his accuser transformed again into his friend. But the glance he got was just as cold.

Floki drew silver from the purse from which he had compensated the farmer. Calling Sheep and Wolfskin forward, he gave each a portion and dismissed them. Gil watched with rising fury as his tormentors returned to the hearthside, smiling broadly. He whipped around and opened his mouth to argue, but his eyes met Aidan's as he did, and again, Aidan silently, and firmly, shook his head.

Struggling to swallow his anger, Gil raised his eyes to Floki's once more. "However long it took you, you are here now," Floki said mildly. "So I will have, now, the cup I entrusted to your care."

"The cup?" Gil cried, astounded.

Floki raised one eyebrow. "Yes. The cup." He paused and his forehead lined with a look of gentle puzzlement. "Is this so unreasonable a request?"

Gil shook his head. "I never ...."

"*The cup!*" Floki's eyes flashed and his counsellors drew back, alarmed. "The cup I left in *your care*. I will have it *now!*" He extended his scarred seaman's hand, palm upwards.

Gil stared at it, mesmerized. "But Floki, I *didn't* have it. You ...."

"Enough!" Floki slapped his hand down and then leapt to his feet and vaulted the table, landing light and certain directly in front of Gil. "Enough," he said again.

Gil saw the hand coming and tried to duck, but a second

later, he was on the floor. Dazed, he looked up. Floki nodded to his two guards, "Take him." Then he walked back around the table and took his seat amid his council and called to his harper for a song.

CHAPTER FOUR

The longhouse doors slammed shut behind Gil. The doorkeepers watched in silence as the guards hustled him away. Beyond the light of the guttering torches, stars faded in a blue-grey sky. To the north, summer's night-long dawn outlined the hulk of the longhouse, revealing a huddle of small turf lean-tos clinging to its walls.

Floki's henchmen hauled Gil to the nearest, raised the bar that secured its plank door, and with bored efficiency, shoved him inside. He glimpsed bare turf walls and dim shapes clustered on the dirt floor. Then the door swung closed and the heavy bar slammed down.

Enveloped in darkness, Gil heard the guards talking casually as they walked away, his fate of no more interest than that of the farmers' disputed ram. Wearily, he leaned against the door, trying it with his shoulder. It creaked and moved slightly. A loose hinge rattled against the wood. Light filtered through chinks in the planks and as his eyes adjusted, the faint outlines of the room and its contents re-emerged.

Awkward, with his bound arms, Gil stumbled across the small space and leant against the nearest object, exploring it with his numb fingers: curved planks of wood, a flat top, a familiar sweet smell. Ale. An ale cask. Beside the cask was another, emitting an aroma of salt and fish. His foot collided with something round and rubbery. A cheese. Ale, fish, cheeses. They had locked him in the dairy, like some disobedient girl.

Angrily, Gil staggered back to the door and thudded his weight against it. The wood gave a splintering crack. Elation flared and then spluttered out like a doused lamp. What was the point of escaping? The island was a sea-bound fortress. There was nowhere to run. The insecurity of his make-shift prison was a testimony to his helplessness.

He gave the door a last petulant shove and then stumbled in a mindless fury around the dairy, kicking savagely at turf walls and wooden casks. His foot connected with something smooth and cold that shattered with a tinkling crash, releasing the delicious scent of fresh milk.

Numbly, Gil stared at the pale pool growing amid the shards of broken pottery at his feet. He sank to his knees and bent forward, hungry enough to drink the sweet puddles from the dirt.

But then his mind flashed to Merlin's Tower, the Golden Knight's terrible prison in the ruins of Camelot, and the Knight himself spilling fresh water on the floor to torture his thirst. And now, the very man who had rescued him from Jocelyn Guidbairn's brutality had taken his place as Gil's tormentor. With his face an inch from the sweet pool, Gil jerked back and turned away.

Grimly he stood and stepped back from the broken milk jug. Leaning once more against the ale cask, he smiled to himself, savoring his one tiny victory over Floki. Then, propping his aching shoulders against the cask, he let himself slide to the floor. Too weary even for anger, he rested his head back against the sweet-smelling wood and closed his eyes. In an instant, he was asleep.

Then, in what seemed like another instant, he was no longer alone. A hand was shaking his shoulder, the fingers cool and light, as if a dream or a ghost had joined him.

Gil jerked awake. A face was bent close to his, surrounded by long silky hair, as grey as the dawn. Two deep, uncanny eyes stared into his own. "Gil?"

"Shony!" he gasped. "You're here!"

"Welcome home," she said.

"Home?" Gil murmured. Blearily, he surveyed his prison in the strengthening light shining through the open door. "Am I free?" he whispered.

She did not seem to hear him. Her attention was fixed on a cloth-wrapped bundle in her hands. "Come I bring you supper."

"Isn't it morning?" he mumbled dully. She unwrapped bannocks and cheese and a basket filled with berries and shook her head.

"The good father sings vigils. It is night." She drew a knife from the belt of her dress and cut his bonds with one quick slash. Gil rubbed his swollen wrists. Day or night, supper or breakfast, it was food. He clutched two bannocks, but a sudden noise outside froze his hand.

"Does Floki know you're here?" he whispered warily. Shony looked surprised.

"Of course. He sent me." She read Gil's incredulity on his face and her own expression hardened. "My son does not starve prisoners," she said.

Gil shook his head in confusion. "Prisoners ... but why am I a prisoner?" he protested furiously.

She gestured to the food. "Eat, Gil. I cannot stay long." She rose and found a stone cup on top of a cask, drew milk from a remaining jug, and offered it to him. Hunger overcame his frustration and reluctantly he took the cup and drank and then ate everything in sight, while she watched approvingly. "You have grown," she said proudly, as if she was his mother.

He remembered her standing alone on the strand of Einar's Holm, as he and his friends sailed away on her son's longship. "Shony," he said looking up into her strange eyes, "I haven't done anything wrong. I never had the cup he says I stole."

"Then you must tell him," she said mildly. "He is not unreasonable."

"But I tried!" Gil burst out and then shrugged and shook his head. "And, anyhow, he *knows*." He held her gaze unflinchingly. "He does know."

"He is not unreasonable," she repeated. "Nor does he set guards about a man with no cause." She nodded toward the open door.

"They're still there?" Gil asked, uncertainly.

"The dawn is very still," she said. "Listen. The waves on the shore. An owl returning to its nest." Gil shook his head, not in the mood for selkie runes. "Every sound," said Shony. She held her finger to her lips.

Gil stared and then suddenly understood. "I get it," he murmured. He wondered grimly if Floki's guards were set to spy, not just on prisoners, but on his own mother, as well. Shony stood, folding the cloth that had wrapped Gil's supper.

"The good father comes now," she said, watching from just within the door. Then, without farewell, she slipped out into the dawn. Gil stared at the grey rectangle of false freedom left by the open door until a tall familiar shape appeared within it, blocking out the light.

"Aidan!" Gil cried joyfully. A smaller shape slipped in at the Ab's feet, its tail hooked in a friendly curve, whiskers twitching at the scent of the spilled milk. "Oh, cat! Noble Cat!" Gil grinned happily, even as his own Cat-hackles rose on the back of his neck. He crouched and extended his fingers. "Well, *I'm* glad to see you, even if *he's* not."

Laughing gently, Aidan lowered the cowl of his worn grey habit and held out two strong arms to Gil. Gil moved forward eagerly, but then he stopped, unable to forget the Ab watching in silence as Floki denounced him. He wrapped his arms around himself and stepped back.

Aidan accepted the rebuff with a smile. He looked Gil up and down. "Well done," he said then. "Well done. You have returned."

Gil stared in astonishment. "Oh, right," he gestured furiously at his surroundings. "Like, in triumph, too!"

Aidan laughed. "And still as outraged by fate." His smile faded. "You have displeased our earl."

"Floki?" Gil cried. He shook his head in frustration. "But I haven't done anything. *You* know that. You saw. *He* took the cup and I took the reliquary. Is *that* what he wants?"

"No. Viking though he is, he knew the true treasure."

"Which *he* had!" Gil shouted. "I'm innocent and he knows it. He's lying, Aidan."

Aidan stepped closer, laid his long arm across Gil's shoulders, and turned him to face the open door. "Do not expect justice in this world, Gil." He smiled and then lowered his voice to a whisper. "And do not use words that call other men to use swords."

The chill of the early morning grew suddenly sharper. Gil moved back from the open doorway. "Aidan, what's happened here?" he said in a small, scared voice.

Aidan stepped back with Gil into the shadows. He found a milking stool and a small bench by one wall. "Come," he said. He took a place on the bench with the cat beside him and offered Gil the stool. "Sit. We will talk. But first," he raised his eyes to the doorway, "There is one who would join us. Come, friend," he called.

Gil shrank back against the wall, expecting one of Floki's listening guards. Or worse, Floki himself. But the figure that slipped in out of the grey morning was slight and boyish, despite his Viking dress. "Ciarnan!" Gil cried.

The Irish boy's eyes lit for an instant, seeing Gil. But, at once, the light in them faded, and he looked down at the dirt floor. Gil stared at his unfamiliar clothes and the sword belt at his waist. "Why is he here?" he whispered to Aidan. "Where's Donal?"

Ciarnan looked up, surprising Gil by understanding his English, at once. "Donal is dead," he said numbly.

Gil flinched, remembering the red glow in the sky as they fled Hy. Ciarnan looked again at the floor. Aidan stood and put his hand on the boy-monk's shoulder. "Tell him," he said.

Slowly, the Irish boy raised his eyes to meet Gil's. When he spoke, the accent of his English was the same as Aidan's. But each word came haltingly, as if it hurt him to say it, as much as it hurt Gil to hear.

"They come seeking you, with swords. Fire. But you are gone. Hy pays your ransom. Soon, everything is burning. Donal runs to the ponies. They kill him there and the beasts as well. The brothers hide me beneath the church. They go, singing, to their deaths. At last, the ships sail away. Those who are left kneel in the ashes. Pray. But I am done with prayer." His eyes flashed suddenly. "I return to my father and ask for a sword."

Aidan kept his gentle hand on Ciarnan's shoulder, but he looked at Gil as he spoke. "Now Ciarnan, too, seeks justice in this world."

Ciarnan turned to face the Ab. "I must avenge my kin. I am a king's son."

"As was Columcille, the great saint of Hy." Aidan smiled and gave the boy a little hug. "But come, my young Viking, your friend has much to learn." Aidan took his seat on the bench and Ciarnan sat cross-legged on the floor at his feet, as he had sat, a day long ago, with Gil and Ismail and Donal, beneath the high cross of Hy.

"At first," Aidan began, "All went well. While you rode so bravely to the North Gate of guarded Pentecost, we made our escape through the gate to the south. And while the usurper's knights pursued you, we circled and then travelled north through Caledon. By lauds we were riding out of the forest onto the high ground beneath the Grey Mountains, and at vespers of that day, we descended to the Great Loch and the ships."

Aidan paused as the Noble Cat stood and stretched, then jumped down and stalked to the open doorway, where it sat, flicking the tip of its tail. Aidan lowered his voice to a whisper and continued. "And there," he said, "We met dissension. The Northmen had seen a sign in the night. Above their heads, the winter dancers had ceased their stately dance and stood still as three great pillars on the hill."

"I saw that!" Gil cried. "I followed it … I thought it would take me north."

"That was wise," Aidan said. "For the Lord's world can never speak of evil, for all of it is good. But the Northmen feared it. They thought it an ill-omen, a warning, and they remembered the dragon and now they refused to sail back the way they had come for fear of it.

"Floki laughed at them, though he is the one who suffered the dragon's fury. Still, men who face bare steel unflinching can yet shrink from shadows and wraiths. And Hakon, too, clings to the ways of his fathers, though he will not admit it. 'Sail east,' he argues, 'Where the waters are wider and there is less dragging of the ships.' And Floki claims that the foe would think with the same mind and await us in the east.

"And then," Aidan said bleakly, "An arrow from the hill above takes Hakon's steersman, and the time for argument is done. The knight, Palamedes, rides to the hill to defend us and we set sail. In the haste, we are divided. Some go with Floki;

some with Hakon. But both ships sail one course, to the east, for the Northmen will have it no other way.

"Again, all at first goes well. By loch and river, we traverse Glen Alban to the sea. But there we meet the danger Floki foresaw. Behind the great headland of Ross, Guidbairn's ships lie waiting. They are many; we but two. We race for the open sea. Winds rise, a storm sweeps over us. The ships struggle and, cloaked in cloud and snowfall, are driven apart by the seas. When the squall passes, Storm Serpent is gone.

"Under oar, we turn back, search, and find, floating, those things – chests, oars – a ship leaves behind when she goes to her death. She is lost, and Floki is beside himself with grief, for his cousin, and for his lady, on his cousin's ship.

"Danni," Gil murmured.

"And your brother, Ismail, as well."

"Janetta?" Gil whispered fearfully.

"Safe with us. Safe, too, my scholar, Rachel, even now at her books, and the child, who never leaves Floki's side."

Gil fought back tears, in a turmoil of sorrow and relief. Aidan laid his gentle hand on his shoulder and smiled. "Have courage. The story is not yet done. Listen: night falls and we sail on then, in darkness; for Floki reads his course in your gift from Tir nan Og. But, by dawn his grief has turned to anger and his heart's course is set on revenge.

"And he is not alone. The Golden Knight, too, seeks vengeance. And though we reach the Northlands, we are not safe, even in our sanctuary. Before we make the Lenten fast, his Raiders fall upon Cille Aidan, with fire and sword." The Ab stroked the Noble Cat's striped back, "Fore-warned by my good advisors, we flee, with what we can save, to Einar's Holm.

"But here, too, the axe falls. For word spreads fast that we have some great treasure, and as well, Guidbairn has set a fine price on our heads. Pirates, Vikings, knights bought and sold for silver, all clamor to do his will. Again, they are many and again, we are few. The flames of Magnus Redbeard's roof light our way to the sea. And we come, at last, here, to Hrolf's Isle, where Floki commands men enough to hold our ground.

"But wild ground it is. And we live that first winter like

the beasts of the fields, indeed we live with them, with sails for shelter and often no shelter at all. The young bear it well, but it takes its toll on the old. Your sweet lady's fosterers both lie in lonely graves."

"Sir Alisander and Grania," Gil said sadly, remembering the ancient knight and his lady setting out so bravely on their last adventure.

Aidan gestured toward the rising land beyond the open door. "I sleep those months beneath the Stone of Odin, singing psalms to the wild birds and the seals." He smiled, "But my Master is, as always, with me. And, come summer, even before he raises his longhouse, Floki builds a church on the strand." He shrugged. "I am as grateful as I am mystified."

"That spring, fields are ploughed. Floki sails to Norway for seed. There is neither time, nor wood, to build properly, so turf is cut to make these walls, beams are raised, sail cloth spread over them. Again, Floki sails away and returns with *Silver Dragon* well laden: those fine panels that line his walls, the tables, goblets, stoneware, even glass. Ale, a cask of wine from Francia. Some paid for with silver, some, no doubt, with blood. By autumn, this fine longhouse stands here and though he laughs at its turf walls, he is proud of it.

"Between sowing and harvest, he sails back and forth, from island to island, paying courtesies to chieftains, paying silver to warriors, hunting deer and otters for noble sport. Then the harvest is gathered in, and the dark nights bring the time for feasting. His table is bountiful. There are games to test warriors. There is music and storytelling. He makes verses with Eoin, the blind harper from Ireland, and they play and sing together, and all are charmed.

"But through it all, his eyes are cold. And if you know him, and I do know him, you know it is all of it, song and verse, feast and play, for one purpose. He is binding men to him with ribbons of loyalty. And when he is ready, he will lead them to war. And so, while his warriors cheer him, I watch with misgiving.

"And then, into the next dark winter, a bright star falls. It is, again, Saint Lucy's Feast. And just as we come forth from Mass, a young man appears, walking alone up the strand. He nears us. We see his face. It is Thorkel, the youngest of Storm Serpent's crew, returned to us, like Lazarus, from the dead. His father runs, weeping, to embrace him, his child thought lost. And then, from him, we learn the true fate of Hakon Sea-Friend's ship:

"Not storm winds, but axe and sword were her undoing. Lost from us in snow and mist, overwhelmed and boarded by Guidbairn's pirates; her crew and passengers were taken prisoner and her fine hull splintered and sunk. Even as we searched the seas for them, our friends were sailing to their captivity."

"They're alive!" Gil cried joyfully. And then he remembered his own capture by Jocelyn Guidbairn. He looked grimly at the spilled milk on the floor. "And in the Knight's prison."

"No," Aidan answered. "Though that was most certainly his wish. But a man who pays for loyalty can be out-bid. This captain served many masters. And from one, an old sea-king in Norway, he thought to win a better price. So, breaking his feeble pledge, he turned his prow east, and sailed beyond the Golden Knight's reach.

"And in Norway, he sold his captives to this chieftain as slaves. Most were scattered amid the fjords. But Thorkel, the king kept, to carry here this message: that Hakon Sea-Friend remained a guest at his court and with him, the girl and the Saracen boy, from Tir nan Og."

Again, Gil felt joy and relief bubbling up inside him, but before he could speak, Aidan shook his head. And Ciarnan, too, looked solemn, as Aidan continued, "Floki sailed at once for Norway. And he took me with him, as a pledge of his good faith. But, arriving at the sea-king's hall, we found the noble chieftain had hidden his guests away, until he could be assured of our affection for them. Assurances he wished expressed in a very great deal of silver."

"They're hostages," Gil said bleakly.

"Of course. Which we expected. But we did not expect so high a price. Floki played the humble farmer, with scarce silver enough to ransom a sheep." Aidan's lips quirked in a smile. "And he played it well, taking care to dress the part; his finery left, with his sword, on the ship.

"But he made one mistake. The king, old and graceless, spoke too freely of Danni's charms. And the humble farmer's hand reached, by instinct, for his Viking sword. So, then, our host knew two things: silver could be found. And the captive lady held captive this farmer's heart.

"We left empty-handed. Floki played his part to the end, promising to return at harvest with the assurances required. And he will. But now he will return with seven ships and two hundred fighting men. The wrath aroused by the Golden Knight will fall first on this old fool. For if Floki made a mistake, the king made a far greater one."

"What?" Gil asked, uncertainly.

"Not killing us both before we left his hall."

Gil shivered to hear the words spoken so calmly by the gentle Ab. But then Ciarnan said suddenly, from his place at Aidan's feet, "He will serve for sharpening our swords."

Aidan laughed gently. "Ah, little brother of Hy," he whispered. "The saint and the warrior vie within you, as they vied within Columcille. As they do," he smiled, "Within every man. Even Floki Magnusson."

Gil studied the Ab then with growing awareness. "So he builds you a church," he said slowly. Aidan nodded. "And he lets you sit beside him at his council." Aidan nodded again, his shaved brow wrinkling in puzzlement.

"And that's it, then?" Gil cried. "That's why you didn't stand up for me? You *owe* him?"

Aidan's puzzlement vanished. He flung his head back, laughing so gleefully that the cat left his place at the door and trotted worriedly to his side. "So you see me a mercenary!" Aidan cried. "A prayer-Viking. For sale to the highest bidder." He laughed again and Ciarnan giggled at his feet.

Gil shook his head, his face burning, but as much with anger as with shame. "Well, why didn't you?" he demanded. "You know the truth. Why didn't you say it?"

Aidan ceased laughing. He held his hands out to Gil as he had at the door and then lowered them. "A man can speak, Gil," he said quietly. "But he cannot make another listen." He paused.

"You were long away. Long, long away." He shrugged. "And he is not a patient man."

"But it wasn't a long time there!" Gil protested. "Time is different there. You knew that. Didn't you tell him?"

"Yes. And as always when he does not understand, he does not listen."

"Well, tell him I was held prisoner. He can understand that."

"Yes." Aidan looked down at his hands, resting on his worn robe. When he looked up, his face was solemn. "He is not your enemy, Gil."

"Oh, right," Gil said sourly, waving his bruised hands at the walls of his prison.

"He is far more your friend than others in his hall," Aidan continued. "Many here have paid a high price for our adventure. Magnus Redbeard highest of all. Driven from his lands and longhouse, a vassal now to his own son."

"Does he blame me?" Gil said warily.

"Not as much as he blames me. Were Shony not here to stay his hand, I would be with my Master already." He paused and shook his head lightly. "But even *he* is not your enemy. Your enemy rules yet in Camelot. He has harried all who oppose him beyond its borders."

"My father," Gil whispered, "Lance'lot?"

"Exiled across the sea in Francia. The Master of Lances rides with him." Relief flooded Gil, again, as Aidan added solemnly, "Others are dead; others, still, in chains."

Gil thought again of the terrible prison in Merlin's Tower and the Golden Knight tormenting him with visions plucked out of time. *I am the eldest of many brothers.* The cruel face blurred and became another, uncannily alike. *Do you perceive why I am always your enemy?*

He looked up at the Ab. "Is it possible," he asked slowly, "For a man to be in two places at one time?"

Aidan looked surprised. Then he laughed whimsically. "Only the saints, Gil, are granted that gift."

But Ciarnan vigorously shook his head. "No. That is not true! Finn MacCoull could do that, with his harp, Time-Heddler. And he was far more warrior than saint."

Aidan smiled. "Indeed, he was. And when warriors grow powerful, their stories grow, too."

"It is more than a story." Ciarnan's eyes met the Ab's boldly. "I have seen the harp myself, at Tara, when I was but a child. My father carried me on his shoulders to the gathering of the kings. And there I saw it, by the pillars of the High-King's seat.

"And with it, the *file*, the King's own harper, and beside him, his son, a child no older than myself. Already this boy studied the harp that only his father could play, for just as the verse-making of the *filidh* is passed from father to son, so, too, the playing of the High-King's harp." Aidan regarded him thoughtfully, his chin resting on his hand. "Ask Eoin," Ciarnan said. "Before he came to serve as *file* to Floki Magnusson, he sang his verses for an Irish king."

Aidan laughed quietly. "From Tara to a turf hall. That is a humbling. Floki must pay him nobly."

"Tell me about the harp," Gil kept his eyes intent on Ciarnan's freckled face. Ciarnan looked uncertainly at Aidan.

"Speak," Aidan said. "I would hear this, too."

Ciarnan hesitated a moment and then began. "Some say Finn MacCoull won the harp from a goblin. Others that he found it in a mountain pool. Either way, it is enchanted. It plays a music so sweet that the warp of time is drawn apart by it, and men can pass through it, as the weaver's shuttle passes through the warp threads of the loom. And so, while time stands still in one world, a man can have long adventures in another. It is said that Finn travelled always with his harper, and three times escaped his enemies, vanishing through the threads of time, the harp yet sounding in the empty air."

Gil looked from Ciarnan to Aidan. Aidan leaned forward. "And you are certain you saw this harp?" he asked quietly.

Ciarnan nodded. "I saw it, for my father showed me it. And it was neither rich, nor beautiful, but plain and dark, without carving or decoration. But all around it stood the High-King's warriors, and none could touch it but the *file* and his son. And yet," he whispered, "It was stolen all the same."

"From Tara?" Aidan said. "That could not have been easily done."

"It was done by treachery," Ciarnan said, "And but one summer past. It was again the meeting of the kings, and again my father was there. There was a great feast, as always, and as always, games and horse racing.

"This year, strangers had come, men from Alba with horses more splendid than anyone had seen, bay and brown, dapple, and black as night. Fairy horses, some said, too beautiful to be of the world of men." Ciarnan's eyes shone, imagining them. "And when they ran, the sun seemed to stop in its course, that they might outrun it!" He dropped his eyes shyly. "Or so my father's household said.

"All gathered, before the great hall of Tara to watch; every warrior, his sword forgotten at his side. And then there came from within the deserted hall, the music of Finn MacCoull's harp. The warriors rushed in, drawing their swords, but already they were too late. For though the notes of the harp yet hung in the air, the harper, the King's *file*, lay dead on the floor, beside his murdered guards. And both the harp and the harper's young son had vanished.

"And when the warriors ran out again, seeking them, the men of Alba and their fine horses were gone too. And though all of green Ireland was searched, no trace of them was found. Horses and horsemen, boy and harp, all had vanished, none knew where." He stopped speaking suddenly, as if stunned by his own story.

In the silence that followed Gil spoke with absolute certainty. "I know where," he said. Both Ciarnan and Aidan stared. "They are in Camelot," Gil continued. "In Merlin's Tower." And then, leaning back and closing his eyes, he added, "And all the powers of the High-King's harp are in the hands, now, of the Golden Knight."

Ciarnan's eyes widened with astonishment. "How ...?" he whispered, but Aidan laid a quick hand on his arm and signaled silence. Quietly, he rose to his feet and stepped to the doorway, where the Noble Cat already crouched with swishing tail.

A shadow fell across the floor as the red-bearded guard loomed suddenly out of the dawn. The man barked a few gruff Norse words and Aidan answered in the same tongue.

Turning back to Gil and Ciarnan, he smiled wryly. "I am summoned," he said, beckoning to the Irish boy. "Come. We must go."

Ciarnan got up quickly and walked, head down, to the door. But Gil jumped up also and caught Aidan's sleeve, holding him back. "Who summoned you? Floki?"

Aidan nodded. "He wishes my counsel," he said, adding quietly, "And I would not try his patience, this night."

"So he wants a report," Gil said. "That's why he sent you, isn't it?"

Aidan's expression did not change, but Gil felt suddenly compelled to release his grip. "He sent me," Aidan said, his voice mild, "for the same reason he sent his mother. To offer comfort to a prisoner."

Gil laughed. "Great. Well, tell him this," he said angrily. "The only comfort I need is to get out of here. I'm innocent and he knows it."

Aidan folded his arms and studied Gil's face in silence. Outside, the guard barked another order and Aidan raised his hand in acknowledgement but did not turn. Then, as if searching carefully for words, he said, "I do not belittle your pain at your circumstance. But I beg your patience. Each man's cause is the only cause, in his eyes. But in his earl's eyes, it is always one of very many."

He paused, as if weighing his words again. Then he said slowly, "Floki is chieftain on this island, and on lands beyond it. All held in trust for men more powerful, but far away. Once a year, an earl will sail from Norway and receive tribute. It is a formality. The islands are too distant to be held from there. They are happy to leave him to rule here, as long as he leaves their shores alone and drives out any who would do otherwise.

"You have seen, this night, how this rule is accomplished. His hall is open to all. Any man can present his grievance, great or small. He addresses them with surprising wisdom, for one so young. In this, I do not fault him.

"He has his council. Four men, already chieftains in their own right. His father, out of filial duty." Aidan smiled wryly, "And me. I do not know why. Some memory of his childhood.

He consults us. At times he listens, at times not. He makes his rulings. And men obey."

"I bet they do," Gil muttered, remembering Floki's lightening leap over the table of counsel; the slap that ended argument.

Aidan smiled again. "The sword that men shrink from is also their protection, Gil. He leads them into battle, always at the front, in the greatest danger. He arms them. Wins treasure for them. Sets out the feasting board.

" But more; he is there when the harvest fails. Or the nets are empty. He will go hungry before they do." Aidan paused again, "In this, also, I do not fault him." He stepped closer to the door and stood looking out. "And now he wants my counsel." He shrugged slightly. "The night is nearly gone and when men are tired, they reach for familiar things. Childhood things."

He turned and fixed his eyes solemnly on Gil's face. "But he has gone beyond his childhood, Gil. Beyond any power, however slight, I had over him. He is the law here. The only law there is."

He went silently out, then, with the Irish boy beside him and the cat trotting at his heels. The door was closed by an unseen hand and the bar thudded into place. Gil sat down on the floor, staring at the dusty beams of light drifting through the worn planks. He leant back against the ale cask and closed his eyes.

A lump prodded his shoulder blades. *Aidan's book.* His treasure, rescued from Cille Aidan for the Ab. He had forgotten it entirely. With a sigh, he sat up, unrolled the cloak, lifted the book out and laid it open on his knees. He ran his finger along a line of the Latin script, trying to sound out the words. But their meaning remained locked away, as indecipherable as the world in which he was imprisoned.

Cradling the book gently, Gil curled on the floor to sleep, clutching the vellum pages against his chest.

CHAPTER FIVE

"Up!" A rough hand slapped his shoulder. Gil groaned, turned his face from the light, and curled tighter around the book. A foot nudged the small of his back. "Up!" Wincing, he opened his eyes and stared blearily up at a fierce, scarred face. *Floki's guard. The other one.* The hand shook his shoulder and the book was snatched from his arms.

"No!" Gil sat up, fully awake. "Give me that!" The guard threw it into a corner, dragged Gil to his feet, and shoved him out the door. He stumbled to his knees. Every part of his body ached from yesterday's punches and last night's cold, exhausted sleep. The guard caught his arm and he was dragged up again, squinting against the light.

To his left, the bright sea glowed blue and green, flecked with white. A longship was heading out to the open sea, her yellow-checked sail tightly reefed and her hull heeled sharply before the brisk wind.

Beyond, a white line marked the great wave that had nearly capsized Sheep and Wolfskin's skiff. Its low, continuous roar and the rippling and snapping of the gale-battered longhouse roof nearly drowned the shouts of his guard. "Go! There!"

Giving up on English, the man poured out a stream of Norse words and pointed. Three shaggy ponies stood waiting, bristly manes whipped by the wind, their reins gathered in the hand of the red-bearded guard. The nearest was buff-colored with chocolate brown legs. *Lionheart,* Gil thought for a joyous instant. But the pony was a stranger, older and heavier, and its companions; tan and cream-colored with dark cross-stripes on backs and shoulders, like all the Northmen's ponies, were strangers too.

The buff pony raised its head and pulled at its rough, rope bridle. Gil felt its fear of the flapping sailcloth. *It's alright,* he said with his inner, Lionheart-soothing voice. *It's noisy, but it doesn't eat ponies.*

The pony cast him a sideways look and shook its mane. The guard shoved Gil toward it and it shied again. *I don't eat ponies either.* Then it stood calmly, while the guard shouted at Gil and pointed at the cinched blanket that served as a saddle. Warily, Gil stepped forward, gripped the animal's mane, and, too stiff and bruised to jump, pulled himself up onto its back.

Straightening up, he saw both guards already mounted on their own ponies. The scarred man jostled closer to Gil, leaned over, and clasped his arms, jerking them roughly behind his back and binding his aching wrists yet again. The other grasped Gil's pony's bridle and kicked his own into a trot up the slope behind the longhouse. Ahead, the land rose, first gently, and then steeply, away from the buildings and fields, toward a heather-clad, rocky summit.

Gil gripped the pony's fat sides with his knees and looked around, baffled. Floki was the law here, Aidan had said. And Floki had tried him and passed judgement. So why were they leading him away from Floki's stronghold, up onto the wild hillside?

He is more your friend than others in his hall. Gil twisted around on the pony's jouncing back, as far as his bound arms would allow, and looked down at the strange, tented longhouse. *Many have paid a high price ... Magnus Redbeard most of all.* Cold wrapped his heart so suddenly that the buff pony felt it and whinnied its alarm. Magnus.

Warily, Gil returned his gaze to his guards, riding in silence on either side. Did they, like the pirates who betrayed the Golden Knight, also serve two masters? This place was full of treachery but even between father and son? *Trust no man,* Floki had told him, long ago.

Gil looked back again. The yellow-sailed longship was farther away, just a bright splash against the blue of the sea. Nothing else moved. Longhouse and barns, fields and meadows; all were deserted. What better time for Magnus to take his revenge, than now, while the men of the council sailed home and Floki's warriors slept off the night's feasting, in their hall?

Gil searched the empty landscape with fearful eyes. But no one, neither friend nor enemy, appeared, and they rode on until the longhouse slipped from sight behind a grassy ridge. And then, just where the green fields gave way to the steepening heather hillside, he saw the figure of a man, seated on a sun-washed rock with a grey, shaggy dog resting its head on his knee. Remembering the dog in the longhouse, Gil's heart leapt with hope. *Aidan!*

The dog raised its ears and watched them approach. But the man only tilted his head at the sound of hoof beats. Wrapped in a fine embroidered cloak, his black hair blowing in the wind, he kept his gentle handsome face turned toward the sun. *Not Aidan, but Floki's poet, Eoin.* Gil's hopes dissolved. He looked wistfully back as they passed, suppressing the yearning to cry out, lest he bring punishment on the blind harper as well.

"There!" A hand slapped Gil's face forward. Instantly, he was back in the ruins of Camelot, riding between two guards to an unknown fate. With a pang of grief, he thought of Janetta, and stole a glance over his shoulder to the landscape spreading out below, where, somewhere, she waited for him, as she had waited two whole years.

The ponies climbed higher on the steepening hill, and each upward step revealed more of the island. The longhouse reappeared far below, its white roof bold amidst the green meadows. Blue-green fields of rippling barley fringed the white strand where two longships yet lay beached, one surely Floki Magnusson's *Silver Dragon*. The thought cheered him, in spite of Floki's betrayal. A ship was an innocent thing, whoever helmed her.

Beyond, was the sea and beyond that, the mainland. In the distance, he saw the surf-rimmed headland around which they had sailed and the little green island with its bars of fierce white water on either side. Other islands appeared, low and blue on the horizon, mysterious and beautiful.

The ponies mounted higher still, into a broken terrain of heather and peat, scrambling over hillocks of rough golden grass and splashing through small dark pools. Gil caught glimpses of the far coast, headlands and coves, white beaches and green pastures. Although birds flew everywhere, and once a herd of deer bolted away at their approach, he saw nothing worked by human hands. Only Floki's longhouse and barns, and the small green roof of the church he'd built for Aidan, revealed men lived here at all.

Gil raised his eyes bleakly to the wild, distant shore. In which hidden bay lay the Viking ship that would take him into slavery, while Magnus walked away with a purse full of silver? Again, he thought of Janetta. At least she would learn he had kept his promise. He had returned. And maybe, like Thorkel, he would return again. Then he lowered his gaze to the near horizon and knew, at once, that would never happen.

A small dark smudge marked the greying sky at the point it touched the land; a standing stone, set up on the island's windswept summit, like the dark twin of the high cross of Hy. *I slept that winter beneath the Stone of Odin.*

Gil's pony skidded down a peat hag and the black smudge sank below the horizon, re-emerging longer and darker as they mounted the next small rise. It vanished as they descended again, and when it appeared a third time, he saw that, unlike the great stones of Cille Aidan, it was hollow. A circle cut through its face, showing white sky beyond.

Brooding and dark, it stood above all the island, like the one-eyed Odin himself. And Gil's path led relentlessly toward it, to a place more terrible even than Merlin's Tower. Far from the feasting hall, far from the church; a place of execution, beneath the Northmen's god of war. Just as Wolfskin's skiff told Gil his life was safe, the Stone of Odin told him it was finished.

He tugged desperately at his bound hands, working one chafed wrist against the other, but the knots held firm. Giving up, he cast quick glances left and right, seeking any sign of weakness in his guards. These were not Wolfskin and Sheep, but hardened warriors. They would do the work they were paid for and sleep untroubled tonight.

Ahead, the hollow stone loomed so close he could see its fretful shadow on the wind-torn grass. He struggled furiously with his bonds and the buff pony rolled its eyes at his panic.

The pony. He could feel its fear at his fear. He could *see* it. Its ears flattened, the whites of its eyes flashed, its coat rippled with nervousness like the grass in the wind. He stroked its sides gently with his toes. "I'm sorry," he whispered. "I wouldn't do this if I didn't have to." Then, wondering why he hadn't thought of it before, he conjured an image of yellow eyes and bared fangs, and shouted in his inner pony voice, *Wolves!*

Whinnying in terror, the buff pony reared and shied, flinging its head up and breaking the guard's grip on its lead. Gil clamped his legs tight and filled his mind with slavering jaws. *Wolves! Wolves! Wolves!"*

Fear leapt from pony to pony like sparks from a fire-striker. Gil's mount shied again, crashing into the beast beside it just as its rider lunged for the lead rein. Caught off balance, he lost his seat, but clung to his reins, dragging the animal's head around as he fell. Panicking, the pony stumbled to its knees in front of the second guard's mount. A moment later, both were down and both riders sprawled on the marshy ground.

Not believing his luck, Gil cried *Wolves* one last time, and the buff pony bolted for the open hill. He snatched a gleeful glance over his shoulder at his bog-wallowing keepers before his mount scrambled up out of the marsh, onto the summit of the island. The Stone of Odin stood ten strides ahead. Whooping in triumph, Gil urged the pony on toward the monolith, and the descent to the wild land beyond.

Then something moved behind the stone. Gil caught a flash of color, and then the pony saw it too. Flinging itself back on its haunches, and planting both fore legs straight, it skidded to an instant halt. Arms bound, and without a hope, Gil flew over its head and landed, face-first in the heather at its feet.

For a moment he lay stunned, aware only of the dark smell of peat and the whistling of the wind above. Then, spitting mud from his teeth, he turned his head enough to see daylight, and as he did, heard a new sound: the slow, measured steps of a well-schooled horse.

The steps came delicately closer until a black feathered hoof appeared beside Gil's cheek. Warily, Gil levered himself over onto his back, and peered up through peat-plastered lashes. Horse and rider loomed above him, blocking out the light. Gil glimpsed a splash of vivid red beneath a wind-whipped azure cloak; a glint of gold on the arm that held the reins.

"That is no way to ride." The voice was barely audible above the wind.

"*What*?" Gil wriggled sideways on the marshy ground and propped himself up against a tussock of grass.

The rider leant forward, holding aloft one leather-wrapped wrist on which perched a fierce-eyed hawk. The hood of his cloak fell back and the wind plucked gaily at the bright ribbons binding his hair. "Floki," Gil whispered.

"A man should use his arms." He smiled slightly and nodded to Gil's bound hands. Then he dropped the reins of his pony, and still holding the hawk aloft, reached to his belt. Gil saw the cold glint of steel. *The only law there is*, he thought dully. He flinched against his clump of grass.

Then, beneath him, the spongy ground trembled with the thud of approaching hoof beats. He heard the shouts of his belated guards, mounted again on their recaptured ponies. Muddy and red-faced, they burst up onto the ridge and then reined their mounts in so hard that they nearly followed Gil into the heather.

Floki whirled his horse to face them, the knife yet in his hand. His eyes narrowed. Pointing with the blade first to Gil and then to his two henchmen, he asked a soft-voiced question.

The red-bearded man swung an angry hand toward Gil's pony, calmly cropping grass beside the Stone. Then he jabbed a finger at his companion, who shouted a protest and raised a fist. Floki sliced the air with the knife, cutting the argument off short. Without a word, he flicked the point in the direction of the longhouse.

White-faced, the guards backed their ponies and then whirled them so quickly that the animals collided again. Half unseated, they pulled themselves frantically into their saddles and galloped away. Gil felt the mud on his face crack as his lips formed an involuntary grin. Then he turned and saw Floki watching him, and the grin died.

"They are not the fools they look at this moment," Floki said quietly. "You do well to escape them. Very well." He nodded his appreciation and sat studying Gil, as if re-considering. But then he twisted abruptly in his saddle and set the hawk onto the cantle. Swinging a leg over the horse's neck, he jumped down, the knife still in his hand.

"Floki," Gil whispered, "I didn't ...."

"Up," Floki said, and he bent, caught the neck of Gil's tunic, and lifted him to his feet.

"I didn't take the cup!" Gil cried.

Floki's hand on his shoulder whirled him around and he sensed the movement of the knife at his back. "You take the cup," Floki said gently. The knife slashed twice at Gil's wrists and the rope bonds fell apart. Gil gasped, feeling the sky whirling above him. "But I forgive you," Floki said.

He returned the knife to his belt and then turned Gil to face him. With a small smile, he brushed mud from Gil's hair. "Hail, Warrior," he said. "Welcome home." He put his arm around Gil's shoulders as if they were the best of friends.

Gil struggled not to shrink away, his thoughts racing. Did he accept this weird pardon? What if it was a trick to make him confess? But did he dare argue? His mind flashed to the slap that felled him in the hall. With the arm yet around his shoulders, Floki walked him to the height of the hill, beside the Stone of Odin, and turned him to look out over islands and sea.

"What think you of my earldom?" He gave Gil's shoulders a little shake.

"It's beautiful," Gil said warily.

"Yes. It is very beautiful." Floki smiled and looked off into the distance. "You take the cup," he said, "And you trade it to the Golden Knight, for your life." He turned to Gil. "A treachery. But I forgive you." He shrugged lightly and released his grip. Pointing out to the small green island amid the race of white water, he said, "That is most beautiful. I like that island most of all." He smiled dreamily. "You are young. You do not want to die."

"No," Gil said under his breath. And then all at once he understood everything. *He's crazy. Not like Crazy Ivan. Not even crazy like the kids at Safe Haven. Total, screw-loose, psycho crazy. And armed to the teeth.* Gil took a wary step back and looked left and right as if there might somehow be somewhere to run. Floki watched him, his brows drawing close in puzzlement.

Then he lifted his hand and before Gil could duck, very lightly tapped the side of his head. "What? You leave this behind in Tir nan Og?" Gil shook his head, still edging backward. "Why do you run from me? I tell you a story!"

"What?"

"A story! A tale for the longhouse! We play a *game*, Warrior!"

"A *what*?"

Floki shook his head like a teacher with his dumbest student. He put his arm around Gil's shoulders again. "This cup ...." he began.

Gil snapped. "I didn't have it!" He jerked free of Floki's embrace but didn't even try to run. "I never had it! Never! Never!"

Floki looked at the sky. "Gods of my fathers," he murmured. "What? Is my mind full of clouds, like old Asa's, that you have to tell me this? Of course you did not have it. *I* had it."

Gil stared and shook his head again. *Okay, it's me who's crazy. Come and get me, Dr. Fairchild. All is forgiven.*

"Warrior," Floki said patiently. "We are alone here. Here, now, I speak without stories. This cup we bring here, from Caledon; men do not know what it is. But they think they do. You say it when you take the reliquary: *this* is what men see. What they will follow. Gold, jewels, silver. Oh, this thing we bring here is far richer," he smiled with the same dreamy look he had for his island. "But they cannot see it. So they follow what they think they see.

"Word spreads, ship to ship, island to island, in markets, in feasting halls, that on Hrolf's Isle there is a great, great treasure. And the gold, the jewels, the silver grow and grow in men's greedy eyes. And they come, with ships and with swords, seeking it." He paused gravely. "And seeking you, who some think carry it yet.

"So I set men all over the islands, seeking you, myself. I set a high price for you; higher, I hope, than the others who would have you. And so you come to me," he said with satisfaction. "*But*," he continued, "You do not bring the cup."

"Because I didn't have it," Gil said, through gritted teeth.

Floki slapped his head lightly. "Speak when spoken to. No, you did not have it because *you traded it to the Golden Knight*. You betrayed me. Every man in the hall hears this. They sail, now, to their homes, their own longhouses. Soon all men know Floki Magnusson has been betrayed. The cup, the precious treasure, is not here. Although," he added with a playful smile, "Of course, it is."

He turned Gil again toward the green island in the white-frothed sea. "There, Warrior, where no earthbound man will find it."

"On the island?" Gil said.

"Where no earthbound man will find it," Floki said again. "I take it home, Warrior, to my brethren of the sea."

An image filled Gil's mind of Floki's selkie mother, Shony, swimming sleek and grey, among the seals. He shivered. "I guess it's safe there," he murmured.

"It is safe," Floki agreed. He grinned suddenly, and tousled Gil's hair. "You see? Our game is done now, and we have won!"

Abruptly, Gil stepped back. He shook off the affectionate hand and shook his head. "No. *You* won. I wasn't playing any game."

Floki laughed. "But you were," he said cheerfully. "Only you didn't know."

"No. I didn't know. I didn't know when I got myself out of Tir nan Og. I didn't know when I came back and found Cille Aidan and Einar's Holm burned and thought all my friends were dead. I didn't know when your gorillas jumped me and threw me into that boat. I ...."

Floki shook his head. "Gorillas? What is this gorillas?"

"*Gorillas!*" Gil said, angry to be interrupted.

Floki looked blank. "I do not know this word."

"Gorillas. They're animals." It dawned on Gil that there weren't a lot of them in the Northlands. "From Africa. The Saracen place."

"I know where Africa is. I am not stupid."

"Okay. They're animals. Hairy."

"Like sheep."

"*No*. Like, oh, sort of bears. But like people." Gil clenched both fists in frustration. "Like … like Bjorn!" he said with a flash of inspiration. "Like big Bjorn, on *Silver Dragon*."

"Ah!" Floki's eyes lit. "Animals like Bjorn. Gorillas! I like this. Bjorn-animals."

"Right. And you had two of them throw me into that boat and bring me here, into your longhouse, for your game. I was cold. I was hungry. I was scared. It was not fun."

Floki looked solemn. "It must be real, Warrior, or no one believes."

"You hit me," Gil shouted.

"Show me. Show me where I hit you."

Gil touched his cheek where Floki had slapped him. He felt nothing and shrugged.

"There is no mark. I know how to hit a man and do no harm, Warrior."

"Well, your gorillas didn't." Gil jerked his tunic up and showed off his bruised ribs. Floki's eyes narrowed.

"They have not my skill," he said quietly. He sighed. "I need many men to find you. Not all are warriors. These are farmers, when they find the way from the ale hall to the fields. You are a boy, and small. And already you show me you are more stupid than cowardly. I think they will be careless. You will try to escape, being stupid and not cowardly. Then they will panic and kill you. I do not want that."

"You could have fooled me," Gil muttered.

Floki looked away as if he had not heard. With his eyes on the horizon, he said, "Warrior, if I wish a man to die, he dies." He turned back. "But I do not wish it. So I tell them you are a great warrior. Schooled by my mother, the seal-wife. Her best student."

He smiled, "Do not concern yourself; I confess this lie to the good father. So now they are afraid. They make no mistake that lets you make a mistake." He looked solemn again. "I am sorry they hurt you. I deal with them."

"No," Gil said. "They did what you made them do. You can't

blame them. And it wasn't them who dragged me up here to die."

"Die? Who is dying?"

"No one! *But I thought I was.* I see that stone and I think I'm going to be executed – sacrificed to Odin!"

Floki's eyes narrowed to slits. He looked from Gil to the stone, and back to Gil "*What?*"

"It's the Stone of Odin. Aidan told me." Gil ducked his head. "I thought you'd kill me here. For Odin."

Floki looked heavenward again. "What are you, a pagan?" He sighed and said patiently. "The Northmen do not put the stone here, Warrior. It is old. But they like the stone and they like Odin. So they call the stone after Odin." He shrugged. "I like the stone, too. It shows my way home from the sea. When I wish to summon my council, I light the ward fire here." He gestured to an open space where the ground was charred and bare. He smiled at the stone, looked at Gil, and smothered a grin.

Then he said, "I'm sorry my game frightened you. But games are necessary. Indeed, Warrior, the longhouse is *all* a game. A story."

Gil looked up sullenly but said nothing.

Floki strode away suddenly and stood by the hollow stone, the wind whipping his beautiful cloak. He held his arms out. "Look at me," he said. "I am not a big man. I am tall, like my father, but I am not my father. He could break me in half, if he wished. And yet," he paused and said carefully, "It is to me the council turns.

"These two," he gestured toward the vanished guards, "I tell you, they are not fools. I choose them with great care. For my own safety, you understand. They are big. They are warriors. There are *two* of them, with axes at their belts and swords at their sides! And yet they run from a little knife I use to cut fishing line." He shrugged, delightedly, and held his arms up, the sunlight flashing from his gold bracelets.

"Yes, I have more skill with the sword than any man in the hall. But more than that. I have more skill *here*." He touched his forehead and laughed.

"I adorn myself as a king's son. This fine fur from Norway," he swirled the azure cloak to show its lining. "Silver and gold from the smiths in Deer Bay." His fingers brushed the twisted golden collar that encircled his throat. "Do I like this? The eyes of the women following me? Of course I like it. But that is not the reason.

"I bring Eoin from Ireland to sing of my feats in battle. And he does not come cheaply. Again, do I like this? To hear my fame in his beautiful words? Of course. And I drink the music of his harp sooner than any man's ale. But neither is that the reason.

"Men follow what they think they see, Warrior. Like the jewels of the reliquary. And there is more power in the words of the *file*, than in thirty benches of Vikings. The mind makes the story, and the story makes the chieftain."

He smiled again and looked away at his green island. "I have a surprise for you," he said.

Gil brushed mud from his face and worked his stiff shoulders and grimaced. "I think I've had enough of your surprises."

"This one, you like."

"Yeah, right."

"We bring two treasures from Caledon, Warrior, do we not?"

Gil groaned inside. *Oh, please. Not again.* "You mean the cup and the reliquary?" he said warily.

Floki looked at him as if he had grown a spare head. "Now, how can I mean that? Surely, they are but one thing, divided. And only one is the treasure, anyhow. *Two* treasures we take from the Golden Knight. The cup and ...." Floki made a beckoning gesture with his fingers.

"And his bride! Janetta!"

"Ah, well done!" Floki slapped Gil's head. "You do *not* leave this behind in Tir nan Og!" He turned then and waved an expansive hand toward the green land and blue water below.

"There?" Gil whispered.

"There."

"In the *sea*?"

Floki narrowed his eyes. "On the island, idiot. How do I keep her in the sea?" He shook his head. "Now I bring you back,

I wonder why I bother. What? You think there is a kingdom, in the depths, where the seal-folk build palaces and dance?" He shrugged. "Men will believe anything. Indeed that is what they do believe and they fear the island and the seal-folk and dare not set foot there. But if wraiths and selkies are not sufficient, the tides will keep her safe.

"See there," he pointed far out beyond the distant headland, "There is the sea of the west." He turned a half circle, "And there, the sea of the east. Twice a day, those seas run to each other, like a man and a woman in love. First, he runs to her," he swept his arm, west to east. And then, she runs to him." He smiled and gestured east to west.

"But to reach each other, they must pass, in all their greatness, through that narrow space." Floki bowed his head solemnly to the white-flecked water far below their feet. "And look! My island stands in their way. Like a proud mother, guarding her daughter's honor!" He held his hand up, as if to stop the tides themselves.

"Still, they meet, as men and women will, no matter what. But, as always where things opposite meet, be it seas or lovers, there is much that is beautiful, but much that is dangerous, as well." He showed Gil the two fierce lines of white water. "Twice a day, the tides must do this. And if the winds are wrong, they do not stop doing it, and there is not slack water, all the day long."

Gil nodded solemnly. "We came through there. The gorillas and me."

"What? Those two? They are idiots!"

"They cut my hands free, so I wouldn't drown if we capsized."

"They are kind idiots. You drown, anyhow. I bade them go around, Warrior." Floki said. He sounded remorseful. "There are men I count good seamen, who sail there." He turned and with one hand swept the far horizon beyond the seaward coast, "And all the way around, rather than pass my island." He paused, with satisfaction.

"I set watchmen on the strand, there, and there," he pointed to raised knobs of land to right and left of the longhouse, "To guard your lady. But they are little troubled." He laid his hand on Gil's shoulder and turned him slightly, "Look, now, that small roof, where the smoke rises?"

Gil stared until his eyes picked out an oblong of green turf, barely distinguishable from the green of the island. A pale, blue smudge of smoke drifted from it.

"There," Floki said, "Is the house I build her, with all she needs. I think she is too fine a lady to spin and weave like a Northman's wife. So I give her a little harp, and make a little bench by the door, where she can watch the sea, and sing love songs to you." He looked down at Gil, with a sparkle of mischief suddenly lighting his eyes. Gil turned warily back to the island. "What, you do not believe me?"

"I believe you," Gil said, a little uncertain about the harp. He paused and still wary, said, "Please. Can I see her?"

"Surely. There is a boat on the shore." Floki turned away then, to his waiting horse.

"A boat ...?" Gil looked down at the fearsome tide race, struggling to keep his terror from his face.

"You would prefer to swim?" Floki said, over his shoulder. Then he turned back in mock astonishment. "Ah, perhaps you do not know the *use* of a boat? That is not a worry. I teach you!" He grinned cheerfully.

"In that?" Gil winced.

"In that." He slapped Gil's arm. "We have fun. Come, I have new surprise."

Oh, wonderful. Gil wrenched his gaze from the turbulent waters.

Floki laid his hand on his horse's flank. "I must attend to my hawk." He extended his leather-bound wrist to the bird perched on the cantle of his saddle. She stepped one claw and then the other onto the leather, and flapped her wings once, as he lifted her down. "So patient," he held her to his face and she nuzzled against his cheek with her fierce hooked beak. "And so gentle." Then he lifted his arm and flung her free. "Fly home, pretty one."

The hawk swept up into the sky and flew off behind a heathery hillock. In moments she came streaking back and flashed over Gil's head and over Floki's, to the great hollow stone. Wings furled tight, she darted through the empty circle at its center, tumbled to the earth beyond, and then jumped up, again, a slender red-haired girl.

"Rachel!" Gil cried.

"Gil!" She gave a happy little sob and ran into his arms, enfolding him in her own. "I missed you!"

"I missed you, too!" He stepped back and dropped his arms awkwardly, staring at her. She was wearing something white with long, fluttery sleeves beneath a rich blue tabard, fastened at both shoulders with circles of silver. Ropes of amber beads glowed golden around her throat and crowned her braided hair. Her face seemed softer and sweeter than he remembered, and her eyes glowed, warm as the amber. Stunned, he hugged her again.

Floki's hand closed on his shoulder. "That will do," he said. "If anyone is to breach this fortress, I would have it be myself. Besides, she has one who courts her already. A young Viking. Is this not so, my Fire-Hair?"

"*No!*" she snapped.

"It is so." Floki said. He turned then to Gil. "See now, how can I sacrifice you, with my pretty hawk watching all the while?" He shrugged. "Otherwise, of course, I do it."

"Oh, Floki, shut up," Rachel said. Gil gasped, but the Northman only nodded thoughtfully.

"My hawk is kinder than you," he said.

"Your hawk likes the treats you give her. Like all hawks."

He smiled and touched the silver clasps on her shoulders. "And do you like the treats I give you? Like all women?"

Rachel met his eyes boldly. "Yes. But you still talk a lot of rubbish."

Floki leaned close to her and whispered, "I think I give that young Viking a farm. It is time he were wed."

Rachel looked up, her eyes blazing, and with both hands against his chest shoved him away. "Then *you* wed him!"

Floki collapsed against his horse, laughing helplessly. "Oh, Warrior," he said, "It is hard being earl. So much ingratitude!" A pony whinnied in the distance, and still laughing, he struggled upright. "Ah, look," he said gently. "Here comes one who will not despise me."

From behind the hillock, where Rachel's Hawk had flown, a rider appeared, small and stocky on a tall brown horse. A smaller animal trotted beside them, tugging fretfully at its lead rein. The led pony was pale with a dark shaggy mane and tail. He raised his head, casting nervous glances all around, and then suddenly stopped, his ears pricked forward.

Gil's heart soared. "Lionheart!" The pony reared and whinnied its excitement, tugging harder at its lead. In the same moment, Gil recognized the brown horse's rider, who struggled valiantly to hold the rein. "Let him go, Percy!" he shouted, and in his inner voice called, *Lionheart! Come!*

The pony broke loose and galloped free, head tossing wildly, the lead rein whipping the heather. Thundering around the standing stone, he clattered to a halt in front of Gil. Then, puffing hot breath into Gil's face, he lowered his head and pressed his nose against Gil's chest. *You left me!*

Gil rested his forehead against the pony's forelock. *I had to. I left you with Floki. He took you home.*

On the ship. Accusation bristled through every fiber of Lionheart's rough mane.

When you can walk on water, we'll skip the ship, Gil said patiently. *Hey, I'm* back *now. How about hello?"*

Lionheart rolled a wild eye toward Floki. *He feeds me heather.* Gil stepped back and looked down at the pony's bulging flank.

You look pretty fat.

He beats ....

Floki turned suddenly from helping Percy from his horse. He lunged past Gil, grabbed Lionheart's forelock and pulled his head around until they were eye to eye. "And I *will* beat you, and flay you, and hang your hide on that stone to feed the ravens, if you lie in my hearing *one more time!*"

He gave a satisfied nod and turned to Gil "Come, someone wants very much to greet you."

Gil looked up and saw Percy hopping from one foot to the other and waving both arms in delight. "Gil's back! Gil's back!" he chanted in a sing-song voice. He gave Gil a hug and a sticky kiss on his nose and then ran to Floki. Worming himself inside Floki's cloak, he hugged him, too. He looked out proudly, from within the cloak's enveloping fur. "I'm Floki's cupbearer."

"I saw that," Gil nodded, impressed.

Percy's arm shot out straight and he pointed at an intricately patterned bracelet encircling his chubby biceps. "Floki gave me this!" he announced. "It's shiny because it's gold." He squinted down his arm and pointed to the intertwined figures enchased all around it. "This is the serpent Fafnir. And this is Our Lord Yesu, Our lady, God's mother, and Saint ...." he paused and looked up at Floki.

"John," Floki said.

"And this is Odin playing with his wolf Fenrir. It's shiny," Percy said again, happily. He held it up so it caught the fleeting sun. "Floki gave it to me." He grinned and then, sliding out from under the cloak, hopped again from one foot to the other.

"You are cold," Floki said.

Percy squeezed his eyes shut and shook his head, "I need ...." he glanced at Rachel and hopped again.

"Well, go then," Floki said gently. "There, behind the stone. Rachel does not look." Percy bolted for the standing stone. When he came out again, shyly hiking up his trousers, he showed his bracelet to Rachel as he had to Gil.

Watching them, Floki said quietly, "The wolf does not play with Odin. It devours him." He slipped the circle of gold from his own arm, and gave it to Gil, showing him the figures. "But I do not tell him that." He smiled. " I see he likes mine," he said, "So I go back to the smith in Deer Bay."

"The smith?" Gil said.

"The jewelry maker." Floki gestured to the gold band in Gil's hands. "I do not steal everything, Warrior. I have him make another, smaller, to fit the child." He laughed as Gil handed the bracelet back. "I like this smith. He pleases all and serves two masters. See," he turned the gold band in his hands, "Here is Aidan's God and his cross, and here, my father's, with the wolf."

He looked up to Percy proudly holding his arm to the sun. "It is worth a year's harvest, but he likes it because it is shiny."

He smiled, and then said, "He is wise, this Holy Fool. Why else do men seek treasure?"

He turned suddenly to face the sea and slapped Gil's arm. "Come, the tides are running, the wind rises, and your lady waits."

Floki helped Percy back onto his tall horse and gathered the reins of his own. Gil reached for Lionheart's bridle but stopped, not sure whose pony he was, now. "Can I ride him?" he asked uncertainly.

"Of course, ride him. Indeed you may eat him for all I care," Floki said. "A more irritating piece of horseflesh has never graced my fields. But first," he pointed to the buff pony who had borne Gil up the hill. "Chase that one off, so my pretty hawk rides with me."

"No, you don't!" Rachel leapt past Gil and caught up the reins of the grazing pony and scrambled up onto its back. Turning to grin triumphantly at Floki, she sent it off in a canter, down the marshy track.

Floki laughed quietly. "Like the deer on the hill, Warrior. The faster they run, the more fun it is to chase them." He mounted his horse and, shepherding Percy before him, followed Rachel down the hill. Gil jumped happily up onto Lionheart's bare back, hugging his fat flanks with his knees. Lionheart gave a little buck of welcome and flattened his ears.

Yeah, I love you, too. And I'm staying on, so don't bother.

They caught up with Rachel where the steep heather slope met the fields above the longhouse. Floki drew his horse up short. Lionheart snorted and nipped at its heels. Floki pointed down to the strand where the longships lay.

"See, there, Warrior, by the side of my *Silver Dragon*?"

Gil shaded his eyes with one hand, struggling to control Lionheart with the other. A long frame of fresh yellow timbers was laid out on the shore. Two men were busy with axes, beside it.

"My cousin Hakon Sea-Friend has lost both ship and helmsman in my cause. So I build Hakon a ship." He gestured toward the workmen on the strand. "I owe him this. And I give him Erling as helmsman. I owe him this, too."

He paused, studying the wooden frame with satisfaction. "The good father tells you I sail to Norway at harvest's end?"

Gil nodded uneasily.

"It is well," Floki smiled. "I ask him to tell you. I would do a little trading there. And I take my friends with me." Gil nodded again. "This leaves, of course, a problem," Floki said. "For I need a helmsman, myself." He gathered up his reins and turned briefly to Gil. "This will be you."

"*What?*" Gil mouthed, dumbfounded. "*How?*"

"I teach you?" Floki reminded him. "Yes?"

He turned his horse toward the longhouse, guiding Percy's mount beside him. "I will be at the strand at None. But first, go with my pretty hawk to her virginal nest," he grinned at Rachel. "And have her feed you well, for you will need it."

"Where?" Gil said, confused.

Floki pointed to the green roof of the church and Gil saw then two small turf structures beside it. "I keep her safely apart from the longhouse," Floki called, as he rode away, "She frightens my Vikings."

CHAPTER SIX

The church was small and dark, tucked into the sand bluffs on the shore. It was built of cut turfs and had no windows, and the green grass roof swept almost to the ground. But a small wooden cross stood above one gable and beside it perched a grey and black bird.

"It's Feannag!" Gil cried happily. The crow stretched its wings and cawed and flew down to a new resting place on the wooden bell frame at the church door. "It's just like Cille Aidan," Gil whispered. His fingers found the stone in his pocket that he had not yet returned to Aidan.

Rachel nodded. "We took everything we could in the time we had. The bell, the holy vessels, the altar cloths, and lights. All the books we could carry. Aidan took them in the fishing skiff, with Percy. Janetta and I took the ponies and the hens. We had to leave the sheep behind."

"They killed the sheep," Gil said.

Rachel didn't answer. Her eyes were on the door to the church where a tall young Northman had suddenly appeared. Lanky and fair-haired, he smiled and ducked his head shyly as Rachel rode by. Gil looked back as they passed. He leaned across and prodded Rachel's arm. "I know him! He's ...."

"The boy from the ship," Rachel said for him. "The one Danni wounded."

"Right. He called you Fire-Hair. *He's* your Viking!" Gil said. "The one Floki's going to give the farm to! But he attacked us!"

Behind them, the bell suddenly rang. Gil looked back at the church. Aidan was standing with the young Viking. Beyond, he saw Shony striding from the longhouse, her grey hair blowing in the wind, and Percy trotting to keep up, at her side.

"What hour is it?" He looked at the sun.

"Only Saxt. Shony keeps the Little Hours with Aidan. Terce, Saxt, None. The angrier Magnus is with him, the more Shony comes here to pray."

"And your Viking too."

"He's not my Viking," Rachel said. "But my house being right beside the church might have something to do with his holiness." She shrugged. "His name is Ragi Ulfsson. He belongs to the High Island. Last winter he walked, unarmed, into the hall, flung himself down on the floor in front of Floki and asked to be killed or to be allowed to sail with him. For my sake."

"Really?" Gil stared. "That's pretty cool."

Rachel raised an eyebrow. "Oh, not you, too," she said wearily. "Floki loved it. He gave him a bench on the longship and put him to work on the farm."

"To work ... he's sort of earning you?"

"Right," Rachel said drily. "Like some Viking Jacob. Only, Floki isn't my father, so it rather misses the point, doesn't it?"

"What?" said Gil.

"Jacob and Laban? It's from the Bible, pea-brain." She drew her pony up in front of a little turf hut and turned to face him. "Haven't learned a lot more back home, have you?" She grinned, but then her grin faded, and she slid down from the buff pony's back. "How long is it there, Gil?" she asked. "How long have we been away?"

"Three months."

She winced. "My father will think I'm dead."

Gil looked away uncomfortably. "Well, missing," he said.

"I'd never run away. Never leave him deliberately. I'd *have* to be dead."

"Or here."

"Yeah. Here," she smiled wryly. "I'm sure York Constabulary will have worked that out by now." Her smile suddenly broadened. "Of course," she said, "He may have found my message!"

"Your ... oh!" Gil cried. "'All will be well!' Rachel, I'm so sorry! I took it. I found it in the ashes in the scriptorium. I brought it here inside a book." He shook his head sadly, but she laughed.

"So?"

"But how will he find it now?"

"The same way he does find it, if he does. Whatever happens here is part of what *has happened*, there. Wherever you move it to will be on the way to where it is there."

"It makes no difference?" Gil said. She nodded. "But if everything makes no difference, what's the point of doing anything? We have no choice."

"Of course we have. Get off your pony."

He shook his head. "I can't stand that."

"Get off your pony."

"Sure," he said disconsolately. He swung his leg over Lionheart's back and jumped down.

Rachel smiled triumphantly. "You just *chose* which side to get off Lionheart. Not to the right. Not over his head. Not down his stupid tail. You chose, and one thousand plus years from now, in Tir nan Og, that's part of history. In that world, what we will choose has already been chosen. That's all."

"All?"

"Gil. Live with it. You have bigger problems. Like your sailing lesson, helmsman." She took Lionheart's reins from him and led both ponies to a small pen built of hazel saplings woven between stakes. He helped her drag the gate closed, his eyes on the bright sea and the green island beyond.

"Do you think he means it? Or is it another of his weird jokes?"

"Oh, you never know with Floki," she said airily. She held open the plank door of the turf hut. "Welcome to my virginal nest!"

He paused, just outside. "What's going on between you and Floki?" he said.

"Absolutely nothing." She gave him a stern look. "Hawk likes him," she added. "But Hawk likes anything that feeds her. Rather like a cat," she grinned. "He flirts with me, Gil."

"He gives you gifts."

"He is earl. He gives gifts to everyone. He loves Danni," she

said. "He could have anyone. He has no one. He only wants her."
She stepped ahead of him into the dark interior and knelt by a
little hearth in the center of the floor. Blowing on the embers,
she fanned a small flame into life. Then, taking a burning twig,
she stood and lit an oil lamp hanging in one dark corner. Its
soft light flared, revealing a bed, a table, and a desk with a book
lying open.

"It's like Aidan's cell," Gil said.

She laughed gaily. "Help! I'm turning into a monk! Quick,
tell Ragi!"

Gil stared at the book. Beside it, on a lined sheet of vellum,
words had been copied out in an almost identical script. "Why
are you doing this?" he whispered. "You really are becoming
one of them."

Solemnly, she shook her head. "No. One day, I'm going
home. And I'm taking all the knowledge I can, with me. The
only thing I can keep from this whole world. The *only* thing,
Gil." She went to the kist beside the fire and took out barley
bannocks and cheese and a stone bowl filled with berries. "I'm
sorry for Floki," she said. "That's why I flirt with him. I like to
see him laugh."

Gil looked up, startled.

"If you could have seen him, that winter we camped on the
hill," Rachel said, "When he thought she was dead ... and then,
when Thorkel came and we learned she and Hakon and Ismail
were in Norway, he was like a little kid. He loves her so much
...."

"So why doesn't he use some of that bling he wears to
ransom her?" Gil said.

"What? Oh, the gold." She smiled. "It's not that simple, Gil.
If he pays too high a price, word will spread among the pirates
and none of his household will be safe. His parents, his priest,
his poet ... me ... any of us will be targets. It's all a game of
bluff. The king pushed too far. Floki has to use force, now." She
laid the food in front of Gil and gestured for him to eat. "Not
that that bothers him. It's his favorite part of the game."

She sat on the floor and laid peats on her fire while he ate.
Looking up, he asked evenly, "Does Floki take hostages?"

Rachel spread butter on a bannock carefully. "He holds none here, now. Nor any thralls. All are free men." Then she raised her eyes to his. "If the circumstances were right, of course he would."

"And that's okay with you?"

She wiped butter from her fingers and shook her head in frustration. "Gil, it's their world. It's nothing to do with me." She leaned closer and said urgently. "Everything is different here. They may seem the same as us, sometimes – men and women, boys and girls, little kids – but they are not. A thousand years of history lie between us. We cannot cross that. Even in our minds."

"Except we have."

"We haven't, Gil. That's my point. That's why I'm sad for Floki. We don't belong here and we don't belong together. Not Ragi and me. Not Floki and Danni. And not you and Janetta, either."

Gil put down his bannock unfinished. "Oh, you really do know everything, don't you?" he said coldly.

"No. But I know this. And so do you."

He ate his lunch in silence, thanked her gruffly, and went out the door, his face turned stubbornly from her wise, gentle eyes.

The strand below the longhouse was deserted, the only sound the crying of gulls and the hammer blows of the distant boat builders. Glad to be alone, Gil strode swiftly along the sand and rough shingle until he reached the two beached longships.

The first was a stranger; its carved figurehead a snarling wolf, painted in red, black, and green. Gil ducked beneath the ship's high stern, splashing through the water pooled in the hollow in the sand where the hull lay. Beyond, *Silver Dragon* nestled in her own sand hollow, her mast lowered as when they had dragged her through the marshes of Glen Alban.

Between the two ships, five Northmen were gathered around the frame of fresh hewn wood Floki had shown him from the hill; not, he saw now, a ship, but the cradle in which a ship was being born. Only the keel had been laid, so far. Beside the frame, two men were trimming long planks with skillful axes, while two others hammered splitting wedges into a mighty tree trunk. More felled trees lay waiting. Gil wondered in what forest they had grown, far from these windswept islands.

The fifth man, with rosy cheeks and a long white beard like a Northmen's Santa Claus, stood watching. He wore a grey smock over his tunic, with a broad pocket filled with tools. More tools hung from his leather belt. When he spoke, his voice was a curt growl and the others nodded nervously.

A fire burned in a circle of stones and over it something sweet and piney bubbled in a black pot. Neat coils of rope lay beside a bundled sheep's fleece and a row of hammers, axes, and tongs. For a fleeting moment, Gil saw his father's workshop in Greene Mountain Falls.

The white- bearded boat builder squinted briefly in his direction, his blue eyes faintly curious.

Gil nodded a silent greeting and retreated to where *Silver Dragon* lay in the sands beyond. Standing in the shadow of her hull, he reached out and laid a hand on the smooth oak strakes. Stroking the wood, he felt his anger with Rachel drain away.

He looked up to the graceful, curving bow and saw to his delight a new wooden dragon had replaced the one splintered by the living dragon of the Great Loch. Trailing his fingers along the wood, he walked around the bow, where the sturdy stem rose up to join the figurehead. He stepped out to the far side of the ship, but kept his hand still on her strakes, warm and dry in the midday sun.

"You would helm my *Dragon* already, Warrior? That is bold."

Gil whirled. "Floki?" He looked up and down the empty strand. "Where are you?" Then his eyes fell on a little skiff drawn up on the shore, half-obscured by blowing beach grass. Within its shallow hull, the Northman stretched lazily on the sun-soaked fur of his cloak.

"I'm sorry," Gil muttered.

"Do not be. I like boldness." Floki adjusted his bare feet on the skiff's rail. "But you are early and you disturb my sleep." He closed his eyes.

Gil muttered "Sorry," again and wondered if he should leave. But before he could move, Floki suddenly sprang into wakefulness, leaping to his feet. Signaling Gil to join him, he began hauling the skiff to the water. At the sea's edge, he stopped.

"Here is your dragon for this day. A little dragon, a young dragon, but fine and playful, as all young things are."

Gil looked at the skiff and thought suddenly of his first ride on a very young Lionheart. "Great," he said.

Floki slapped his upper arm. "We have fun," he grinned. Then he leaned into the skiff and, throwing his cloak aside, scooped up a sword and shield. "Yours." He handed them to Gil. Then he retrieved the small, bone-handled knife that had been Gil's father's. "And this. I am sorry to have disarmed you, but it was the only way."

He paused and added, "There was also a book. But unless you become very holy in Tir nan Og, I think it is the good father's." He paused and said cautiously, "You do not become very holy?"

Gil shook his head, as he strapped his sword belt around his waist and slipped the knife through his belt. "It's Aidan's. I found it."

"Good. That would perhaps have made a problem."

Gil looked up quizzically, but Floki only grinned. He climbed lightly into the boat and standing on two ribs, lifted the pine mast that lay, with spar and sail, diagonally across the hull. He pointed to an arched and tapered block of wood rooted firmly over the center of the keel. "Mast-fish," he said. "And, below, the kerling – the old woman, we call her – who holds the mast." He raised the pine pole vertically, slotted its foot into a waiting hollow in the wooden block, and wedged it in place.

"Here, the rakke." He lifted the long spar with its furled sail and showed Gil the ring of rope securing it to the mast. He tugged at the halyard attached to it, "With this we raise and lower sail. This is alike on any ship. Everything is alike. What you learn here, you learn for there," he pointed to his beautiful warship. "Come."

Dragging the skiff into the sea, he stood in the water by the steering board and drew Gil close beside him. "Steering oar. See?" He pointed down into the water, "It is fastened below, and above it is yet loose." He pivoted the smooth blade, then swung it up. "Here, when we beach her, and now, here," he lowered the blade into the water and with swift hands fastened the upper length of the oar to the skiff's side with a strap of leather. "For the sea." He flipped the strap free. "You do it."

Clumsily, Gil repeated what Floki had shown him. "Do it with care. Without the steering oar, the sea does what it wishes with her. You do not like that." Gil checked the strap again, peering at it intently. Floki nodded, with a small smile.

He waded out, dragging the skiff until the prow slipped into the water and floated free. Then he leaped lightly aboard. Gil pulled himself up out of the waist deep water and flopped over the side, envious of the Northman's swift grace. *What do I expect?* He reminded himself. *He's half fish.*

Floki handed him the steering oar. "Yours." Then he took up a set of oars and with powerful strokes rowed them out from the lee of the shore. "Head her up," he said, shipping his oars, "into the wind."

Struggling to find the wind direction amid the shifting eddies, Gil obeyed, while Floki loosened the square sail and hauled the spar up the mast. At once, the skiff spun sideways, lurching under the force of the wind. "Head her up," Floki said, his voice as mild as milk.

Gil worked the unfamiliar rudder, pivoting the little craft into the wind, and then beyond. The half-secured sail blew back over his head and the skiff lurched again. Floki jumped beneath the sail, laughing, and caught the flapping sheet. Securing it, he gently took the steering oar from Gil's hand. The little skiff came alive. Its sail billowed taut, its sleek hull heeled sharply, and it bounced across the choppy sea like a happy puppy.

Floki sat down on the bench beside Gil, put the steering oar back in Gil's hand, and kept his own over it. He guided the oar until the wind spilled from the sail and the woolen cloth sagged and fluttered.

"The wind is a proud woman," he said. "She scorns us if we face her too boldly." He nudged the oar beneath their hands and the prow dipped toward the beach at their left. The sail filled and the skiff rode landwards. "But if we bow to her, yes, she will play. But look," he pointed to the right edge of the sail, fluttering backward toward the mast, "She tricks us. Hold course," he said.

He got up quickly and took up a light spar, fitted one end into a notch near the foot of the mast, the other into a little pocket at the foremost edge of the sail. "Now, we trick her," he said. He took his place beside Gil and laid his gentle hand on the oar again, nudging it slightly. The sail kept its trim curve and the skiff picked up speed. "But wait!" Floki cried, "Where does she take us?" He looked pleadingly at Gil.

"Into those rocks?" Gil said, pointing nervously at the shore.

"Ah, she is cruel, this woman. But we outwit her." He turned the oar beneath their hands and the prow of the skiff swung out to the right. The sail fluttered briefly, and then caught the wind from the other side. Floki jumped up and switched the little spar to its new leading edge. He took his seat again, but left Gil alone with the steering oar, and to Gil's amazement, he held their course.

"Good. Good. You outwit that proud lady. But now we grow bold, Warrior. Bold enough to seek her embrace." He took the steering oar from Gil and swung the prow sharply around to the right. The sail lifted and billowed and the little skiff bucked like Lionheart and plunged forward, with the wind full at their backs. "Take the spar." Floki pointed to the sail with his bare foot, while he managed the rudder with one hand and loosened the nearest sheet with the other.

Gil jumped up, took down the spar, and adjusted the other sheet until both were equally taut. "Yes!" Floki smiled. "Good." He returned the steering oar to Gil. Looking up at the sail, he said, "Now, she is our lover; she gives us all of herself." He smiled again and lightly adjusted the sheet. "But she is a very vigorous woman, I must warn you."

He showed Gil a low blue silhouette behind them. "Soon, we leave the lee of the Spear Island, there, and there is nothing between us and the open sea." He pointed forward, "There, where the white horses play, you will feel her vigor. Take care you do not run too fast, lest your sea pony stumble, as *Silver Dragon* does, in the Great Loch, when I break her mast."

He glanced up. "This mast does not break. It is slender, and not stayed. It will bend like a woman at the harvest." He made a graceful gesture with his hand. "But she will plough deep and the sea will drag her under."

"Right," Gil said uneasily. He kept his eyes on the skiff's sharp prow, slapping against the waves. Ahead, the small green island was barely visible in a haze of spray. He could hear the low roar of the tide-race over the wind and the rippling sail.

"It is called the Holy Isle," Floki said. He leaned lazily back against the rail, trailing one hand in the rushing sea. "Fathers, like Aidan, lived there once. They are gone now. See there, that white strand?"

Gil peered ahead and glimpsed a streak of pale sand between the sea and the greenness.

"Make for that. Beyond, there is that place where sea meets sea. We save that lesson for another day."

"Right," Gil said again, tightening his grip on the steering oar. Floki stretched out on his fur cloak, twisting around to lean over the rail.

"Ah, my brethren."

Gil looked to his left and saw two dark heads bob up in the water. A sinuous dark back slipped through the waves, yards from the flying skiff. Yelps and cries surrounded them and again Gil remembered Shony on the strand of Cille Aidan. Floki laughed, reaching out as if to touch the nearest.

"Do you know what they're saying?" Gil asked uneasily.

"Of course." Floki flicked water at the beast's whiskery snout. "They say that at the bottom of this sea lie the bones of many men."

"Great," Gil muttered.

Floki turned and smiled. "They are like all creatures, Warrior. They talk of what interests them. In their case, fish." He stretched again, rolled onto his back, and folding his arms beneath his blond head, closed his eyes.

Gil stared. "What are you doing?"

"I talk all night with chieftains and ride, hawking, in the dawn. Now, I sleep. You sail her."

"By myself?"

"That is right."

"What if I miss the beach or something?"

"Then we will go in the tide-race and sink," Floki said sleepily. "You know, Warrior, this does not worry me."

"Well, it worries me!"

"Then do it right. And quietly," he added.

Gil glared and, for an anarchic moment, looked for something to throw. But the sail and the steering oar demanded his attention. *He's like Ivan,* he thought suddenly. *Work it out yourself or die trying.* He remembered his escape from Safe Haven; the flaming torches and Ivan's great horse galloping ... no. No horse. No torches. Something else ... something else. Gil gripped the steering oar and fixed his eyes on the green Holy Isle in its veil of spray. The future was gone. All that was real was the wind and the sea and the steering oar beneath his hand.

And an arrogant sleeping Northman. Gil reached over the rail, scooped a handful of water, and flung it at Floki, splashing his face. Floki smiled without opening his eyes. "There is something I have always wondered," he said.

"What?" Gil snapped.

"Do cats swim?"

Gil reached for another handful of water, but suddenly the wind slapped into the sail, doubling in strength, as they lost the lee of the blue island. The gale battered Gil's back, whipping his hair into his eyes. The skiff took off like a bird. Breaking waves rolled and frothed on every side and the little boat leaped from crest to crest. Gil's breath caught in his throat. *Too fast. Head her up. Lose the wind.*

He leaned hard on the steering oar. The skiff slewed sideways, her rail dipping into the sea. Water rushed over his arm. Frantically, he swung the rudder the other way, but the little boat slewed wildly again. "She won't turn," he muttered. The skiff tore on like a runaway pony, rearing up the backs of waves and plunging down the breaking crests.

Then suddenly there were two waves, jammed together, a great wall of water. The prow hit it first, cutting through it like a knife, and then buried itself in the blue green depths of the second. Cascading water flooded the hull, sweeping Gil from his bench and flinging the steering oar from his hand. He felt the skiff roll and grabbed wildly for the rising rail.

Then, from nowhere, Floki was beside him, one hand on the steering oar, the other on the neck of Gil's tunic, hauling him upright. The skiff settled level again, water sloshing in her bilges. A moment later, she was sailing sweetly across the wind, her obedient prow aligned with the low white strand of the Holy Isle.

Gil sat shaking on his bench.

"You are cold?"

"No. Scared. She wouldn't turn for me."

Floki laid his hand lightly on his shoulder. "She would. When she was done frightening you, she would turn. Next time, hold fast."

"I thought I was going to drown."

The hand tightened on his shoulder and then released him. "Let loose that sheet, Warrior. We beach her now." Floki smiled, his eyes on the strand. "You do not drown when I am here," he said.

He leaned over the rail, swiftly loosed the leather strap, and raised the steering oar. "Jump, now, and pull her in."

Gil ducked under the sail, climbed up onto the curving prow, and jumped down into the shallow water, relishing the solid ground beneath his water-logged boots. Floki lowered the sail and dropped the mast, and then waited until the prow touched the strand before stepping ashore, as if disdaining to wet his bare feet. Then, together, they dragged the little skiff up onto dry sand. "Warrior, where is high tide?"

Gil looked around blankly and then, with Floki watching, trudged up the beach until he reached a line of dead seaweed. "Here?"

"And in a storm?" Gil trudged further, until he was surrounded by beach grass. Floki nodded. When they'd hauled the skiff up into a grassy hollow, he sent Gil higher, still, to a rocky outcrop. "Three stones." He measured a small boulder size with the gap between his hands. He stood by the skiff, re-fastening his cloak, while Gil hauled rocks. "In the skiff. Carefully. Do her no harm."

Gently, Gil laid three stones into the bottom of the hull. Floki re-aligned his gold armbands and smoothed the windblown hair of one of his be-ribboned braids. "Winds and tides can run higher than any man imagines, Warrior. The day will come when you want a ship in a hurry, and you will thank me." He turned toward the sea. "I leave you the skiff. I do not advise you to use it."

"Leave?"

"I would call upon my brethren."

"What? But what about me?" Gil looked up and down the empty strand.

"Warrior. Your lady is here. Do you forget?"

"*No*. But … I mean, like, just me? And her?"

"It is the way it is done, is it not?" Floki smiled and pointed inland. "Just up the hill, there. It is a small island. You will find her." He turned and trotted to the edge of the breaking waves and stood with the water foaming about his bare ankles. He looked grave. "It is customary for a warrior to thank his earl for a gift."

Gil cast a terrified glance over his shoulder. "Thanks," he grinned weakly. "A lot."

Floki kept the stern look for a moment longer and then dissolved in laughter. "I wish you a good night." He ran into the sea and turned, still laughing, and waved to the high ground of the little island. "If she proves too much for you, light the ward fire. I come and help!" Still laughing, he dove into the waves and vanished, leaving Gil staring in outrage at an empty sea.

After a long while, two sleek grey seal heads appeared far out, among the white horses, but if either was Floki, Gil had no way of knowing and they dove at once, re-appearing farther away, remote and unreachable as any wild creature. Gil picked up a stone and hurled it at them both. "I hate selkies!" he shouted uselessly. He snatched up another stone.

"No! They are good! Do not hurt them!"

Gil whirled. She was standing on a little green knoll, just above, clasping a hank of her wind-whipped black hair in one hand. Her other was raised in a determined fist. The fist slowly uncurled. Gil dropped his stone. All his apprehension vanished and he felt his face break into a huge, mindless grin.

"It is you?" she whispered. He nodded happily. She released the hank of hair and let it blow free across her face. For a moment, she stood with her hands holding down the edge of her braid-trimmed tunic, the sleeves of her white dress fluttering in the wind.

She was taller than she had been, and older, and he knew, at once, she had abandoned the child's toys she had played with in the Mews Tower. But she had not abandoned him. She lifted her hands from her dress and then she suddenly shrieked joyfully and ran down from the knoll. She reached the sand and with arms outstretched, leaped at him like a bounding cat. He caught her, mid-air, and she wrapped her arms around his neck, and her legs around his, her bare feet crossed behind his calves. Without a hope, he fell backwards, onto the strand of the Holy Isle, with her warm weight on top of him, enveloped in her curtain of shining hair.

Thank you, Floki, he thought joyfully, all doubt vanishing in the warmth of her embrace. *Thank you. Thank you. Thank you.* For a dizzy moment he wondered if he should ask permission to kiss her again. But then she was kissing him. *A second kiss!*

She pulled back just enough to look into his eyes. Hers sparkled like the sun on the sea. Then she bent down and he was lost in the shadows of her hair, as she kissed him again. *Three times! Would there be four? Five? Did people count them forever?*

He felt everything move far away until there was nothing left but the warm sand at his back and the warm girl in his arms. No one to discover them. No Golden Knight to run from. Just him and her and this wonderful island, the sea surrounding them like a moat.

She raised her head again, staring into his eyes.

"You don't have to stop," he mumbled.

"I missed you so much. You were all I thought of. For two whole years. Even when my foster-parents died," she whispered, "You were still first in my prayers." She slipped from him and sat up, suddenly sober.

"I'm sorry I wasn't here," he said, sitting too.

"The good Viking promised me, always, that you would

come. I tried so hard to believe him.

"The *good* Viking?"

"Our earl!" she said, as if there could be no other. "Come!" She leapt up. "I will show you the house he built for me. It is all of earth and grass grows on its roof, and yet I love it more than King Arthur's own tower!"

She reached for his hand and pulled him up, too, and then, with her fingers entwined in his, led him up the green slope, away from the sea and the skiff in its hollow in the beach grass. He saw, ahead of them, the little green turf roof Floki had shown him from the hill and was filled with a weird mix of terror and joy.

Would it be like kissing her the first time? Would he magically know what to do? *Work it out yourself or die trying.* He cast a belligerent glance at the highest point of the island. One thing was for sure: no way was he asking fish-breath for help.

The wicker door of the turf house was standing open, secured with a hemp cord to the little bench beside the wall. Gil followed Janetta into the single room and stood blinking in the dusky light.

A shaft of sunlight, slanting through the doorway, dimmed the fire in the hearth and cast a dusty glow over the cooking pot on its chain. He saw three wooden kists, a bench, and a table with a stone lamp and a prayer book. On the floor by the hearth, a board with gaming pieces lay beside a basket filled with driftwood and peats. On the other side of the fire stood a little harp, just as Floki had claimed.

Gil's eyes swept over all and fastened, against his will, on the fur-strewn bed built into the far wall. It was no narrow couch, like in Janetta's Mews Tower, but really big, broad enough for two people, at least. His heart thudded.

"Do you like it?"

He turned. She was standing with her hands clasped in front of her, as if in prayer, her face shining with eagerness.

"Um, *yeah*. It's … great."

She held her hands out to him then, and he stepped toward her, just as the shadow fell across the door. He saw her half-turn, her eyes widening with surprise. Then a wedge of steel flashed across the room and slammed into the earth at his feet. Janetta screamed. Hand on sword hilt, Gil spun to face the darkened doorway. He glimpsed a huge frame, a halo of wild red hair, the glint of another battle axe, gripped in a burly hand; and, bizarrely, the fluttering sleeves of a *dress*. And then the second axe flew.

Chapter Seven

With a whacking thud, the axe head buried itself in the floor at Gil's other side. Janetta screamed again as he leapt back, drawing his sword. A blade flashed at once, in the burly hand, but Janetta moved faster still. Flinging herself in front of Gil, she stood facing the doorway, arms outstretched, her body his shield.

"No!" He struggled to wrestle her aside. She thrust his arm away.

"Grimhildr!" she cried. "He is mine! He is mine!"

Sword raised, Gil faced his huge adversary with Janetta's words ringing in his ears. *I'll die happy!* he thought giddily. But then his opponent slowly lowered the weapon and stepped sideways through the door. Sunlight flooded again into the room, revealing a figure as tall and broad-shouldered as Magnus Redbeard, with the sweet, dimpled face of a girl.

"My companion, Grimhildr," Janetta whispered. She stepped primly aside and stood an arm's length from Gil. The woman strode closer, her boots thudding on the smooth earth floor. She wore a white linen dress, like Janetta's, a blue woolen tunic, cinched in by leather belts for her axes and sword, and a linen headdress from which bushed a mane of fierce red hair. A large knife was sheathed at her waist and, dangling incongruously beside it, a pair of scissors and a comb on a silver chain.

Her eyes, dark and suspicious under pale brows, fixed firmly on Gil. She put her free hand against his chest and gave him a little shove. "No men!"

"But this is *Gil!*" Janetta stepped quickly forward. "My Knight of the River. I am pledged to him," she added boldly. "We are betrothed."

Again, her words filled Gil with giddy delight and he struggled to keep a fatal smile from blossoming on his face. Grimhildr's suspicions remained written on hers. "And I am pledged to defend your honor," she said.

"Oh, my honor is safe!" Janetta cried. "It could not be safer!" She nudged Gil with her elbow. "Is this not so?"

"Yes!" he lied valiantly.

Grimhildr walked in a circle around him, her headdress brushing the sooty rafters above. "Where is your boat?"

"On the strand," Gil said quickly. "Floki told me to leave it there. He … left."

Grimhildr nodded slowly. She sheathed her sword and bent to retrieve her axes. Holding one in each hand, she stepped closer. "You may stay until he returns," she said. "If you are lying, he will kill you himself." She sheathed her axes, dusted her hands briskly, and stepped to the cooking pot. "You will have broth?" she said.

Gil nodded. "Thank you. Broth would be great," he said, adding silently, *No. Fish-breath will not kill me. Because I'm going to kill him first. I cannot BELIEVE he set me up like this.*

Janetta stole a kiss while Grimhildr bent over the cooking pot. "She likes you," she whispered happily.

Later, they walked on the modest heights of the island, looking down on the blue sea all around. Grimhildr strode behind, a little spindle dancing beneath her hands, magically drawing yarn from a sack of fleece.

"She is very kind," Janetta whispered, glancing back. "But very strange."

"You must be so lonely," Gil said.

"Oh, no!" She smiled. "We play the little harp and sing. She sings very sweetly. We tell stories and play at board games." She dropped her voice further. "Rachel flies to see me, as often as she can. But it must be secret." She smiled again, proudly. "I have grown quite accustomed to Change-Things. I do not fear them at all. But Grimhildr is full of terrors of witchcraft. Just like her brother."

"Her brother?" Gil whispered.

"The big man whom they name so unkindly. Surely he

breaks no more necks than any warrior."

"Break-neck! Bjorn Break-neck is her brother!" Janetta nodded. Gil glanced back. *Bjorn Break-neck in a skirt. Cool move, Floki.* "I should have guessed," he said.

"Yes. They are alike. It is the eyes, I think. Both dark."

It's the biceps, Gil thought. He grimaced. "I'm glad you see Rachel," he said.

"Oh, yes. And our earl himself sails his little boat to take me to Mass. Sometimes he comes to work in the garden." She paused thoughtfully. "He is also strange; an earl with his hands in the dirt. But I like that, because my Fool comes, too, and it is like long ago in the Garden of Pentecost, when we were together. I wish he could stay, but he is the earl's cupbearer now, and has duties.

"But still, I do see him. And each week, as well, the good father comes to hear my confession. So, body and soul, I am cared for," she said cheerfully. She glanced over her shoulder and seeing Grimhildr had turned back to the turf house, she stole another kiss.

"You are so good," he said fervently. "What could you have to confess?"

"The thoughts of my heart." Her cheeks turned pink.

"Are they bad?"

She giggled. "Only until I am wed." She kissed him quickly again, and Gil swore then, in his own heart, that he would marry her or die.

The late dusk was falling when they reached the turf house. The smoke rising through the hole in the roof smelled sweet and welcoming, and Gil thought of the fire's warmth with regret. Floki had not returned for him and he would have to go back to the skiff and sleep under its sail.

But when they entered the house he saw that Grimhildr had spread three fur rugs on the broad bed at the end of the wall, and after they had shared a supper of hen's eggs and oatcakes, she directed Gil to one side and Janetta to the other, leaving a wide space between. Then, after covering the fire with ash and extinguishing the stone lamp, she lay down between them, stretched out straight, in all her clothes and her headdress, too, as sure a guard as a castle wall.

Gil lay on his back, staring up at the sky through the smoke hole in the roof, wanly remembering his terror as Floki abandoned him on the strand. *Alone with her. If only, if only.*

Almost at once, Grimhildr began to snore, a low grumbling like a surf in a cave. A single star appeared in Gil's circle of grey sky, wrapped in a skein of smoke. He sighed, and the sound came back to him in a whisper. "Does she sleep?"

"Janetta!"

"She is snoring! Here!" He sensed movement above Grimhildr's head and reached out. Small, determined fingers touched his. He linked them with his own. "Do you think of me?"

"*Do I?*" He moaned softly. "Oh, nothing else."

"And I of you. I dream it is our marriage day. And all the guests are dancing and the harper plays and sings and our earl recites his tales of love and battle. But you and I are far away, high in a loft, above the great hall ...."

"Stop!" he said.

"Does it not please you?" her voice trembled.

"Yes. But I'm afraid."

"Of me?"

"No." *Not anymore.* "I'm afraid of what happens if you talk about dreams. They fade ... you can't remember them."

"Oh!" Janetta cried. "That must not happen!" She sat up straight in her distress. "Quick, pray to Our Lord to guard our dreams." Still holding his hand, she hurriedly clasped her own together, tumbling Grimhildr's headdress over her face.

Grimhildr surged up between them like the prow of a longship. Flinging the headdress aside with one hand, she grasped the front of Gil's tunic with the other. In an instant, she was on her feet, dragging him to the door.

"Grimhildr!" Janetta shrieked. "It was me. He tried to resist!"

"No, I didn't," Gil said stubbornly. Grimhildr kicked open the door with her boot and flung him through it. Pin wheeling like starfish, Gil tumbled across the close-cropped grass and landed with a thud on top of a sheep. It baaed in panic and scuttled away, leaving him sprawling flat on the ground, gasping for breath.

Something clattered beside him. He reached out and felt his sword belt and ducked as his shield landed at his other side. "No men!" Grimhildr shouted, slamming the door. With a clunk of finality, the bar fell into place.

Gil sat up slowly, rubbing a bruised shoulder. He heard Janetta sobbing inside the house, and Grimhildr's voice, surprisingly gentle, comforting her. A patter of rain damped his hair. He wrapped himself in his cloak and shivered. Looking up, he saw a dim, cloudy sky; even his star had deserted him.

Still – rain, cold, cloud – all were nothing. Every word she had spoken was aglow in his heart. *It is our wedding day.* With a dumb grin plastering his face, he strapped on his sword belt, slung his shield around his neck, and tramped back toward the strand and the skiff.

And then, suddenly, he stopped. Why sleep on a windy beach, wrapped in a wet cloak and sheltered by a sail, when all around him were dry, grassy nooks and hollows, just the perfect size for a cat?

He looked back at the turf house and his grin broadened as he unbuckled his sword belt, re-buckled it into a circle, and laid it on the ground. Jumping inside, he recited fervently,

"Bless to me my sister,
Bless to me my brother,"

A shiver of delighted anticipation swept over him.

"Bless to me, O Changeless One,
My Change-Thing, my Other."

The weird pummeling began at once and his body shrank downward. "Gil, one! Wonder-woman, zero!" he shouted. The last word came out as a hair-raising feline yowl.

All around him, night was instantly vanquished. House, garden, even the island's summit, stood clear against the dim sky. Whiskers trembling, he surveyed his surroundings. Then, raising one tentative paw, he sniffed the air, opening his mouth to savor it better. Myriad scents, all promising, washed over him.

He lowered the paw with a satisfied chirrup, leapt out of the circle of his sword belt, and trotted toward the beach. Claws and fins were rustling in pools by the sea. Sleep could wait.

Two crabs and a tide-stranded fish later, he was crouched, full-bellied, beneath the prow of Floki's skiff, fending raindrops with twitching ears. Peat smoke from Grimhildr's hearth teased his nose. He thought longingly of the warm fire, the snug bed-furs, and the warm girl beneath them, until, with purposeful paws, he crept out of his shelter and trotted inland.

At the closed door, Gil's human self hesitated, remembering his uncompromising ejection. But his feline Other was already scratching at the planks. Someone stirred within the turf house. Footsteps sounded on the earthen floor. He scratched harder and added a pathetic meow, staring upward with wide innocent eyes.

The door swung in and Janetta was there, peering into the dark. He meowed louder, and looking down, she cried out with delight and scooped him up in her arms.

"Who goes there?" Grimhildr jumped from the bed and snatched up her sword.

"It is but a cat!" Janetta cried, clutching him close.

Grimhildr strode across the floor, her hand yet gripping the weapon. She stared suspiciously at Janetta.

"A *little* cat," Janetta pleaded. "And see, his poor fur is wet." Cat flattened his ears.

"There was no cat. How is there now a cat?"

"Surely, the earl brings him, to eat the mice?"

"I see no mice."

"But there may be!" Janetta leant close and made a scuttling motion with a hand. "There *may* be a rat!"

Grimhildr shuddered and turned her face aside. *So there is something that could frighten even the wonder-woman.* Cat snugged his face against Janetta's shoulder and thought about rats.

"May he stay? See? He is gentle." Cat swished his tail.

"Until dawn," Grimhildr grunted. "Cats hunt at dawn." She re-adjusted her headdress and lay down again on the bed. Still clutching Cat, Janetta crept in beside her.

"Poor Pussikins in the cruel rain." She tickled under his chin.

Oh, please. Gil winced. *Not Pussikins. And not the tickle thing.*

But Cat rolled shamelessly onto his back, his fierce clawed feet as soft as butter.

Hey. She's MINE. Like, don't forget.
Cat purred.

He awoke at first light with a hand gripping the loose skin at the back of his neck. He yowled and Janetta cried out and clung to him. But the hand hauled him free. A moment later he was pinwheeling into the dawn. "Hunt!" Grimhildr ordered and slammed the door.

Cat landed perfectly, on all four feet, between the sword and the shield. Washing off the derangement of his scruff, he sat down to think. The warmth of the bed faded under an onslaught of interesting smells. As usual, he was hungry. And cats did hunt at dawn.

He prowled for a while behind the turf house, looking for mice. Or, better yet, a rat, whose bare, bony tail he could leave at Grimhildr's door. But he found neither, gave up, and returned to the tide pool and ate another crab.

Crunching a last crackling leg, he sat down on a smooth rock and washed. The perfect circle of the tide pool nudged at his human conscience. *Time to go back.* But the sun was up now, warming his fur. He smoothed a last hair into place. And then, with a yawn, he closed his eyes to slits and dozed, paws tucked beneath him and his tail stretched out lazily on the sunbaked stone.

The straight tail was a mistake. He knew it the instant the thing closed over it, startling him awake. He yowled, but the thing bore down hard. Hissing, he scrabbled around and slashed at the bare human foot arrogantly pinning him to the ground. A hand closed on his scruff and pulled him up short.

Gentler than Grimhildr's, but just as firm, it lifted him, wide-eyed, numbed, and furious, into the air. "Ah, *now* I find the answer!" Cat rolled an eye and caught a glimpse of Floki Magnusson's white grin, before the hand swung him over the round tide pool and let him drop. Claws scratching air, furry belly exposed, he splashed full length into the vileness of water, hissing his outrage even as cat paws transformed into human fists.

"Ah!" Floki cried delightedly. "They do not swim. They turn

into Vikings!" Then Cat's last paw swipe caught the edge of his bearded jaw and sent him sprawling.

Gil clutched his stinging fist and stared in horrified disbelief. *Idiot Cat! You've just punched the lights out of the only law there is!* He turned to flee, but Floki sat up, shaking his head and laughing too hard to speak. "It is well, it is well," he gasped, beckoning Gil back. Warily, Gil obeyed.

"Warrior," Floki said at last. "You are not happy! Your lady does not please you?"

"*My lady* pleases me fine."

"Then?"

"Grimhildr?"

"Ah."

"You could have told me."

Floki blinked innocently. "Did I fail to do that?" Gil fought the desire to punch him again. "Ah, the affairs of my earldom distract my mind." Floki collapsed into helpless mirth. "Come, Warrior," he begged, "Help me up. I am weak."

Gil extended a cautious hand, expecting a trick, but Floki got meekly to his feet then, rubbing his jaw. "That is good," he said. "I feel that." He gave Gil's head an affectionate whack. "We make a warrior of you yet. Go bid your lady a good day, helmsman. Your other woman awaits." He smiled at the wind-rippled sea.

CHAPTER EIGHT

The moment the skiff was afloat, Floki stretched out in the sun on his cloak, and left Gil to sail her alone. The day was brisk and beautiful, blue summer sky above, sun sparkling on blue water below. Even the tide-race sang a muted song. Gil was glad, since Floki barely stirred himself all morning.

Once, he sat up and adjusted the tacking spar as Gil turned across the wind, and twice he rose and laid a momentary hand on the steering oar. Each time, as the little craft surged ahead, he went promptly back to sleep. Gil had sailed nearly to Spear Island before Floki roused himself to suggest they return.

Gil brought the skiff downwind and took down the spar himself. He played a little with the steering oar and tightened both sheets. The skiff skimmed across the wave crests like a bird.

"That is good," Floki murmured, without looking. Then he said suddenly, "Surely, you do not think I leave your lady unguarded."

Gil kept his eyes on the skiff's prow slicing through the water. He shrugged uncomfortably. "I thought the island was safe."

"It is as safe as anywhere can be. But I am not the only man who can helm a ship." He paused, reaching to tighten a sheet without bothering to get up. "I say I take two treasures from the Golden Knight. Indeed, I take three," he said. "I have his Cup. And I have this." From a leather pouch he wore around his neck, he drew out the gold and amber necklace he had stolen for Danni and held it up to the sun. "This," he whispered, "He never claims."

"But more than the Cup, and more than the treasure of her

dowry, I have his bride. Do not doubt the insult that is to him, nor what he will do to win her back. She must be well guarded indeed."

He looked briefly somber as he returned the necklace to its leather pouch. "But who do I trust? Her worth is known to all." He paused, wrinkling his brow in remembered distraction. "Men are weak, Warrior. A debt owed, a grudge to be repaid, a night of ale and stupidity, and she is sold to the highest bidder, like my lass and my cousin across the sea." He opened his eyes briefly and shrugged.

"But then I remember Grimhildr; as loyal to me as her brother, Bjorn, and alone with him on their father's farm."

"I guess she isn't married," Gil said, unsurprised. He looked across the steering board toward the white roof of Floki's longhouse, and wondered where they were going.

"She has had two husbands," Floki returned at once. "And buried them both. And now she bids me find her a third." He paused and murmured shyly, "How do I say this to one so young? She is like the wind, a very vigorous woman." He laughed sleepily, "Now *she* is gorilla!"

"Uh, *no*." Gil glanced quickly at Floki and then back at his course. The mist-wrapped Holy Isle lay amid its tide-races, straight ahead.

"No?"

"Women are never gorillas," Gil said firmly. He could feel the skiff losing way, despite her taut sail. Wave crests crisscrossed on either side, as the incoming tide met the tide in retreat.

"No women gorillas?"

"None." The water tugged at his steering oar. The roaring of the wave came to his ears. Its spray was already on his face. He stared mesmerized at the approaching white line. "Floki," he nudged the Northman's bare ankle with his boot. "Are we going in the tide-race, or what?"

"You are helmsman," Floki said, without opening his eyes.

"O-*kay*." Gil felt a murderous calm descend. He checked his sail, gripped the steering oar hard and with the infuriating realization that Floki had gone back to sleep, guided the slender prow into the heart of the wave.

Sheep and Wolfskin did it, he told himself as the skiff reared up and plunged down, *and they're even stupider than me.*

For a moment, he thought he'd won. The skiff regained her balance and surged forward, over the cascading back of the wave. Then something tugged him to one side, and then the other and he was caught in an eddying whirlpool like a giant Indian Kettle. His sail lost wind and fluttered back against the mast. Then the whirlpool spewed him out and the wind slapped back into the sail.

The skiff heeled hard onto her load-board and he felt the steering oar lift clear of the water, snatching away his control. Desperately, he grabbed for the nearest sheet, scooping all the wind he could find into the sail. The crest of the wave slapped his face and cascaded over Floki in the hull.

Floki woke up slightly and shook his head. "How are there *more* gorillas?" he murmured plaintively.

"Look," Gil said, clutching the steering oar, "Trust me on this one, okay? I'm kind of busy here." The prow lifted at last and the hull settled level. He felt the oar bite deep and joyously set his little ship back on course. A last wave drenched him with spray, but he was free, sailing bravely toward the open sea.

"You do well," Floki said.

"How would you know? You've been asleep the whole time."

"I know because I am not swimming." Floki smiled and stretched. "Besides, a Northman can sail in his sleep. Take us home, now, Warrior. We play with the sea again."

Gil turned the skiff up into the wind. "You mean *I* play with the sea again," he said, setting the tacking spar.

The return was easier. The skiff sailed best reaching across the wind. He relaxed a little, liking the firmer set of the sail, the steadier feel of the hull with the wind across his shoulder. He crossed the fierce wave again and with the running tide behind him, made good speed. The longhouse roof was in sight again when Floki sat up. "No one is ever alone on a ship," he said.

Gil blinked and shook his head. "What?"

"You are not alone. Even if I am not here at all. There are with you the ghosts of every hand that sails her. And every hand that builds her, as well. Come, now," he pointed to the strand. "Bring her in by *Silver Dragon* and I show you the man who teaches you to helm a ship."

"I thought that was you," Gil said uncertainly.

Floki smiled and pointed at the strand. "Beach her there," he directed, "between my *Dragon* and the *knarr*. Gil saw, then, the third ship resting on the strand, beside the wolf-prowed longship and Floki's own.

It was shorter and broader, with decking built higher at stem and stern. Its mast was down, resting on its cradle and a stream of men and boys were unloading the contents of its hold. He recognized one of them, at once, by his bushy blond beard and bright blue eyes. "It's Erling," he cried happily, waving.

"I am happy to see him, also," Floki said. "He has brought me fine timbers from Norway. But if you do not turn your oar, we will beach sideways, and both look fools."

Still grinning, Gil straightened his course. "Is Erling going to teach me?" he asked.

Floki smiled again. Then, as the skiff rode gently up onto the strand, he pointed to the wooden frame with its new-laid keel, now surrounded by a dozen men, all wielding tools. In their center, the white-bearded Santa Claus stood with folded arms. "There," said Floki.

"That old man?" Gil stared, disappointed.

"That old man," said Floki sharply, "Is Eyolf Grimsson, Master Shipbuilder. And you would be honored were he to teach you to wipe your arse. But since you know how to do that already, he will teach you to helm a ship. And no man in the Northlands teaches you better."

Gil gave Floki a nervous glance and nodded hurriedly. "Okay. Right." He paused. "Is he a better helmsman than you?"

"Of course not," Floki said disdainfully. "Nor was he ever. But the sea is in his mind and the wind is in his heart. And both mind and heart guide his hands. No finer shipbuilder ever lives." He smiled. "My fifteenth summer, my father sends me to Eyolf. He builds my *Silver Dragon*, and at his side, my hands the shadows of his, I build her, too.

"When we are done, she is part of me. Her ribs and strakes my bones, her rigging, my sinews, the wind in her sail, my blood. This is what makes a helmsman. Now," he said solemnly, "I give you the gift my father gave me."

Awed, Gil nodded in silence, and then warily murmured, "Thank you."

Floki laughed, his solemnity vanishing. He slapped Gil's arm. "Go. And see if you thank me at nightfall." He strode off to his longhouse and left Gil to approach Eyolf alone.

Gil found the old shipbuilder immersed in thought, studying an odd-shaped piece of timber held out to him by a respectful young Northman. Turning the wood one way and the other, he seemed oblivious of Gil's presence. At last, he traced a line on the timber with his finger and returned it to the young man. Abruptly, he turned to Gil, a bushy eyebrow went up and his long moustache twitched.

"Floki sent me," Gil blurted. "You're supposed to teach me ...." His voice trailed off as Eyolf stared blankly at him. *Oh, great,* Gil groaned inside. *No English. What now?*

But then Eyolf's huge, gnarled hand landed on his shoulder. He turned Gil and marched him to the cradle supporting the new ship. Parting two workmen, he pushed Gil's face close to the long, curving keel, where it met the rising stem. His calloused fingers stroked the joint of the two pieces of oak and settled on a round peg, split by a small wedge, and hammered deep within the timber. "Tree-nail," he growled.

Taking Gil's hand, he traced his fingers along the joint, over the peg. Then he pointed to a group of boys sitting cross-legged around the fire, heads bent intently over hands. "Tree-nails." He shoved Gil toward the boys, folded his arms, and walked off.

The boys all looked up, and Gil saw that one of them was Ciarnan, and another, Rachel's Viking, Ragi. Ciarnan grinned. "I think I leave monks' labors behind at Hy." He shrugged, displaying a row of little pegs. "Here. I show you," he whispered, with a wary eye on Eyolf.

Ciarnan held up a short tree branch, severed it neatly with an axe blow and showed Gil the smooth core within its concentric rings. Shaving the wood with his axe, he exposed the core, chopped it into short lengths, smoothed one with his knife until it resembled the pegs in his row, and notched one end. "Tree-nail!" he announced proudly. He handed Gil a small axe of his own and went back to work. Thinking it looked pretty easy, Gil settled beside Ciarnan, unsheathed his father's bone-handled hunting knife, and took up a tree branch himself.

Two cut fingers and a bruised palm later, he decided it was definitely not easy. By the time the women and girls arrived on the strand with baskets of bannocks and a huge pot of broth, he was hot and dusty, his neck ached, and all his fingers stung. But in front of him twenty tree-nails lay in a proud little row.

He grinned at the pretty blond girl handing him a frothing ale horn and stuffed bannocks into his mouth, before he saw Eyolf bearing down on him, white beard flying. Jumping up, he stood with the other boys, hiding the food and drink behind his back.

Eyolf squatted in the sand and surveyed his work. Lifting a tree-nail, he turned it around, held it up to his face, and then, with a snort of disgust, hurled it over his shoulder into the fire. "*Eldivdr!*"

"What?" Gil mouthed to Ciarnan. Eyolf picked up another tree-nail and another, flinging them over his shoulder. "*Eldivdr! Eldivdr! Eldivdr!*" Gil stared in horror as the fresh-carved wood hissed in the flames. "*Eldivdr!*" The old shipbuilder's eyes bored into his. He held up three pegs of Gil's treasured twenty and nodded. "Tree-nail. Tree-nail. Tree-nail." He laid them in a row in the sand and turned to the next boy in line.

Ciarnan fared better. Eleven of his thirty survived. Ragi managed twenty out of twenty-five, but that was top score. Eyolf stamped off, boots thudding in the sand. "It means 'firewood,'" Ciarnan whispered. But by then, Gil had guessed.

When, hours later, at the ringing of Aidan's vespers bell, the boys trudged wearily to the longhouse, Gil had provided fifteen successful tree-nails toward the building of the ship. He had also stripped a bundle of willow shoots of their bark and watched in awe as Eyolf bound strakes to ribs with them, weaving the ship together as if wood were yarn. And, as dusk fell, he had twisted pitch-soaked sheep's wool into ropes of caulking, his fingers following Eyolf's down the grooves between strakes. Back aching, hands burning, stinking of sheep and pine, he entered the longhouse and felt like he had walked into another world.

Torchlight flickered on the beautiful paneling and shone silvery on the goblets set on the High Table, and the brooches and pins adorning women's dresses and men's cloaks. Magnus Einarsson and three older men lounged on the broad, fur-strewn benches by the walls, with board games spread before them. The *file*, Eoin, played his harp by the fire, with Floki, dressed again in his finery, seated beside him. Percy hung over Floki's shoulder, arms clasped around his neck, bouncing and jiggling, as the two men sang together.

Floki looked up at the end of a verse and jumped to his feet. "Warrior! How fares my ship?"

Gil nodded slowly and pulled from his pocket a small, perfect peg. "Brought you something." He held it up for all to see and then, with glorious abandon, he hurled it into the fire. "*Eldivdr!*"

"Yes!" Floki laughed with glee. "*Eldivdr!*" He mimed throwing something over his shoulder and screwed up his face, pretending to stroke an imaginary drooping moustache. For a fleeting moment he actually looked like Eyolf. "*Eldivdr! Eldivdr!*" He turned, laughing, and called to his father. "Redbeard! Do you remember?"

Magnus looked up from his board game, and glowered briefly, and then suddenly his face relaxed into a grin. "He walks away," Magnus said.

"Five times," Floki laughed. He threw his hands in the air like a petulant teenager, pretending to stalk out of the longhouse. "Redbeard sends me back. I storm. I shout. I throw things. *Eldivdr! Eldivdr!* Five times, my patient father sends me back." He lowered his hands and smiled fondly at Magnus. "Come to table, Redbeard," he said. Then he laid his arm across Gil's shoulders. "You, also."

The long room was filling up as men and women returned from the fields and the strand, the dairy and the weaving sheds. Ragi's eyes followed Rachel longingly when she walked into the hall, deep in conversation with the Ab.

Floki stopped suddenly on his way to the High Table and turned Gil to face a group of well-armed men. "Here he is," he

announced, "The warrior who fells his earl!" They grinned at
Gil and raised triumphant fists and at least one looked envious,
as if Gil had got away with something he'd yearned to do for
years. Floki led him all around the hall, introducing him in
the same way and Gil realized he had told everyone what had
happened on the island.

"I can't believe you punched him," Rachel whispered,
slapping her forehead.

"I can't believe I did either," Gil murmured. Anyhow, it
was obvious Floki had forgiven him. With a flourish, he led
Gil up to the High Table. Then Gil suddenly understood that
the circuit of the hall was not the playful accident it appeared.
Floki was telling every man in the longhouse that Gil was
pardoned of the theft of the Cup, and they must pardon him,
too.

With the eyes of all on him, he seated Gil at his side in
the place held by his father, two nights before. Gil watched
uncomfortably as Magnus sat down in silence, two chairs away.
But then Aidan joined them, and Rachel, and Shony directed
the serving of the meal, and as Percy proudly filled the wine
cups, the conversation turned to the ship, and the crops, and the
gossip of the islands, and Gil forgot his concerns.

The plates were cleared away and the wine cups re-filled,
when Magnus finally spoke. "A great warrior, indeed, this *boy*,"
he said without looking at Gil, "He escapes the Golden Knight
when others, three times his strength and courage, fail."

"My father helped me," Gil cried at once, seeing in his mind
Lance'lot far below as he climbed the eerie arc of the Rainbow
Bridge. "He disarmed the Golden Knight and took the key to
the bridge to Tir nan Og!"

"He disarmed the Golden Knight?" Magnus stared hard at
Gil. "Then why did he not kill him?"

Gil shook his head. "I don't know," he murmured.

Magnus laughed coldly. "Perhaps there *was* no disarming,"
he said. "Perhaps he paid a ransom. Indeed, perhaps he paid
two. So he walks free in Francia, and you sit at my son's High
Table, while my fosterling wears slaves' rags, and my hall hosts
the raven and the fox."

"My father couldn't pay ransoms," Gil protested. "He hasn't any silver. He's poor."

"He had us," Magnus growled. "And so did you. What did you tell them that brought them here on the first fair wind from the south?"

"Nothing!" Gil cried. "And neither did my father." He half rose, but Floki's hand on his shoulder sat him down hard.

Floki leaned past him and addressed his father softly. "You will take that back." Magnus stood with a rough laugh. "Do not leave my table, Father," Floki said, in the same quiet voice. Magnus stepped back from his chair. *"Do not leave my table."*

The room went suddenly quiet. Magnus stood unmoving, for a long uneasy moment, and then, with a grunt toward Gil that might have been an apology, sat back down in his chair.

Floki nodded and said evenly, "The boy's father is a fool like Palamedes. He did not kill him *because* he was disarmed. For any sensible man, the best time to do the thing, but not for an idiot knight."

He leaned back in his tall, pillared seat. "Eoin, I would hear your sweet harp." At once, music filled the hall. Floki closed his eyes. "Your house will be avenged, Father," he said, "And my foster-brother freed." He paused and added, "If you had not filled his head with pagan foolishness, we would have sailed west as I wished and all made safe landfall."

"The gods of your fathers are not foolishness," Magnus said.

"Oh, they are all foolishness," Floki answered wearily. He looked to Aidan then, and shook his head. "I am sorry."

Aidan smiled. "I do not deny I preach a folly to Greeks."

Rachel gave a little laugh. But Magnus growled, "Oh, you preach a folly, indeed, good father, and better men than you pay for it." He turned warily to Floki who sat again with closed eyes, listening to his harper. "I would play at King's Table," Magnus said. "If my son permits me."

Floki roused himself from the music. "Of course, Father," he said gently, "Go."

Magnus rose and stamped off into the hall without speaking. Floki watched in silence, until Magnus had taken his place among the men with their gaming boards. Then he said quietly, to Aidan, "This beautiful thing we bring from Caledon might as well be a sword. We are as divided as the cows and calves at weaning. And just as sorrowful."

Aidan looked out over the hall. "'Father against son, and son against father.'" He turned back to Floki, "But does that make the thing less beautiful?"

Floki shook his head wearily. He turned suddenly to Rachel. "What say *you*, gentle one?" he asked. "What course would you have me sail?"

She answered without a moment's hesitation. "You must take the fight to the Golden Knight and defeat him in Caledon. Or there will be no peace there, or here, ever again."

Gil stared at her, stunned, but a slow smile crossed Floki's face. "I think my hawk is speaking," he said. But Gil realized it was not Hawk, but Rachel, and as usual, she was right. He thought of the High-King's harp.

"And no peace even in Tir nan Og," he said softly.

Floki beckoned Percy and the child came, yawning hugely, from his place beside Eoin and poured more wine. The torches had burned low and the women were smothering the long fire with ash. The room grew quiet, but for the notes of the harp, the low voices of the game players, and the whispers of young men and women in the shadows. The old, and those who had drunk most, were already sleeping under the furs; men one side of the hearth, women, the other.

Percy set down his wine jug and yawned again. Gil leaned closer to Rachel. "Where does he sleep?" he whispered. "I'll take him to bed."

"He stays with me," Floki said. He called Percy to him and Percy climbed up onto the high seat beside him and curled up, one arm around the young Northman. He buried his face against Floki's shoulder, sucking his thumb.

"He's really tired," Gil said. "Let me take him ...."

"*He stays with me.*" Floki gestured to his fur cloak hanging on the back of a chair, and Rachel quickly handed it to him. Wrapping it all around Percy, he leaned back again and said to Eoin, "I would hear a verse, friend." He paused and added tiredly, "Speak of Ireland. I knew a lass there, once."

Eoin's fingers drifted gently across the strings of his harp and in a voice halfway between speech and song, he began to recite. The Irish words meant nothing to Gil, but the sound alone aroused images of seas and ships, towers, and torch-lit halls.

Aidan rose quietly and Rachel rose with him. Gil was startled to hear her speak to Floki in his own Norse tongue. Aidan laid his hand on Percy's tousled hair and then briefly bid Floki goodnight with the same gentle gesture. They left the table and Gil rose to leave, too.

"Stay," Floki said without opening his eyes. Gil sat down again, uncertainly, and when Eoin's poem ended, Floki stood and scooped Percy up, still wrapped in his fur cloak. He turned toward the door in the wall behind the High Table and nodded to Gil. Gil jumped up to open it.

Beyond, the room from which Floki and the council had first appeared was plainer and simpler than he expected. A low fire burned in a central hearth. On one side was a bed, on the other, a table with benches. The small flame of a stone lamp revealed more of the painted paneling disguising the turf walls. Aside from the gaming board on the table taking the place of a book, the room was not that different from Aidan's cell.

On the floor, beside the bed, furs were piled in a thick heap. Floki laid Percy down on them and drew another fur over him for a blanket. He straightened and smiled at Gil, but Gil only stepped backward and closed the door between them and the hall. "Is that where he sleeps?" he asked quietly.

Floki nodded. He unbuckled his sword belt and laid it down beside the bed.

"On the floor?" Gil said.

"Yes, on the floor," Floki answered. "On a king's ransom of furs, Warrior, as well."

"But on the floor." Gil said again, fighting to keep his voice from rising.

"What?" Floki laughed, sitting down on the bed, pulling off a boot, "You would have me share my bed with him?" He shook his head. "That is reserved for his sister. Besides, he is nearer the fire than I. He does not suffer."

"Oh, no," Gil murmured. "Of course he doesn't suffer. You wouldn't let a dog suffer, would you?"

"No." Floki's voice was mild, but his eyes had lost their laughter. "What are you saying, Warrior?"

"He's not a dog," Gil said. He felt his hands clenching again into a fist. "He's not your pet dog to do tricks for you and sleep on your floor."

"No," Floki said, his voice still mild. "He is not my pet dog." He nodded his head as if in agreement and pulled off the other boot. Then he leapt up from the bed and crossed the room in two savage strides. He grasped Gil's hair with his left hand and shoved him against the wall. Without a sound, he thrust his right forearm across Gil's throat and pinned him against the paneling so hard he could not breathe.

"He is not my pet dog," he whispered, with more menace in the whisper than any shout could carry. Gil struggled and clawed at the arm across his throat. He felt the room fading and realized that Floki could and would kill him here, so quietly, that Percy would not even wake.

"You're choking me," he gasped.

"I wish to choke you." Floki jerked his arm away, but before Gil could draw a full breath, he wrenched his head around and propelled him toward the far wall. With his free hand, he grasped the edge of the paneling and yanked it aside, revealing the black turf behind. "What is that?" he demanded and buried Gil's face in the turf.

"A wall!" Gil cried frantically.

"No, it is *not* a wall!" Floki hissed and again Gil sensed madness. But then Floki punched his head against the turf and instead of a solid thump of resistance, he felt a crumbling, a rustle of straw, and a rush of cold air. Outside, the grey night sky beckoned serenely. "It is not a wall," Floki whispered again. "It is a door."

He jerked Gil's head back and spun him around, gesturing to Percy, and then the gaming board. "King's Table," he whispered. "That piece in the center is the fist," he raised his own, "The power. The king. All is played for him." He pointed to the sleeping child. "He, too, is king. And all is played for him.

Capture him, and the game is over."

Gil nodded, but Floki's hand gripped his hair harder and thrust him back to the hole in the wall. "And when they come seeking him and burn this roof over my head, as they burned my father's, *there* is where I flee with him to safety.

"For him I abandon my father and my mother. My warriors I am sworn to defend. Aidan, who is under my protection, and my poet who is helpless because he is blind … all." He dropped his voice even further. "When I do this, I abandon everything." He paused as if searching for words. "I abandon *myself*. I abandon who I am. Do you understand?"

Gil nodded and gulped.

"All for this child. I pledge his sister I guard him always." Floki looked down at Percy under his furs. "And so I take him as my fosterling. He is to me as Hakon is to Redbeard. He is not my dog. He is my son."

"I'm sorry."

"Good. Now, get out."

"Floki, I didn't understand."

Floki nodded with a small, strained smile. "Please, Warrior," he begged, "Learn to keep silence when you do not understand." He held up one hand as if fending something off and turned away. "Now, leave me, please, before I do you harm."

Out in the hall, Gil found a place on the sleeping benches between two snoring warriors and lay down. Despite the fire and the furs, he was trembling in every limb. The room filled gradually with the sounds of the fire and gentle laughter, where men and women had found each other in the dark. Faraway, the tide-race murmured, soft as the poet's harp. He thought of Janetta in her turf house and his fingers, remembering hers, clasped empty air.

CHAPTER NINE

*T*he ship is on me. Lionheart flattened his ears and shook his mane mournfully. Gil shifted the weight of the great oar on his own shoulder and winced. *Only part of it. And half of that is on me.*

Lionheart hunched his back, trying to unseat the creel-harness. *Not going to happen.* Gil hung on grimly. The sturdy strap over the pony's withers held Eyolf's tool-filled creel on Lionheart's right, and one end of the oar, slung from a loop of hemp, on his left. The other end settled hard on Gil's shoulder as they climbed.

The ship is on me.

"Better than you on the ship," Gil muttered. Ahead, Eyolf strolled, hands in pockets, whistling, as boy and pony struggled under the new steering oar. Gil squinted into the September sun. "Like it would hurt so much to lift a finger?" he murmured, in English. He thought of Floki, lazing uselessly in the little skiff while he struggled to learn to sail. "Hey, maybe he learned *that* from Eyolf, too."

"*Hvat?*"

"Fine day," Gil answered, in Norse.

"*Neinn,*" Eyolf returned. "Rain soon. Bad for harvest. Bad sailor. Bad farmer." He went back to whistling, striding higher up the hill.

Great, Gil thought. *If it's weather, parts of a ship, or insults, I've got Norse cracked.*

"*Dar.* There." Eyolf stopped suddenly and pointed to a shallow gully dividing the green meadowland. Gil saw the bright splash of cascading water. Eyolf came back and took

Lionheart's bridle, pulling him toward the tumbling burn. Lionheart made his neck long and his ears flatter, and with slow, stiff steps followed the old ship builder to the gully's edge. Below, the water raced, smooth and black, in a narrow chute.

Like the waterfall of the Indian Kettle. Gil realized, suddenly, he hadn't thought of home for weeks. He turned from the water and carefully laid his end of the new rudder on the ground and began unbinding the cord holding the oar in the sling. He hadn't had *time* to think of anything, he told himself truthfully. But it hadn't stopped him thinking of Janetta.

He stopped, dreamily, his hands still on the cord, his eyes drifting instinctively to the green island in the wind-frothed sea.

"Work!" Eyolf gave him a shove. Gil hurriedly untied the oar, ducking his head to hide a love-sick grin. He wondered if Eyolf had ever been as young as him and as much in love. He decided both were impossible. Eyolf probably grew in some forest and got hewn out, like a ship's keel, by a Northman's axe.

Eyolf shoved him again. "Dream less." Together they dragged the oar to the edge of the burn. "Up! Up!" Gil lifted his end, which was holed already, awaiting the tiller, and Eyolf lowered the broad blade into the deepest channel of the rushing stream. Gil braced one foot against a rock and teetered on the edge of the bank, struggling against the pull of the current.

Eyolf knelt and peered down into the water, his white brows drawn close, twitching like bleached caterpillars. Occasionally he slapped Gil's leg and pointed, and Gil turned the blade left and right. "*Dar!* There!" Eyolf crowed. "See! *Illr!* Bad!"

Gil leaned over the black stream and peered into the water. Eyolf's gnarled forefinger jabbed at the oar. At first, Gil saw nothing, but gradually the pattern of the rushing water took shape; two smooth curves of current on either side of the wood, joining downstream in a tail of foam. "Bad," Eyolf jabbed again. On the left side, the curve was broken in a swirl of bubbles. "Hah! *Reida!* Up! Up!"

Straining, Gil dragged the heavy rudder back on land. Eyolf's finger went at once to the small, raised lump in the smooth wood that had broken the current. As he glared at it in outrage, Gil ran to Lionheart and the creel full of tools. The creel had shifted sideways and Lionheart was nudging it with his nose to move it further. Gil hauled the harness back in place and tightened the girth wearily.

I can't breathe.

Then leave the creel alone! Gil loosened the harness a compromise notch; then retrieved an adze from the creel. Hurrying back to Eyolf, he knelt beside the oar, but before he could raise the tool, Eyolf snatched it from his hands. Gil stood back resentfully. Surely, he'd learned to use an adze by now. He felt he knew every strake of the new ship and could feel the tools in his hands just looking at them. Eyolf ignored him, shaving the wood of his precious oar with slow, sure strokes. "Up!"

Gil crouched and levered the oar upright. *I may as well be Lionheart. Beast of burden.* Eyolf stood staring at the rudder standing proud against the sky, as if it would part the winds instead of the seas.

Gil stared suddenly, too. He looked down to the strand where the sea birds dipped and soared, and then back at the oar. That shape, that bird's wing shape. And the way the water flowed around it, like air around a bird's wing. It meant something important. Something about the sky. *But why? Ships don't fly.* He watched a white gull, hovering overhead. *Why do I know this? What does it mean?* But the idea was gone. It was something from Tir nan Og; something of the future he had lost. Resignedly, he turned back to Eyolf.

Three more times they lowered the oar into the stream for Eyolf to study and pulled it out again. Lionheart had gone to sleep, standing, in his weird pony way. The sun had risen high enough to warm the land and draw in an onshore breeze, drying the silver fields of ripe barley. Gil saw figures below, going out into the fields. He stepped from foot to foot, restless to be with them.

Everyone worked at the harvest; men, women, boys, and girls, even old people hobbling on sticks. Floki put aside his finery and took up a sickle and Aidan left his books and worked beside him. Percy followed behind, painstakingly gathering cut stalks and tying them into sheaves with twists of straw. When he was not with Floki, he was with Shony, and both mother and son were always armed.

Each day, Gil sailed the little skiff to the Holy Isle and brought Grimhildr and Janetta to work, too. He had crossed the tide race so often, now, it felt like a friend, and he had to remind himself, sometimes, that the skiff was Floki's, not his own.

Eyolf beckoned him again. Gil sighed and went back to the burn's edge, reaching to lift the oar. But Eyolf stayed his arm and pointed into the water, with the twitch of his moustache that passed for a smile. "*Heill!* Good!" The two currents of water swirled perfectly around the oar in a silky ellipse.

In his mind, Gil saw the oar beneath the ship's hull, gliding through the sea. Then, suddenly, he imagined the small distortion in the wood dragging relentlessly against his helmsman's hand, and understood, at last, Eyolf's persistence. He grinned. "Good!"

Eyolf's moustache twitched again. When they had the oar loaded once more in Lionheart's harness, he suddenly bent and lifted the lower end himself and reached for the long rein. Gil handed it to him uncertainly. Eyolf pointed to the tide race and the island where Janetta waited. "Go." Gil glanced warily at Lionheart's flattened ears. "He goes home now," Eyolf said blandly. "No problem."

Gil nodded and stepped back. Lionheart's eyes rolled in convincing terror. *I don't know him!*

You'll like him, Gil lied, and bolted for the strand, before Eyolf could change his mind.

I was wrong! he thought gleefully. *He's actually human.* Running headlong down the close-cropped fields, scattering small black sheep and gently protesting cattle, he tried to imagine a young Eyolf with a girl of his own. *Probably someone like Grimhildr.*

He grinned to himself, thinking of all the ways Janetta had contrived to distract Grimhildr, while they stole a kiss behind her back at each day's end. A bird in the sky, a dropped spindle, an imagined sail on the horizon ... actually, he realized, as he slowed to a trot behind the longhouse, Grimhildr was gullible.

Yesterday, she'd taken forever to examine her headdress for stray straws anyone could see weren't there.

The startling thought that she might also be human flitted through his mind. *No. Not possible.* He slowed to a panting halt, listening to the sail-roof flapping in the wind.

His eyes went to the hidden door of the room where Floki slept alone, with Percy on the floor by the fire. For a moment he imagined the whole great roof aflame, and Floki fleeing with the boy he had pledged to protect. *Abandoning everything.*

Gil heard a far, raucous cry and looked up. In the sky above the longhouse, a black speck circled. *Feannag. You're why I'm here. And I'm why everyone here is changed; even Floki.* The weight of responsibility settled on him, chilling him, despite the September sun on his back.

Sobered, he walked around the longhouse, toward the strand. He saw Rachel in the distance with Aidan and two of the farm girls, all carrying sickles. He strode quickly on, averting his eyes to avoid the silent judgement in hers.

Rachel worked as hard at the harvest as anyone and sat at Floki's high table like one of his council, even sharing jokes with him in his own tongue. But still she held something of herself back. *We don't belong here.*

Well, maybe I do, Gil answered rebelliously in his heart. There were days when the farm, and the shipyard, and Janetta seemed like his whole life. No past, no future, in this world or in Tir nan Og. Only the ripening barley and the ship growing day by day, as beautiful as a girl on the Holy Isle strand.

More than once, sailing back alone to Hrolf's Isle, his hand easy on the steering oar and the setting sun coloring the waves, he was hit suddenly with a cold splash of guilt, that from dawn to dusk he had not thought once of Danni and Ismail, held hostage across the sea. If Rachel disapproved of him, what would Danni say?

"They're safe," he murmured. "Probably more comfortable than I am." For despite Magnus's dark talk of slave's rags, Aidan assured him that hostages really were treated as guests, at least as long as a ransom was promised. But still, they who had been his closest friends now seemed faraway shadows, as if his love for Janetta had emptied his heart of care for anyone else.

Bewildered, he stopped and stood forlornly on the white strand, between Floki's *Silver Dragon* and the new ship in her stocks. Her pine mast lay ready beside her in the sand. Her graceful curving prow lacked only its figurehead; whichever fierce animal – dragon, wolf, or bird-of-prey – would go before her.

Then she'll be ready, he thought grimly. Ready to set out from these shores with laughter and song and return with blood-stained swords and other men's silver. *And the hand of every man who builds her and every man who helms her, goes with her, too.*

He looked vainly in the sky for Feannag. Everyone had changed. But he'd changed most of all.

"Hey! Gil!" Ciarnan's dark head appeared above the sheer strake of the new ship. "Come see!"

Gil scrambled up the makeshift gangplank. Ragi was sitting on the bright pine decking, laying the last plank down. Shaped exactly, and unfastened, either by twisted willow or treenail, it fitted into its place like a piece of a puzzle. Ragi jumped up gleefully, "Done!" He hung over the side of the ship, grinning.

"Soon we wet her keel," Ciarnan announced proudly. "Then, battle!" He raised a triumphant fist. Ragi cheered and Gil raised his own fist, a little feebly, in reply.

"Great," he said, feeling as hollow as the word sounded. "Got to go." He leapt down into the sand and ran to his little skiff, nestling in the grass. He raised the mast and dragged the boat over a log roller to the water. Jumping aboard, he lowered the steering oar with practiced hands. The wind was brisk and suddenly cold, as if winter lay waiting in the mists beyond Spear Island.

When harvest is done, I sail to Norway. I take my friends with me. Suddenly, it seemed much too soon, and Gil was glad when the sail filled, driving the skiff out into the bright sea, where wind and water claimed all his attention and Janetta waited on the white beach of the Holy Isle.

By the time he returned with his passengers, the wind had risen to a gale and milky clouds were washing the blue from the sky. Grimhildr's headdress stood up like the wings of a gull as she clambered from the boat. Shepherding Janetta before her, she strode up the strand.

Gil saw Shony leading Percy to where Floki and Aidan waited with sickles, at the edge of the fields. Grimhildr clutched hers and hurried off to join the line of reapers. "Pray the rain away, good father," she called. "Pray a fair wind."

Floki laughed. "A fair wind for the barley. A stout wind for the sea. A fine husband for Grimhildr. The tasks of Lord Yesu are without end."

Aidan smiled. "The time of Lord Yesu is without end," he said. He swung his sickle in a smooth arc and the rippling barley fell with a whisper at his feet. Percy ran forward and gathered the stalks, tying them into a sheaf.

Shony followed Floki, binding sheaves, and Janetta followed Gil, bending and stooping at every step. It was hard work, but swinging the sickle was harder. Gil's hands, calloused from the shipyard, yet blossomed with blisters. His arms and back ached like in his first days of sword practice. Sweat glued his tunic to his back and his face was caked with dust.

Still, when the serving girls brought ale and bread into the fields, a third of the remaining barley had been cut and little tepees of gathered sheaves stood starkly amid the stubble.

They worked all afternoon, and though clouds darkened and lowered, no rain fell. The day, dreamy with the scent of the harvest and the cries of sea birds overhead, gentled everyone. Rachel bound sheaves behind Ragi, laughing and joking with him in the Northmen's tongue. Shony and Magnus exchanged smiles as they passed in the fields. Even Eyolf managed a grin, stamping by with straw in his beard. Only Grimhildr remained untouched, muttering darkly, "Harvest sloth makes winter hunger," when, with three sickle-widths of their field yet uncut, Floki called for a rest.

Gil flopped down and lay flat in the stubble, wiping sweat from his face with his sleeve. Janetta caught up his sickle. "Let me. I do this with the good sisters when we reap our little field. I am good!"

Gil shook his head. "It's too heavy. And you are too small." But, struggling with the sickle's weight, she lined it up with a stand of barley and swung with all her might. The stalks fell cleanly and Floki cheered her. Gil got up and gathered the grain into a sheaf and tied it, as Janetta swung the sickle again.

"See! I am as good as you!"

"But I'm not very good," Gil laughed, binding another clumsy sheaf.

Magnus grunted. "That is true. Indeed, she is better. Give her your sword and take up her spindle," he said. "She makes the better man."

Gil shrugged and gave Magnus a grudging smile. But Janetta's eyes flashed. She flung the sickle down at Magnus's feet. "It is not so! He is as good a man as ever will be!" she cried.

Magnus's dour face broke into a grin. "And what would you know of men, little wildcat?" He looked up at Floki, watching with narrowed eyes. "Here! Find this one a real warrior! One to match her fire." He brushed her chin lightly with a playful finger.

"Don't you touch her!" Gil shouted. He lunged forward, his hand reaching for his sword. The laughter died on Magnus's lips, replaced by an outraged scowl. Then Floki's iron arm caught Gil around the waist and threw him aside.

Floki stepped firmly between his father and Gil and held up his hands, "Redbeard, the day grows long and I am thirsty. Let the young work. You and I drink ale."

Magnus rubbed his bearded chin and glared at Gil. Then he shrugged and allowed his son to steer him toward the longhouse. Floki turned, as they passed, whispered, "Idiot!" and slapped Gil's head with the palm of his hand.

Then he called to Aidan and Shony, "Come with us. I would have your judgement on a matter of great concern." He grinned suddenly at Grimhildr and strode away with his parents and his priest, Percy trotting contentedly behind.

Gil and Grimhildr reaped together, then, with Janetta binding sheaves for both. At the bottom of the field, where the barley faded into sea grass by the strand, they laid down their sickles and built a final stack of sheaves.

The late sun broke through the clouds, casting long blue shadows across the fields and turning the heather hill ruddy, above. Gil looked up and saw Floki returning, with a short, sturdy figure at his side. "Grimhildr!" Floki called. "Lord Yesu answers my prayers!"

Grimhildr straightened her back and shaded her eyes. Floki left his companion at a distance and loped down the stubble field until he stood in front of her. "I bring you a husband," he said.

Grimhildr faced him eye to eye. "A warrior?" She peered at the distant figure.

"And a farmer. His name is Ulf."

"Which farm?"

Floki grinned. "Do you not wish to know the color of his eyes? So you can dream of them, as she dreams of his?" He nodded toward Janetta and Gil.

"All eyes are dark in the night," Grimhildr said. "Which farm?"

"Two farms. One from his father, and one from his wife, who is dead; the first on the Horse Isle and the second, here. And his eyes are blue." He smiled winsomely. "Good farms, Grimhildr. And he is a good man." He held out his hand. "Come, he would meet you."

Grimhildr hesitated, her own eyes on Janetta and Gil.

"Come," Floki repeated. "Whatever tasks remain here, these two will surely manage. Alone down here," he nodded solemnly, "Where none will see."

They walked quickly away, Grimhildr's headdress fluttering in the wind, her long legs matching Floki's, stride for stride. "I don't believe it," Gil murmured. "He's human, too." A slow grin spread across his face. He turned to Janetta. She held out her arms and he flung himself into them and they tumbled, laughing, into the sheaves of barley.

It was late in the evening when Grimhildr returned, pink-cheeked and unusually cheerful; and later still when Gil returned from the Holy Isle. Floki was waiting for him on the strand. Together they dragged the skiff to her nest in the sea grass and then, with his hand lightly on Gil's shoulder, Floki crossed to the new ship and stood beneath her curving bow. He laid his palm on her stem and looked up. "What think you, now, of Eyolf?"

"Wonderful," Gil whispered.

"He is. As is this ship. She must have a name. What will you call her?" He turned and looked straight at Gil.

"*Me?*" Gil stuttered.

"You build her. You name her. She cannot sail without a name." He looked suddenly stern.

Gil stared up at the ship, feeling like he'd been given the biggest gift of his life. "I can't think ..." he murmured. But then he could.

Eyes like the dawn-lit sea.

Hair like the raven's wing.

"Sea-Raven," he said. "I name her Sea-Raven."

Floki's face softened into his sweet, white smile. He slapped Gil's back hard. "Ah, the bard! The bard! Good! A good name. A Viking name. There could be none better."

He looked up again at the bow. "Sea-Raven, Saint Matthew's Day we fledge you. At lauds, you fly the nest!" He laid his hand again on Gil's shoulder and together they walked the strand to where the tent-roof of the longhouse glowed in a rising moon. Outside the great doors, he suddenly stopped.

"Warrior," he said softly, his eyes yet on the entrance, "You come to us a boy. The burden of a boy's errors is borne by others. A man bears the burden of his own. Do not cross my father again. I will not again defend you." He turned and nodded slightly and then entered his longhouse, leaving Gil to follow, wary and alone.

Gil rose before first light, the morning of Saint Matthew's Feast and launched the skiff into the dawn. The sea was grey silk, the sail barely filling in the whisper of wind. The gathering tide clutched eerily at his steering oar.

He wrapped his blue cloak close. The air was wintery, the night now as long as the day. Raising his eyes to the low, mist draped hills of the Horse Isle, he imagined Cille Aidan and the Wandering Pool glistening amid the ruins. Saint Matthew's Feast; the equinox. The door to Tir nan Og lay open. "The door to home," he whispered. But the words vanished in the song of the tide race.

Even were Aidan's stone yet in his pocket, he would choose no landfall but the white beach of the Holy Isle. He thought of his father riding with Guinevere in the lost Forest of Caledon. *This is what he felt. This is why he stayed.*

On his return, with Janetta and Grimhildr, a great longship overtook them, surging past under oars, her fierce wolf figurehead glinting in the sunrise. Two of Floki's council stood, with swords and shields, beside her bare mast.

When Gil reached the shore of Hrolf's Isle, the longship was already beached and two smaller boats were approaching the strand. On the hill above, men on horses trotted out of the mist, descending to the shipyard where others were dismantling the stocks around Sea-Raven.

The crew of the visiting ship examined the newly built hull, while the chieftains conferred with Eyolf. All of Floki's longhouse company milled excitedly on the shore. The thud of hammers, the shouts of men and boys, and the laughter of the watching women drowned out even Aidan's bell. Yet, when Gil followed Janetta into the turf-roofed church, he found Floki himself within, kneeling in the candlelit shadows, like the quiet center of a storm.

The stocks around Sea-Raven were gone, when they came from Mass, and four men were raising her tall pine mast. Ponies waited in harness either side of her hull. Gil ran to help Ragi and Ciarnan lay log rollers beneath her stern.

When they rejoined the waiting crowd, all eyes had turned from the ship to the weaving sheds behind the longhouse. Rachel squeezed into a place beside them. Ragi hung over her shoulder, but in her excitement she forgot to push him away. "Look!" she pointed to where a line of women and girls had appeared, carrying a long white roll of cloth, like a great snake, between them. "The sail!"

The women spread out across the hillside and in a slow, stately dance, unrolled the cloth until the whole length was unfurled and held up like a roof above their heads. Then, with a joyful shout, they ran toward the shore, the white sail cascading down the hillside like the breaking crest of a wave.

Cheers greeted the sail as the women laid it proudly at

Floki's feet. Cheers broke out again when it was rigged to the spar in its cradle aboard the ship. Ciarnan and Ragi rode the ponies into the sea, tautening the ropes and turning to wait as Eyolf distributed oars to thirty men.

When Grimhildr's farmer, Ulf, received his oar, she, too, stepped forward, took up an oar of her own, and waved it at her future husband. He shook his menacingly back and cheers erupted again.

"So be it," Floki ruled. "She rows, and he rows. And the first to weaken makes up the marriage bed." He turned to the boys on their ponies. "Go!"

The ponies strained and men and boys took up ropes of their own, and with a silken lurch, Sea-Raven broke free of the sand on which she was born and slipped, stern-first into the sea. The crew clambered aboard on either side, slotting their oars through the oar-holes. Floki lifted Janetta and Rachel into the ship and jumped aboard himself. But Gil was so entranced by the sight of the strakes he had shaped and caulked afloat, he forgot to board at all. As the oars dipped into the water, Ciarnan and Ragi hauled him up by the seat of his pants and dumped him on the deck.

Gil scrambled to his feet to watch Erling lower the steering oar that Lionheart had borne up the hill. Then, while Eyolf the shipbuilder stood, arms folded, on the strand, Floki laid his sure hand on the tiller and Sea-Raven turned her unadorned prow to the open sea.

The wind had strengthened with the rising sun, and a sharp chop buffeted the untried stem. Within a hundred yards of the shore, oars were shipped and the white sail hoisted up the mast. Floki turned into the wind until the sheets were secured and the tacking spar rigged. Then, with a flick of his hand, he regained his course.

Gil felt the wind across his shoulder, strong and steady. The sail billowed taut, the prow lifted, and the ship heeled hard on her steering board. Floki watched the sail and the sheets a moment longer, then nodded with quiet satisfaction. "Take her, helmsman," he said.

Gil looked around for Erling, but Erling was in the bow,

talking to one of the chieftains. "Take her." Floki looked right at Gil and pointedly dropped the tiller.

"You mean me?" Gil stammered.

Floki raised his eyes to the heavens, and then gestured to a gull perched on the masthead. "No. I mean that shitty-arsed seabird in the rigging. *Take her*, helmsman." Gil leapt up and grabbed the swinging tiller. At once, it steadied under his hand. "*Thank you*." Floki flopped down on a sea-chest and leaned back against the rail, with a grimace of exasperation. Then he murmured, so quietly that only Gil could hear, "She is the same as the little skiff you sail so surely, Warrior. Only larger."

Gil nodded grimly. She was so *much* larger. Her mast towered above his head. The sheer power of the sail and the weight of the great hull strained against the steering oar. Even the solid oak of the tiller was too thick for his boy's hand. He felt small and useless, as if he was suddenly on the back of the huge monkish plough horse, after riding Lionheart.

Even the sounds of the ship overwhelmed him. The mast creaked and groaned; the rigging thrummed. The bow wave roared like surf. Gulls screamed overhead and the raucous crowd of warriors shouted and cheered.

Only Floki was quiet, sitting beside Gil on his sea chest, eyes half-closed, as if listening to a voice no one else could hear. Ahead, beyond the lee of Spear Island, white horses tumbled before the stiffening wind. The sail caught the first gust and the ship heeled hard.

Gil felt panic rise in his throat. *I can't do this.* His hand slipped on the spray-soaked tiller and the ship shimmied like a skittish pony.

"Hold her," Floki said, without looking up.

I can't. Struggling with the tiller, Gil turned despairingly to the young Northman, so calm and so immovably arrogant. *Look at me, damn you. I'm just a kid!*

And so was he, his own voice argued back. *Fifteen. Sixteen when he raided the Irish coast.*

"I'm not you!" Gil shouted.

"Hold her," Floki said again, and smiled.

Fury swept over Gil and in its midst, he suddenly

remembered Floki striding petulantly across the longhouse floor, mocking his own younger self. *Fifteen.*

Biting his lip so hard it stung, Gil gripped the tiller until he felt the rush of the sea trembling the steering oar beneath his hand. In his mind he saw the cascading dark flow of the burn drawing its perfect ellipse around the polished wood. Then the burn became the salt water beneath their keel; the rudder passing silkily through it, drawing their course.

He looked forward at the proud curve of the strakes, and saw them also beneath the waves, twisting, sinuous as an eel in their fetters of willow. He could feel again the adze in his hand, shaping thwarts and ribs, each solid treenail, each flexing strake slipping effortlessly through the deep. The mast fish; a single piece of sculpted oak, bracing the mast against the power of the wind. The mast itself that Ragi had trimmed and smoothed for days, bound in place, bending like a living tree.

She's alive, Gil thought. *Every part of her is alive ... her ribs my bones, her rigging my sinews, the wind in her sail my blood ....* We are all part of her and she is part of us. Bjorn lowering the great kerling into place. Lithe Ciarnan climbing the thirty foot of mast. He, himself, soaked in pitch, caulking every strake. And Eyolf, standing firm as the great oak keel, so sure of his ship he need never leave the shore. Gil swung the tiller slightly, feeling the response through hull and rigging. *Every man who builds her and every man who helms her goes with her, too.*

They rode out beyond Spear Island, far into the wind-driven sea, until nothing but mist and Norway lay beyond. Floki turned at last. "Helmsman," he gave Gil a brief nod, "take her home."

Gil nodded back. He called to Ciarnan and Ragi to man the sheets and take down the tacking spar. Then he swung Sea-Raven down the wind and let her fly.

CHAPTER TEN

The ship is on me.

It's not the ship. It's firewood.

Lionheart hunched his back under the creel harness. *The ship is heavy.*

The ship IS heavy. But it's not on you. Gil clambered up the muddy path, steadying the nearest creel with his hand.

The ship ….

It's firewood. I told you. Firewood.

Lionheart's mane bristled. His eyes rolled, showing a wild white rim. *The fire is on me.*

Gil sighed. *I'm so glad I came back. I missed this like so much.* He looked up the hill to where the Stone of Odin stood, black against the evening sky. He felt a little stupid, remembering how afraid he'd been of it.

Ciarnan was already unloading wood from his own pony's creels onto the fire-blackened turf. Ragi piled it around a core of pitch-soaked straw. Gil added his own wood, stacking it high.

When they were done, Ciarnan pointed to the fire striker slung from Gil's belt and grinned. Gil looked down the hill to where Floki followed with Percy, riding at Percy's leisurely pace. "We better wait," he said dutifully. He took the fire striker from its pouch and turned it over in his hand, stroking the finely worked dragon heads rearing up at either end.

"It is very beautiful," Ciarnan said shyly.

Gil handed it to him. "Erling gave it to me. I borrowed his in Glen Alban and he wouldn't take it back unless I took this one." He shrugged, remembering the helmsman's astonishment at his return. "I think it's my reward for staying alive."

Ciarnan smiled as he gave the fire striker back. "A better reward than you had from the earl." But Gil thought of Sea-Raven on Saint Matthew's Day, and quietly shook his head.

He led Lionheart away then and tethered him carefully where he wouldn't see the flames. When he returned to the Stone of Odin, Floki was kneeling beside it, patiently helping Percy master a fire striker. At last, the kindling at the heart of the stacked wood flared. The fire roared and crackled, casting flickering shadows over the hollow stone and lighting the dusky hilltop.

Floki drew Percy safely back from the flames and stood with his hands on the boy's shoulders, looking out across the Holy Isle's tide-races to Horse Isle beyond. Far across the dim water, a ruddy light suddenly appeared, high on a hilltop. "Look." Floki gently turned Percy, pointing, until the boy crowed with delight.

A second light flared, and Percy squealed and giggled. Further still, a red pinpoint in the lowering dusk marked a third. For a long while, Floki stood watching as the ward fires flickered from hill to hill. Then he smiled down at Percy. "Come," he said softly, reaching for the reins of their horses. "Now, we play."

He helped the boy up, and then mounted his own pony and turned abruptly to Gil. "Harvest is done, helmsman, and I would pay courtesy to a king. At Michaelmass, my *Dragon* sails east. With thirty men." He paused and looked malignly at Lionheart. "And four ponies, that one included."

"Ponies? But he's a sea-king." Gil looked down to Floki's longhouse, sited like any Northman's dwelling, a stone's throw from his ship. "Doesn't he live, like, by the sea?"

"He does that," Floki agreed. He smiled quietly. "A sea-king is like a swan, Warrior. Splendid on water. Clumsy on land. Come." His smile broadened into a grin. "We pluck this haughty bird."

At dawn on Michaelmass, when Gil returned, one last time, from the Holy Isle, six ships lay on the Hrolf's Isle strand. Grimhildr, her possessions packed in a sea-kist, named each of the newcomers as they passed. "*Wave-Loper*," she rolled the words out like a chant. *"Tide-Trampler,"* she sang on to the chime of Aidan's bell, *"Sea-Stag, Foam-Steed."*

"Such beautiful names," Janetta whispered. She leaned on Gil's shoulder as he guided the skiff ashore, admiring the richly painted figureheads. "Such beautiful ships!"

Grimhildr snorted, adjusting the axes at her waist, "Warships. They leave nothing beautiful behind."

By Terce, the ships were afloat; their oarsmen holding them steady in the shallows. Erling turned *Sea-Raven's* fierce-beaked new figurehead seaward, grinning like a proud father. Gil stood at the helm of *Silver Dragon,* struggling to believe he was really there.

The ponies were loaded and the last warriors came aboard. Janetta smiled at Gil from within the black tent she shared with Rachel. Percy perched on Floki's sea-kist, looking anxiously around.

"He's there," Gil said gently. He pointed to the strand where Floki walked in the distance with Aidan, Aidan's grey robes blowing gently in the soft wind, his head bent attentively. "He's coming," Gil added, though Floki seemed in no hurry.

Erling, too, pointed and shouted, "Save your confession for your return, Floki Magnusson. You'll have better stories to tell!" But Floki only smiled and waved.

Magnus, standing beside Shony amid the longhouse company on the shore, raised his head and bellowed, "You miss the tide!"

Floki laughed and waved again, but he turned and still talking with Aidan, slowly walked back. "I am here, Father," he said smiling gently. "Mo'Aidan bade the tide stand still, and behold, it has."

"Do not mock me," Magnus growled. "Four chieftains wait, and you are at your prayers?"

Floki shook his head. He turned then to Eoin, who sat waiting on a driftwood log, his grey dog beside him, and laid a hand of farewell on his poet's shoulder. "Sing us to sea, friend," he said solemnly, "That I may reap a fine harvest for your harp."

As the poet's fingers swept across the strings, Floki held out his hand to Magnus. "Come, Father," he said, "Sail with me."

Magnus hooked his thumbs through his sword belt. "And who will guard your household?"

"I leave warriors enough to guard it. Come."

"As they guarded Einar's Holm?"

Floki bowed his head, accepting the rebuff. "I sail for my foster-brother, Redbeard. I would have you at my side."

"You sail for a woman. You do not need my help."

Floki shook his head. He smiled wistfully and again he extended his hand. "If I cannot have my father, I would have my father's blessing," he said.

"Go to your priest for blessings," Magnus laughed. "I am a farmer." He turned his back. Shony reached out to him, but he shrugged her off and strode away.

Floki watched him go and then slowly turned, mounted the gangplank, and took his place beside Gil. Percy threw his arms around his neck and he closed his own around the boy. "Take me to Norway, helmsman," he said softly. "I grow weary of this shore."

Gil signaled to his oarsmen, and as they moved into deep water, to Ragi, to lower the steering oar. He felt the tide swirl around its blade and for a moment he was on the hillside with Eyolf and Lionheart. He raised his eyes to the mast but the day was so calm that he heard the sound of Eoin's harp, light as birdsong, over the dip and splash of the oars until they were far out from shore.

Spear Island was a blue silhouette behind them when they at last met the wind. Gil looked up at the masthead. The regal gold pennant Floki had bound there fluttered bravely. He turned hopefully for direction. But Floki was oblivious, intent on a gaming board, playing King's Table with Percy.

With a wary shrug, Gil called to Ragi and Ciarnan to raise sail. The spar rode, creaking, up the mast, and the blue-striped sail filled and tautened. Around them, the sails of their five companions billowed free. Floki adjusted his gaming board to the new angle as *Silver Dragon* heeled before the wind.

Gil waited a moment, and then, setting his eyes on the unfamiliar horizon, tightened his sweaty hands on the tiller, while his cheering oarsmen brought their oars clattering inboard. Grimhildr and Ulf bowed formally to each other as they stowed theirs side by side.

"My sister rows like two of him!" Bjorn Break-Neck crowed, mimicking Grimhildr's powerful stroke. "She is winner."

"Not so!" Arnkel Fish-Tail shouted back. "He saves his strength for the marriage bed. There *he* has the bigger oar!" He gestured cheerfully with his fist.

"Silence!" Floki looked up sternly. He nodded toward Janetta and Rachel, busy soothing the stamping ponies. "Hold your coarse tongues. What are you, Vikings?"

He turned then to Gil. "Warrior," he said mildly. "Were I at the helm, I would keep that island farther from my load-board." He gestured easily to the ship's left.

"What island?" Gil shaded his eyes and peered into the blue haze.

"The one that you cannot see because it is low and small and in the mist. Listen." Gil heard the rush of the sea against the hull, the snapping of the pennant, the low voices of the relaxing Northmen. Then, gradually, beneath them all, he heard the murmur of waves breaking on a rocky shore. He turned the dragon prow quickly windward until Floki held up his hand, and then signaled to Ragi to adjust the sail.

"Good," Floki said. "For although it is low and small, it would wreck you all the same." He rose and put away his gaming board and sent Percy to join the girls. Then he took his place beside Gil as they sailed on and, talking quietly the while, guided him past islands and skerries, through straits, and invisible shoals, naming each and its hazards as they passed.

"See, there, Warrior, that red cliff? There, always, you keep far out. There are rocks below. Ahead, that white line? Not water enough to float the little skiff." He touched the tiller, nudging their course. "Now, look, who swims there?" Gil saw a dark shape below the surface. "The Great Fish, Warrior. He goes to the open sea and so do you. Follow him."

Floki leaned back against the rail, his eyes on the grey sky. "The maas fly seaward. Soon this south wind turns to the west and carries us east and north." He looked up at the pennant.

"Hold course, helmsman. We set foot this night in my foster-father's hall."

"How do you know which *is* west?" Gil protested. "The sun's gone."

"I am in the waters of my childhood, Warrior. Here, Hakon Sea-Friend and I played, as boys." He smiled suddenly. "But look. I make it easier." He held something out, flat on his hand. It gleamed, silvery and small.

"My father's compass!" Gil cried.

Floki nodded. "The Falling Star." He said then, gently, "Will you have it back, now, Warrior? As it was your father's?"

Gil shook his head. "I gave it to you," he said, and then with a strange certainty, he added, "You will need it, one day."

"More than you?"

"Yes. But let me see it." He took the compass from Floki and aligned it north. Then he looked up at the pennant at the masthead, fluttering boldly north-eastward before the southwest wind.

Floki laughed. "You doubt me. Come. Soon we leave Sand Isle behind and there is nothing but open sea. There, we play a game."

Quite suddenly, the air grew cooler, and a sharp shower of rain reminded Gil how exposed the steersman's raised decking was and how stationary his stance at the helm. Shivering, he tightened his cloak around himself and drew the hood close over his wet hair. Floki took furs from the sea-kist and tossed one to Gil, before wrapping himself in the other. Gil grinned gratefully, retreating into its shaggy grey warmth. He saw himself as Erling; a man-wolf hunched over his oar.

Turning, he searched the seascape for their companions. *Sea-Raven* was nearest, a hundred feet off his load-board and beyond, *Tide-Trampler* with its stallion figurehead. Wolf-prowed *Wave-Loper* trailed *Silver Dragon's* stern, with *Sea-Stag* and *Foam-Steed* following, beyond a grey squall of rain.

Despite the showers, the air was clearer, now, so that the color of each chieftain's sail shone brightly, striped or checkered in yellow, blue, and green. Beyond the last ship, Sand Isle was a thin blue line, and when Gil looked again, it was gone. Floki handed him the compass again. "Now we play," he said with a smile, "Where is north?"

Gil turned the instrument until the needle touched the 'N.' "There." He raised his hand from the tiller to point, and then lowered it. Floki grinned, his arm extended already, exactly in line.

"The air is clear. The squalls come. It is cooler. The wind is in the west. So there is north." He pointed again. "When the hail bites your face, you will know the wind also turns to the north. But not yet."

Gil nodded, reaching to return the compass, but Floki shook his head. He leaned back, looking at the sky, and then sat up again and directed Gil's gaze above the mast. "There, Warrior, listen and you will hear them cry."

Far above, Gil's eyes found the vee of dots from which drifted the faint calling of a skein of wild geese. He thought of Danni, and wondered if Floki thought of her, too. But the Northman only smiled and said, "Michaelmass, and they fly southward, for winter comes. They rest in my cousin's islands, and then my own. So, from whence they come, we go." He extended his arm, north-easterly, toward their goal. Gil looked down at his compass and smiled.

The light was fading when Rachel and Janetta appeared with salt fish and ale. Gil ate with one hand on the tiller, as he had seen Erling do. Percy came and curled up beside Floki, after his supper, nesting in a mountain of furs. "We play again, Warrior," Floki murmured, his hand resting on the sleeping child's head. Gil checked his compass and, again, Floki found north before him. "We are midway, Warrior. And there is an island here."

"Where?" Gil cried, looking around in alarm.

Floki laughed. "Hidden beneath the sea, like the land of my brethren." He shook his head. "Beyond our sight, Warrior. It is Far Isle, and were its ward fire burning, you might see the glow on the clouds above. We pass it off our steering board. But look," he pointed to where swift, dark seabirds darted against the grey sky. "They fly homeward, at day's end, and so we know it is there."

Dusk fell, and then night. There was no moon, though

fleeting stars appeared in the gaps between clouds. Still, the sea carried its own light and even in the darkness Gil glimpsed the ghostly sails of their companions. When Floki next asked, "Where is north?" he looked first to the sky, seeking the Plough and the Pole Star. But the familiar shapes were lost in cloud. Defeated, he reached again for the compass. Floki stayed his hand. "Look, Warrior," he touched Gil's shoulder, turning him to look behind. Beyond the shadowy curve of the dragon tail, the sky was clear, lighting their wash with starlight.

"See," Floki pointed to a line of three stars. "There Frigga carries her spindle." He raised his hand, as if gripping a distaff. "She is Odin's wife, but each night from Michaelmass to Lentron, she rises from his bed and climbs the southern sky, spinning the clouds into yarn.

"Now is but the first watch of the night. Mo'Aidan sings Compline, and Frigga begins her climb, there, in the east. So there, now," he moved his hand in an arc, "Is south." He turned and gestured straight ahead, "And north lies there."

Gil dutifully checked his compass. He looked back at the three stars. "Orion," he murmured. "We call them Orion's Belt."

"Now, why would you do that?" Floki sounded exasperated. "It is clearly a spindle." He cuffed Gil's head and leaned back against the rail. "Ah, Warrior, now we need play no more. Look."

Gil saw the glow begin on the northern horizon, even behind the veil of clouds. And then, as the veil broke apart, curtains of rippling cascading light swept up the sky.

"Odin's maidens dance," Floki said.

"They hang their shields on the stars," Gil whispered. He rested both arms on the tiller, entranced. Then he straightened up suddenly. "Doesn't his wife mind? She's out spinning and he's dancing with maidens all night?" He ducked, expecting another slap. But Floki was silent for a long while. Then he gestured to the darkened deck.

The girls had retreated into their tent. The ponies were dozing shadows in their pen; the crew huddled lumps under cloaks and furs. "When you are alone at this helm," he said very softly, "And all are asleep. And around you is nothing but sea and night – laugh, then, at my fathers' gods."

Gil nodded warily. "Am I going to do this alone?"

"Yes. But not this night." Gil glimpsed his white smile in the eerie light. "It is hard work, Warrior. I take her now."

Gil nodded again, suddenly aware how tired he was, his eyes burning with the strain of peering through darkness, his hands frozen, and his legs so stiff that when he rose, his knees wouldn't unbend. "Go, now," Floki said. "Sleep." He took the tiller from Gil and the ship responded at once to his hand, light and swift, like a hawk at her master's command.

Gil lay down on the deck, wrapped in his fur, and was so instantly and so soundly asleep that when he awoke, nudged into consciousness by Floki's foot, he could not have said if he had slept ten minutes or ten hours. "Warrior. What is the scent?"

"Scent?" Gil mumbled, his face buried in fur.

"Sit up. Breathe. What is it?"

"Ponies?"

"Beyond ponies." Floki nudged him harder. Gil sat, rubbing his eyes blearily. Ponies. Salt. Wood. Harvest. *Harvest.* His mind leapt to the sheaves of fresh cut barley, the sweetness of the scent, and the sweetness of the girl in his arms. "Janetta," he murmured.

"*What?*"

"Harvest. I smell the straw."

"And *why* do you smell straw in the middle of the sea?"

"Land!" Gil cried. He got to his feet, swaying on the moving deck. "Where?"

"Too far to see. But the wind carries the scent of Ragnvald's harvest." Floki swung the tiller, heading up. "See to the sheets, Warrior. We seek these fields."

The Northern Lights grew so brilliant overhead, that Gil could see the colors of their companion's sails as they tacked across *Silver Dragon's* wake. Ahead, the outline of an island appeared, black against the shimmering sky.

"It is well we come as friends," Floki pointed to the dark summit of the island. "They have seen us."

Gil saw a red flame flare and flicker. "The ward fire," he said uncertainly.

Floki laughed. "It is good. They will have time to prepare our welcome."

The aurora was fading into midnight blackness when they slipped into Ragnvald Sveinsson's sheltered cove, but still men ran to draw the ships ashore. Helping hands unloaded kists. Two young boys joined Ciarnan, leading the wild-eyed ponies down the gangplank. Gil heard Lionheart's panicked neigh with a pang of guilt, but his new role earned him a new status, whether he wished it or not.

While the girls were spirited away to the care of the women, and Ragi and Ciarnan slept under the black ship tents, Gil was provided a place in the longhouse and a seat among the chieftains at the next night's feast.

The longhouse, though well-built of stone and wood, with a green turf roof sweeping almost to the ground, was dark and gloomy within. Its somberness seemed to flow from Ragnvald, himself; a lean, grey-bearded man who walked with a shuffling limp and took his place on the high seat with a wince of pain.

There was no harp here, no poet, and little laughter. Floki's sail-roofed hall, for all its makeshift structure, seemed to Gil a brighter and a happier place. Awed and shy, he sat in silence as around him men spoke of battles past and the battle to come, in a tongue he yet struggled to understand.

But then Ragnvald's wife, Magnus Redbeard's sister, Gunnhild, took a place beside him. Though she shared her brother's height and ruddy features, she was as gentle as Magnus was gruff, and as cheerful as her husband was dour. She fussed over Gil, finding the best morsels for his plate, and showing him the little lapdog that slept at her feet.

"She is Hakon's," Gunnhild said sadly, "And she whines for him every night." Though Cat's hackles rose, just at the thought of it, Gil patted the little dog to please her.

When the feasting board was cleared and the ale horns replenished, Floki rose from his seat, his bright, braided hair a splash of sunlight in the darkness of the hall. Bowing first to his foster-parents, he recited a courtly poem, telling of the battle that had cost Ragnvald his fitness, and lauding the bravery with which he had fought, even after a falling mast had shattered his leg.

It was a story known, no doubt, to every man at the table. But, embroidered with graceful rhyme and bright phrases, it became less a tale of loss than one of heroic achievement, and Floki's lilting recitation, almost a song.

Still, Gil saw the true grace was in the message that lay beneath: that Ragnvald's courage was proven and needed no further testing. The duty of Hakon's rescue had passed from the crippled father to his foster son. Gunnhild listened gratefully, and thanked Floki with a kiss, and Ragnvald, too, nodded and smiled.

But when, before dawn the next morning, they left for Norway, his ship sailed first.

The day was bright and cold; the sea mottled with the shadows of flying clouds. With a stiff wind yet in the west, they set out, due east, and raised sail at once. As soon as the encircling arms of the cove slipped behind them, Floki left Gil alone at the helm.

He wandered the deck; playing games with Percy, flirting with Rachel, teasing Lionheart with tufts of straw, as if the ship were of no more interest to him than some merchant's knarr on which he had taken passage.

Rapidly, the islands slipped behind, dropping below the horizon. For a while, Gil felt safe, following Ragnvald across the empty sea. But, even under his novice hand, *Silver Dragon* was the faster ship. They drew abreast of the blue-checkered sail of Ragnvald's *Bright Wanderer*, and then beyond.

Gil held to his compass course, his eyes sweeping the waters around him for those signs Floki found everywhere. Birds flew overhead. Gulls followed their wake and rested on the dragon's tail. Shoals of fish rippled the sea's surface, like rain. But without Floki's guidance, their paths and their journeys were a mystery.

Gil looked forward. Floki was stretched out beside Percy on the sun-splashed deck, the gaming board between them. Janetta saw Gil watching, and he waved. She smiled, and seeing him without his teacher, shyly approached the helm.

Gil jumped up from the sea-kist and stood beside her, one hand on the steering oar, the other on her shoulder. Her black hair whipped in the wind like the pennant on the masthead.

When she turned to him, her eyes sparkled with love for him like the sun on the sea. Beneath his hand, *Silver Dragon* carried him through the waves as nobly as the monkish plough horse had borne him through the Forest of Caledon.

Then suddenly he saw the ship as if from above; his hand on the tiller, Janetta at his side; as he had seen it through the window in Merlin's Tower. *This is it,* he thought joyfully. *Where I would be if time stood still. This is Time Out of Time.*

But even as he thought it, the moment had passed. He tightened his grip on Janetta's shoulder. She smiled and laughed; but the wind at his back grew cold. Time did not stop. It was the ship no man could helm, ploughing the sea no man could sail. And it sailed on.

CHAPTER ELEVEN

At dusk they saw the snows of Norway. Floki joined Gil at the helm, his eyes on the line of brighter white above white banks of cloud. "They are tall mountains, Warrior. We are yet far out to sea."

He turned Gil's course southward. "We follow the coast. There is a bay beneath that highest point. We make landfall, there, this night." He grinned. "It is not courteous to call on strangers in the dark." He gave Gil's arm a friendly slap. "Good. A good crossing. You do well."

Hurriedly, Gil aligned his compass with the distant snowy summit. Floki turned and looked over his shoulder to Ragnvald Sveinsson's longship, trailing in their wake. "Now, head up and stand by."

Gil turned the prow into the wind. The sail slackened and sagged. Floki signaled *Bright Wanderer* and Ragnvald's helmsman brought the ship alongside. "Close in." Floki stood up on the rail, "Take care with the oar."

Gingerly, Gil steered *Silver Dragon* nearer, his eyes on the vulnerable rudder. Floki nodded. "Hold course," he said mildly, and then, as easily as if stepping from his longhouse door, he leaped out over the rushing sea, landing, light as a cat, on the deck of Ragnvald's ship. He turned with a smile and waved Gil away.

"*What?*" Gil mouthed.

"I would speak with my foster-father," Floki called, as *Bright Wanderer* moved seaward, to resume their south-easterly course.

Gil stared at the widening gap of water between them. "You're just *leaving?*" he shouted. He grabbed for the tiller as, free of the shadow of *Bright Wanderer's* sail, *Silver Dragon* caught the wind in her own.

"I come back," Floki said cheerfully. Then he pointed to their dragon prow already edging ahead. "If you do not outrun us."

"But how ...?" Gil protested wildly. *Silver Dragon* plunged forward like Lionheart fleeing a wolf.

Floki laughed. "Clip her wings, Warrior!" He waved at the spar, straining at the masthead, and still laughing, turned away.

Gil stared numbly at the spar and then suddenly woke from the shock of abandonment. "Ragi! Ciarnan!" he shouted. "Reef the sail!"

With the spar lowered and an eighth of the sail rolled and tied, *Silver Dragon* sailed tamely as a lady's palfrey. Gil aligned the nose of her figurehead with *Bright Wanderer's* mast and kept it there as he shadowed the other ship toward the coast.

His white mountain disappeared behind nearer, lower hills, as they drew closer, and he set his course by the dark headland that lay below it. The light was fading when the white sands of a sheltered bay suddenly appeared between two rocky promontories.

Bright Wanderer's sail was but a pale smudge against the dusky sky, and Gil watched her, warily, terrified he might be left to beach the ship alone. But at last Ragnvald's helmsman altered his course, bringing his ship again alongside.

Floki jumped across, and took the steering oar from Gil, as calmly as if he had been no further than the stem of the ship. "I take her in, now, helmsman."

Gil released the tiller from his sweaty grip and got to his feet, stumbling on shaking legs. Floki smiled and nodded at the mast. "Women, ships, and ponies, Warrior, always ask for more. Give them less, and they love you." Then he called for full sail, turned down the wind, and ran *Silver Dragon* into the bay and up onto the foreign strand.

When the seven ships were beached and secured above the tide, Floki looked around the hidden cove with satisfaction. "*Now*, we are Vikings." He grinned mischievously at Gil. "You may have your lady, if you wish."

Janetta's smile lit up her face, but Grimhildr strode between them, showed Floki the blade of her axe, and with her hand gripping Janetta's elbow, marched her back to the ship. Janetta waved forlornly from the black tent, and Gil waved back. Then he lay down beside Ragi and Ciarnan on the beach, and slept a cold, sea-haunted sleep.

Too soon, it was dawn, and a hand shook him awake. "Come. We ride hawking."

Gil squinted up out of his cocoon of wolfskin. Floki stood above him in the grey light, holding the reins of a pony in one hand and wrapping his wrist with leather, with the other.

"*Hawking?*" Gil shook his head blearily. "But you haven't got …." He saw Rachel, then, mounted on a pony already and giving him her "idiot" look. "Oh. Got it." He staggered to his feet and stumbled to Lionheart who looked sleepier than he felt, if that was possible.

On the crest of a hill, just out of sight of the ships, they halted the three ponies. Rachel jumped down and drew her circle in the grass with the point of her sword. Then she stepped within and with a calm smile, recited the blessing. Floki watched as she took her other form and mounted the sky.

"She sees the world as I never shall," he said softly. He gestured to the mountains above them, and the sea below, grey and smooth in the dawn. "I envy no man, but I envy her."

"It's beautiful," Gil said.

Floki looked at him oddly. "What say you?"

"I've seen the world like that," Gil murmured. "I don't know how." The memory dissolved as he sought to grasp it, like so many memories of Tir nan Og. He shook his head.

Floki's eyes narrowed warily. Then he laughed. "Of course. A cat that swims must also fly." He ducked, as if expecting another punch.

Then Rachel came streaking back and he held up his leather-bound wrist. She alighted, fierce claws gripping the leather, wings outspread. "And again," he whispered, and sent her aloft once more. This time she swept out over the bay where the ships lay, and beyond, before returning to his arm.

A third time, he sent her out. She was away so long that Floki began to pace nervously, scouring the sky for a glimpse of her. When at last she flew back, he held up his looped sword belt that she might return to him, her human self.

She tumbled into a tangle of low growing shrubs, breathless and laughing, her red hair spread out over their russet leaves. Then, soberly, she got to her feet and with perfect recall described the structures and defenses of the sea-king's hall, lying just beyond the dark promontory of their bay.

"A man watches at the top of the hill." She pointed to the summit above the promontory. "But the bay is concealed by the ridge between and he looks beyond, out to sea. There is something beside him, covered in sailcloth."

"Wood for the ward fire," Floki said. "He may keep it safely dry, for he will not use it."

"There is a stockade all around the hall. The gate at the front faces the sea. There are two guards. Four more wait on rocks above the harbor."

"And behind the hall?"

"There is another gate. It was open. I saw five girls driving cows through it."

Floki's face suddenly softened. "Was my lass among them?"

"No." Rachel shook her head, puzzled. "Would he use her to milk cows? Wouldn't you mind?"

He shrugged, his eyes cold. "He could use her for worse. Wish for his sake that he has not." He paused; then shook his head. "The gate ... did they close it?"

"No. No one has, all summer. I flew to the gate post. Grass was growing over the lowest poles."

Floki smiled. "A clumsy swan, indeed," he said to Gil. "He looks only to the sea." He turned back to Rachel. "And what ships were there?"

"Five on the shore. One in stocks. And five at anchor."

"And the hall?"

"Thick smoke above the roof. Men standing outside the door. Some well-dressed. Some poor."

"Awaiting their earl," Floki murmured. "And he? Did you see him? A big, broad man ...."

Rachel laughed, "With a grey beard to his waist! He is in his bed yet. There is a fine room at the rear of the hall, with two windows. I alighted on a shutter. He did not see me. He was ..." she giggled and glanced aside, "...busy with his wife."

Floki laughed delightedly. "May he enjoy her. He has an interesting day to come." He mounted his pony, still laughing; then turned to Gil, struggling to pull Lionheart out of a half-eaten shrub. "Come, Warrior," he said. "Now we play King's Table."

Back on the shore, Floki knelt in the sand and drew a map of the hall and its defenses for the chieftains and his foster-father. He tapped his drawing of the king's harbor. "Two on ponies circle the longhouse and take the farthest watchmen. Two on foot, take the nearer. A third of the men of each ship cross the hill and approach the hall through the landward gate. They take the door guards and bar the doors and windows with all within."

"Ah, hah!" Bjorn Break-Neck roared cheerfully. "We burn them!"

"*No*, we do not burn them." Floki gave Bjorn a pained look. "One day I burn you." He smiled then and looked around his gathered warriors. "I only ensure my hosts are at home when I come. It would pain them so to miss me."

A ripple of laughter spread through the crowd, but Floki grew suddenly serious. "I come to this shore to pay a ransom. I would do so peacefully. Harm no one you have no need to harm. Do not seek battle where none is required. Hostages are the first to pay the price if things go wrong."

The older men nodded solemnly. The younger shrugged and looked disappointed. Floki turned to Gil and Ciarnan. "Ride, now, to the ward hill that no beacon announce our coming. I am but a humble farmer, unworthy of such honor." He smiled. "Go. And waste no time. We sail on your return."

They left the ponies a hundred feet below the crest of the hill. Lionheart lowered his head at once, munching greedily. *Don't get too fat to run*, Gil warned him as he and Ciarnan went on, on foot, crouching low and moving cautiously from rock to rock.

The guard had his back to them, when they reached the summit, hands at hip level, peeing a yellow stream in the direction of his earl's hall. They waited until he'd finished before they rushed him. He whirled, still hitching up his trousers, boyish eyes wide with amazement, as Gil dove for his knees. With a belated grab for his sword, he went down, shouting and struggling.

Skinny and scared, he was still stronger than he looked and Gil fought to hold him. Then Ciarnan landed a punch on his beardless chin and he fell back, stunned. "Get his sword belt!" Gil sat on the boy's chest, while Ciarnan disarmed him, throwing the belt over his own shoulder. "That cloth!" Gil nodded to the sailcloth covering the stacked wood of the ward fire.

Grinning, Ciarnan hauled it off and together they rolled the struggling guard in it, tying him with the hemp lines that had bound it to the wood. The boy wriggled like a caterpillar, shouting curses in the names of Odin and Thor. Gil grinned uncomfortably, seeing his own self wrapped in the gorillas' fishing net at Einar's Holm.

Then suddenly the young guard's mouth froze, silencing his last curse, and his face went white. Gil turned, following his terrified gaze. Ciarnan was standing calmly holding his upraised sword, hands clasped on the hilt as once in monkish prayer.

"What are you doing?" Gil cried.

"I say thank you," Ciarnan whispered, raising the blade like an executioner's axe. "For Donal."

Gil looked in horror from his still, determined face, to the boy on the ground. "*Him*? But *he* didn't burn Hy!" He thought suddenly of Ismail, chastising him for his own vengefulness, in Glen Alban. "He didn't kill Donal!" Ciarnan paused, the sword trembling slightly in his hands. The boy looked at Gil with pleading eyes. "And, anyhow," Gil said sharply, "Floki told us ...."

Ciarnan's eyes shifted from the guard to Gil. "Who will know?" he said coldly, "If we don't tell them?"

Gil thought of Ismail, again. "You will," he said sadly.

The hill fell silent, but for the wind and the whimpering of the boy. Then, looking suddenly lost and confused, Ciarnan lowered the sword and with shaking hands slipped it into its sheath. "Come," he murmured, turning back to the ponies. "They wait."

Riding down off the hill, Gil stopped in amazement above the beach. The ships now rode at anchor out in the bay, but *Silver Dragon* lay just offshore, afloat on the incoming tide, her gangplank resting on the wave-lapped sand. Down the full length of each rail, her hull was adorned with the bright-painted shields of the Northmen. With the gold pennant fluttering from her mast, and her depleted crew standing ready at their oars, she seemed bound not for battle, but a wedding feast.

Before her, on the strand, Floki waited, with Percy beside him, both dressed in the blood-red tunics and white linen shirts they had worn at the Council of the Chieftains. Floki's azure cloak, thrown back over one shoulder, revealed the glint of gold at his arms and throat. His sea-tangled hair was freshly combed and bound in ribboned braids.

He beckoned to Gil, as they arrived, surveyed his face sternly and then pointed to where a fresh-flowing burn tumbled into the sea. "Go," he said, "Wash yourself."

"Wash?" Gil blinked. Ciarnan grinned and crept away with the ponies.

"Yes. Wash." Floki looked heavenward. "With water."

"Why?"

"*Why?* Because you are filthy!" he leaned over and lifted a chunk of Gil's wind-whipped hair, then dropped it in disgust. "And comb your hair."

Gil heard a muffled giggle and saw Rachel and Janetta smothering laughter behind their hands. Floki turned and saw them, too. "Go help him," he said wearily. He pointed toward the burn and then strode off to his ship.

The girls took one of Gil's arms, each, and marched him to the burn. He stripped off his tunic and doused himself in the freezing water. Janetta splashed him cheerfully and Rachel shoved a linen towel in his face. "Scrub, Gil. Make *some* kind of effort."

"What is he, my mother?"

Rachel looked back at the ships. "He is an earl, calling upon a king. And you are his helmsman. Fine clothes and jewelry say he's rich. That means he's powerful. It's a message, Gil. A warning." She smiled faintly, "Don't worry; he can fight just as well dressed like that." She handed Gil his tunic. "But fighting costs lives and ships. No matter how much he might enjoy it, he will avoid it if he can."

Janetta took out her deer horn comb. "Come on," Rachel pushed him and they hurried back to the ship, Janetta tugging at his tangled hair as they walked.

Aboard *Silver Dragon*, Floki gave him a linen shirt to wear under the tunic, and to Gil's surprise, it almost fit him. Janetta combed the last snarl out of his hair and, untying a ribbon from her own, reached to bind his with it.

Gil held up both hands. "I don't do ribbons."

Rachel shrugged. "Floki does."

"I think he's proved his masculinity a while ago," Gil whispered. "I'm still working on mine. *No ribbons*." He dropped his hands and bolted for the helm.

The wind had veered northwest and the seven ships rounded the headland and entered the king's cove under full sail. Ahead, the valley rose, green and narrow, walled in by lofty mountains, their summits white with autumn snow.

Gil spotted the dark walls and turf roofs of scattered farm buildings amid cattle-dotted pastures. Fields of stubble stretched down to the sea, and beside them stood a roofless barn with blackened timber walls, half fallen in. He thought of Einar's Holm. But whatever the fate of the barn, the king's longhouse stood untouched within its wooden palisade.

It was a noble building, made of dark, upright timbers, with a great sweep of green turf roof, sprinkled with late summer flowers. Splashes of color brightened its eaves and shuttered windows. Blue smoke drifted peacefully above.

Floki directed Gil to take the lead, and with three ships on either side, they sailed landward in a broad vee stretching across the bay. Gil's eyes swept across the line of colorful sails. "I thought we were supposed to surprise them."

Floki laughed. "They are surprised already. Look." He pointed to the stockade gates standing open to the sea and a flash of steel at the longhouse doors where their advance party waited with drawn swords. Then he swept his hand around his elegant ship. "When he peeks out from his fine window, now, I give him something fine to see."

He looked down, then, at the water, gauging its depth. "Drop anchor, here, helmsman. Lower your sail, but do not bind it. Eight men remain on each ship, ready at their oars." He glanced up at the pennant. "This wind we ride so grandly, will face us, on our return. And we may be in some haste to leave." He slapped Gil's back. "Come. Let your lady see the warrior she has won."

The water at *Silver Dragon's* anchored stem was only just above Gil's knees. But Floki and Bjorn graciously carried each of the girls to dry land and even Percy got a piggy-back. Bjorn returned to the ship, snatched his shield from the rack, and then splashed back to the beach, carrying three great grappling-irons in his enormous hands, their coils of rope piled over his shoulder.

Keeping two, himself, he gave one to Grimhildr and, clanking with swords and axes as well, brother and sister strode toward the longhouse, at the head of the warriors of all seven ships. Ignoring Lionheart's pitiful whickers of abandonment, Gil tramped behind, his own shield slung over his back, his sword ready. Floki followed last, with one hand on Percy's shoulder, his shield looped around his neck, and a long, linen-wrapped bundle carried lightly over his other arm.

At the gate, they were greeted with cheers and laughter by their grinning shipmates, who played at barring their way, then bowed and ushered them through. More of their own men guarded the hall itself. Rough timber torn from the palisades jammed the carved doors shut. Gil studied them as Floki joined him. "But won't they be barred inside, too?"

Floki gave him his pained look. "Oh, I hope so, Warrior. Surely, he is not *that* stupid?" He looked down the ranks of his swordsmen, waiting in two lines, before the entrance. He nodded briefly and they nodded back. Then he looked up to Bjorn, swinging his three-pronged grappling-irons like a child's toys. "Go."

Bjorn's black-bearded face broke into a huge grin. He dropped one of the grappling-irons at his feet and began swinging the other in circles around his head. The iron whirred through the air, its arc widening as the rope ran out through his hands. At a safe distance, Grimhildr began swinging her iron, too.

With a last heave, Bjorn flung his up and over the peak of the longhouse roof. With a thud that brought shouts of alarm from within, the hooks bit into the turf. Bjorn tried the rope; then, slinging the second iron over his shoulder, he braced his feet against the wall and climbed hand over hand up the rope, to the sloping eaves.

Grimhildr flung her grapple, too, and with her white headdress streaming like a flag, and her skirts hiked up to her thighs, mounted the wall to the roof, as well. Side by side, brother and sister worked their way up to the smoke-wreathed ridge.

Then, standing with a foot on either side, they loosed their axes and swung fierce blows at the roof. The shouts of alarm grew louder, until, with a cascade of falling turf, Bjorn broke through. Securing his grappling-iron again, he dropped the line inside the hall, gripped it in both hands and, roaring with delight, leapt feet first into the hole. A moment later, Grimhildr followed him, her white headdress vanishing, last from sight.

"Go!" Floki shouted to his swordsmen. In seconds, they kicked down their barricade. Then the great doors swung outward, revealing Grimhildr's pink-cheeked, smiling face. Gil glimpsed the dark interior of the longhouse and Bjorn standing beside the hearth, swinging his second hook in fierce, whirring circles of deadly iron, while men and women shrank terrified against the walls. Then the swordsmen charged through the wide-open doors.

Gil ran to join them, but Floki barred his way. "Stay." Erling, too, was ordered to remain, and behind Floki, Ragnvald, the chieftains, and the girls waited.

Within the longhouse, the swordsmen unreeled themselves in the space Bjorn had cleared. Backs to the hearth, swords upraised, they spread out down the hall until every man in it was facing steel.

The last warrior took his place. The thuds of boots and cries of fear and anger stilled. Floki tapped Gil's shoulder and nodded to Erling. With Percy clinging, wide-eyed, to his cloak, and his helmsmen at either side, he strode calmly into the sea-king's hall.

At the far end, before a table strewn yet with an abandoned breakfast, a bulky, grey-bearded man stared in disbelief. By his side, a lean, handsome young woman and a young boy and girl with white-blond hair, stood frozen in fear.

Floki waited until astonished recognition lit in the big man's eyes. Then, with his three attendants, he walked in silence the length of the hall. Kneeling, he unwrapped the linen bundle in his arms and laid a sheaf of Hrolf's Isle barley at the sea-king's feet.

"Harvest is done," he said. "I bring you a farmer's silver." Then he stood and rested his hand on his sword hilt. "I will have my people now. The ransom is paid."

The king stared at the barley sheaf and then slowly raised his gaze until he met Floki's. He gave a sad little shrug and shook his head. "They are not here."

Floki narrowed his eyes, studying the king's face. Then he whispered, pityingly, "Do not lie to me, old man."

"I do not lie." The king raised empty hands. "They are not here."

Floki shook his head. He looked up at the roof of the longhouse, as if confronted with one of Gil's bigger stupidities, and smiled faintly. He turned to Erling. "Kill him." With a little tug at his beard, as if asked for a surprising change of course at sea, Erling stepped forward and drew his sword.

"No!" There was a flurry of movement and the girl with the white-blond hair dashed forward. "He does not lie!" The first swordsman whirled from the line, but Floki waved him back, catching the girl's arms with his own hands. "My father does not lie!" she cried again. "They are not here."

Floki nodded and gently pushed her away. "Go back to your mother, child."

"I am not a child." She held her ground. Then she looked angrily at the lean woman. "And *she* is not my mother."

Floki's icy eyes locked with hers. "So where are they?"

The girl wavered, and though Gil could see now she was not at all a child, but Rachel's age, or more, she seemed to lose her nerve. She glanced at her father and he sighed.

"Deer Bay," he said. "By now." He looked sorrowfully at Floki. "They bring me nothing but misfortune. From the day I take them under my roof. In the winter, my eldest son's ship is lost. My second son dies of a summer fever. All I have *left* of sons is here, wearing his brother's sword." He drew the fair-haired boy close.

The boy was small, no more than ten, the sword belt almost doubled around his waist. The king stroked his cheek. "I fear I offend Odin. But my wife says, 'It is the girl. She is a witch.'"

"She is *not* a witch." The king's daughter whirled furiously to face her stepmother.

"The kitchen maids saw her," the lean woman snapped back, "Drawing her circles in the sand."

The blond girl looked at her father. "She is not a witch," she whispered. "She is a Change-Thing. She wanted only to fly. And so I let her. She pledged she would return, and always, she did. *She* kept her word."

The king dropped his eyes. The girl turned back to Floki. "Besides, she would never leave until you came for her. Her heart would not allow it." She looked briefly toward the lean woman and then spoke clearly for all the hall to hear. "The girl is not a witch. She is my friend. As were they all," she murmured passionately. She raised her voice again. "But the girl is beautiful. And my stepmother has little fondness for beauty in this hall."

The king shrugged, weary of women's quarrels. "The day Thor's Hammer strikes my barn alight and half the harvest is lost, the trader from Deer Bay drops anchor. I take it as a sign. You would do the same!" He looked at Floki pleadingly. "You had not come. He had. So I sell them on."

"In chains!" the girl shouted at her stepmother.

Floki's hand tightened on his sword hilt until the knuckles turned white. "What day?"

"Ten days past."

Floki closed his eyes, holding one hand up toward the king,

as once, in fury, he had done to Gil. Then he shook his head, opened his eyes again and let his gaze wander all around the hall before returning it to the king.

"These are my terms," he said, in the softest of voices. "I will have every man of my cousin's ship returned. If any are dead or harmed in any way, I will have silver in compensation. Three of your chieftains and three of mine will judge the price. This will be done by spring sowing. I will have, too, the price of my cousin's ship."

"It is not my doing, the sinking of that ship!" the king protested.

"You profited by it. Now you will pay." Floki turned away, then, and looked briefly around the hall. "I will have a pledge of your good faith." He gave the king a sour smile. "Your word will not do." His eyes swept the hall again and then he pointed to the king's son. "I take him."

The old man's face turned grey. A desperate muttering went around the hall as he spoke in a shaky voice. "He is a boy."

"He bears a sword. He is a man. I take him."

The king suddenly crumbled. Whatever had been powerful in him vanished. The hand that reached out to his son was trembling. "Please ...." he begged. His eyes brightened suddenly. "I give you a ship. and its crew. To sail with you to Deer Bay ...." Floki shook his head. "Two ships," the king cried. He held up his hands. "Sixty men!"

Ragnvald stepped forward and laid his hand on Floki's shoulder, bending his solemn head close. "This is a good offer," he said softly. "The men with me have farms and wives. They cannot follow you to Northumbria. Nor can half of yours."

Floki listened courteously and laid his own hand on top of his uncle's. But he shook his head. "He is selfish and dishonest. He pledges lightly what he cares little for. But for his son, he keeps his promise." He looked up and signaled to Bjorn Break-Neck. "Take the boy."

Bjorn strode forward, smiling within his beard. The child shrieked and flung his arms around his father's neck. Again, his sister slipped in between. She stood before Floki with hands clasped, her pale hair framing a face as fearless as it was beautiful. Gil thought suddenly that she was not unlike her adversary, and if Floki had had a sister, she would look like this.

"I wish my friends and your good cousin only well," she said. "But I beg you, spare my brother. I will see my father's word is kept."

Floki's face softened slightly and he gave her a gentle nod. "If you were the warrior I see in your eyes, I have no doubt you would. But you are too young, yet, to rule a king." He smiled suddenly. "Though in years to come, you may indeed." He paused. "I will keep your brother safe. But he comes with me."

She stepped back, studying him sorrowfully. "How strange," she said, "That you and Hakon Sea-Friend share blood; he like the night, and you, the morning sun. But though he is as dark as you are fair, I think his heart is the fairer."

"This is true," Floki agreed. "But he wears chains and I command seven ships." He turned away, then, and Bjorn stepped forward. The blond girl, seeing her cause lost, ran to a kist and brought out a warm cloak for her brother.

Then, approaching Floki the last time, she slid a ring from her finger. "Take this to Hakon, that he believe Gudrun's word is better than her father's." Her eyes flashed defiantly as she pressed it into his hand. Then she kissed her brother and whispered. "You are a man and a king's son. Accept your fate."

But the boy clung, sobbing to his father's neck until Bjorn pulled him away and slung him over his shoulder. "Papa!" he cried, "Papa!" The king reached to him with both hands, tears glistening on his cheeks, and tried to stumble after. Floki's swordsmen stepped in between. "Have pity," the old man sobbed.

Floki's eyes turned to ice. "You sell my kin into slavery and you want pity?" Then he turned, and with his arm around Percy, who stared after the crying boy with baffled eyes, thrust Gil ahead of him. "Go. Now," he said urgently.

Ragnvald and the chieftains swept the girls from the hall. Gil, Erling, Floki, and Percy strode behind; the swordsmen backing in defensive precision behind them. "Papa!" the boy shrieked one last time, as the great longhouse doors slammed shut. Bjorn was already halfway to the ships, when the blocking timbers thudded in place.

"Quickly, now," Floki whispered to Gil. "That will not hold them long. Run to the helm. We must raise sail before they reach the strand."

They left the harbor under oars. Beyond, the wind had veered further into the north and east, and Gil called for the sail. As it rode up the mast, and the splash of oars fell silent, he heard the boy sobbing, still.

Crouched, like a small, frightened animal, beneath the dragon's tail, he kept his eyes glued to the vanishing shore of his home, until there was nothing to be seen but mist. Percy knelt by him, patting him gently and Janetta leaned over him, murmuring encouragement. She looked up and met Gil's eyes. He glanced forward, to where Floki stood looking out to the cold northern sea as calmly as if they sailed to Holy Isle.

"He's a monster," Gil whispered.

Janetta looked surprised. "But he is right. The king does lie, and now he keeps his word." Gil stared at her, uncomprehending. He shook his head and turned to Rachel, watching silently.

"I can't be part of this," he said.

She gave him her most pitying look. "You already are."

CHAPTER TWELVE

L ionheart heard it first. He snorted and stamped a worried
hoof. Gil, alone at the helm, shifted his eyes from the dragon
prow carving the dark sea, to the deck. His gaze swept across
the huddled forms of sleeping men, and the black outline of the
girls' tent beneath the billowing sail, to the pony pen before the
mast.

The animals were dozing hulks in the starlight. Except
for Lionheart. Gil saw the flick of a frightened ear as the pony
struggled to turn in the narrow pen.

What's the problem?

Cat thing.

Cat thing? We're in the middle of the sea, Lionheart.

Cat thing. Lionheart snorted again, an eye flashing white. Gil
shrugged wearily.

Anything you say. He returned his eyes to the sea and checked
his course by the star-filled sky. The night was clear and cold, the
wind light, from the northeast. The great sail bowed gracefully
as they rode on for the coast of Alba. In the north, the aurora
flared, brightening the sky further and lighting the distant sails
of their companions.

Floki had taken the helm as they fled the lee of the sea-
king's shore, calling to Gil and Ragi to trim the sail, winning
every mite of speed from the fickle wind. Four times he sent
Ciarnan up the swaying mast, seeking following sails. Then,
as the snow-topped mountains sank beneath the horizon and
the wind grew true, he called the boy-monk down, and gave
the tiller again to Gil. Certain they had lost any pursuers in the
vastness of the sea, they returned to their own pursuit, sailing

all day, south-westward, before the wind.

As night fell, the sea-king's son at last abandoned his hopeless watch, curled beneath the fur Rachel had found for him and, clutching his brother's sword close to his chest, went to sleep. He had not spoken, nor eaten, since they left his father's shore. Gil wondered sadly how long the boy would survive.

Lionheart tossed his head and snorted again. *Cat thing!* Gil sighed. But a memory tugged at his sleepy mind. *Cat thing.* Lionheart's warning in Glen Alban; the attack from the tree! His eyes shot to the mast. But there was nothing on the mast but spar and sail, ghostly and beautiful in the flickering aurora. *Sorry, Lionheart. That's the only tree we've got.*

But some of Lionheart's restless fear entered his heart. His eyes swept the sleeping forms again, the straining mast, the taut sail, and beyond, endless water, endless sky, all pulsing with the strange, shifting light. *When you are alone at this helm ... laugh, then, at my fathers' gods.*

"I'm not laughing." Gil tightened his hand on the tiller, peering into the dark and saw not what was there, but what was not. *The boy. The sea-king's son.*

The place on the deck where the boy had sheltered was empty. The small, childish shape, its forlorn smudge of pale hair half-buried in fur, was gone. With a lurch of horror, Gil pictured the terrified child slipping unnoticed over the rail and making his own awful end to his captivity.

He half rose, searching among the sleeping men for Floki. His eyes fell on the bright splash of his mane of yellow hair, distinct even in the dim light. Lionheart whickered and pulled at his tether. Then Gil saw a second bright splash, paler and smaller. His heart flooded with relief as he watched the pale blur bob up and down as the blond child crept across the deck.

Despite Lionheart's frantic stamping, Gil laughed quietly. *Just looking for somewhere to take a leak, poor kid.* Then he saw the sword, shining silver in the aurora, raised by two small ,determined hands, above Floki's head.

"No!" he shouted. He dropped the tiller and as the ship slewed sideways, dashed forward. Roused by Gil's shout, a dozen men leapt into awareness. In the center of them was

Floki, on his feet, one arm around the squirming boy's throat, the other fending Bjorn's unsheathed sword.

"Leave him. Leave him. He is a child."

"A child who murders!" Bjorn lunged for the king's son. Floki swung the boy safely aside. Deftly, he removed the outsized sword, still clutched in the boy's fist, and laid it down. With both hands, he turned the struggling boy to face him. Hatred glowed in the child's eyes and he kicked futilely at his captor and spat in his face.

Floki nodded quietly. "Now we talk," he said. He raised his eyes to the sail. "Helmsman?"

"I came to help."

"Thank you. Help now by steering my ship." Floki nodded to the unmanned tiller, flopping as the ship rode at the mercy of the wind.

Chastened, Gil returned to his place and laid a shaking hand on the steering oar, straightening *Silver Dragon's* course until the sail tautened once more. Beneath it, Janetta and Rachel emerged from their tent, staring around in confusion, and Percy, awakened by the noise, stumbled to Floki, trailing his sleeping fur behind. Floki sent him back to the girls with a gentle word, his eyes never leaving his young opponent's face.

"Sit down." He released the boy. "There."

The child seemed to regain sense. The fury cooled in his eyes and he crouched, and then sat on the deck, watching Floki warily.

A shout off the steering board caught Gil's attention and he turned to see *Bright Wanderer* drawing close to their stern. Ragnvald's grey-bearded face strained toward them from the helm. "What befalls you?"

Floki looked up and waved him away. "It is well. Sail on."

As the ships drew apart again, Floki looked around the deck and waved his own crew away, as well. Then he sat down, cross-legged, facing the boy in the shimmering silver light. He lifted the boy's sword and laid it across his own knees.

"What is your name?" he said.

The boy bit his lip but stared back in bold silence.

"Answer him!" Bjorn raised a fist. Floki shook his head, gave

Bjorn a warning look and returned to the boy.

"What is your name?" he repeated.

"Eirik."

"Good. Eirik, I take you by force from your father's hall. You hate me and wish to murder me. This is reasonable." He tapped the boy's sword lightly. "But not practical. There are thirty men on this ship, Eirik. They are not pleased with you, if you do this." He shook his head. "Besides, a warrior does not kill in anger. He does not win that way. Here," he lifted the sword and laid it across Eirik's knees.

The boy stared at it, as if afraid to touch it. A muttering rose from the watching crew, drowning the soft rush of the bow wave. Floki ignored it. He closed the boy's fingers on the sword hilt. "I do not take your brother's sword," he said. "But I take your pledge."

The boy looked up. "I will not serve you," he said at once. "I serve my father."

Floki smiled faintly. "Very well. Serve him. I ask only that you do not use this sword on me, until I return you to your father's hall. Then, you are free. Free to grow and sail a ship and come, then, and kill me in battle. That would be fair." He paused, studying the boy's small, pale face. "Do you pledge?"

Slowly, the boy nodded and in a childish whisper said, "I pledge."

"Good. Now, go to your place and sleep. You are up too late."

The boy rose, obediently, and padded away, the sword clutched tightly in his arms. Gil watched as he rolled himself again in his fur, pulling it up over his head. He had no doubt now that Eirik would survive. But the thought brought little comfort.

"Warrior?"

Gil looked up. Floki was standing beside him, his hand resting on the tiller, nudging it slightly. With his eyes on the sail, he said mildly, "You do not leave this helm unmanned, Warrior. Never, ever."

"He was going to kill you."

"So be it. I am one man. On this ship are thirty. In your hands." He tapped the tiller. "Never leave the helm."

"Right," Gil said, ungraciously. *Next time I won't bother.* His eyes strayed to the treacherous boy. Floki slapped his face around.

"There!" he said sharply, pointing ahead to the sea. "That is your concern. No other."

"Right," Gil said again, through clenched teeth. Then, looking firmly ahead, he said, "Do you trust him?"

There was an unnervingly long silence. "Yes," Floki said at last. "I judge him more his noble sister than his lying father. I trust him."

"What if you're wrong?"

Floki shrugged. "All men die, Warrior." He looked at the sail again, and the stars, then stretched and yawned. "I too am up too late. Are you well here?"

"I'm well."

"Then I sleep again." He turned to go, then turned back and pointed out to sea. "Your only concern."

Gil nodded. Resting both hands on the tiller and looking again at the dragon prow sweeping its tumbling silver bow wave, he said evenly. "Are you afraid of *anything*?"

Floki laughed and slapped his shoulder. "Of course, Warrior. I am afraid of many things."

"Like what?"

"Many things."

"Name one."

"Ah." Floki fell quiet. Then he said, triumphantly, "Yes, Warrior! Those small animals."

"Small animals?"

"Very small. That creep under stones. I do not know the name. Long and thin, with many, many legs." He made a small scuttling motion with his fingers, on the tiller.

"Centipedes?"

"Yes. I am afraid of those."

"Those," Gil murmured.

"Aidan assures me they have a purpose in the White Christ's world," Floki said dutifully. "Though he fails to tell me what that might be. Those frighten me." He gave a girlish shudder.

"Centipedes," Gil said again.

"That is well, then?"

"Oh, yes," Gil said fervently. "That answers, like, everything."
He turned his eyes back to the sea with a weary shrug.

They were in sight of Alba, before Gil really believed the
boy would keep his word. Though he ate the food offered
to him and even spoke a little, mostly to Percy who couldn't
understand him, he still drifted about the ship like a small, pale
ghost, clutching the deadly sword.

But on the last day, he lay on his stomach watching Percy
and Floki play King's Table and when Floki slid the board before
him, he smiled for the first time. Gil studied him playing against
Percy and then against the man he had tried to murder, his face
screwed up with childish concentration, his sword forgotten,
for the moment, at his side.

He thought suddenly of Ismail, a nine-year-old soldier in
his African home and wondered if he had found boys' games to
play, even as he fought a man's war. His mind went back to the
sea-king's hall and then forward to Deer Bay, picturing Ismail
a prisoner again.

Danni had found a friend in the sea-king's daughter. Had
Ismail fared as well?

Grimly, Gil realized it did not matter. Friendship had not
been enough to save Danni from the slave market, or Hakon
Sea-Friend, either. And being a king's son had not saved Eirik.
All were as powerless as the ivory figures on Floki's gaming
board, in this world ruled solely by the sword.

"Helmsman?"

Gil looked up. Floki had put away his game and stood
balanced, now, on the rail, one hand grasping a shroud, and his
eyes sweeping the dark, distant shore. Beyond, the forested hills
of Alba rose against a blue autumn sky. "Head up," Floki looked
back over Gil's shoulder to the six sails following in their wake.
"It is time we make our farewells."

Gil turned the dragon prow into a north wind so light that he
barely had steerage. The sail fluttered, gentle as a handkerchief,
while they waited for their companions to join them.

The crossing had been startlingly calm. Twice the winds
had dropped to nothing; sails and masts were lowered and the

long oars came out, to the sound of aggrieved grumbling. Once underway, the rowers grew playful, racing each other across the gentle blue sea, until the wind rose again enough to sail onward. Three days passed before they saw shore birds and only on this, the fourth dawn, was land at last in view.

Grey clouds piled already over the mountains, and, as Erling brought Sea-Raven in by their load-board, Floki murmured, "A dusk as wild as the dawn is tame, Warrior. But we sleep this night on Alba's shore. Come, hold her steady." He stepped down from the rail, took up a light grapple, and with an easy swing, caught *Sea-Raven* like a fish, drawing the two hulls side by side.

One by one, the remaining ships joined them, lowering their sails and drawing in close, until all were roped together, as if prepared for battle. But the meeting aboard was more like a feast.

Clambering from ship to ship, the chieftains gathered, as they had in Floki's hall. Floki retrieved a small cask of wine from beneath the steersman's raised decking, and as the warriors seated themselves on a row of sea-kists, Percy filled silver goblets for each. Beards and hair wind-tangled, cloaks stiffened with salt and faces grimy from days at sea, they yet maintained a lordly dignity.

Standing before them, Floki drank to their health, thanked them for their service, and then, with formal grace, released them from their pledge. "You have done all we agreed and done it well. Sail on to the north and your farms. My two ships are all I need among our southern friends."

The men laughed, returned the toast, and swallowed their wine. Then each, as formally, protested his release and proclaimed his willingness to follow his earl. But when Floki smiled and shook his head, they looked relieved.

Only Ragnvald repeated his protest, with firm voice and solemn eyes. "The chieftains of Deer Bay are new to their hearths. The embers of old fires yet smolder there. A puff of wind," he blew a breath into the air, "And flames flare. You sail for my son. What risks you take should be my own. I go with you."

"I sail for my brother," Floki answered quietly. "And there

is little risk in a town full of merchants. Silver is their chieftain. Besides, two ships are always faster than three. However fine the third." He made a courteous gesture toward *Bright Wanderer*. Then he smiled again. "But I do ask this, uncle – there are three of my crew I would send home to Hrolf's Isle. Would you spare me three of yours?"

All, but Bjorn, among the older men looked hopeful; each of the young, dismayed. "I sail with you!" Ragi cried. He cast a yearning look at Rachel, busy helping Janetta to calm the land-eager ponies. "No one is stronger on the oar!" He raised a sinewy arm.

"And I!" Ciarnan cried. "Who can climb your mast faster than I?" He pointed proudly to the masthead thirty feet above. "And I carry a king's own sword!"

Floki laughed softly. "One for love and one for vengeance. True Vikings both. Be at peace. You both sail on." He turned suddenly and caught Gil's arm and raised it. "And this one, whether he wishes or not. His place is here." He gave the steering oar a hearty slap. Gil struggled to keep himself from grinning with pride.

Floki's eyes swept his crew. "But you, Gunnar, you are worth more on land. I do not deprive my hall of a smith. And you, Sigurd, you learn too well the carpenter's skill. Who else raises the fine roof I build this winter?"

"And, ah! You, Einar! Is not your wife yet *again* ...?" Floki mimed an enormous pregnant stomach. "And no doubt twin sons a third time!" Einar, young and slight with a drooping sandy moustache, hung his head as the crew stamped and cheered. "Go home!" Floki cried. "Back to the trade you practice so well! Soon we crew a longship with your seed!"

Reluctantly, the three loaded their sea-kists aboard *Bright Wanderer*, as the chosen Shetlanders crossed to *Silver Dragon* with their own. Then, as the laughter continued among the crew, Floki and the chieftains sat down to the serious business of rewarding those whose work was done.

A sizeable metal-bound box was produced, not from Floki's sea-kist, but from Bjorn's. From a linen pocket tied around her waist, Grimhildr drew forth a key. When the lock was turned and the lid raised, Gil saw why the box was left in their formidable care. Piled to the brim with silver, it glimmered like a fairytale treasure.

With Bjorn and Grimhildr standing stalwart on either side, Floki counted out heaps of shining arm-rings, sliced hunks of once beautiful jewelry, piles of coins, and a thing that brought a shiver of discomfort to Gil – a small, cross-shaped clasp that had once fastened a holy man's book.

Ragnvald untied a leather bag from his belt and drew from it a finely wrought set of scales. Solemn as a banker, he weighed out portions of coins, sawn silver, and rings, until each of the chieftains was allotted his share. Then the treasure box and the scales were returned to their places, and with wine goblets replenished by Percy, a final health was drunk.

"A good winter, Foster-Father," Floki raised his silver cup, "With peats on the fire, meat in the pot, and your son again at your hearth."

Ragnvald smiled and nodded and embraced his nephew with sudden warmth. "As Odin wills," he said.

"As I will," Floki grinned cheerfully. But Ragnvald shook a disapproving head and gestured to the sky, where the grey clouds drew closer as the wind backed to the west.

"A man who mocks the gods before a journey leaves wisdom behind him."

Floki only laughed, and then, as if he had thought of it in that moment, he recited a poem, recounting all the story of their adventure in Norway, with praise for each of the chieftain's deeds, and even a mention of the sea-king's beautiful daughter.

Then the ships were un-roped and poled apart, and with cheers and song they set out; five to the north and two to the south; across the rising wind.

By nightfall, a gale was blowing, as Floki had promised, but well before dusk the ships rested on the sand of a sheltered bay. Men strode about ashore, stretching their legs and gathering firewood as they did. Released from their shipboard restriction, Lionheart and the Hrolf's Isle ponies galloped in sandy circles, neighing and snorting, then set eagerly to grazing the rough beach grass.

Shielded by dunes, cooking fires were lit and fresh water carried in leather buckets from a burn. Then, with bows slung over their shoulders, Gil, Ragi, Ciarnan, and a young Shetlander saddled the ponies and rode to the forest to hunt. With a happy shout, Janetta came running after them, and ignoring the laughter of the boys, pulled herself up behind Gil, brandishing a bow of her own. Despite his double load, Lionheart pranced like a foal in his new freedom, and Gil felt the same delight in solid ground beneath him and the wind-blown branches above.

The forest was rich with game. Ragi and Ciarnan bagged two wood-doves, each, and the Shetlander, a huge black bird with a great fanned tail. But when, deep in a sheltered glade, they surprised a roebuck, it was Janetta's arrow that brought the animal down. And it was Janetta who, with skirts tucked up and sleeves rolled, gutted the dead beast, while Gil trimmed the small, hoofed feet with his axe.

With the lightened carcass loaded on one pony, and Ciarnan and Ragi doubling up on another, they turned back to the sea. Dusk was falling and the trees clattered overhead in the gale. Janetta tightened her small blood-stained hands around Gil's waist and rested her cheek against his back with a sigh of contentment. "It is like it was. You and I, and the Forest of Caledon," she whispered. "Soon, all will be well."

Gil closed his calloused hand over her small fingers. The sights and sounds of that time arose before him like images in the windows of Merlin's Tower: the Mews Garden, where they met; the maze where they played pony chess. The Guarded Forest of Pentecost, its chapel rising from unearthly flames. Lance'lot's cave-house and the Convent of the Grey Sisters.

And beyond: a whole landscape of memory rolled out before him. The blizzard on the hill; Palamedes black war horse turned white by snow. The Great Loch and its dragon. Glen Alban and the battle with Sir Owain. And beyond, again, the Western Sea, and the fearsome glow of the burning of Hy.

A new sound jerked him back to the present. Beneath the roaring of the wind and the creaking of branches, he heard the rumble of surf on the shore. His mind flashed to his ship, beached above the lines of weed and driftwood. Yes, she was high enough; he had thought of tide and storm.

He turned from the dark forest, so vast and wild that his own shipwrecked father had wandered months there alone, and rode eagerly to the welcoming fires and sturdy black tents of their Viking camp.

In the morning, the wind had dropped only a little. Struggling against the surf, they launched the ships into a grey, angry sea, and set out under oars until clear of the shore. Then, wrapped in furs and soaked in spray, they raised tight-reefed sails and rode south, following the rain-shrouded coast.

The weather that had been so fine, turned foul. Each short, stormy day was a misery to be endured before early dusk drove them to shelter. Twice more the fires were lit on deserted strands. Then, on the third day out, they sighted an island *muinntir* off their steering board. Floki bade him pass far out to sea, though more than one pair of northern eyes surveyed its fine buildings hungrily.

"We do not sail for plunder," Floki reminded them. "But for my cousin. Do you go short of silver?" With a shaking of heads they turned from the challenge in his eyes.

Floki rested his hands on the rail and said quietly to Gil, "Still, plunder in plenty you will find there." His gaze drifted lazily across the neat turf roofs. "And not one sword to defend it."

Rachel, surveying the *muinntir* with fascination from a perch on the dragon's tail, turned sharply to face him. "It's Lindisfarne," she said reproachfully, "It's Aidan's home."

"As well I know." He gave her a cold look. "And for Aidan I restrain my hounds. But not," he added, "For a hawk. However pretty." She met his eyes unflinchingly, until, with a soft laugh, he turned away.

As night approached, Floki returned to the helm and showed Gil a small, dark breach in the rugged cliffs of the coast. Gil peered at it, rubbing his salt-reddened eyes with a grimy hand.

"A bay," he murmured. Concealed from the sea by rocky headlands, and from land by steep cliffs, the tiny cove sheltered a strip of white sand just broad enough for a pair of longships.

"Einar's Bay," Floki said. My grandfather found it when my father was a boy. And it was my father who showed it to me. It is our inheritance." He grinned and gestured grandly, "I give it to you."

Gil grinned uncomfortably back. A perfect Viking lair, a day's sail from Lindisfarne. *Just what I always wanted.* "Thanks."

"Take her in."

"Me?" Gil stared, horrified, at the narrow, froth-edged opening.

"You must learn. I am not always here." Floki leaned close. "The channel is straight and true, the strand safe. But if you hit those rocks, Warrior, every one of us will die. I wish you to know that. Now, take her in."

He turned his back and strolled up the deck to the pony pen, and with a devilish glance back at Gil, pulled both of Lionheart's ears.

If I survive this, I will kill him, Gil promised himself. *Save Eirik the trouble.* He swung the tiller and headed up, spilling the wind from his scrap of reefed sail. While *Silver Dragon* wallowed in the rolling seas, he swept the bay with uneasy eyes.

Sea birds were mobbing the fresh-washed strand. A white line at the cove's mouth marked the clash of falling tide and wind-driven waves. He thought of the Holy Isle with sinking heart.

Choppy seas would pitch oar blades clear of the water; crosscurrents beguile his steering. Lose way and the ship would flounder, turn broadside, and be driven onto the rocks. Gil remembered Hakon Sea-Friend at Pentland, bringing *Storm Serpent* in under oar, while Floki rode recklessly before the wind. As often, he wished Hakon were here.

But then a weird thought struck him. *Storm Serpent* lay at the bottom of the sea. And Hakon, not Floki, was in captive's chains. "Okay," he whispered to himself. He turned across the wind again. As the sail filled and Ragi adjusted the sheets, *Silver Dragon* swept past the cove and headed out to sea, Erling's *Sea-Raven* following obediently in her wake.

Gil felt Floki's icy gaze upon him but kept his own stubbornly on his course. Close-hauled against the southerly wind, he tacked eastward until the cove was only a dark smudge against the dim shore. Then, with a glance at the masthead pennant, he thrust the tiller hard to the steering board, jibing down wind. As Ragi and Ciarnan re-set the sheets and the tacking spar, he lined the dragon's head with the dark smudge and sailed back north-westward on a racing broad reach.

The prow surged through the crests, gale-whipped froth splashing over the deck. The reefed sail strained and snapped, the mast creaking. Gil fixed his eyes on the rapidly approaching shoreline, until the cove mouth yawned between its fierce promontories and the thunder of crashing breakers reached his ears.

Tightening white knuckled hands on the tiller, he glanced once more at Floki and then shouted, "Full sail!" Ciarnan jerked the reef knots free. Ragi hauled on the spar, and the sail tumbled to its full length and billowed taut, lifting the dragon prow high.

Gil saw a flash of astonishment cross Floki's face and ducked his own head to hide an insane grin. *Silver Dragon* hit the roiling water at the cove's mouth, throwing up sheets of spray. Then, plunging over the tumbling surf, she swept through the rocky gates, flying headlong for the beach. Gil lunged to free the steering oar and seconds later, the keel grounded in the soft sand with a thud that threw him to the deck.

Noise engulfed him; the flapping of the loose sail, the shouts of stunned men and squeals of terrified ponies, and, rising above it all, Floki's exultant cry, "Behold! A Northman is born!"

Laughing, Floki dragged Gil to his feet, swung him in a circle and embraced him in a bear hug. Then he dove for the steersman's decking and retrieved the wine cask. "Northman, I baptize you!" He raised the cask high over Gil's head, dousing his spray-soaked hair with a precious golden stream. "Warrior of Tir nan Og, earl's helmsman!"

Then, grasping two of the silver cups from which he'd drunk the chieftains' health, and with the wine cask on his shoulder, he leapt down into the sea. "Come!" He stood in the surf, filling a goblet, and when Gil landed beside him, he held it to Gil's mouth, tipping it. "Drink!"

Choking and spluttering, Gil drank. The wine, rich and

golden, tasted like honey in the cold, salty air. He drank again, more willingly, as Floki filled his own cup. "Warrior!" Floki cried happily, as they slogged together up the beach, "Those things that frighten me? There is now one more! You free the sail; that frightens me." He turned to look back at his ships, both safe now on the strand. "Yes. I am afraid. But, oh, Warrior," he smiled slowly, "I am proud. I am proud."

He ruffled Gil's wine-soaked hair and then withdrew his hand with a grimace of disgust. "Do you never wash, helmsman?" He sighed. "I live among barbarians. But come," he slapped Gil's shoulder and filled his cup. "This night, other men work. You and I drink wine."

CHAPTER THIRTEEN

Gil awoke by the embers of a campfire with a head pounding like a surf and a mouth that tasted like Lionheart smelled. He rolled over on the damp sand and pulled aside the wet fur covering his face. White light seared his eyes.

"You will eat?" said a sweet hopeful voice. Squinting, he made out Janetta's slender silhouette. "I bring you bannocks. And fish." The smoky fish smell hit him and with a desperate gulp, he leapt up, clutching his head, and ran for the nearest rock.

"Are you ill?" Janetta called sadly.

"No!" he retched, waving her away. But then Rachel appeared as well and threw him a wet cloth. He mopped his face, shuddered, and then forced himself to meet their eyes. "Did I do anything stupid?"

"Of course you do not!" Janetta cried. "How can my Knight of the River be stupid?"

Rachel looked pained. "You sang a duet with Bjorn. Wearing Janetta's cloak and Grimhildr's headdress." He covered his face. She shrugged. "Not entirely your fault," she conceded drily, "Considering your role model." She jerked her chin toward the shore where the ships were already afloat.

Floki looked up and grinned, "Fair wind, helmsman."

Gil nodded painfully and hurried to join him. But Floki took the helm himself, and with another cheerful grin, released Gil to a quiet corner of the deck and a day of queasy sleep.

"Now you know what sea-sick feels like," Rachel informed him, when at last he surfaced.

Floki beckoned from the helm. "Look, Northman. A sweet

sight." He pointed to the coast where a long, low strip of sand dunes ran to a hazy horizon. "Hrafn's Ayre. It guards the entrance of this great river and shelters a strand as welcoming as a woman's arms." He smiled and pointed again. "And we are not alone."

A bare mast appeared, moving behind the sand dunes as if a ship sailed dry land. Then a broad-beamed, sturdy hull emerged at the end of the sand spit, rocking gently as a sail was hoisted up the mast. The ship seemed lightly manned; just four pairs of oars being drawn in, and a handful of men moving about the deck.

Gil watched as it heeled before the evening wind and saw its helmsman's wary attention fixed on *Silver Dragon's* approach. Floki raised a friendly hand as the small ship sailed past, and the helmsman nodded.

"A merchant's knarr," Floki said mildly. "He has finished his trading and sails home with goods and silver." He watched the ship with the same drowsy attention he had given Lindisfarne.

Then he pointed to the curved end of the sand spit. "Call for your oarsman, Warrior. The tide that takes him to sea, will keep us here 'til morning. But we will have a cheerful night."

Gil smiled wanly at the thought but gave the order to strike the sail. They rounded the spit under oars and at once he smelled wood smoke and heard distant voices, raised in laughter and song.

The landward shore of the long sandbar formed a perfect harbor, with a gently sloping beach on which rested a row of ships. Some were small, like the merchant's knarr they had passed; others larger, with spacious holds crammed with casks, or leather-wrapped bundles. One held a flock of sheep; another, crates of noisy white geese and seven goats. But none had the fierce elegance of Floki's longships or their cargoes of warriors and arms.

Voices stilled and watchful faces turned toward them as *Silver Dragon* and *Sea-Raven* rode in side by side. Floki again gave a friendly wave and as soon as their keels crunched into the wet sand, he set his men to innocent domestic tasks, unloading the ponies, pitching tents, and lighting fires with wood carried from the Forest of Caledon.

"Helmsman," he beckoned as Gil returned from tethering Lionheart amid the beach grass, "let us do some business."

"Here?" Gil looked around the windy sand spit.

"A Northman will trade anywhere. Come," he gestured to Ragi and Ciarnan to follow, and set off down the beach, examining the cargo of each of the ships as they passed. "They wait, as we do, for tomorrow's tide to take them to Deer Bay. But our silver is as good as any they will find there."

He stopped before the knarr loaded with baaing sheep, paid farmer's compliments to the sturdy farmer-trader, and then fell to bargaining. The exchange swept over Gil in a torrent of Norse words and gestures, but in the end, the trader smiled and spilled silver coins into his purse, and Ragi and Ciarnan bore a sheep each back to their camp.

Floki wandered off again, with Gil trailing and by the time they turned back to their ships, Gil was weighed down with sacks of flour, cabbages, and apples, and Floki carried a cask of ale on his shoulder and an enormous cloth-wrapped cheese under his arm.

"Wait, Warrior."

Gil staggered to a halt with his burdens and looked back. Floki had stopped beside a well-built knarr, whose master sat cross-legged on a rug on the sand. Before him, rows of brooches, bracelets and necklaces glinted in the evening light. The trader's face was darkly tanned and his hair bleached white from the sun. He wore baggy trousers and a long tunic, and when he spoke to Floki, Gil couldn't understand a word.

But Floki set down the ale cask and the cheese and knelt to examine the merchant's treasures. Then he rose, suddenly, and stepped away. Turning his back on the merchant, he drew a handful of silver from his purse. "The necklace in the center, with the red and white stones – it comes from the East and is finer than he knows. Buy it for your lady." He dropped the silver into Gil's hand.

Gil stared at it, feeling like a kid given pocket money. Then he shook his head and reached to give the silver back. Floki stared and then repeated, as if Gil were stupid, "Buy your lady the necklace."

Again, Gil shook his head. Floki put a brotherly arm around his shoulders. "Warrior, she is very beautiful. Other men notice. If you do not give her gifts, other men will."

"It won't *be* my gift. It'll be yours. It's your silver."

"And you are my helmsman." Floki shook his head and looked at the sky. "Gods of my fathers. A man who refuses silver."

"Besides," Gil said firmly. "She'll love me even if I never give her anything. It's not that I deserve it," he said hastily. "It's just the way she is."

Floki kept his gaze heavenward. "And now the man who refuses silver teaches me about women." He slapped Gil's head. "You think too much, Warrior. And not well. Buy the necklace."

They walked back to the ship, the sacks again on Gil's shoulders and the necklace a wonderful warm secret tucked inside his tunic. Floki shifted the ale cask and said, "Mo'Aidan tells me that all there is in the world belongs to his Master. So I have nothing, Warrior. And thus I give you nothing."

After days of smoked fish and stale bannocks, mutton and cabbage stew tasted like the best meal of Gil's life. He stuffed himself and then lay contented by the crackling fire, listening to the singing from the merchants' camp. Janetta sat beside him, proudly fingering her new necklace. When their eyes met, she blushed with pleasure.

Grimhildr passed with the ale jug, giving them a watchful look. But Gil saw that she, too, wore new jewelry; two splendid silver brooches clasping the shoulders straps of her dress. Ulf smiled to himself as she poured his ale.

If you do not give her gifts, other men will. It was the way things were done. A skill to be learned, like helming a ship. Gil felt a little guilty for not thanking Floki and looked around for him now.

He heard Percy's sharp squeal of laughter from the beach and to his surprise, saw Floki there with Eirik, playing at sword-fighting. Eirik wielded his brother's heavy weapon with determination, battering away at Floki's blade, his face, in the flickering firelight, uncannily fierce. Percy cheered and shouted, backing one and then the other, delighting in the game. But to

Gil it didn't look like a game at all. He was glad when it ended.

"He is good," Floki announced, flopping down on the sand by the fire, still breathing hard. "Swift of foot and sharp of eye." He laughed. "If I teach him too well, I may pay for it."

"Then why teach him?" Gil said uneasily.

Floki looked puzzled. "But surely he must learn the use of a sword." He paused. "I take him from his father who would teach him. The task now falls to me." He shrugged and called to Grimhildr for ale, and when Gil still looked worried, he laughed. "It does not matter, Warrior. He is but a boy. And I will be dead before he is a man."

"What?" Gil whispered. Floki began setting up his playing board for King's Table. Gil shook his head. "Why do you say that?"

"Because it will be so." Floki looked up mildly from arranging the ivory figures and beckoned Percy to come and play. "I know these things." He smiled and shrugged. "It does not trouble me, Warrior. Why should it trouble you?" Gil shook his head. But the sadness stayed with him anyhow.

Still, in the morning, he woke to Janetta's smile as she held out bread and fresh goat's milk. He shared the cup with her and they stole a milk-tasting kiss, and death was the last thing on his mind.

The sun was not yet up, but the whole camp was awake and at work. Rachel and Ciarnan were leading the ponies back from grazing. Floki, Bjorn, and Ulf lowered *Silver Dragon's* mast. In the grey dawn light, Gil saw the merchants were also readying their ships.

Floki jumped down from the deck and turned Gil to face the sea. "Tell me of the tide." Gil looked at the dim water lapping the shore. He counted seven waves. Each broke lower than the last.

"Ebbing."

"True. What next?"

"Slack water," Gil said, puzzled at the question.

"As well you would expect. But not here." He pointed inland. "This river, so broad where it meets the sea, grows narrow; but still all the tide flows all the way to Deer Bay. Where can all that water go?"

"It's like the Holy Isle," Gil cried. "Like the tide-race."

"It is simpler. There, there are two seas. Here, but one. But like there, a great sea must run into a small place, and as it narrows ...."

"It runs faster."

"Faster than you might imagine. And when it turns, it has not time to wait, but turns at once. Soon, you will see it, but we must be afloat and ready, when it does. And then, Warrior, we have fun."

Hastily, they launched the two longships into the falling tide. Once safely free of the sandbar, the oarsmen rowed steadily. Working hard against the flow of the water, they left the slower merchant ships far behind. The sun rose, lighting the marshes and heath land of the distant shores. Ahead, Gil saw another sandbank, narrowing the channel of the river, and beyond, it grew narrow still. It felt tame and safe after the days of open sea, but as they approached, Floki joined Gil on the steering board. "I take her now."

Gil stepped back, disappointed. "I took her into Einar's Bay," he said.

"And very well," Floki agreed. "But men older and wiser than I have stumbled here." He smiled gently. "What say you of the tide?"

Gil looked down at the muddy brown water eddying past the still oars. "Ebbing. No. Slack."

"Not for long," Floki smiled. He pointed behind them. Gil saw a little ripple stretch across the wide river, low, like a lost breaker come in from the sea. He watched, fascinated, as it ran toward them, foam tumbling before it.

"Welcome," Floki whispered. Then he shouted, "Go!" to his oarsmen, and thirty oars bit deep at once. Floki swung the tiller and the ship surged out into mid river, just as the tumbling water passed. "Yes!" he cried gleefully, and suddenly water was rushing by on either side and *Silver Dragon* was riding the racing wave, her prow just feet behind its tumbling crest. Floki turned and waved to Erling, and *Sea-Raven* slipped into the flow behind them.

With a ship's length between them, they rode on, their

oarsmen straining to increase the speed. Floki stood up at the helm, resting his weight against the steering oar, his eyes never leaving the swirling water ahead. "See, Warrior!" he cried, shifting their course between banks and shoals, "We ride Freya's Chariot! I am wrong, once, and she takes us to Valholl!"

The sun was high in the sky, the sweating oarsmen stripped of their tunics, when a broad sand flat rose before them. A river flowed in at either side. Floki pulled on the steering oar and *Silver Dragon* swung hard to the steering board, entering a new, narrower channel.

Confined by closer banks, the tide raced faster. "Warrior!" Floki beckoned from the helm. Gil relinquished the oar he was manning to Rachel and Janetta and joined him. "There, look," Floki pointed ahead to a brown shadow beneath the water. He turned the steering oar and as they swept past, Gil glimpsed the golden glint of sand. "And there!" A shudder of ripples disturbed the surface at an approaching bend.

"Shoals and sandbanks swim this river like fish. No helmsman can know them long. Go," he pointed forward to the prow, "Ride the dragon. See there what I cannot see from here."

Gil raced up the deck between the ranks of sweating oarsmen, scrambled past the pony pen, and mounted the curving neck of the wooden figurehead. Perched high there, he scanned the river far ahead, seeking the subtle shadows that would end their flying journey in disaster. "Load-board!" he turned and shouted, and Floki swung the tiller. "Steering-board!" The prow beneath him shifted the other way. Behind, Erling snaked his course after them, trusting blindly, as he must. As Floki was trusting Gil.

The riverbanks rose; dark walls of glistening mud swept by on either side. There was nowhere to beach, no escape. Gil thrust from his mind the image of the racing keel grounding in an instant and the great hull swinging broadside into the merciless current, with Sea-Raven bearing down at unstoppable speed.

The only thought more terrifying than dying in that maelstrom, was surviving it, having wrecked both Floki's longships in one go.

Intent on the muddy water, Gil barely noticed that the sun

had tipped westward, that the banks had lowered, and, at last, that the current was slackening. "It is well, Warrior," Floki called. He waved and smiled. "Come down. I take her in now."

Gil slid from the dragon's neck. His hands were numb, his legs shaking. Ahead, he saw a breach in the low bank and a broad curve of slow-moving water, rimmed by marsh grasses. *Silver Dragon* slipped into the reeds, amid quacking and offended ducks. The rowers drew in their oars and Bjorn and Floki poled the ship into a resting place beside a grassy bank. *Sea-Raven* came alongside, and Ulf and two of the Shetlanders roped the hulls together. And then, stumbling with exhaustion, both crews clambered ashore and collapsed onto sweet, dry land.

When the tide came, the next morning, they were ready and waiting at the edge of the channel. Gil saw the breaking wave ride up the river and took his place at his oar. But at the last moment, Floki stepped back from the steering oar and beckoned him. "Come. You helm Freya's Chariot now."

Gil grinned uncertainly, even as his eager hand reached for the tiller. "Are you sure?"

Floki shrugged. "A man who does only what he is sure of, leads a dull life. Do you wish me to be my cousin?" He suddenly mimicked Hakon Sea-Friend's look of wary caution, revealing a brief, startling family resemblance. Gil laughed, and stepped to the helm, though it occurred to him that Hakon's life among slave-traders could hardly be dull.

Floki took his vacated rowing bench, leaving the prow unmanned and Gil to choose his course unaided. Gil could see at once it was easier now. The river was wider, the tide less fierce. But there were sandbanks and shoals in plenty and his eyes never left the channel until Percy's shouts told him he had reached his goal.

The current slackened, the river grew wider still. Gil raised his eyes from the water and saw, rising above the low landscape, a white stone building with a square tower and a timber roof. He thought at once of both Camelot and Hy. Clustered beneath it were rows of wooden structures with steep, thatched roofs. Beyond, lay a mighty wall of turf and silvery stone. Rachel and

Janetta joined Gil at the helm and Floki rested his oar and came to stand beside them.

Lines of beached ships appeared along the shore, masts on cradles and groups of men gathered around their hulls. Sounds drifted across the water; geese and cattle, horses and dogs; and voices called along the waterfront as the two longships approached. Then suddenly a new sound stirred the still air, sweeping Gil back to Hrolf's Isle and lost Cille Aidan.

"Listen," Rachel whispered.

"A church bell," Janetta cried happily, as if she, too, thought of home.

Rachel pointed to the white building. "The minster," she whispered, awed. "The *old* minster."

Floki's eyes widened with surprise. "What, Pretty Hawk? You have been, before, to Deer Bay?"

She shook her head and smiled. "No. But I will be born here," she said.

CHAPTER FOURTEEN

Gil turned, astonished, to face Rachel. "You *know* this place?"

"It's York," she said simply. "It's my home. York, *England*," she added drily, "Except England hasn't happened yet."

"It is Deer Bay," Floki said. "*Djurvik*. And how can you be born here? You are born already, and indeed, well grown."

She smiled to herself, her eyes searching the town hungrily. "*Djurvik* becomes Jorvik, and Jorvik becomes York. Words change. And people change, too."

"This is true," Floki agreed amiably. "It was not always Deer Bay. It has an older name, hard for Northmen to say. Nor were there always Northmen here." He paused, his gaze drifting across the pale stonework above the thatched roofs. "It is old. Like the Stone of Odin on Hrolf's Isle. Other men raised its walls. Northmen use them."

He laughed suddenly, "We are like those small animals, Warrior!" He pointed to the plain wooden houses huddled below the fortifications. "We creep about beneath stones." Still smiling, he turned back to Rachel. "You do not answer my question."

She shook her head. "I cannot."

Floki's smile faded. He looked from Rachel, to Gil, and said quietly, "Does Deer Bay, too, lie in Tir nan Og? Across that sea I cannot sail? Even though I see it here before me?"

Gil nodded uneasily. "Rachel?" he said softly. "Do you recognize it? Like the Great Stones?"

Her confidence seemed to waver. "It's all so different. Even the minster, *our* minster, isn't here yet. And *it's* eight hundred years old! But the wall!" she cried triumphantly. "Look! The old

Roman wall. It's *still* *there!*" She shook her head in awe. "The Romans built things to last."

"Romans raised the walls?" Floki said. "Men came from Rome to Deer Bay? Why?"

She smiled. "Why do Northmen come?"

"Trade. Treasure. Women."

"They were the same," she said. Her eyes returned to the wall. She pointed to a massive corner tower. "*There* ... I was standing there with my friends from school ... Helen stood up on Dan's shoulders and climbed ... I kept saying, 'you'll get in trouble ...'" her voice trailed off. "It feels like yesterday!"

She reached her hand out to the distant wall. Gil saw tears glistening on her eyelashes. "I feel so close to my father. Like he's right here, behind a curtain. A thin, thin curtain."

Floki brushed her wet cheek with his fingers. "So, if he is so close, Pretty Hawk, let us go to him. Then you have no need to weep."

She shook her head.

"Why not? I would meet your father. Is he a merchant?"

"No." She smiled suddenly. "Not a merchant." She paused. "He studies books. And writes them."

"Like Aidan," Floki said quickly. "He is a holy man. Perhaps he is at that church." He gestured toward the white stone building; then pointed to the wooden wharf that lined the river shore. "Take her in there, Warrior, beyond the last knarr, and make her fast. We seek out this holy man."

"Floki ..." Gil protested.

"Do it, helmsman."

Gil swung the tiller, aligning the prow with the open stretch of river front. Then he said carefully, "I can take you ashore. But I cannot take you to Rachel's father. He is in Tir nan Og. In Deer Bay, but in Tir nan Og. We can't go there."

"You go there. And you return. I would see this place, now. And I would see this man who has so fine a daughter. Show me how."

Gil cast Rachel a frantic glance. She raised her hands and shrugged. But then, suddenly, Floki stayed Gil's arm on the tiller.

"Wait, Warrior. Bid your rowers raise oars." Baffled, Gil called the order, while Floki turned and signaled to Erling, following behind. With the two ships gliding silently on the slackening tide, Floki pointed again to the shore. "What see you there?"

Gil followed the direction with his eyes. Three men had appeared at the foot of a narrow alley running between the wooden houses. Two were on horseback, the third on foot. All wore trousers and tunics, like Northmen, but instead of cloaks, long lengths of multi-colored cloth wrapped around their waists and over their shoulders. "Men of Alba," he whispered.

He watched, warily, as they came down to the waterfront and stood looking out over the river. When they turned and made their way back, as they had come, he said, "The Golden Knight's men?"

Floki shrugged. "Men of Alba trade like other men. Bring her in." But he kept his eyes on the alleyway, as Gil steered *Silver Dragon* to her mooring. And when *Sea-Raven* came alongside, he joined Erling on her deck, and the two talked quietly until the ships were roped together and secured.

Gil, Ragi, and Arnkel Fish-Tail stretched black tent cloth over the lowered mast and spar to form a sheltered awning. Beneath it, the Northmen searched their sea-kists for dry clothing and purses of silver for the merchants of Deer Bay.

Grimhildr donned a clean linen headdress. Giggling and holding hands, the girls hurried to their own tent to prepare. Ragi grinned and showed Gil a handful of coins. "I save all winter for Rachel. I buy her bride-gift. Like you, for Janetta."

Gil smiled uncomfortably and murmured, "Great." His eyes strayed uneasily to the girls' tent.

"Helmsman?"

Gil turned quickly. He saw a flash of movement out of the corner of his eye and the next moment a sheet of water hit his face. "Wha …?" he spluttered. He swept his soaking hair out of his eyes. Floki was standing before him with an empty bucket in one hand, and a linen towel in the other.

"Wash yourself." Floki threw him the towel. "We call upon an earl."

"I was *going to!*" Gil grumbled, but Floki had turned to Ciarnan. "And you." Ciarnan stopped grinning and ducked away from the bucket. "And dress yourself as would do honor to your father."

Ciarnan went in search of fresh water and Gil pulled off his drenched tunic and replaced it with the linen shirt Floki leant him in Norway. Dropping his salt-sticky fur on the deck, he wrapped himself in the blue cloak Danni had woven at Cille Aidan.

Floki threw him a comb and gestured to his tangle of shoulder length hair. "Comb it, or I cut it off with my sword. Starting here," he drew a line across Gil's throat. Gil tugged frantically at snarls and knots, while Floki stripped off his own sea-worn garments and dressed himself again in the red tunic and fur-lined cape he had worn to the Sea-King's hall.

Then he seated himself on a sea-kist, and while Grimhildr combed and braided his hair for him, he washed Percy's smudged face and helped him into his best tunic, too. "An earl's cupbearer is a man of high rank," he said gently. "He must appear so. Go, now, and play, until I call you." Grimhildr tied a last ribbon, and Floki pointed then to Eirik, watching warily. "Now wash that child, please, and make him presentable. I take him, too."

"No!" Eirik pushed her away with both hands. "I am a man. I wash myself."

Floki struggled to repress a smile. "Then do it." He looked up and beckoned his warriors to his side. "Beside the great church upon that hill," he gestured beyond the awning, "Lies the earl's longhouse. A noble structure, befitting a man as noble as he imagines himself to be. But Deer Bay is a marketplace, and he is a merchants' earl. If our people are here, he will know where, and in whose keeping. And he will tell me," he added, his voice taking a sudden steely edge.

"But first, I must win entry to his hall. New earls are more prideful than old, and I am but a farmer." A low laugh spread among the warriors. "It is true," Floki smiled. "But I travel with the sons of kings." He bowed grandly to Ciarnan and Eirik, and another wave of laughter swept around the ship. Floki shook his head. "They may be young, but they outrank me. And they outrank the chieftain of this town, as well."

He stood then, and stepped from beneath the awning and surveyed the town, up to the heights of the minster. "But since the words of a king have proved empty, on this voyage, I will have assurances against the word of this earl. Half of you are to go out about this town, as you wish. Buy goods for your farms and trinkets for your women. And ask every trader for news of Hakon Sea-Friend of the Northlands, and of the Saracen, and the girl they call a witch. You may learn more than I.

"But return with time to spare before nightfall, that the others may then go, and no man's wife have reason to complain. And be wary, lest you find the hunter becomes the hunted." He nodded to Gil. "Come, helmsman, I have you as my guard." Shepherding Ciarnan and the children before him, he led the way to the gangplank. With a surge of startled pride, Gil followed.

"Wait!" Rachel called from behind him. The girls burst from their tent, fresh-scrubbed in spotless linen dresses and bright-braided tunics.

"We are ready now," Janetta cried, blushing and giggling as the Northmen cheered. But Floki turned, resting his hand yet on Percy's shoulder, and shook his head.

"Rough winds may blow about this town," he said solemnly. "I keep my hawk safe in her mews."

The eager smile left Janetta's face but she bowed her head obediently. Rachel stared in disbelief. "But it's my home," she whispered.

"Your home is in Tir nan Og, as you yourself say," Floki returned. "And this is Deer Bay; a slave-trader's town, where friend and enemy may wear the same face. It is not by chance I leave thirty men to guard my ships. And my women."

Again, Janetta nodded obediently. But Rachel stepped forward and reached out both hands. "Please. It's still my home. Even though a thousand years stand between. I can't bear not to see it." Again, tears brightened her lashes.

Floki drew back, startled. A gentleness softened his lean features. "My proud one begs," he murmured. He turned abruptly to Gil. "Helmsman, you take them." He beckoned to Ragi. "And you. See what she wishes to see, and no more. And watch, watch always." He paused, shaking his head again. "When kings and seas are conquered," he said wryly, "Odin sends women to undo a man. Wait, Warrior."

He left them and scoured the deck until he found a scrap of the kindling they carried from Caledon. Trimming it with his axe, he stripped the bark from one side, and then scored the surface with the point of his knife, slashing a double line of angular symbols into the wood. "Should any man trouble you," Floki handed Gil the marked branch, "Show him this. But do not draw your sword."

Gil studied it uncertainly. "Runes?" Floki nodded. "What does it say?"

"It is for the eyes of others," Floki said, with a small smile, as Gil slipped the wood into his pocket. He nodded to the girls. "Guard them well, Warrior. I will take Bjorn." He signaled to the big man and at once Bjorn was at his side. Then he hurried his charges down the gangplank. Rachel and Janetta dashed after, with Gil and Ragi positioned stoutly before and behind.

The waterfront was lined with traders' wooden stalls, offering pottery and soapstone bowls, stags' antlers and walrus tusks, furs and amber. One, beside a sun-weathered knarr, was festooned with bright silks. Floki paused, took down two silken shawls, threw silver to the dark-eyed trader in his strange, foreign clothes, and draped a shawl each over the girls' heads. "I veil my women like a man of the east," he said, "Lest men of the north be tempted."

Gil sighed, yearning for the day when he could throw silver down like a Viking. But Ragi's eyes darkened. "She is not yours," he said.

Floki turned sharply, an icy glint in his eyes. "Nor yours, Man of the High Island. Nor will she be if you do not live long enough to claim her." But he smiled and laid a forgiving hand on the boy's shoulder. Then he thrust a handful of silver into each of their palms. "Go, now. Spend your silver on a beautiful comb for your Fire-Hair."

He pointed down a muddy lane. "There you find the

comb-makers. And over there," he gestured toward a cluster of houses beyond a pig sty, "are leatherworkers, for fine belts, silversmiths, and an old man who works in amber. I must leave you, now, and call upon nobility."

He turned to where the bell tower of the minster rose above the thatched roofs, then suddenly whirled, leapt behind Gil, and swept his hands over his eyes. "Do not look!"

But Janetta cried out in dismay, "Oh, the poor pussikins! How cruel!"

"What?" Gil pried Floki's fingers apart and then winced. Before him, suspended from a wooden frame, were the soft striped pelts of half a dozen cats. The hackles rose on the back of his neck and he felt phantom ears flatten against his skull and a phantom tail sink low. The growl that rose in his throat came out as a cry of fearful disgust. "Yeeuch!"

"Fine furs," said the smiling trader, tugging his beard, "Look, feel! Gloves for the pretty wives!" He beckoned Janetta.

"No!" she cried and Rachel screwed up her face. Floki waved the trader away with an imperious hand. "I told you I live among barbarians," he said wearily. "But have no fear, Warrior. Should such a fate ever befall you, I swear never to use you as gloves." He grinned cheerfully and then strode away with his retinue. At the end of the lane, he turned and shouted, "No matter how cold the winter!"

"Try sealskin!" Gil shouted back. But Floki had vanished into the maze of tightly packed houses.

Ragi stared angrily after him, clutching the silver resentfully. "One day he goes too far," he muttered.

Rachel folded her arms and shook her head. "One day *you* go too far. Am I supposed to be honored when he kills you?"

"I work for your bride-price. And he makes free with you."

Rachel's eyes narrowed. She waved a finger under Ragi's nose. "*No one* makes free with me, Stupid Man of the Stupid High Island!"

"Please," Janetta whispered, "Do not argue. Our earl means no harm. See," she raised the silken shawl Floki had draped over her shining hair, "He gives me gifts, too, though he truly knows that body and soul, I am my knight's." She cast Gil a glance that made his heart melt. He stepped closer and kissed the top of her head. Trust Janetta to see only good, even in Floki Magnusson.

Rachel shrugged and suddenly grinned. She waved her shawl at Ragi. "Oh, body and soul I am *not* Ragi Ulfson's." But she let him take her hand as they ran together up the muddy lane.

Gil felt a burst of exhilaration, like the moment on a school trip when the teachers left you alone to buy souvenirs and explore. "Which way?" he asked.

Rachel spun in a circle of excitement. "I can't choose! There's so many places, so many things ... oh, if my father could *see* this," she said fervently. "Let's see the minster, but first, that corner of the wall. The place I remember. I'm sure I can find the exact stone I stood beside!"

She led the way eagerly, stopping from time to time to orient herself by the river or the minster tower. The town was a maze of narrow passageways between houses and workshops; animal pens, plots of leeks and cabbages, and stinking, wicker-walled latrines. Some streets had walkways of wooden planks; others were only mud. One, wider than the rest, was paved with stone cobbles.

All were strewn with the trampled rubbish of every trade. They found the comb-maker by the scraps of antler discarded outside his door, and the leatherworker by the stench of fresh hides.

Gil and Ragi bought the girls silver-inlaid combs, and at the leatherworkers, Ragi chose a belt with a bronze buckle. Gil found a sheath for his bone-handled knife, decorated all over with fierce, tail-biting beasts. As he slipped the blade into the leather casing, a memory flashed into his mind of his father doing the same, on a camping trip in Greene Mountain Falls.

Then Laurent Lake's youthful face faded into the weather-beaten features of Lance'lot. Gil felt a pang of yearning for both, as if they were two separate people, both loved, and both far away.

Out in the autumn sunlight once more, they joined the broader stone-paved street and followed it toward the minster tower, until it ended abruptly in an open square beneath the great wall.

There, beside the looming stone gateway, a farmers' market

stood beneath canopies of striped sail cloth. Cattle, sheep, goats, geese, and chickens filled the air with farmyard sounds and farmyard smells.

Ragi admired a splendid ram with ribbons tied to its horns. Janetta found two baby goats. "Get Floki to take them back to the Holy Isle, and they're yours," Gil promised. He wandered, smiling, amidst the crowds of bargaining, arguing people, their children clamoring for treats and toys.

"It's just like home," he said to Rachel, who had suddenly appeared beside him. "It's like Saturday at the mall!"

She shook her head. "Listen."

Over the squawks of hens and lowing of cattle, Gil heard a soft singing voice and the delicate notes of a harp. At the edge of the square, a young girl sat with the instrument, her fingers flying over the strings as she sang. Beside her, a handsome, slender youth played a small flute.

A cluster of people stood around them and Gil thought them, at first, an audience. But they seemed sad and subdued, and the girl, for all her music, had a face full of sorrow. Rachel's face was sorrowful, too. "Look," she pointed to the girl's bare feet on the cobbles of the square. The tarnished links of a chain ran from a metal cuff around her slim ankle, to a matching cuff on the leg of the youth.

"Slaves," Rachel said. "And the others. It's the slave market. See," she caught Gil's sleeve and turned him so his gaze fell on two well-armed men before a table. One weighed silver in a set of scales like Ragnvald's. The other gestured toward the singing girl and mimicked the harp. Then he said something to a crowd of watching men, laughed roughly, and slapped his thigh. Something inside Gil clenched like a fist.

"Not really like home, is it?" Rachel murmured. Gil's mind was racing. He swept the huddled slaves with his eyes and pulled free of Rachel's hand.

"Let me go. I have to see."

"They're not there," she said. "I've looked." But she stood waiting patiently while he searched among the forlorn, chained captives for his friends. Then, suddenly, the slave trader blocked his way.

Holding a young blond girl before him, he called, "Here, Viking. A serving maid for your wife." He leaned closer and grinned, "And a bedmate for you. Young, pretty, no man has touched ...."

Gil spun around and strode back to Rachel. "Let's get out of here," he muttered, taking her arm. She nodded, her face white. Hurriedly, he gathered the others and, ignoring their confused protests, hustled them out of the square. He chose the first alleyway he saw, heedless of direction, wanting only to get away from that place and the thoughts it forced into his mind of Danni and Ismail and quiet, noble Hakon, at the mercy of men like that.

In no time, he was lost. He looked in vain for the landmark of the minster, hidden by overhanging roofs. Each alleyway curved and meandered, blocking any glimpse of the river. He turned to Rachel, but she seemed more confused than he was. "It's all different!" she cried. She looked blindly around, shielding her eyes with one hand. "It looks so different!"

Gil shook his head, "Of course it does," he said sharply, "It's a thousand years earlier. *You* said ...."

She wasn't listening. Still shielding her eyes, she shrank back against him and pointed at the sky. "Look! Look! The tower! The tower's burning!"

He turned. "The minster? But we can't see it!"

"The tower!" she cried, pointing frantically at the serene blue sky. "It's on fire!"

"*What* tower?" Gil cried.

"I see no tower," Ragi stepped closer to Rachel and Janetta reached out comforting arms. Rachel thrust them both away.

"It's burning. And the houses! The houses are burning. And the children. Oh, the children!" Her voice rose to a cry of despair.

"Oh my God," Gil whispered. *Cille Aidan. The Wandering Pool. Rachel beating out flames with bare hands ... flames only she could see.* He leapt forward and grasped her shoulders, turning her to face him. "Rachel, it's not here. It's another place. Another time."

But she broke free, running down the alleyway, crying out for help. "Fire! Fire!"

Alarmed faces appeared at doorways. Men and women ran out into the alleyway, staring up at the dry thatched roofs. A man in a potter's clay-stained smock caught Rachel's arm. "Where is fire?"

She pointed at the sky. "Help me! Please! The children!"

He stared and then shrugged and stepped warily back. "Where?" another shouted.

"She says her children are burning!" a woman cried.

The potter shook his head. "There is no fire. She is mad." His eyes fell on Gil. "You care for her?"

Gil nodded, reaching pleadingly to Rachel. But she pulled away and clutched at the potter, pointing again at the clear blue sky. Over his shoulder, Gil heard laughter, and then, from farther away, a new, ominous cry, "Fire! A madwoman lights fires!"

Rachel turned again to run, begging for help from all she met. They drew back, fearfully, and a big, rough youth suddenly stepped forward, snatched at Rachel, and when she eluded him, turned on Gil. "If you can't stop her, we will."

"It's a trick," a shrill woman cried. "They are thieves! Watch! Your houses are empty behind you."

"Saxons!" cried a pretty girl. "Murderers!" she shrieked.

Gil swept his arms around Janetta. Ragi lunged for Rachel, but the brutish youth stepped between them. Ragi reached for his sword.

"No!" Gil shouted. "Floki said no. Wait." He dug in his pocket for the rune-marked wood. Clasping it, he held it up in front of the youth, praying he, at least, could read it. The youth screwed up his eyes and shook his head. But the potter stepped between them and took the wooden message. His eyes, scanning the markings, grew wide.

Quickly, he beckoned the youth and two other men who had pushed to the front. They conferred in low voices and the older men shook their heads and backed off. "Go," the potter said to Gil, thrusting the wood back in his hands, "We mean no harm. Take the girl and go." A murmuring passed through the crowd and as quickly as they had gathered, the people melted away.

"Come on," Gil muttered to Ragi, "Before they change their

minds." He clasped Rachel's arm and walked quickly away, ignoring her struggles and pleas.

Behind him, the youth said clearly, "I do not run from *any* Northlands Viking."

"Then *you* fight him, lad," the potter returned.

"Madwoman!" the youth shouted. "Fire! Fire! Fire up your skirt!"

Ragi whirled in an instant, his sword in his hand. "No!" Gil groaned, but it was too late. He turned to face a row of shining blades.

CHAPTER FIFTEEN

Gil flung his shield up, drew his own sword, and closed in, shoulder to shoulder, with Ragi. The big youth jeered, "Your sword is bigger than you are! Go home and give it back to your father!" He swaggered, waving his own weapon. His face was marked by deep pitted scars. A sweaty moustache darkened his upper lip.

Seventeen, eighteen, Gil thought. His eye ran down the line. Five of them. All at least as old. A sixth stepped forward to join them. Gil cast a desperate glance back at Rachel. She was as good with a sword as he was, but she stood clinging to Janetta's shoulder, her face a mask of confusion, and the weapon forgotten in its sheath.

"Take her," he shouted to Janetta. "Run. We'll catch up." He turned back to Ragi. "Your three," he murmured, with a quick nod to his left. He looked to the right, "My three. Let's go."

He picked out the middle boy of his group, hovering behind the pock-marked leader. The boy's sword tip wavered as he chewed a nervous lip. He ducked his scruffy brown head behind his shield, peeking at Gil over the rim.

Gil screwed his face into a calculated scowl and charged, swinging his sword in a flamboyant arc. The boy vanished behind his shield, stumbling backward into the lad at his left. Both staggered, and Scruffy-Head fell to one knee.

Way to go! Gil feigned another dramatic swing and then whirled, shifting the blow toward Pock-Mark's now undefended ribs. Startled, the big youth spun from his attack on Ragi and met Gil's sword with his own. Steel clashed on steel and sparks flew in the dim alleyway. A shout arose from the gathering crowd, and cries for more.

"No!" The potter stepped forward with upraised hands. "Enough. Go home," he waved at the crowd. "And you," he turned to Gil and Ragi. "Go your way. We want peace here."

"They begin it!" shouted the tall dark boy now facing Ragi. Out of the corner of his eye, Gil saw Ragi charge the boy and with quick flicks of his sword, batter him back. Relieved, he returned full attention to Pock-Mark, raising his gaze uncomfortably to meet the leering youth's eyes.

He was a head taller than Gil, and three times as broad. A man, except for his childish taunting. Suddenly Gil felt like a kid again, facing Magnus Redbeard at Einar's Holm. Then, as suddenly, he saw Shony, dancing light as sea spray around her fearsome husband, wielding a blade not even he could match. *A warrior need not be big ... if he is swift.* Shony's words. Shony's silken voice. Shony's unearthly grace. *You are my shadow.*

In some secret place within, Gil aligned himself to the slender form of the selkie. He leapt forward, slicing beneath Pock-Mark's shield. Steel ripped through cloth. A smear of blood brightened Gil's sword. Seeing it, Pock-Mark swung ferociously.

Gil crouched, weaving low on bent knees, Shony's shadow. Pock-Mark's blade swished above his head. Gil jumped up and danced back, shield raised. Pock-Mark swung again. Gil parried and again steel rang on steel. But the youth followed, his long arms keeping Gil at bay. Grinning, Scruffy-Head joined him.

Gil backed again, and cast a glance at Ragi as Ragi's own opponents closed in. "Too many," Ragi grunted. He jumped backward, colliding with a stack of wooden casks, tumbling one into the roadway.

The lid clattered free and a torrent of salted fish poured onto the muddy ground. Pock-Mark's lunging foot splatted into it. He skidded, shouted his alarm, and fell, with a splashing thud, flat on his back.

"Cool!" Gil kicked over another cask, and sent it rolling into Ragi's pursuers, spilling its own slimy trail. Ragi lifted a third cask and hurled it. Splintering on the ground, it enveloped their attackers in a cloud of flour.

Laughter burst from the watching crowd. Coated white and stinking of fish, Pock-Mark struggled to rise, slipped, and slammed into Scruffy-Head, bringing him down, too. Gil met Ragi's eyes, and, as one, they bolted up the alley, after the girls.

They found them around the first bend, crouched in the shelter of a wickerwork gate. Three shaggy ponies reared and whinnied behind them. "You were supposed to run!" Gil cried.

"I do not leave my knight." Janetta's eyes met his with a flash of green fire. Rachel stood stalwart behind her, sword in hand.

"I'm sorry, Gil," she murmured. "I sort of lost it ...."

He shook his head, helping Ragi haul them back over the gate. "There!" he pointed up a wooden walkway branching to the left. "They're right behind us. Go!"

Ragi swept them ahead with outstretched arms. As Gil turned to follow, the ponies whickered and neighed, kicking against the gate. *I know. You're scared.* Gil ran three steps and then skidded to a halt. *And you're about to be a lot MORE scared.* With fingers fumbling in haste, he untied the rope latch and swung the gate wide.

Wolves! Shoulder to shoulder, the ponies thundered out into the roadway. Flinging his arms out, Gil turned them down the alley, just as a floury, fishy Pock-Mark bulged into sight. *Wolves! Big, big wolves.* He watched for a gleeful moment as the youth turned before the stampede; and then ran, laughing, to join his friends.

They grinned and cheered as he caught them. He shook his head, "Keep going! That way," he pointed ahead to another opening between two tall wooden barns.

"Where are we going?" Rachel cried.

"Worry about that later," Gil grunted, diving deeper into the maze of Deer Bay. "Try and lose them first." Sheathing his sword, he took Janetta's hand. Ragi grinned and grabbed Rachel's, and before she could argue, ran on.

"We do it!" he cried, ducking into a third entrance, his boots thudding on the muddy wood. Gil looked ahead, glimpsing the Minster tower above the crossed beams of a gable.

"Yes!" And then his heart froze. Slamming his boots into the boardwalk, he skidded to a halt. Janetta crashed, giggling, into him. "Stop!" Gil shouted.

But Rachel had seen them, too: four plaid-wrapped figures,

standing guard across the lane. "Men of Alba," she whispered. Janetta's eyes grew wide. She looked back, over her shoulder. Already, Gil could hear shouts and pounding boots. His eyes fell to the mud-caked wood of the walkway. Their footprints led back the way they had come, totally betraying them.

"We're trapped," Janetta whispered and Gil again drew his sword.

Steel flashed across the alley in response. Ragi drew his own blade and thrust Rachel behind him. She barged past him, sword in hand. But her eyes, meeting Gil's, were dark with fear.

"This is not good," Ragi muttered. He nodded toward the Men of Alba, and then back to their pursuers. "Yours, mine?"

"We can't win this," Gil said evenly. Ragi shrugged. He gave Gil a small smile, like Floki would, when things looked grim. He turned until they stood back-to-back, each facing impossible odds. Gil glanced once at Janetta, watching him, as trusting as a little kid. Then he nodded to Ragi, raised his shield, and charged the waiting four.

He was a sword length from the nearest, when suddenly the man leapt aside with a shout of amazement, "Warrior!"

Gil skidded past him and whirled, expecting treachery. "Warrior of Tir nan Og!" the man cried, and then, raising his sword high, "Our king lives!"

"Our king ...." Gil whispered. He stared and then shouted with joy and relief, "Morians!"

A loud cheer rose from the other three. "Darras!" Gil cried, clasping the hand of a dark youth who ducked his head shyly. "Gareth!" He turned to a grinning, black-haired boy, and punched his shoulder gleefully. "Am I glad to see you!"

The tallest of the four bent his head to Janetta, "My lady."

"Elias!" she cried happily. "How are you here, so far from Caledon?"

Before he could answer, a shout of triumph echoed in the narrow alleyway behind them. Pock-Mark burst into view, flanked by a small, angry army.

"Watch out!" Gil cried. Lunging forward, he shoved Elias down as an arrow shot past and smacked into a wooden lintel above them.

Elias' eyes flicked from the quivering feather tail to the bowmen approaching. "Who are *they*?"

"Tell you later!" Gil grabbed Janetta. "Run!" Morians and Elias gauged their approaching opponents and flung their shields over their shoulders.

"We run."

Ragi caught Rachel's hand again, and with the Men of Alba closing ranks around them, they sprinted up the muddy boardwalk once more. Panting with exertion, Morians matched strides with Gil. "How long are you in Deer Bay?"

"Half a day."

Morians grinned. "And already you make friends!"

Gil grinned back. Then he skidded around a steep-roofed gable end and stumbled to a gasping halt. Ahead, his way was blocked by a solid face of earthworks and stone. At either side, houses abutted the barrier, built right into the turf. Morians and Darras mounted the grass slope, scrambled a few feet up the smooth pale stone, and slid hopelessly down.

"You won't climb it," Rachel said softly, "No one ever could. It's the Roman Wall." She stretched up and laid a hand on the stone for a moment, and then turned to Gil. "There's no way out. I'm going for help."

"What?" he whispered. But Pock-Mark's furious howl, echoing off the white ramparts, drowned her answer. Gil spun around and drew his sword. Ragi followed, and the Men of Alba lined up on either side. In moments they were engulfed by a mob of taunting youths, the leaders brandishing swords, and the rest, weapons fashioned from anything at hand.

One swung a barrel stave at Ragi's head. Another had a length of pot chain, its heavy iron hook as lethal as a mace. A noisy ring of boys and women surrounded Rachel, chanting, "Fire!"

Gil ran to rescue her, but something was happening within the circle. He glimpsed her turning, dragging her sword tip on the ground, and then, suddenly, taunts turned to cries of horror. A whir of brown wings arose above the heads of Rachel's tormentors, and Hawk streaked away over the roof tops. The youths scattered and a woman shrieked, "Witch! Witch!"

"Where is she?" Ragi shouted.

"Safe," Gil answered, "Which is more than we are."

The crowd closed in, their shouts and jeers hushed by fear. Even the peace-making potter wore a menacing scowl. "We need no witchcraft here," he growled.

"Burn them!" a woman muttered coldly. "Before they burn us."

"I smell smoke!" a child shouted and several more joined in the cry. "Smoke! Smoke! They light witch-fires!"

Gil and Ragi aligned themselves along the wall, with Janetta between them and two of the Men of Alba on either side. The crowd grew larger still, jostling against each other, packed in between the house walls flanking the alley. Pock-Mark, his eyes scrunched up with hatred, closed on Gil, one wary step at a time.

Gil retreated up the turf banking until he felt cold stone behind his back. The Wall. The old Roman Wall. *It's still there*, he thought numbly. *Will anyone ever know we died here?*

The crowd surged, the leaders thrust forward by a disturbance at the back, as if those at the rear strained ghoulishly to see. But suddenly the solid wall of angry faces broke up, turning this way and that in alarm. A whispering swept through the gathering and then a clear angry voice sounded over the turmoil, "Leave them. They are mine."

Gil gasped with giddy relief. A gap appeared in the roadway as men, women, children and even yapping dogs, shrank back from the tall, yellow-haired man striding through their midst. Only Pock-Mark held his ground. "Who are you?" he demanded, sword yet in hand.

The potter laughed drily. "He is Floki Magnusson. And you, lad, are on your own." He brushed his clay-stained hands together and slipped away into the crowd.

Huge grins spread across the faces of the Men of Alba. But Floki did not smile; nor did he draw his sword. He strode onward, with Percy stumbling cheerfully at his side, until he was within reach of Pock-Mark's half-raised blade. Ciarnan and Eirik fanned out at his right; Eirik fiercely poised behind a shiny new shield. Beyond, towering over the heads of the crowd, Bjorn glowered within his beard; two axes at his belt and his mighty sword in his hand.

Eye to eye with the belligerent youth, Floki stopped. With his fur-lined cloak flung back over one shoulder and the glitter of twisted gold at his throat, he looked as much a king's son as the two he travelled with. Pock-Mark's forehead dampened with sweat, but he did not move. Floki nodded courteously. Then he leaned forward. "Drop the sword," he said softly, "Or I will kill you where you stand."

Pock-Mark hesitated for a last foolish second, and then, as the watchers scurried further away, he let the weapon fall. Floki nodded again. "I thank you."

Eirik dashed forward and scooped up the surrendered blade, and Floki smiled for the first time. But when he turned back to Pock-Mark, his face was solemn. He gestured lightly toward Gil and Ragi. "What have they done, that you pursue them?"

Pock-Mark looked around, wild-eyed, for support. The crowd that had egged him on shuffled and turned away. But out of their midst, Scruffy-Head suddenly appeared. "They begin it!" he pointed an accusing finger. "They draw swords!"

Floki's eyes flicked to Gil and Ragi. "Do they," he said. But he turned back at once. "And have they reason?"

"No reason!" a man, emboldened by Scruffy-Head, stepped forward.

A woman shouted, "The witch lit fires. We only defend our houses!" The crowd began to jostle and grumble, remembering its grievance.

Floki looked around with undisguised contempt. "I see no witch."

"There was!" a man far back shouted. "There was a girl!"

Floki looked at Janetta. "This girl?" he said innocently.

"No." The woman shook her head. "A girl with red hair."

"As witches have!" another woman shouted.

"Then my father is a witch," Floki growled. "For his red hair. I see no red-haired girl."

"She is gone," the woman whispered. "She grew wings. Like a bird. And flew!"

Floki looked hard at the woman, and then raised his eyes to the sky above the Roman Wall. "Gods of my fathers," he said. "Why is it when I leave the Northlands, I leave all intelligence behind?"

Then suddenly he threw back his cloak and raised his left arm, revealing the creature whose fierce talons gripped his leather-bound wrist. Hawk flashed golden eyes at her erstwhile tormentors and a gasp rose from the crowd. Floki drew the bird close to his face and kissed the smooth feathers of her head. Then he lifted her high again and swept the gathering with scornful eyes.

"Here is the bird you see. No witch, but my pretty hawk. I release her that she may stretch her wings, and she stoops over your heads, pursuing a dove. And while you make fools of yourselves, the girl flees."

He stroked Hawk's wing and with a weary shrug murmured, "Idiots. Next you will tell me that in the Northlands, men turn into seals."

A woman giggled and then another laughed aloud. Pock-Mark glared and half-raised a fist, and then froze, as Floki quietly drew his sword. "I go now to find the poor frightened girl," he said. "And if she is harmed in any way," he raised the sword and looked down its shining blade at Pock-Mark, "I will find you, no matter where you run."

"I do not hurt her!" Pock-Mark protested. "I promise!" A muttering of agreement echoed his words.

Floki suddenly smiled. "Good," he said. "Then all is well." He nodded to the townspeople as if all were friends and turned, shepherding Percy before him. "Come. Let us leave these good people to their work."

Gratefully, Gil wrapped an arm around Janetta's shoulders and hurried her past Pock-Mark's looming bulk. Ragi, Ciarnan, and the Men of Alba closed in around them, with Bjorn standing guard until all had safely passed.

Then suddenly, the hush of the alleyway was shattered by a high-pitched howl. Gil whirled and saw Eirik fly past Bjorn's knees, small face screwed up in battle fury, his unwieldy sword aimed at Pock-Mark's chest.

"*No!*" Floki flung out a long arm, caught the boy around his middle, and lifted him, squirming and shouting, off his feet. "Not *now* King's Son. I make *peace* now." With a grimace, he flung the still struggling child over his shoulder, sword, shield, and all.

When they reached the open marketplace, Floki lowered the boy to the ground. "Go, and behave yourself," he said. "If I know, then, how much trouble you are, I take your sister." He paused, and turned suddenly to Gil, astonishment at his own stupidity lighting his face. "Now what was I thinking, Warrior, that I do not do that?"

Gil shrugged warily. Floki looked from him, to Ragi, and then back to Gil. "And which of you idiots draws a sword?"

Gil glanced at Ragi and shrugged again. "We both did," he muttered.

"They mocked her!" Ragi cried.

"So it was you." Floki slapped the side of Ragi's head. "Which would pain her most?" he said. "To be mocked? Or to see you dead at her feet?"

He walked off in silence until they came to a quiet lane approaching the river front. There, he unbuckled his sword belt and held it up before Hawk. "Come home, pretty one," he whispered, bending again to kiss the creature's sleek head. "We would have you in our world."

The bird spread her wings and sprang from his wrist. She rose high above their heads, wheeled, and then plunged downward, sweeping through the circle, and into his arms, a sobbing, terrified girl.

"Pretty one," he whispered, alarmed. Rachel clung to him, her own arms clasped around his neck, her face buried in the fur of his cloak. He lifted her chin with gentle fingers and looked into her eyes. "They hurt you."

"No." She shook her head. And though her face was dirty and her hair tangled, she bore no marks.

"But they frighten you. It is enough." He raised cold eyes to the wall from which they had fled. "I deal with them."

"No. Please, they're just stupid. It wasn't them." She paused, her eyes clouding with remembered fear. "I saw something. I see things. I see things no one else sees."

He nodded solemnly. "I see things, too, Pretty Hawk. I cannot change them. Nor can you."

"I must try," she whispered. He shook his head sadly. But she turned in his arms then and faced Gil and the others with a little smile. Eirik hid behind his shield, peeked over, and hid again. Ragi stared at Rachel in silence, his jaw slack, and his eyes wide with astonishment. She smiled again and gave a little wave.

"You ...." he found his voice at last. "You are a Change-Thing."

Rachel shrugged. "Looks like it."

Floki laid a protective hand on her shoulder. "So, Man of the High Island," he said coolly, "Do you yet save for a bride-price?"

Ragi drew a hand across his eyes, drew it away, and stared again at Rachel. Then a slow, wondering smile crept across his face. "Yes," he murmured, "Oh, yes. As fine a hawk as she is a woman! I pay *twice* the bride-price!"

Floki laughed delightedly. "Well spoken," he cried. "And with such a wife, your table will not lack for game." He let go of Rachel's shoulder and gave her a gentle shove. "Go, pretty one. Reward the warrior who fought for you. However stupidly." He smiled again, but he turned deliberately away as Ragi claimed his Fire-Hair's kiss.

Floki's eyes fell on Morians, who he seemed quite unsurprised to see. "Tell me, Man of the Forest," he smiled, "What word of the mighty and honorable Palamedes? Has he found at last his shadowy Questing Beast?"

"No," Morians answered, "Nor will he, unless the Beast itself is exiled to Francia. For there the great knight rides, champion of all the tournaments."

"And there, soon, you ride yourselves," Floki said. "Far from the snows of Caledon."

"This is true," Elias had joined them, "But how do you know?"

Floki laughed. "Indeed, I know more: that you lay down the last of your silver for shields, and mail, and Saxon swords. And travel on, as penniless as pilgrims."

"It is necessary," Elias said stiffly. "The tournaments are not for beggar knights." He looked offended, but Gareth laughed cheerfully.

"We will win it back twice-fold!"

"Thrice-fold, I am sure," Floki smiled.

"How *do* you know?" Gil asked, puzzled. Floki gave him a slow grin. "The chieftain of this town is as fond of gossip as a woman at the washing," he said. "By his courtesy, I now know the comings and goings of every man, woman, child, and beast in Northumbria."

"Has he heard of the hostages?" Gil cried eagerly.

"They walk these streets but three days past," Floki said. He nodded grimly to the slave market behind them. "And leave, again, in chains; slaves now to a Viking chieftain, cousin to this earl."

"Three days," Gil whispered sadly. Already they must be far away.

"Three days of what was ten, Warrior," Floki returned exultantly. His eyes took on their battle light. "We take seven from their lead. And now we ride the evening tide. The ebb is gentler than the flood. We make our way by light of stars, and by the morrow's nightfall, set sail from Hrafn's Ayre to Francia."

"Francia?" Gil said. "But he's a Viking."

"A Viking born among the Franks. He holds a stronghold on an island off the coast."

"Mont Tombe!" Morians cried. "I know the place!"

"As well you should, for it is famous for its tournaments."

"And for its defense," Elias said soberly. "You will not easily take it."

"This I do know," Floki gave him a cool look. "Nor shall I try," he grinned. "For there is no need." He looked away at the Minster, its tower pink in the evening sun. "Come. The day ends and we have much to do."

He led them on toward the waterfront, with Elias and Gil trotting, puzzled, at his heels. "This southern chieftain," he continued, waving a hand toward the earl's unseen hall, "springs from northern seed. Indeed, by a lawless bedding he is cousin to my father, and hence, cousin to me." He grinned again. "I turn a stone from Ireland to Denmark and find my kin. This is good. I do not like him and he does not like me. Nor does he like his Frankish brother, either. But blood is blood."

Floki smiled and turned to Gil, "I bear his greeting to our kinsman and his plea for Hakon Sea-Friend's release. For the others I must pay silver – they are not kin – but he bids him set an honorable price."

He reached into the leather purse at his waist and drew out a folded sheet of vellum. "Though he is a pagan, a Minster monk records his words. And they are here," he held the vellum out to Gil, "Scribed in Latin which neither he nor I can read."

"I can read it," Rachel said.

Floki grinned. "And this, also, I know. Though he does not." He nodded to Gil who gave the vellum to Rachel. "Does he betray me?" he asked mildly, as she read.

"No." She handed back the message. "It's what you said."

"That is well for him," he said, still mild. He folded the vellum carefully and put it away.

He turned to Elias, then, and smiled. "Why take a fortress when I win my cause with silver and courtesy? Unless," he laughed softly, "I catch them first at sea, for if I do, I take what's mine with steel."

He glanced from Elias to his three companions, and then back to the tall young knight. "Come. You travel to Francia … sail with us! Perhaps we have fun along the way."

Gil grinned hopefully, but Elias only bowed his head. "I thank you for this honor. But we travel with others, Knights of Arthur, all. Bound, like us, for the tournaments. They wait for us, now, with our horses, at a camp beyond the town. We follow the pilgrim road and take sea passage in the south." He paused, and added with dignity, "They, too, are poor, for their lands lie in the grip of the usurper, and like us, they have no other way to earn their bread."

"It is no shame to be poor," Floki said quietly. "The man I rank the highest, is poor." He paused and added, "And what news have you of your noble overlord? For I owe him, too, a courtesy."

"Courtesy?" Morians' face darkened with indignation.

"He burns my father's house," Floki said bluntly. "I would return the favor."

Elias shook his head. "This you will not achieve," he said. "Nor is he even there to receive you."

Floki's eyes narrowed. "And where is he, then, if not at Camelot?"

"He makes pilgrimage, sir," Darras said innocently. "To Holy Rome."

"Pilgrimage?" Gil cried incredulously.

"Yes," Morians laughed suddenly. "He lays his case before Saint Peter, to prove his right to Arthur's crown. Oh, now he is a pious, Christian king! But do not expect bare feet and wooden staff. Guidbairn dresses his humility in Cloth of Gold."

Darras and Gareth laughed with him, but Elias looked hard at Floki. "This is no Frankish Viking," he said, "To be won by silver or steel. Go back to your Northlands, friend, and live in peace."

Floki bowed his head graciously. Then he looked up and smiled. "Allow me to judge my enemies," he said. "And allow me to choose my peace."

CHAPTER SIXTEEN

They sailed at sunset, from Hrafn's Ayre, in the same haste with which they had left Deer Bay. Then, the ebbing tide had been a friend, carrying the freshly provisioned ships through the night. Now, it was an enemy, threatening to imprison them amid the shifting sands.

The ponies were dragged, reluctant, from their grazing; the last cask of water loaded aboard, and the last grumbling Northman roused from his few hours of sleep. Hauling the ships from the clinging sand took the strength of every man of the crew; and threading a course through the dwindling tide streams, all of Floki's skill.

Safely in the channel, Floki stepped back, and Gil took the helm, with a wistful backward glance at the merchants' campfires. Around him, the Northmen bent to their oars without laughter or song. Hunched over his tiller, wrapped in his steersman's fur, Gil understood. Dusk was falling. Time to be roasting game, not heading out into a wintry sea.

The flickering fires faded to pinpricks, behind them. Under oars, they rounded the tip of the sand bar. At once, the pennant at the masthead rippled and snapped. Gil called for the sail, and as *Silver Dragon* heeled before a brisk west wind, he felt his pulse quicken, despite the hour. He grinned at Ulf, somberly stowing his oar, but got no grin back.

Gil shrugged and looked out to sea with a wry smile. The Northmen were like ponies leaving their home fields; the further south they sailed, the more uneasy they grew.

Eagerly, they had followed their young earl to Norway; willingly, on to Deer Bay's rich markets. Now, they had spent their silver, and with sea kists packed with treasures, their minds were set on home. Floki's stories, of Frankish women yearning for Northern husbands, fell on deaf ears.

Silently they headed out, and soon Hrafn's Ayre was only a thin pale line between grey waters and grey land. Ahead, the sea was empty, but for a single, distant sail. Some merchant, Gil thought, as determined as Floki to ride the late tide. The sail looked small and lonely, and made him feel the same. He looked up to a darkening sky, as sullen as the mood of Floki's crew.

With oars stowed, they settled in fur-wrapped clumps, grimly chewing cold smoked fish. Their voices were a low murmur, like the seas breaking beneath the bow. Then, suddenly, one voice rose above the others. "How long," asked Grimhildr, "Are the farms of Hrolf's Isle left to old women and boys?"

Gil stiffened and stared. Grimhildr held her fluttering headdress back with one firm hand and met Floki's eyes, unblinking. Around her, men nodded, though none spoke. But Floki only smiled. He looked out to the sea, where the merchant's sail bellied before the wind, and then up at the sky.

"It is All Saints Eve, this night," he said mildly. "The Dark Time comes now. Fields lie fallow. Beasts graze close to their byres. There's little work to do; less light to do it in."

"There is fishing," quiet Ulf said boldly. "There is work in the smokehouse."

A muttering of agreement swept the crew. "My roof needs mending before the snows." Svein Snaggletooth shot Floki a quick rebellious look, then ducked his head.

"The women wait," said a solemn voice from the back. There was a peal of laughter.

"Mine waits!" cried Arnkel Fish-Tail, "But yours, Thorbjorn? She's off with the selkies before our keel is wet!"

Thorbjorn roared in outrage and dove for Arnkel. Floki caught him by his plaited hair and sat him down hard on a bench. "The selkies would not have her," he smiled. "She is a Christian. But do not trouble yourselves," his eyes were again on the sea and the merchant's sail.

It was closer now. *Silver Dragon's* sleek hull cut the water at half again the speed of the sturdy knarr. "The women will wait a little longer, and the more eagerly they will greet you on your return." He smiled again. "And now we give them reason to love you more."

Leaving Thorbjorn with a warning slap across the ear, Floki came and stood beside Gil. He pointed ahead at the knarr, which had veered its course so that it now lay off their load-board. "Bring us closer," he said.

"But he's turned north," Gil said, "And we're going south, aren't we?"

"Indeed," Floki agreed. "But we may sail north a little first."

Puzzled, Gil adjusted the tiller until the dragon swung northward, following the knarr like a curious pony. As Ragi set the sheets, Floki looked back and signaled to Erling, and he, too, changed course.

The distance closed. Gil saw the dusky brown of the merchant's sail, and the faces of the men aboard, all turned toward them. "I know him," Floki said, "He is at Hrafn's Ayre, the first night. A fur trader from the land beyond the sun. Fine furs. And amber, also. His hold is empty, now, but his purse, full." He looked up again, a glint of amusement in his pale eyes.

Erling's Sea-Raven now rode parallel, the two ships closing on the knarr from either side. Floki waved and Erling waved back. Gil saw the broad white grin within his bushy beard. Floki touched Gil's shoulder lightly and nodded at the knarr. "Take him."

"What?" Gil looked from the knarr, to Floki, in confusion.

Floki's eyes narrowed. "*Take him*, helmsman." He pointed ahead, "Bring her there, so Bjorn may throw." Gil saw Bjorn playing out the rope of his iron grapple. He stared at the knarr.

"We're *attacking* them?" he cried, stunned.

Floki shook his head. "Surely, he will not call for that." he said innocently. "Two longships? Sixty men?" He shrugged and smiled. "We talk, Warrior. We make agreement. Then he goes his way, and we go ours." He gauged the narrowing gap. "Drop your sail."

Gil called the order. Ragi freed the sheets. Ciarnan loosened the halyard, lowering the spar. Practiced hands swung it onto its cradle, as *Silver Dragon* glided alongside the knarr.

Bjorn's grapple flew, thudding onto the merchant's deck. Bjorn hauled on the rope, securing his hold. A second iron, flung from *Sea-Raven*, clattered over the knarr's high rail. Together, the rope men drew their ships in close, until the fierce figureheads bowed to each other across the merchant's prow.

"What's happening?" Gil looked up to Janetta's voice. The girls stumbled from their tent, alerted by the slowing of the ship and the shouts of the knarr's crew.

"Go back," he waved urgently, but, eyes bright with excitement, Janetta ran to join him. And, uncomfortably, he realized there was little danger to her, or any aboard *Silver Dragon*. Or *Sea-Raven*, either. Like a pony between two warhorses, the knarr lay imprisoned.

Her crew watched warily as Floki grasped a shroud and stood up on the rail, surveying her. The merchant, a big, dark man with a beard tucked into his belt and a face lined by sun and wind, stared back at him in silent suppressed fury. His men clustered around, bitter in their helplessness.

"A fine ship," Floki called graciously. "She rides this wind well."

"As well as is needed for peaceful trading," the merchant said quietly.

"Indeed," Floki smiled. Then he sprang to the deck of the knarr with a leonine suddenness that surprised even Gil. An instant later, Bjorn landed at his side. And then Eirik appeared from nowhere, and, sword flashing, flung himself across the sea and crashed at Floki's feet.

Floki looked down in disbelief, and then, with a sigh, picked him up by an arm and a leg and tossed him back. "Forgive him," he said to his unwilling host, "He has royal blood. You know what kings' sons are like."

The merchant stared stonily. "I know nothing of kings," he said. "I am a poor man. Our earl, like most earls, keeps the best land for himself."

"The world is not just," Floki agreed.

"Odin sends a wind that flails my harvest before it is reaped."

"And the gods," Floki shook his head sadly, "Unjust as well.

But," his face brightened with another smile, "A good winter in the North for furs. I seldom have seen finer at Hrafn's Ayre."

"They do not fall from the sky, friend. I work hard all winter for them."

"The bear and the wolf work harder still. Their loss is your gain. Your loss, mine." Floki's smile vanished. "I would see your silver-kist, *friend*. Before Bjorn seeks it out with his axe."

It was the numb resignation with which the merchant succumbed that hurt most. *Fight*, Gil cried silently. *Do something.* But he knew, as the merchant surely knew, how bloodily pointless that would be.

A wooden box was produced, its lid raised for Floki to inspect the contents, and then closed and latched and handed over to Bjorn. Bjorn smiled the way Percy might, and clambered aboard *Silver Dragon* clutching the prize.

The merchant stared, with sagging shoulders, as his year's labors passed from his ship. Floki watched and then looked up at the knarr's loosened sail, flapping forlornly. "A fine wind, friend," he said, his voice softened.

"I have seen finer."

"It will carry you easily homeward."

"For what purpose, now?"

Floki shrugged. "The hearth of home is purpose enough."

"Six hungry mouths to feed? Grain enough for four?"

Floki said nothing. He turned, gripped *Silver Dragon's* shroud, and swung himself back aboard.

"How do I feed my children?" The anguish in the merchant's voice cut into Gil's heart.

Floki looked back, and then bent suddenly, and lifted one of the big casks of meal they had loaded at Deer Bay. Swinging around, he hurled it, without speaking, to the merchant's deck. He looked up then, and his eyes, pale and cold, met Gil's. "Helmsman, raise sail." Gil held the icy gaze unflinching. "*Raise sail*," Floki repeated.

"In a moment." Deliberately, Gil turned, closed his hands on the next meal cask and with a gasp of effort, lifted it, swung it around, and flung it after the first. Amid shouts of astonishment, he reached furiously for a third.

As he gripped the heavy cask, he sensed a flicker of movement: Floki reaching as if to help. "Thanks," he grunted, with a startled smile. Then the Northman's hands closed on his shoulders, wrenching him back. The iron grip shifted in an instant to his arm and his leather belt, lifting him off his feet and swinging him in a savage arc. He glimpsed deck and rail and then the amazed face of the merchant, as he flew through the air.

He hit the water off the knarr's high stern. The cold snatched his breath and thumped his chest like it would stop his heart. Gasping, he swallowed a rush of salt water, and then the light and the ship vanished and darkness closed over his head.

Swim, his mind cried, but arms and legs stayed frozen in shock, while boots and sword belt dragged him down. Darkness became blackness. Then a thin, high scream cut through the cold and the fear and the sea itself. *Janetta. Janetta!* Strength of desperation surged through his limbs. He flailed and thrashed, clawing the water until light broke through. Gulping sweet air, he sought the ship's deck with salt-stung eyes. *I'll kill you if you hurt her!* The words howled in his brain but his frozen mouth made no sound.

Janetta screamed again, and he saw it was not Floki holding her, but Grimhildr, clutching her tightly about the waist as she fought to throw herself after him, into the sea. "Help him!" she begged, reaching out her small hands to the stunned, watching crew. Ragi stepped forward, but Ulf pulled him back. Ciarnan ran to the rail. Three men blocked him, their wary eyes on Floki. Bjorn hopefully held out an oar. Floki shook his head. Crestfallen, Bjorn drew the oar back in.

Floundering desperately, Gil turned to the knarr and the man he had tried to help. The merchant looked down with the same sad hopelessness as when his treasure was taken. But he stepped forward and reached out one big hand.

"Leave him!" Floki drew his sword and aimed it at the merchant's chest. The merchant straightened, his defeated eyes clouded with misery.

"Sorry, lad."

"Raise your sail and leave us," Floki ordered.

The knarr's crew put out oars, rowing clear of the two longships. Gil heard the creak of her sail riding back up her mast, and despair swept over him.

Stirred by his fear, Lionheart whinnied wildly and thudded the bars of his pen. *You're safe*, Gil cast the thought, like a last farewell pat, to the terrified beast. *You're safe*. Another wave swamped him, and when he surfaced, the knarr had gone, revealing *Sea-Raven* riding just beyond, bushy bearded Erling at her helm. Gil strove to reach out a numb hand.

"You, also!" Floki swung the sword to Erling.

Erling shook his head. "He is a boy, Floki. Have mercy!"

Without answering, Floki sheathed the sword and stepped to the helm. Percy tugged bewilderedly at his cloak and pointed at Gil in the sea. Floki rested his free hand on the child's head and looked up to Ulf. "Raise sail."

Gil saw the spar swing around and heard the rakke ride up the mast. He felt the water stir as *Silver Dragon* caught the wind. He fixed his eyes on Janetta, struggling against Grimhildr's imprisoning arms. She ducked her head, as if unable to watch him drown, but he kept his own gaze locked on her wind-blown hair, a last sweet sight before the emptiness of the sea.

Then suddenly, she turned back, triumph lighting her face, and Grimhildr's long-bladed sheath knife in her hand. Grimhildr shouted in alarm and reached out for the knife, and Janetta broke free.

"No!" Gil croaked. *Don't die for me*. But it was not the sea she sought now. Racing across the deck, she flung herself at Floki with murderous force. Blood splashed his sleeve as he fended the blade with his forearm. She stabbed at him again, slashing his tunic.

Silver Dragon slewed as he stumbled back from the helm, and Janetta slashed at him a third time. With a look of amazement, he flung the tiller over, heading the ship into the wind. Then, in one quick lunge, he caught Janetta around the waist, spun her around, and lifted the knife from her hand.

Still, she fought, scratching and biting, but he wrapped both arms around her, pinning her effortlessly against his body, until she was still. Then with the blood from his wounded arm soaking both their clothing, he slowly raised his head. "Bjorn," he shouted, with a quick nod toward the sea, "Catch your fish."

Bjorn ran with his oar to the load-board rail. So many helpers crowded around him, that *Silver Dragon* lurched dangerously until Ulf drove some back. Bjorn's big happy face, surrounded by eager reaching arms, swam before Gil's water-blurred eyes. He reached for the extended oar and gripped it, but it dissolved in his hands. He tried again, and again it vanished. *Like that dream*, he thought sleepily, *where you get up, only you don't, over and over ....*

"The oar, Gil!" Ragi's voice cut through, "Hold the oar!"

Gil tried a third time, and suddenly the wet wood was solid in his numb fingers. He heard cheers and then Bjorn's huge paw had the collar of his tunic and he was dragged by a dozen hands, drenched and frozen, over the rail.

His arms flopped, leaden, and his legs folded when he tried to stand. Eased down by gentle supporters he collapsed onto the deck and sick darkness closed around him. A finger came out of the night and poked him sharply in the ribs. He opened his eyes and the blackness faded back into dusk. Percy's round face beamed over his. "Gil! Gil! Wake up, Gil!"

"Awake," he mumbled, struggling to make his mouth work. Ciarnan was beside him, tucking a fur around him. Before him, Rachel stood; her face strangely expressionless; holding out another fur. He looked past her, seeking Janetta.

"Here," she called, "I am here." Floki still held her, but she stood now without struggling, tears of joy wetting her cheeks, her eyes alight with longing.

Gil raised his gaze from her face to Floki's. "Let her go," he croaked.

Floki shook his head in amazement. "Or what?" he said softly, "You swim again?" He leaned back slightly, and half-closed his eyes. "Oh, Warrior," he whispered, "Learn. *Learn.*"

Then he straightened and shot Gil a look of cold fury. "You are alive," he said, "For one reason only. Because you are so good a helmsman. If you are *this much* less good," he lifted one hand for an instant and held thumb and forefinger a fraction apart, "*this much*, I leave you to drown. That is the reason you live. The *only reason.*"

"Let her go," Gil said again. Behind him, a man groaned.

"He does not hurt me," Janetta whispered.

Floki tightened the grip of his bloody hand around her and suddenly dropped his head, resting it briefly against her hair. "No. Two reasons. Because of this wildcat, also," he said quietly. Still leaning over her, he murmured, "Come now, if I let you go to him, do you murder me?" He raised his head and smiled and released her.

She flew, like a bird from a cage, to Gil, throwing herself down, with all her warm body pressed tightly against his, sobbing as if she could never stop. He held her, and caressed her hair, and then, embarrassed, sat up, bracing himself shakily on one arm.

Arnkel Fish-Tail was at the helm, holding the ship steady into the wind. Floki leant over a sea-kist, then straightened and strode back to Gil, with his fine, fur-lined cloak bunched awkwardly under his uninjured arm. One-handed, he threw it at Gil. "Warm yourself."

Gil caught it, staggered upright, and threw it back. It landed at Floki's feet and another groan rose from the watching men. Floki patiently knelt, picked it up, and stood, stumbling suddenly as he did. Rachel hurried forward with a bundle of linen bandages, but he waved her away, and tossed the cloak back to Gil. "Warm yourself. You are useless to me ill."

Ulf laid it over Gil's shoulders, leant close and whispered, "Silence. *I beg you*. Silence."

Gil nodded. He wrapped the beautiful fur around himself and in its shelter, stripped off his wet garments and replaced them with dry. Then, still wearing the cloak, he walked to the helm, flexing his tingling hands. He took the tiller from Arnkel, looked up, and signaled to Erling on *Sea-Raven*. Then he swung the prow across the wind and returned his ship to her southern course.

Floki watched him, casually bunching the sleeve of his torn tunic to staunch the blood that yet ran down his arm. Rachel stepped forward again, with her bandages, and before he could argue, pushed him down on a sea-kist below the steering board.

"Let Odin's Maiden mend it," he said cheerfully, "Since it is her work." He half rose, looking laughingly for Janetta, who had retreated to the girl's black tent, to change her blood-stained clothes.

"Floki, if I don't stop this," Rachel pressed her fingers against the wound, "You will bleed to death. You will. I promise."

He shrugged and leaned back against the rail, as she wadded linen against the wound and held it firm. "I die happy. Slain by a *Valkyrja*."

Rachel drew back, her fingers still firm on the linen. "What is it with you men? You're worse than Ragi."

Floki grinned and turned suddenly to Gil. "Helmsman! I tell you once that I envy no man, and this is true. But a night lies ahead for you ...." he smiled dreamily and nodded toward the tent, "Ah, Warrior. I envy you that night!"

"I can't believe it," Gil said to Rachel, as they made camp at dawn on a desolate Northumbrian shore, "He thinks he's still my friend."

She looked up from the meal she was kneading on a flat rock by the fire. "He is."

"*What?*" Gil stared at her. Then he said evenly, "No, he is not. And if you side with him over this, *our* friendship is finished, too." He crouched beside her and whispered hoarsely, "He tried to murder me, Rachel." Then he shook his head. "You didn't even say anything."

"It wouldn't have helped." She thumped the ball of dough with clenched fists; then raised it and shook it in his face. "You gave him no choice, Gil," she said fiercely. "You took the food he needs to feed his crew. You endangered his ship. And you defied him. He gave you an order, and you *defied* him."

"I was right. Those people will starve because of us."

She sat back and looked out toward the strand, where Ciarnan and Ragi and Arnkel Fish-Tail were raising the black tents for a few hours rest before they sailed on. "Maybe you *were* right. But what about the next man who thinks he's right? Say, maybe a couple of them want to take women aboard from the slave market? Or, six of them decide they won't row unless they get more food? Or half would rather raid Lindisfarne than sail to Francia at all? If he lets you challenge him, why should any of them obey him?"

"Because he's a murdering tyrant."

She shook her head. "He's just one man, Gil. He can't fight them all. He can't watch them all. They could kill him in his sleep. *Eirik* almost did, and he's ten."

She bashed the dough ball flat and laid it on the hot stones of her hearth. "They obey him," she said quietly, "Because he's strong – strong enough to protect them." She met his eyes, her own dark and troubled, "There's no government, Gil. No police. No armies except the armies of other earls, strong enough to call themselves kings."

She paused and then said suddenly, "Do you remember what Aidan said when I was mad at Ismail for hunting the deer?"

"'You've never been hungry,'" Gil murmured.

"We haven't, Gil." She gestured toward Floki, out on the strand gathering driftwood, with Percy, and now Eirik, too, trotting behind him. "His cousin, the girl he loves, the boy who fought bravely beside him – all of them now in chains. Only he can save them. But he can't do it alone. He needs ships. He needs men to crew them. He needs to make it worth their while. Worth leaving their homes and risking dying in some far-off place."

She looked back at *Silver Dragon*. Bjorn was carrying the ale cask down the gangplank, singing one of his lullabies. "They're happy now. They have silver. They'll sail on." She spun around and looked straight into Gil's eyes. "What would you do ... what would you *be*, if you were born in Floki's world?"

"Aidan was born in Floki's world."

"Aidan's a saint. Are you?"

He rocked back on his heels and looked up at the brightening sky. "No. I'm not a saint. But I will not live the way Floki lives. I'll find another way."

She smiled and shook her head gently. "I really respect that, Gil. But you won't."

He stood up and walked away.

Far down the strand, Janetta, astride Lionheart, led the Hrolf's Isle ponies out to graze. The sea wind made streamers of their manes and her long black hair. The rising sun haloed them all in gold. His heart thudded, like in the cold sea. *A night lies ahead for you.*

He closed his eyes, not daring to imagine. But in the darkness, another certainty came, as if he, too, could see through time. A day, also, lay ahead: a day when he would face Floki Magnusson over the blade of a sword.

CHAPTER SEVENTEEN

By nightfall, Gil was again at the helm and they sailed on under fitful stars. For four days, Floki drove his crews against the weather and against the wind. Sleep was snatched aboard, or under guard on hostile Saxon shores. Food was salt fish and sodden bannocks; drink, stale water, tasting of wood.

Gil helmed his ship with teeth-gritted determination until at last they sighted cliffs of white stone, gleaming through a mist of fine rain. Beneath them lay a grey strand crowded with ships, men, and horses: the pilgrim port of Dofras. He ordered his sail lowered and his oarsmen to their places, and as *Silver Dragon* glided closer, Floki raked the shore with hunter's eyes. But no Frankish longship rested there; their quarry had kept his narrowing lead.

Gil brought his ship ashore beside a cloth-shrouded knarr; *Sea-Raven* scraping the gravel at the merchant's other side. Under the knarr's dripping awnings, men turned wary faces to watch. Floki raised a curt hand, his mind on other things. The keel grounded and he leapt down to the strand. "See to the camp," he called to Gil. "I will learn the news." He strode off into the crowds, bright head bare to the rain. Pilgrims, traders, and ferrymen all stepped back to let him pass. Gil directed the rope teams to haul the hull above the tide; as startled to see weary men obey him, as he was to be left in charge.

When her captain returned, *Silver Dragon's* mast was down and the black awnings stretched over it. Driftwood from the tideline crackled on a newly lit fire. The water casks had been replenished from a spring in the pilgrims' camp. Rachel and Grimhildr kneaded barley bread by the flames. Floki sniffed the wood smoke appreciatively and laid a companionable hand on Gil's shoulder. "I speak with the ferrymen, Warrior. Our friend leaves Dofras two days past. This night he is in Francia, and a day hence, at Mont Tombe. Set the beasts to graze and take your rest."

"We've missed him," Gil said morosely.

"For now."

"We should have been faster."

Floki shrugged. "We were as fast as the wind allowed. Perhaps Odin wishes that he live." He smiled, and with Percy and Eirik trotting after, went to barter with the merchants on the shore.

Gil took Janetta with him to lead the ponies out to grass. With three mounts to spare, she rode bareback behind him on Lionheart. Nudging his shield aside, she pressed her small chin between his shoulder blades. "Look," she cried, "knights."

Beyond the shabby tents of the pilgrims, stood a colorful pavilion topped by a fluttering blue and gold pennant. Whinnying horses were tied in a long line at one side, and before the pavilion, a cluster of young men watched two others, mounted on chargers, facing each other with lances raised.

They wore padded linen coats, but no mail, and their shields and blunted lances were battered and plain. Older men, more finely dressed knights, stood among the watchers, but most were young boys, beardless and pink-cheeked in the cold, damp air. Gil searched wistfully among them for Morians and the Men of the Forest, but the journey from Deer Bay that had taken five days by sea, would take longer, still, overland.

A few of the pilgrims had gathered, also, to watch. Some were lean, serious men, like the men of Hy; others had the look of warriors, despite their simple dress and wooden staffs. They cheered as the two knights lowered their lances and galloped toward each other over the sand.

Both were unseated in the first charge. Janetta giggled, burying her face in Gil's cloak. "They are not as good as you."

He laughed shyly. "You say I'm good at everything."

"Because it is so," she answered. The boy knights mounted again. The watchers shouted encouragement and the nearest knight responded with a wide grin. "He is like Ismail," Janetta said. The young man was dark-haired and lithe, but it was his cheerful white smile that brought the African boy to Gil's mind, too. He watched as the two knights laughed and teased each other, feeling a homesick yearning for his friend and the adventures they'd shared.

The boys met in a second charge, both lances missing their targets. Whirling their horses, they galloped away to the ends of the list. Gil peered after them through the wind-blown rain, his fingers twitching on Lionheart's rein. Janetta leaned close over his shoulder. "Go. Show them."

He laughed, but she suddenly snatched his knife from his belt and slid down from Lionheart's back. Wrapping her cloak against the wind, she ran up the beach to a gale-battered copse and returned bearing a slender hazel sapling. "Here!" she hacked a last green branch off with his blade. "I arm my knight!"

He grinned shyly. "Joust bareback?"

"It is but a game. Like Pony Chess in the Mews Garden. See?" she said, as the young knights unseated each other a second time. She took the leads of the Hrolf's Isle ponies and thrust her lance into his hand. "Surely they will run at the sight of you!"

Gil shook his head, laughing, but he slipped the greenwood shaft under his arm. His heart thudded with remembered excitement as he turned Lionheart and cantered toward the rain-drenched list. The knights and pilgrims looked up to the drumming of hooves on the beaten sand. "Behold!" one shouted, as Gil and Lionheart emerged from the mist, "Lance'lot rides forth from Caledon!" The dark-haired boy shaded his eyes. Then, with a cheerful grin, he turned his mount and lowered his lance. Lionheart skidded to a halt, shied sideways like a crab, and whirled to flee. "And now he rides home again to Guinevere!" Laughter swept the crowd.

Gil hauled on his lead-rope rein and pulled Lionheart back into line. *Like you've never seen a lance before?* Before him, the boy braced himself in his sturdy saddle, raised his shield, and kicked his mount into the charge. Gil dug desperate toes into Lionheart's furry flanks and, clutching his sapling lance, galloped to meet him. Then a memory flashed into his mind, of a younger, carefree Floki teasing the knight Palamedes in the farmyard of Einar's Holm.

Grinning, he steadied his lance and raised his shield as the knight thundered closer. Two strides away, he flung both aside and ducked flat on Lionheart's mane. The straining boy's lance whisked through empty air, and with a wild shout the boy followed it, tumbling forward over his horse's head. A cry arose from the crowd, half cheer, half condemnation, as the knight sprawled on the sand. Gil drew Lionheart up and jumped down to help the fallen rider. "What kind of fight is this?" a man's gruff voice called.

"A Northman's fight?" Gil grinned apologetically and reached his hand down to the dark-haired boy.

"Then go home to the North," the man growled, "We need no Vikings here."

But the boy Gil had defeated took his hand and bounced cheerfully to his feet. "He is no Viking, but a true knight!" he cried. "See, he rides with no saddle and defeats me with this!" He retrieved Gil's greenwood lance and held it high, laughing. "And look!" he turned to pat Lionheart, "His charger is scarce bigger than a lady's palfrey." Lionheart flattened his ears and bared his teeth. Gil hauled his head aside and got himself between the teeth and the young knight. "Do you ride to the tournaments, sir?" the boy asked.

Gil smiled and gave a regretful shrug. "No. I sail with my earl to Mont Tombe in Francia. To visit his kin," he added cautiously.

The boy nodded, but as Janetta joined them with her clutch of ponies, the second young knight said boldly, "Would your earl grant passage to us as well? We, too, travel to Mont Tombe, for the first of the tournaments is held there."

"The ferrymen take all the older knights first." The dark boy cast a shy glance at Janetta. "They have more silver and we must wait."

Janetta smiled willingly, but Gil shook his head. "There's no room for your horses. We have these four ponies already."

"But we have none!" The second knight, a stocky, sandy-haired lad, gestured toward the two chargers. "These are but leant to us that we might learn." As he spoke, an older man collected the reins of both animals and led them back to the line of tethered beasts.

"But how will you enter the lists?" Janetta asked.

"As we do here, my lady." The dark boy dropped his eyes when she smiled again. "We will borrow horses."

"And in the melee, we will capture others," his bolder friend cried.

"Then we ride those and capture more and ransom them for silver," said the dark boy.

The other laughed. "You may ride for horses. I will capture the son of some Frankish lord. His ransom will buy horse and armor, both, and make of me a fine knight."

The watching men laughed. "Oh, no doubt," one cried. "But for now, see to cooking our supper."

The dark boy bowed his head meekly, but his friend caught his arm, holding him back. He faced the man who had spoken, and then nodded toward Gil. "If I am to serve, I'll serve this Viking's master. He has a ship, and you do not."

"Sail with the Vikings and they'll sell you as slaves," another shouted. "And who will pay your ransom? Your father," he pointed at the sandy-haired lad, "is as poor as you are. And yours," he nodded to the dark boy, "is a hostage himself."

The boys looked uneasy, but when Gil and Janetta returned from tethering the ponies, they fell into step on either side, clutching their meagre gear and grinning hopefully. As they passed the pavilion with its fluttering pennant, a powerfully built old man, wearing pilgrim's garb and carrying a wooden staff, stepped out of the crowd. "You sail on the longship *Silver Dragon?*" he raised a scarred hand toward the strand. Gil nodded. "So you sail with Floki Magnusson."

"I'm his helmsman," Gil said shyly.

A grey-haired knight laughed. "And I'm King Arthur."

But the big pilgrim shook his head. "Brains, not brawn, make a helmsman. And that," he nodded to the site of Gil's triumph, "was clever." His craggy face lit with a smile.

"I learned it from Floki," Gil said.

The man threw back his head and laughed. "Yes," he said.

"No doubt you did. And would Floki Magnusson bear a penitent to Francia?" he asked.

"Surely so," Janetta cried. "For it is the duty of every man to aid a pilgrim."

The old man smiled down at her. "I doubt it is the duty of every Viking. Still, the young lion may show courtesy to the old." He nodded to Gil to continue, with an authority that belied his humble robes. Warily, Gil led his growing party back to the ship.

He found Floki kneeling with Percy and Eirik in the shadow of *Silver Dragon's* stern, fashioning a moated sandcastle at the water's edge. Percy shouted a happy greeting and waved a driftwood boat. But Floki got to his feet in one swift move, his eyes never leaving the old pilgrim's face and his hand firm on the hilt of his sword.

"A fine ship, Floki Magnusson." The penitent's smile again lighted his dour features.

"She is that." Floki's eyes flicked to Gil and then to the pilgrim.

"Too fine to come to grief on Irish shores."

"Nor shall she," Floki said softly. "And you are far from those shores, Padraic Njalsson." He looked the pilgrim over carefully. "Where is the sword that sparked fire from mine?"

"Laid down before the altar of Saint Colum's church, that I might better grasp the pilgrim's staff." The old man lifted it lightly from the sand and then leaned easily on it again.

Floki laughed suddenly. "When we battle on the strand, that day, I do not imagine I meet you next on the pilgrim road. What brings you here?"

"What brings any man here? Nightfall. I have served your aged kinsman long enough. It is time I see to my soul."

Floki nodded. "And how fares that noble earl?" he said quietly.

The pilgrim shrugged. "Well contented with a new young bride, held safe from young lions of the North."

"May the gods pity her."

"And may Our Lord pity you, for the work you did there." The old man gave him a bleak smile. "You know I am sworn to kill you."

"I know."

They stood regarding each other in silence. Then the pilgrim raised his wooden staff and shrugged. "It will have to wait. I would cross this sea." He glanced at the beached ship. His fingers brushed his small satchel, "I have only a pilgrim's coins."

"I do not own the wind," Floki said. "I do not sell it. Come." He gestured toward the campfire where the crew were settling for supper.

"Good sir?" The bolder of the two boy knights stepped forward. "You will take us, too?"

Floki's eyes were on the old pilgrim's back. "What say you?" he murmured.

"We must cross the sea as well."

"We have these." The shy, dark boy held out a handful of little coins. Floki looked down, brushed the hand aside, and pointed wearily to the fire.

He turned then to Gil and Janetta. "Anyone else, helmsman? Knights? Pilgrims? Perhaps a farmer and some sheep? Why be an earl when I may be a ferryman?" He looked sourly at his warship, turned, and strode away.

They set sail the next morning, on a still winter day. Floki and the pilgrim sat with a gaming board between them, talking quietly, as Gil steered the ship from shore. The two young knights stood by the dragon prow and cheered lustily as the sail rode up the mast. The old warrior wrapped his cloak around his bare feet. "They think themselves Vikings."

"They could be worse." Floki moved a playing piece. "A Viking is an honest murderer; a knight, the same, but less honest." He nodded at the board. "And I have won."

They made landfall on a beach as crowded with travelers as Dofras, only long enough to set the penitent warrior down. He thanked them for the crossing, and then, leaning on his staff, he nodded kindly to Floki. "When next we meet, young lion, I keep that pledge. Be ready." With a wave and a gruff smile, he set out on the road to Rome.

Floki watched him go and then suddenly grinned at Gil and

slapped his shoulder. "Take us to sea, Warrior, before you find me any more old friends."

They sailed south and east then, following the coast for four more days, making camp each night on deserted, marshy strands. In the evenings, Gil and Ciarnan and the two young passengers from Dofras rode the ponies out for grazing, playing at jousting along the way. After dark, they sat together around the campfire talking of armor and horses and the skills and tricks of the tournament.

The sandy-haired boy boasted of the fame and fortune he would win, and how he would be knighted by some great lord. "And then I will ride forth," he said, "On my own great warhorse, as white as snow, trapped in crimson and gold, and when the heralds cry out my name, 'Sir Garlon!' the women will blush and faint and whisper in their pavilions, 'Garlon! Most noble Garlon!'"

Janetta giggled and Rachel looked up from sewing a patch on Eirik's trousers and rolled her eyes. "And what about most noble Allein?" she asked the dark boy. "We will all blush and faint over you?"

He smiled and shook his head. Then he told how his father had lost his lands when Camelot fell and had gone to Francia to fight as a mercenary, leaving Allein with his mother and sisters in the Forest of Caledon. "But he has fallen captive to a Frankish lord. I ride to raise his ransom." He ducked his head. "I am not a good knight, but there is no one else."

"I am sure you will be a good knight," Janetta touched his arm. "It is not too much to learn." He reddened with shy pleasure and stared, blinking, into the campfire.

Gil leaned forward, about to speak of their quest for their own hostages, but then he thought suddenly of the warrior pilgrim he had brought to Floki's camp. The boy knights seemed innocent, but so had he. For all its distances and its emptiness, this world was bound together by ties of kinship and friendship, and of enmity, too. He prodded the embers of the fire with a driftwood branch and said nothing.

They came to Mont Tombe on a hazy, calm morning, the air as warm as spring. The island appeared shadowy through the mist, its rocky heights rising suddenly from the sea. A small church clung to its feet. On its summit, a fortress surmounted sheer cliffs. "There is a fair landing beyond the church," Floki said. "Take her around."

"You've been here before?" Gil swung the steering oar and signaled to Ragi and Ciarnan to set the sail.

"I have sailed past. The island was the preserve of monks, then. I did not call upon them." He smiled, his eyes on the fortress. "I thought then some sea-king would make it his. And so, one has."

"It is a holy place," Garlon the boy-knight said reprovingly. "No warrior should hold it. It is pledged to Saint Michael."

"A warrior's saint," Floki smiled again. "There, helmsman." He pointed to a stretch of sand beyond the little church, where ships were drawn up below the cliffs. But then suddenly he stayed Gil's hand, his eyes intent on the beach. "Oh, kinsman," he whispered, "This was not wise."

"What?" Gil said.

Floki nodded toward the ships. "What see you there, helmsman?"

Gil studied the shore, uncertainly. He counted seven ships, beached side by side. Four were longships; three, smaller, broader knarrs. One warship stood out from the others, longer by half, and beautifully painted from stem to stern, in red, blue, and gold. The awnings stretched over her lowered mast were striped gold and blue and fringed with crimson. "It looks pretty special," Gil said. "Somebody important, I guess."

"Indeed." Floki turned to Garlon. "And what say you?"

"All know that ship," Garlon whispered, awed. "It is Camelot's new king."

"The Golden Knight," Gil cried. "He's here!"

"Yes," Floki said, "and my noble cousin in Deer Bay speaks not a word."

"Maybe he didn't know," Gil said.

"That old gossip? He knew, Warrior. This is a trap." He pointed inland. Ripples and eddies darkened the moving water amid yellow streaks of sand. "This sea is barely a keel's depth. The tide flows faster here than at Hrafn's Ayre. Faster than a man can run." He glanced at the sky. "By None, all this will be dry land. Ground our keel on that shore, and we are there until nightfall. By which time, we are dead."

He slapped the tiller. "Out to sea, helmsman. Before we are left stranded like a fish in a tide pool." Gil swung the oar and Floki signaled to Erling on *Sea-Raven*. "Take her out."

A groan went up from the sea-weary crews. Erling flung both arms in the air. "Now? We can smell their cooking fires!"

"You smell your funeral pyre. Out!" Floki watched Ragi re-set the tacking spar. Then he sat down quietly beside Gil and turned his eyes to the sea. "The old fool will pay, Warrior," he whispered. "He will pay."

They beat far out to sea, and then sailed back northward until Mont Tombe was a far silhouette on the horizon. Floki pointed inland. "Beach her there, helmsman. Where that river meets the sea, and we can sail again on any tide."

Gil found a landing at the river's mouth, broad enough for both ships. They set up camp beneath a sandy bluff and led the ponies out to graze, while the Northmen settled resentfully to another meal of dried fish. Before them, the tide rushed out, leaving nothing between them and the distant island, but a sweep of yellow sand.

The sun came out and a heat haze shimmered over the tide flats, the salt marshes inland, and the dark forest, beyond. A clear musical note sounded on the meadow-scented air. "A hunt!" Janetta cried.

"No, my lady," Garlon's eyes were shining. "It is the tournament. The herald gathers the knights." He turned to the sand bluff behind them. "If we climb, we may see the pavilions."

They scrambled up the slippery sand slopes and turned, shading their eyes. At the dark forest's edge, a row of tents appeared to float on the marsh grass like bright-sailed ships. The note of the herald sounded again. Garlon gripped Allein's shoulders. "We are here! And soon we are famous and rich!" The dark boy looked at his feet. Garlon turned to Gil. "We must go now, my friend. While the land lies bare of water." He gestured to the shining seabed. "Come with us! No finer sight can be seen! The greatest knights, in armor burnished like the sun. The finest horses, trapped in silver and gold!"

Janetta's wistful eyes sought the distant pavilions. "Once, our land, too, held such sights," she murmured.

Gil took her hand. "Come." They ran together, slipping and sliding, down the bluff to where Floki stood alone on the strand, his eyes on the Frankish chieftain's island. He shifted his gaze to the forest, when Gil described what he had seen from above.

"Listen," Garlon said. "There is music, too." The high notes of faraway bagpipes joined the herald's horn. "It is the Vespers of the Tournament," Garlon explained. "All the ladies come to watch the knights arrive. Sometimes they even joust, like men." He smiled. "We must go now." Then he nodded to Gil and Janetta, and added helpfully, "And they would come to see, as well."

"Would they." Floki gave Gil a grim look, but his eyes settled on Janetta. "Music is for the feasting hall. And battle is not for the amusement of women. Why would you wish to see such a thing?"

Janetta hung her head. "Because it is not real battle, only play. And it is pretty."

Floki looked down on her shining black hair for a long moment. Then he turned abruptly to Gil. "Return before the tide. And take ponies for yourself and your lady. They may outrun the sea. You never will."

"Oh, I thank you!" Janetta cried. She reached out, as if she would embrace Floki, and then blushed and dropped her hands. He struggled not to smile, and then pointed a finger at Gil.

"*Well* before the tide."

Gil grinned and ran to catch and saddle Lionheart and the fastest of the Hrolf's Isle ponies and hastened to join the two knights. Janetta rode behind him and the boys doubled up on the Hrolf's Isle pony, cantering over the tide washed sand. A narrow track threaded the marshes beyond, busy with the traffic of the tournament. Knights jangled by on finely trapped mounts. Farm lads on plodding plough horses jostled donkey-drawn carts. As they neared the bright, flapping pavilions, Lionheart looked back over his shoulder and began chanting despairingly for the ship.

Which you hate, Gil reminded him.

Garlon pointed ahead and shouted, "Behold, the lists! There I shall make my name!" Before them stood a long palisade of rough wood, banked with earth like the Roman wall in Deer Bay. Beyond its shelter, knights were practicing on a great field that stretched far out into the autumn haze. Opposing pavilions appeared as distant smudges of color amid copses of trees.

Behind the palisade, workmen in carpenters' smocks scurried around a tall wooden platform, roofed like Floki's hall with sail cloth. The air rang with the blows of axes and mells, the neighing of knights' chargers and the shouts of the herald announcing a new arrival. The knight galloped back and forth, brandishing his pennant-decked lance. Three young girls mounted the stairs to the unfinished viewing platform, cheering.

Garlon grabbed Gil's arm. "Look!" he gestured at the pennant. "Those are the colors of the great Sir Danane. And there," he turned Gil to face a pavilion on which hung a red shield with a crouching lion wrought in gold. "There Sir Brandel resides. He has a young son, new to the field and dear to his father's heart. Think of the ransom he will bring!"

Close to the palisade, the view was obscured by crowds mounting the earth banks or standing on farm carts. Janetta stood up on Lionheart's back, her hand resting lightly on Gil's shoulder. "It is so beautiful!" she cried.

Gil craned his neck and glimpsed a double line of armored knights cantering onto the field, pennants flying from upheld lances. Behind them, pairs of ladies rode with flower wreaths for helms and lances gay with ribbons.

Garlon scrambled up from his shared pony's back, onto an overhanging tree branch. "'Tis the Joust of the Ladies!" he called, climbing higher. "Ah, there I would set my lance!"

Two women, watching from a cart laden with timber, laughed coarsely. The older, whose unbound hair mocked her worn face, called up, "I will joust with you, lad. And a fine ride you'll have, if you have silver for a mount!"

Her companion was scarcely older than Janetta, and she clutched a small lapdog, like a doll, but her voice was bold. "He

has none! Look at his clothes. He has slept in a ditch, the night!"
She held up the little dog, "Sit and beg me, like my pretty one!"

Janetta hid her face. But Garlon's own features darkened,
and he shouted down, "When I am a great knight, 'tis you who
will beg me!"

"No doubt she will," a man's voice rumbled. "But no
knight mocks a lady. Even such as they." A tall man with grey
hair tumbling from beneath his helm stepped from behind a
merchant's booth.

"Good Uncle!" Garlon cried. "And are my cousins here?"

"They, and your sworn-kin as well. And all their company."

"Horses?" Garlon cried eagerly.

The knight smiled. "And I thought the joy in your eyes was
for me. Yes, horses. Enough for all." He nodded to Allein, who
smiled shyly, and to Gil.

Garlon turned to Gil, too. "This is my mother's brother, Sir
Malegrine," he said proudly. "Come ride with us."

Gil shook his head. "I promised Floki."

"The tide does not turn yet," Janetta said. "You might ride
a little."

"And I will repay your kindness with a proper mount," said
Garlon. He slid from the tree and gave Lionheart's haunch a
dismissive slap. Lionheart's lip curled back. Gil flicked a rein
against his nose.

"Lionheart is fine," he said.

Sir Malegrine laughed, and he laughed again when Gil rode
out beside Allein and Garlon, he with a borrowed lance, and
they with fine borrowed chargers as well. But Janetta stood up
on the earth bank, shouting his name as loudly as any cheering
their champions in the crowd.

An armored knight stepped from the pavilion with the lion
shield and stood adjusting his helm as one young esquire took
down the shield, another brought him his lance, and a third led
forth a black warhorse. He mounted the horse and the crowd
roared in a babble of English and Norse, Irish and the Frankish
tongue. It roared again as he rode through an opening in the
list and onto the tournament field, a red lion pennant fluttering
from his lance. He cantered in a circle, halted, and lowered the

lance until the pennant touched the ground. "Sir Brandel," Garlon whispered. "He vows to take on all comers, in courtesy." Garlon pointed to the banner. "Did he not bid his lion bow, all would know he rode with feutered lance, prepared to die."

A young man on a tall, dappled horse rode out, dipping his lance to Sir Brandel. The girls on the stand cheered and the two women on the timber cart waved ribbons. Esquires ran to take the pennants as the knights turned their mounts haunch to haunch. Then, to cheers from the crowd, they cantered gracefully to the far ends of the palisade.

"Silver on Brandel," a man cried behind Gil.

"Mine's on the challenger," another answered. "Brandel's an old man."

But when the herald's horn sounded and the two knights thundered to a ringing clash, it was the challenger's shield that splintered, the younger man flung over his horse's rump. Even as he limped from the field, another rode out to face Sir Brandel. He lasted two passes before landing in the trampled meadow grass. A third drew a tie, with both riders' lances shattered. But, fighting then on foot, he begged mercy before the old knight's swift sword.

One after another, challengers took their turns, but rock steady on his black horse, grey beard blowing in the wind, the champion faced them all and rode undefeated from the field.

"Fantastic," Gil whispered.

Garlon shrugged, "Weak challengers make any knight a champion."

Janetta smiled sweetly. "Then you must try," she said.

Garlon reddened and looked away. "I save myself for the melee tomorrow." But then he turned and cried, "No. This champion I do meet!" He pointed joyfully at the field. A second knight rode out, carrying the red lion banner.

"Brandel's son," said a voice in the crowd. "Now, there's a prize." The rider was young and slender, with blond hair, as pale as Floki's, flowing from beneath his helm, and a boyish face set in lines of determined courage. Still, he looked scared when Garlon trotted out to challenge him, and his horse seemed too big for him as he cantered up the field. When he turned, adjusting his lance and shield, Gil thought of Eirik with his brother's sword.

Garlon rode out to his end of the list, spun his mount with a savage jerk of the reins, and galloped back, shouting and waving his lance. The blond boy sank down behind his shield, and suddenly steely as a sword, met Garlon's flamboyant charge. His lance smashed into Garlon's shield and the stocky lad flew from his saddle and sprawled flat on his back, staring in amazement at the sky.

As Garlon dragged himself up on his horse and rode defeated from the field, a group of young knights laughed gleefully from the earthen bank. Brandel's son shook his head, but they laughed louder. "Wait 'til tomorrow," Garlon muttered as he rejoined Gil and Allein.

The dark boy shrugged and rode out to take his turn. He met the young knight in a cautious charge, but caution worked no better than bravado, and he, too, tumbled into the grass. The knights on the earth bank jeered. Two other young esquires made their own hapless challenges and met the same fate. "How does he do it?" Janetta whispered.

Gil laughed as he swung up onto Lionheart. "Guess I'm going to find out." He rode out and dipped his borrowed lance to the young defender. The boy smiled, a sunny, friendly smile, and accepted Gil's challenge. Lionheart's ears twitched back and his nostrils flared as the two animals stood haunch to haunch. The knight's charger galloped away, but Gil's pony stayed rooted to the ground. Laughter swept the watchers on the bank.

Gil kicked his mount's stubborn flanks. *What's the problem?* Lionheart shied sideways and turned a white-rimmed eye back at him.

The horse is old.

Good. You can run faster. Go! Gil thumped him harder and Lionheart broke into a reluctant trot, took his place at the end of the list, and stood trembling until Gil goaded him into the charge. Gil raised his lance to match the boy's higher seat, jammed his feet into his stirrups, and snugged his butt down into the saddle.

Three strides away, the knight's big charger leapt into the

air and hurled himself forward. The boy's lance slammed into Gil's shield, lifting him from his saddle, while his own shaft skidded harmlessly aside. Gil dropped the reins, grabbed a fistful of Lionheart's thick mane, and kicked his feet back into the stirrups. At the far end of the list, Lionheart shuddered to a halt and blew air through his nose. *The horse is old. He knows everything.*

Gil nodded. An old horse, schooled by Sir Brandel through many tournaments, trusted, now, to keep his son safe. The boy was good, but the horse was better. Gil turned Lionheart for a second pass. Lionheart shook his mane and shied backward.

Okay. He's old. So you do something young. Like when you try to buck me off.

Lionheart's ears pricked forward then, and he snorted happily as he broke into a gallop. Halfway to their opponent, he hunched his back and bounded into the air, landing on four bunched feet. Gil grabbed mane with his shield hand but hung on. Lionheart bucked again and threw in a backward kick, winning gleeful laughter from the crowd. Thrown up over his pony's ears, Gil glimpsed the knight's charger swerve and then slow to a canter, turning his head aside in disdain. *Now! Go for it!*

Lionheart's back flattened and he leapt again into his agile hill-pony gallop. Gil caught a look of amazement on the young knight's face, before his blunted lance whacked into the center of the crouching lion shield. With a startled shout, Sir Brandel's son somersaulted to the ground.

A roar of disapproval rose from his watching friends. Gil swung down to the ground to help his fallen opponent, but Garlon shouted, "No! Up! Run! They seek hostage!" Gil looked up and saw five of the boy's supporters mounting their chargers. He leapt into his saddle and struck out at a gallop, with a thundering pursuit on his heels.

Lionheart looked once over his shoulder and squealed in terror. *The ship! The ship!* Gil's eyes swept the horizon for some refuge, but only small clumps of trees broke the expanse of the tournament field. Then he heard Garlon again, shouting his name. He and the dark boy were balanced on top of the palisade, waving frantically. Beside them, Janetta pointed to her right. "The recess!" Garlon called. He gestured toward a gap in the palisade, a hundred yards ahead.

Gil set his eyes on the gap and drove Lionheart toward it. A black equine nose edged into view at his left. Another, grey, at his right. His ears were filled with conflicting shouts; his pursuers demanding he halt, his friends urging him on, and in his head, Lionheart crying *Home! Home! Home!*

A hand reached out and grabbed at Gil's reins. *My tree!* Lionheart begged. Gil flung his lance at the hand and hunched over Lionheart's neck as the pony scuttled through the gap in the list, into a walled enclosure cut off from the field.

Suddenly cheers erupted all around as Lionheart stumbled to a muddy, exhausted halt. Smiling faces looked down from the earthen bank, among them Allein and Garlon. Then Janetta was beside him, proudly clutching Lionheart's bridle and parading him triumphantly before the crowd.

Gil stared at the five angry faces of the knights, halted just outside his sanctuary. "It is the recess," Janetta said primly. "You cannot be followed. The rules forbid it." And to Gil's surprise, his five pursuers turned then, and rode away. Safe from pursuit, Gil walked Lionheart in cooling circles, rubbed him down with bunches of dried grass and left him tied beside the Hrolf's Isle pony, while he and Janetta enjoyed the sights of the tournament.

Beyond the cloth-roofed viewing stand, merchants had set up tented booths like at Hrafn's Ayre, selling nuts and apples and roasted meat, as well as glass beads and ribbons in the colors of the competing knights. An armorer displayed swords and mail, and safely distant from the tented booths, a blacksmith hammered a shoe for a charger, beside his white-hot fire.

Stern knights and noble ladies, boyish young esquires and clamoring children bargained with the vendors. Penitents, travelling to and from the pilgrim road, bought new, coarse-woven cloaks like Padraic Njalsson had worn, or replaced staffs and purses worn out on the long way home. A lean man, darkly tanned by southern suns, strode by on calloused feet, around his neck a silver badge. "Saint Peter's keys," Janetta whispered. "Barefoot, he has walked to Rome."

Gil bought roasted chestnuts and sausages from a Frankish-speaking vendor, bargaining with sign language and coins from Deer Bay. Then they stood together on the earthen bank, eating them greedily and watching the show.

Several more knights rode out to accept challengers, as Sir Brandel had done. Though more seemed content to watch and criticize, saving themselves for tomorrow's melee. When the last defender had vanquished his last challenger, the herald blew a note on his horn and a hush fell over the ground. Then, riding in pairs as they had paraded earlier, a dozen women came out onto the field. Now, as well as flower crowns, each bore a wreath of oak leaves and autumn roses, tied with a ribbon at the end of her lance.

'The Joust of the Ladies!' Janetta cried. She clasped her hands in delight at their dresses of jewel-toned velvets, their flower-trimmed shields, and the fluttering silks of headdresses and banners. "And are they not the most beautiful in any land!"

Gil grinned, looking down at her. "No," he said. "But they're okay, too. Do they really fight?" he asked Garlon, who had climbed up beside him, a fire-blackened sausage in each hand.

"It is only for show," Garlon said, munching. "They must claim from each other the flower wreaths. But they're never any good."

Gil watched a pair of young women turn at the end of the lists and bear down on each other in an authentic charge. "They can ride," he said.

Garlon shrugged. "The horses are well trained," he said, as the two closed, their lances aimed, tip to tip, at the swinging wreaths. Gil remembered Palamedes schooling him and Ismail with rings of straw held firmly in a mailed fist.

"She's got it!" Allein cried. One girl rode off, the other's flower ring slipping down her upraised lance. Flipping it off, she caught it and tied it by its broken ribbon to her pommel.

"*That* is hard," Gil said.

Garlon shrugged and ate another sausage.

"I have done it," Janetta said calmly. She didn't look at Garlon. "But my horse was well-trained." Gil grinned and Garlon stopped chewing, mid-sausage.

The winning lady, tall, with a serious face and honey-blond hair, took on another challenger and rode away with a second wreath adorning her saddle. One by one, she met opponents, and though she lost two wreaths, the rest were hers. "Set her against Sir Brandel," shouted a voice from the crowd. But, although Sir Brandel made cheerful pretense of mounting his charger, no other challenger appeared. A new wreath, golden with ripened wheat, was carried out and set on the lady's head: the winner's crown.

"She deserves it," Gil said.

Allein nodded.

"She is very good."

"But I am better," Janetta said, and smiling sweetly at their astonishment, she untied Lionheart and rode out onto the field. Cries of surprise greeted her, but the newly-crowned Queen of the Joust only smiled, and signaled to the herald for shield and lance for the new challenger. Janetta held a snorting Lionheart in check as a flower wreath was tied to the lance's tip. Then, with its fragile ribbon fluttering bravely, she cantered to the end of the list.

Even on Lionheart's modest back, she looked tiny, dwarfed by the outsized shield. But she hoisted the over-long lance with surprising ease and held her dancing pony with a steady hand. Lionheart jumped in the air at the herald's note and broke into a wild gallop. *Slow down!* Gil called to him, but Janetta urged him faster with hands and heels, and he flashed by the lady's charger in a pale buff blur. A moment's silence fell over the ground, and then the crowned champion turned, laughing, displaying her bare lance.

"Yes!" Gil shouted. Janetta raised the wreath in the air, showing her trophy to all, then, cantering by the list, tossed it to Garlon. He stood dumbly clutching the circlet of flowers as she returned to the joust.

The champion settled firmly in her saddle, her tanned chin jutting forward. But as the pony and its small agile rider swept by a second time, her lance was again plucked bare. She laughed in cheerful amazement, and ruefully adjusting her wheaten crown, returned to her end of the list. Allein caught the second wreath, held it high, and bowed to Janetta on the field.

On the third charge, the Jousting Queen sat bolt upright, and adding her full height to her charger's superior size, held the lance temptingly above her opponent's head. Janetta rose up in her stirrups, swaying wildly as the horses thundered together. Losing her balance as they met, she pitched onto Lionheart's neck. The crowd gasped and Gil closed his eyes. But when he opened them, Janetta was secure in her saddle again, and a third wreath dangled from her lance. Eyes shining, she galloped right up to him and threw her newest trophy into his hands.

The herald came forward to replace it, but the champion waved him away. Smiling graciously, she rode to Janetta's side, lifted the wheaten crown from her own sweat-dampened hair, and held it up for all to see. Then she leaned down, placed it gently on Janetta's head and, turning her charger, rode from the field.

At once, Janetta was surrounded by cheering supporters. Children gathered, offering Lionheart apples. Ladies tossed silk favors to Janetta. But her eyes sought only Gil, struggling to reach her through the crowd. Hemmed in by jostling horses and looming, good-natured knights, she strained to glimpse him, and then, scrambling up on one knee, she stood up on Lionheart's back, laughing and waving.

So thick was the press of the crowd, and so loud their cheers, that Gil never heard the drumming of approaching hooves, until horse and rider were almost upon them. With shouts of alarm, the throng burst apart. Children scattered, chargers reared, knights reached belatedly for swords. But Janetta stood frozen on Lionheart's back, her hand reaching yet to Gil, as the great black warhorse stormed past, its rider mail-clad and helm-shadowed, one gauntleted arm outstretched.

Janetta called Gil's name, just once, before the arm swept her from Lionheart's back, and up before the knight. In moments, they were gone, out across the field, flashing through stands of trees, and vanishing into the dark forest beyond.

CHAPTER EIGHTEEN

Suddenly alone, Lionheart whinnied in terror and bolted for Gil. Gil met him halfway and swung up into the saddle. "Wait for us!" Allein called. The two young knights ran to collect their chargers, but Gil only drove Lionheart harder for the forest. The drumming hoof beats were already fading, and when he reached the edge of the trees, all was silent.

"That way!" a young voice shouted from behind. Gil turned and saw the smiling face of Sir Brandel's son. The boy pointed to clods of loose turf kicked up by the fleeing charger. Gil grinned.

"Thank you!" He reined Lionheart toward the broken ground, and with the blond boy's mount on his pony's heels, plunged into the forest.

Gnarled oaks and dark firs shaded the woodland floor. Beyond, twin rows of beeches cast amber light on an ancient bridleway. Stirred and trodden leaves revealed the passage of the fugitive horse. Gil followed the trail at a gallop, and the old charger matched Lionheart's pace. Far behind, he heard Allein and Garlon shouting encouragement.

But then the trees grew closer, their branches lower, as the path narrowed. Small and agile, Lionheart outran the heavy chargers. Sir Brandel's son fell back and soon even the sound of following hoof beats faded. Ahead, the trail ended suddenly in a wall of glistening holly. Gil reined in his sweating mount and swung to the left of the barrier, but met a monstrous fallen trunk, wrapped in vines. "Other way," he muttered, and turned his pony to the right.

A faint pathway wound into the shadows. Lionheart's ears flicked back and his forelegs braced. *Go*, Gil said. *It has to be this way.* Lionheart shook his mane, bucked, and reared.

Horse.

Yes. We're following him. Go!

Lionheart reared again, and then, out of the forest stepped a horse as black as the shadows all around. On his back sat a huge knight in burnished mail, his faced masked by a chain *ventaille.* A black curling beard tumbled down his chest, and beneath his helm glinted eyes dark as night.

Gil whirled his terrified mount, and both pony and rider froze. A second knight blocked his retreat, his great white charger filling the narrow path. With sinking heart, Gil drew his sword.

"No!" The black bearded giant held out empty hands. "Put up your blade, my noble friend." Gil hesitated, and then the knight reached up and unhooked the chainmail veiling his face, revealing a huge white smile.

"Sir Palamedes," Gil gasped.

"Welcome!" The Saracen knight stretched his arms wide, "A hundred, thousand welcomes, Gil of Tir nan Og!"

Gil stared, and then slowly turned in his saddle to the rider on the white horse. His eyes fell upon the Green Tree of Caledon shield. "Lance'lot," he murmured, "Dad!"

The knight unhooked his *ventaille.* His face, so familiar and at once so strange, was lined and weary. But his eyes lit with joy. "Oh, Gil. I never thought I would see you, ever again." Swinging down from his saddle, he held out his arms. Gil slid from Lionheart, and ran, half laughing and half crying, into his father's embrace.

The big white charger shook its mane and snorted. "It's you!" Gil cried. The monkish plough horse that had carried him through the Forest of Caledon pushed forward and pressed its nose against Gil's chest. Gil rested his head against its warm forelock and then looked up at the sound of distant hooves. Coming to his senses, he turned to mount Lionheart again. "They've taken Janetta," he cried. "Help me!"

Palamedes rested his mailed hand on Gil's shoulder. "Have no fear," he smiled, "She is safe."

Gil shook his head, but Lance'lot said quietly, "She is with us, Gil." He sighed. "Forgive us, but there was no other way. Guidbairn was on the field. We had to take her, before she was seen."

"Guidbairn," Gil murmured, feeling sick.

"He came with his retinue from Mont Tombe. He would ride in the melee tomorrow. He wished, like any knight, to see the ground."

"But the knight who took her ...."

"Her father," said Palamedes.

Gil's cry of protest was cut short by a crashing of branches as Sir Brandel's son burst into their midst. He reined his charger to a halt and stared open-mouthed at Gil's companions. "Sir Lance'lot," he whispered. He slid from his saddle and bowed his head. Then he looked up and cried, "But it is not safe!"

Gil's father smiled and held his hand out to the boy. "It is safe, Briant. I am well hidden and well protected." He whistled, then and a dozen armed knights stepped from the forest as if the trees themselves had come to life. Some young, some old, clad in the gartered trousers and long tunics of the Franks, or the plaids of Caledon, they stood in a silent, watching circle.

A moment later, Garlon and Allein galloped out of the forest, and with shouts of alarm, reached for their swords. "No!" Gil cried.

"It is Lance'lot," the boy, Briant, called, "My father's friend."

"And friend to your father, too, Allein. From old, in Caledon." Palamedes bowed solemnly. "How fares that noble knight?"

Allein hung his head. "Pitifully, sir. He is a prisoner. I ride tomorrow for his ransom."

"Then he is blessed," Lance'lot said, "prisoner or not, to have such a son." He smiled gently at the dark boy. "The lady you seek is safe in our care. You must go now," his gaze took in all three young knights. "Rest and prepare. The day will be long." Allein looked at Gil.

"It's okay," Gil said, with a wary glance at his father. "I'll see you tomorrow at the tournament."

"We'll come for you at Lauds, and we'll ride together!" Garlon grinned and raised a bold fist. "And we will win ransoms enough to buy a kingdom!" He turned with the same bold look to Lance'lot. "Will we see you there?"

Lance'lot laughed. "We may be there, but you will not see us." He watched the boys go and then turned to Gil. "Come," he said as he mounted the white horse, "Your lady waits for you." Escorted by Palamedes and the guard of knights on foot, he led Gil and Lionheart into the forest.

Lionheart whinnied suddenly. Gil smelled wood smoke in the air and through a break in the trees glimpsed a pavilion of un-dyed cloth, a fire burning brightly before it. Were it not for a line of tethered chargers, it might have been a pilgrims' camp.

A burly, red-faced knight, his forehead yet creased from the helm he turned clumsily in his hands, faced a tall woman over the fire. A small child, clutching a wooden sword, tugged at his tunic for attention, but the man's pleading eyes never left the woman's face. She glared at him fiercely, her arms around a weeping girl.

"Janetta!" Gil cried.

She looked up from within the curtain of the woman's golden hair and her tear-stained face brightened joyously, "Gil!" She pulled away from the gentle embrace and ran toward him, but the man caught her around the waist.

Gil jumped down from Lionheart. "Let her go!"

Pinned by the knight's arms, she reached out to Gil. "I am his!" she cried to her captor. "He is my lover. I have given him my honor and I am worthless to any other!"

The red-faced knight's eyes fell on Gil, widening with fury. "Is this true?"

"Yes!" Gil glared back.

"You see!" Janetta cried.

"Gil." Lance'lot spoke softly from behind. "Is this true?" Gil felt the weight of a mailed hand on his shoulder. He turned and his eyes met his father's. "Is it true?" Lance'lot repeated.

Slowly, Gil shook his head. Then he raised his gaze to the angry knight. "But I wish it was!" he shouted.

"And I!" Janetta cried. Kicking and biting, she wriggled around, broke free, and fled to Gil. Safe in his arms, she turned bitter eyes on her captor.

The man stared at her, mournfully rubbing his bitten wrist.

"Do not run from me, daughter," he said quietly. "I would sooner see my soul in Hell, than return you to Jocelyn Guidbairn." He sighed. "I was all the fool my lady, Ingirid, said and more." He nodded to the blonde woman.

The child dropped his toy sword and ran suddenly to Janetta's father and wrapped small arms around his legs. The knight rested a gentle hand on his head. "I thought to win bread for our mouths and a roof over our heads. Instead, I have lost home and hearth, my lands, and now my daughter, too." He reached tentative fingers toward her then dropped his hand and shook his head. "I am Martin de Troye," he said then, to Gil. "Father to the lady who shows you such devotion." He held out his hand again. "Come, daughter. You, also," he said to Gil. "Neither need fear me."

Warily, Janetta released her desperate grip and, stepping away from Gil, approached her father. Gil followed and when both were standing before him, Martin de Troye bowed slightly to Gil. "I thank you for worthily protecting my daughter. I do not ask for a better suitor. But she is young." He sighed again. "Will you come home to us, child? Your brother misses your games. He stroked the boy's curly head and the child grinned shyly. "And your good stepmother, Ingirid, weeps at night for you. As do I," he whispered.

Janetta looked at Gil and then at her father. When her gaze shifted to her stepmother, tears brightened her eyes. But Ingirid smiled and shook her head. "No," she said. "They must make their own way, now. They are young, indeed, but the world is theirs." Janetta nodded joyfully and slipped back into Gil's arms. He rested his chin on her hair, too happy to speak.

Martin de Troye called then for wine, and silver cups were filled and set on the forest floor. They settled around the fire, with the silent guardian knights in a circle, facing outward toward the surrounding trees. Gil told his father all that had happened since they parted at the Linn of the Rainbow Bridge; his arrival amid the ruins of Cille Aidan, his capture and delivery to Floki at Hrolf's Isle, his apprenticeship as helmsman, and the long pursuit of the hostages. But he kept to himself the story of the knarr, saying only how he hoped to raise silver to match Floki's, tomorrow, at the tournament.

"And how is that noble Viking?" Lance'lot smiled.

Gil looked into the fire. "The same as always," he said.

Lance'lot raised an eyebrow, but before he could question more, Sir Palamedes spoke from across the fire. "The hour grows late," he said. "The forest is not safe at night."

"Night!" Gil looked up. Golden light slanted in long shafts through the ancient trees. The sun was setting, and twilights here were briefer than in the Northlands. He jumped to his feet, reaching his hand to Janetta. "We have to go. The tide …."

They made their farewells; she, tearfully, he, restless to be moving. Lance'lot walked with them to the edge of the clearing, where Lionheart grazed happily. He kept his hand on Gil's shoulder and talked in an urgent, low voice of the day to come, as if he could teach all his skills in the few moments remaining.

He helped saddle the pony and when Gil was seated on Lionheart's back, with Janetta astride behind him, he looked up and said solemnly, "The tournament is play, Gil, until someone chooses to make it war. Beware the sheltered copses, the hidden ditches, any place beyond the sight of the many. There, vengeance is wrought, scores settled. There, men are killed."

Gil nodded. "I'll be careful."

"Yes." Lance'lot looked back to the distant campfire and then said quietly, "Your mother, Gil? You saw her?"

Gil nodded again. "She doesn't believe me. She says you're dead."

Lance'lot closed his eyes briefly and then looked up once more. "That is so, Gil. I am. He reached inside his padded hauberk, drew out a stained leather purse, and took from it a small, white stone, hollow in the center. He held it out to Gil.

"A seeing stone," Gil murmured, taking it. "It's the Golden Knight's! From Merlin's Tower."

"It's Merlin's," Lance'lot corrected him. "Merlin's key to the Rainbow Bridge. I shall not return to that world, Gil. But one day, you shall. Take this, and when that day comes, may it take you safely there." He stepped back and raised his hand in a salute as Gil turned Lionheart and rode away.

The forest was dark and forbidding already, the arched

avenue of beech trees shutting out the sky. Lionheart trotted
eagerly to the distant tournament field, lit yet by the last rays
of the sun. When they reached the deserted viewing stand,
the merchants were gathered around their cooking fires. The
Hrolf's Isle pony, tethered alone by the chestnut vendor's booth,
whickered an eager greeting. Gil untied it, and Janetta slipped
from Lionheart's back to its saddle, and they set out at a gallop
for the shore. The track through the marshes was deserted now,
and they made good speed. But the sun was down when they
reached the strand.

Dark against a dusky sky, Mont Tombe floated above a bank
of mist. Between the island and the shore, the golden sands
of the tide flats were, once again, a stretch of shining sea. Gil
turned Lionheart's head hurriedly toward the light of Floki's
campfire, across the bay.

The twin lines of hoof prints that marked their morning
passage across the sands, ended, midway to the far shore, in
rippling waves. "It's shallow still," Gil said, "We'll make it if
we're quick." And with Janetta riding at his heels, he urged
Lionheart down onto the sands.

As soon as they left the shore, the mist was all around
them. Land and water blended in the eerie light. Rivulets of
encroaching tide wound on either side, and in the thickening
murk, Gil struggled to guide Lionheart amidst them. He heard
a splash and a shout behind and whirled to see Janetta urging
her pony up out of a swirling tide pool that grew as he watched.
The sand at its edge crumbled and liquefied, dragging at the
frightened pony's legs. With a squeal of terror, it clambered
out, pushing up against Lionheart for comfort. Gil turned
and grasped its bridle, lest they be separated again, and drove
Lionheart on.

They came to a rushing inlet and crossed it with the icy
water up to the animals' bellies. The next was even deeper and
for a chilling moment, Gil felt Lionheart swimming beneath
him. The third inlet was a raging river. "Where?" Janetta cried.
Gil looked behind. Water swept over their tracks. To left and
right smaller streams ran. They were on an island, and the
island was shrinking as he watched.

Around them, fog combined with nightfall to wrap the tide flats in darkness. The fire of the Northmen's camp faded to a pinpoint of light. Gil fixed his eyes on it, wishing for the compass he'd given Floki long ago. Then a tongue of windswept mist wrapped itself around them and the light vanished.

"Come on," he murmured, "We have to cross this. There's no other way." Lionheart reared. Gil kicked him hard. *Don't argue with me. There isn't time.* Shaking his drenched mane, Lionheart snorted and plunged in, the Hrolf's Isle pony skidding stiff-legged after. Freezing water swirled around Gil's saddle. Janetta gasped behind him. He turned and saw her white face as she clung on, light as a leaf in the torrent.

Lionheart, his hooves barely touching the bottom, swerved sharply to the right. *No.* Gil cried. Lionheart whinnied.

He's there. He's there.

Then Gil, too, heard, over the rush of the sea, a voice calling "Warrior!"

"Floki," Janetta whispered.

"We're here!" Gil shouted. Lionheart whinnied again and an answering whinny came from the right. A dim shape of horse and rider emerged from the cloud bank and then suddenly Floki was beside them. Without speaking, he lifted Janetta from her pony, up before him, on his. Then, with one arm clasping her tight, he caught the pony's reins and Lionheart's, too, and looped them around his saddle pommel. With the animals in a tight cluster, he rode into the sea.

In moments, all three were swimming. Gil clung to Lionheart's neck as his body floated from the saddle. He began to swim, with one arm, as hooves churned all around him. Floki half-turned to help, but Gil gasped, "No. You've got enough. Save her." He went under and lost his grip on Lionheart's mane. Reaching out wildly, his fingers caught the high cantle of the jousting saddle. "Last chance," he muttered, even as his grip on the slippery leather failed.

And then suddenly there was mud in his face as Lionheart's kicking hooves touched ground. He hauled himself up, half-swimming, into the saddle. Beside him Floki was urging his mount toward the shore, where the light of the fire was bright again. Dark figures clustered on the strand, beside the hulls of the beached ships.

Snorting with terror and relief, the animals clambered up out of the sea and splashed through the last of the tide flats to the grassy bank. Gil slipped from Lionheart's back and fell to his knees on the sweet dry grass. Then a huge hand caught his tunic and dragged him upright. "Ho! My fish!"

"Thanks Bjorn." Gil grinned weakly, then ran to catch Floki, who strode toward the fire, carrying Janetta in his arms.

Grimhildr barged to the front. "I take her." Snatching Janetta from Floki, she glared at him as if he were as much at fault as Gil. Then she wrapped Janetta in her warm cloak and hastened her to the fire. Gil started to follow, but a hand, fiercer and less friendly than Bjorn's, caught his drenched hair and jerked his head back.

"And you," Floki growled. He took a cloak offered by Ulf and slammed it against Gil's chest. "Change your clothes. There. By the fire. The women will not see. And if they do, they'll only laugh." He half released him, and then tightened his grip and whispered, "If I wish you to drown, I drown you. You are not permitted to drown yourself." He gave Gil a hearty shove toward the fire and stalked off.

CHAPTER NINETEEN

Garlon and Allein came for Gil at first light, their chargers' legs wet from the falling tide. Garlon raised his hand in a happy salute. Gil, rolling his sleeping fur at the edge of the camp, touched a finger to his lips and quickly signaled them to join him. The horses' shod hooves rang on the shingle above the tide line. Gil looked warily to the river mouth where Floki stood talking with a Frankish man, who had beached his fishing skiff on the strand. "Quiet," he whispered, as the young knights joined him. "I'll get Lionheart." He glanced again at the two men at the water's edge, and then crept away to the grazing ponies.

He had avoided the earl since their return, snatching his supper amid a crowd of Northmen and retreating to eat it far from the fire. He made his bed up alone, in the shadow of the sand bluff. When Ciarnan and Ragi joined him, full of curiosity, he recounted his adventures in the forest in a whisper.

Gil had Lionheart armored and saddled, and was riding him surreptitiously behind the beached ships, when Floki saw him. Floki turned from the fisherman and strode, head down, back to the camp. Gil wheeled Lionheart defiantly to face the Northman. But Floki greeted him with a cheerful smile. "Behold! Our knights return." His eyes swept the pair. Allein ducked his head. Garlon grinned. "And what seek you here, in a Viking's camp?"

Garlon's grin broadened. "By Vespers we will be knights indeed. And so will he," he pointed cheerfully at Gil. "We ride together in the tournament."

Floki looked at Gil. "I see only a Viking's helmsman, with a hill pony from Einar's Holm. What use has he of tournaments?"

Garlon seemed less certain, but Allein raised his eyes to meet Floki's. "Please, good sir. He rides well in the Vespers."

"Yes," Floki said. "So well that he forgets time, duty, and the sea. To be a knight, he fails as a helmsman. I see no gain in that."

"But there's more!" Gil burst out. Lionheart jumped and he reined him in a dancing circle. Floki reached out and caught the pony's bridle.

"And you be quiet," he whispered, drawing the animal's head close. Then he looked up at Gil. "What more, and of such import, that it is worth drowning yourself and the girl I entrusted to your care?"

Gil bit back a treacherous flare of anger. "I met my father," he said. "And Sir Palamedes. And Janetta's father, too. He caught her and rode into the forest. I had to follow."

Floki's cold eyes took on a brief amused sparkle. "Into the arms of an outraged father. That was bold, Warrior."

Gil shrugged. "It would have been if I knew who he was. Anyhow, he's changed sides."

Floki smiled. "Or so he says. And your own good father? For whom does he ride, now?"

"For Arthur!" Garlon shouted.

Floki waved him, silent. "And Palamedes, Warrior?"

"You know the answer to that," Gil said coldly. "Traitors don't sleep in the Forest, do they?"

"No," Floki agreed. "And, fools that they are, they are not traitors. Well, they may stay in the Forest in knightly foolishness, helmsman. You and I have work to do."

"Today?" Gil cried. He looked at the young riders in despair. A small crowd of sleepy Northmen had gathered. Ciarnan and Ragi stood watching uneasily. Ulf, returning from the spring with a leather bucket filled with water, paused, too. "But we're riding in the melee, today," Gil said. "I promised them ...." He trailed off, flinching away from the ice in Floki's eyes. He saw Ulf quietly shaking his head.

"Helmsman," Floki's voice dropped again to a whisper. "Your time is not your own. You make no promises without my word. And this promise," he looked squarely at Garlon and Allein, "Is broken. Go."

Allein turned his horse. Garlon sat stubbornly on his. "I am not your servant," he said. "I am a knight."

In a flash of dawn light, Floki's sword tip was resting beneath Garlon's chin. "A dead knight and a live one are all the same to me."

Garlon shrank back and with a quick, angry shout, turned his charger and galloped out of the camp. Floki sheathed the sword, reached up casually, and with one hand hauled Gil off Lionheart, and walked away. Staggering back to his feet, Gil raced after him. But another hand closed on the neck of his tunic and Ulf's patient voice murmured in his ear, "At this moment, a dead helmsman and a live one are the same to him as well."

"I don't care!" Gil shouted.

Floki whirled. "Warrior," he whispered, "Had I less need of you, I would send you to join your foolish father and be done." He raised a hand toward the misty tide flats. "More men have died in those sands than in all the tournaments of Francia. You do not cross again." Ignoring the fury on Gil's face, he nodded calmly, then, and said, "Come."

Ulf shoved Gil from behind. "And keep your mouth shut."

Gil walked with stiff, angry steps behind the earl until they stood in the shadow of *Silver Dragon's* hull. Floki stretched up and laid his hand on the weathered wood and picked at a small white crust, until it broke free. Setting it on his palm, he held it out to Gil. "Warrior, what do you see?"

Gil shrugged. "A barnacle?" he muttered.

"Yes." Floki looked sourly at it. "There is a little animal inside. It makes this shell. And those." He gestured down the length of the barnacle-speckled hull. "They are many, these small animals, and I do not like them. They make my *Dragon* slow." He narrowed his eyes, squinting down the curving strakes. "And they do not look pretty." He slapped the barnacle into Gil's hand. "Take them off." He turned toward the small circle of watching Northmen. "Ulf will show you how."

Silently, Ulf drew his knife and scraped it along a strake,

prying a cluster of shells free. He stepped back and Floki nodded to Gil. "Begin."

"Now?" Gil cried with a desperate glance to the distant tournament pavilions.

"Of course, now. Would you prefer a day in the midst of the sea?"

Ulf handed Gil the knife and stood back. But Erling, still half-dressed from washing at the spring, suddenly protested, "That is slaves' work, Floki. It is not right for a helmsman."

Floki nodded thoughtfully. "A slave may become a helmsman. Or a helmsman, a slave. It is not a matter of rank, but of knowledge. While he works, he will think. And when he is done," he slapped the hull and smiled at Gil, "he will remember that a helmsman does not forget the sea. I do him a courtesy, Erling Maiden-Face. And now I do you one, also." He smiled pleasantly, but his eyes were cold. "Take charge of my camp while I am away. And do not cross me again."

Erling rubbed his beard and looked aside. "Where do you go?" he asked then.

Floki turned toward the man with the fishing skiff, waiting yet on the strand. "I have found a ferryman to take me to Mont Tombe. I will learn a little of this fortress."

Erling nodded solemnly. Ulf said, "Do not be seen. A warrior's fame is also his burden. You are known."

"Of course I am known. I am Floki Magnusson." Floki laughed and gave Gil's shoulder a companionable shove. Gil fought the urge to return it with a punch. "I will not be seen," Floki said. He called to Gil, "Make her beautiful by sunset, Warrior, for so she deserves."

Fist clenched around Ulf's knife, Gil watched the skiff sail into the dawn. Then he turned to unsaddle Lionheart before he began his task. Ragi and Ciarnan were standing either side of the pony, holding the reins. Gil reached for the bridle, but Ragi shook his head and offered him a leg-up to the saddle, instead. "If you're quick, you will catch them still."

"But the ship!"

"We'll do it," Ciarnan extended his hand for Ulf's knife.

Gil grinned slowly. But he hesitated, his gaze shifting warily between the fisherman's sail and the beached longship. "You sure? He might be pretty mad."

"There's two of us," Ragi said. "We'll be done before he gets back."

Gil's grin broadened. "Thank you!" he cried gleefully. "Thank you so much. I'll pay you back somehow, I promise. I'll get my armor and tell Janetta." He glanced up at the girls' shipboard tent, where Janetta remained under Grimhildr's guard. "I'll be right back."

He raced to the ship but skidded to a halt. Grimhildr knelt at the foot of the gangplank, kneading dough on a flat stone. Beside her, Percy copied her with his own ball of barley meal. Grimhildr looked up and saw Gil. Casually, she drew one of her two throwing axes, slammed it into the wood of the gangplank, and returned to her bread dough.

"Okay," Gil muttered. "I've got the idea." He met Percy's wide-eyed gaze and silently jerked his chin aside, beckoning hopefully. Percy shook his head.

"Floki says I have to stay right here!" He pointed to a patch of sand a foot from Grimhildr's skirt. "By Grimhildr." Grimhildr cast him another stony glare and laid a hand on her second axe.

But then Rachel appeared, braiding her hair at the door of the black tent, and he waved frantically. She fastened the braid and came down the gangplank, stepping delicately around Grimhildr's axe, and joined him on the sand. He led her away out of earshot and whispered, "Tell Janetta for me that I'm riding in the tournament, okay?" he glanced up at the tent. "I can't get near her. Grimhildr's like some kind of guard dog."

"What about your barnacles?"

"Ragi and Ciarnan are doing them." She raised her eyebrows. "They offered," Gil said.

"Then they're as stupid as you. You never learn, do you?"

"Not if learning means being Floki's slave." She raised her eyebrows again. "He needs me, Rachel," he said stubbornly.

"Not that much." She gave him a cool smile and then waved her slender hand toward Mont Tombe, golden in the early sun. "And once he has Hakon, he won't need you at all."

"Well, I'm helping him get Hakon. And Danni and Ismail,

too. I'm riding in this tournament and he'll be glad I did."

Rachel shrugged and then suddenly smiled. "What I like about you, Gil, is your modesty. I'll tell Janetta," she said.

He nodded happily. "And while you're up there ...."

"Your mail and your helm?" she grinned.

"And my lance. Please."

The heralds were calling the knights into the lists, when Gil reached the tournament ground. The field itself was barely visible through the crush of boys and men gathered on the earthen banks. Cut flowers, piled all along the lists, were gathered by children and tossed onto the passing horsemen below. The red and blue pennants of the herald's men dipped and soared above, like dragon flies.

"Where do I go?" Gil murmured. Lionheart reared and rolled a fearful eye in response. Gil strained up in the saddle, seeking a glimpse of a familiar face. But all around were hundreds of strangers.

The viewing stand, hung now with tapestries like a lord's hall, was crowded with ladies in jewel-toned dresses and fur-bordered cloaks. Knights paraded past, their horses' trappings fluttering boldly, as favors were thrown to ornament helms. Gil turned Lionheart in a ring, feeling the pony trembling beneath him with the same lost uncertainty he felt himself. *Home!* Lionheart pleaded. *The ship!*

Gil grinned. *Next time you've got all four feet rooted to the foot of the gangplank, I'll remind you of that.*

He urged the pony forward, worming a path through the jostling chargers to the tree Garlon had climbed. Beneath it, the chestnut seller's booth was surrounded by new stalls selling jewelry and leatherwork and furs, like at Deer Bay. Gil sniffed the sweet charcoal smell, hungrily aware he had missed breakfast. He reached into his purse for coins, but suddenly a mailed hand closed on his shoulder. "My friend!"

Gil whirled. Garlon's happy face loomed over him as his big charger nudged Lionheart sideways. Lionheart bared his teeth but Gil snapped the reins, grinning back at the young knight. "I couldn't find you."

"How do you escape the earl?" Allein cried, driving his mount in at Lionheart's other side.

Gil's grin weakened. "Tell you later. Where do we go?"

"To the lists." Garlon grabbed Lionheart's bridle, winning a snort of indignation. "Come! It is time!" Three abreast, they cantered through the gap in the earthen banks, and onto the field. There, the chaos of the audience was magnified ten-fold. Knights cantered back and forth, stretching their chargers' legs. Others, dismounted, stood adjusting stirrups and bridles. The herald's men galloped in circles, their shouts barely heard above the beating of drums, the neighing of horses, and the high, pure notes of the horn.

In the midst of all, a small, stout man sat on a grey charger with the authority of a king: the herald. With brief snaps of his fingers, or bursts on his horn, he captured the attention of one and another cluster of knights, directing them to positions on the field. Before Gil's eyes, the chaos formed itself into two long, wavering lines at opposite ends of the lists.

The horn blew and the pointing finger was suddenly aimed at Gil's chest. "What now?" Gil gasped.

"Choose your side," Allein said.

"I choose ...?"

"Or he will," said Garlon. He shrugged. "It matters little. It must be made to look even at the first charge, so the heralds divide us. After that, it is each for himself." He shrugged again. "Red or Blue?" But he paused, then, as a sudden hush fell over the field.

Three knights appeared from the far side of the tournament ground, riding through a gap in the distant earth bank. Several dozen armored men rode in ranks, a respectful distance behind. Their supporters were a blur of bright colors and pale faces along the lists, their excited shouts a buzz like angry bees. But as the three leaders rode closer, both sides fell silent.

The central rider was tall and imposing, his armor and helm glittering with gold. From his upraised lance, a golden banner rippled and snapped in the brisk sea wind. "Guidbairn," Gil whispered. In an instant, he was in the Forest of Caledon, riding for his life beneath the Northern Lights. He felt his hands shaking on the reins and fought to still them before the pony panicked, too.

"The new king," Garlon said quietly.

"No," Allein answered. "Though he name himself one, he has not the soul of a king."

Garlon laughed and unsheathed his sword. "Here is a king's soul!" he cried. "Come. He rides with Red. Let us join him."

Gil shook his head. "I won't ride with him. King or not."

"Better than riding against him," Garlon said. "For his side will surely win, and with them, we take more hostages." But Allein, too, held back.

"He has no honor."

Garlon shrugged. "I ride for silver. When I am rich, I will be Lady Honor's knight."

But then Gil held up his lance to the herald seeking riders for Blue and rode out at his command. Allein cantered to join him, and with ill-grace, Garlon followed. Shoulder to shoulder, they took up their places in the long, jostling line of knights, and turned to face their opponents. Far down the field, a solid wall of men on horseback waited, shields raised and lances held high. The herald's horn fell silent. Suddenly there was no sound but the uneasy creak of leather, the nervous jingle of a bridle. Lionheart blew through his nose and pawed the ground, ears flat against his head.

It's just a play fight, Gil said. *A game.* Lionheart wrinkled his furry lip and showed his teeth to Garlon's charger. *And he's on our side.*

Garlon grinned at the force arrayed against them, beneath its cloud of glittering lance points. "This is what war feels like," he said. Gaily, he punched the air.

Gil gave him a stiff nod. But his gaze sought the golden banner and his mind could think of nothing but the piercing blue eyes beneath the golden helm, tormenting him in Merlin's Tower. "Just a game," he whispered, as the herald blew the charge.

Suddenly, the air was filled with a deafening rumble of galloping hooves, the rattle of chain, and the shouts of comrades. Swept up in the excitement, Lionheart hit his gallop before

Gil's heels touched his flanks. Choking on dust, Gil ducked clods of earth flung up by the heels of the leading horses and peered through the murk at the rapidly closing gap between the lines. Around him, the tight formation fragmented as each man sought out a target. Gil's eyes fell on a lean brown horse, trapped in yellow, whose rider hunched warily behind a yellow shield. "Young. New at it," he muttered. "Like me."

And then they were five strides apart and nothing existed but Lionheart's bobbing head and beyond, the brown horse and the yellow shield. *Go for it!* He cried, inside, but Lionheart was already stretched in his wild pony leap. Gil's lance struck the shield so hard that his own arm went numb. Two yellow halves spun to the ground. The young rider's stunned face swept by and his swaying lance grazed Gil's mailed shoulder. And then they were gone.

Gil whirled Lionheart, but the lines of the charge had disintegrated into a chaos of men and horses, milling in the dust. Small factions lined up for a second charge. Others galloped after rider-less horses, worth a hefty purse of silver. Gil saw Garlon and Allein pursuing a disarmed opponent like hounds after a hare.

He turned Lionheart again and confronted a pack of unseated knights, fighting on foot, dragging mounted opponents from their saddles. A man in a ragged linen undercoat reached for Gil's stirrup, but Lionheart's quick teeth sank into his poorly protected arm. Howling outrage, he brought a fist down hard on the pony's nose.

Lionheart squealed and before Gil could reach for his sword, his shaggy charger was galloping for open ground. *The ship! The ship! Home!*

Gil hauled on the reins. *Stop! We're not finished!*

He hit me!

You bit him! But Lionheart wasn't listening and not for the first time Gil realized he was no match in strength for a hill pony determined to run.

The battling knights were far behind when Gil regained control. Lionheart slowed to a trot and then a walk. Then he lowered his head and began to graze. Gil jerked the reins. *I'm supposed to be raising ransoms. Not taking you for a stroll. And it's not lunchtime.* Lionheart munched an unfinished mouthful. Gil looked around.

They were nearly at the edge of the forest, in a little dip in the field, where a stream ran through a small stand of willow. The autumn sun shone and dry grasses swayed. But for the distant shouts and ringing steel of the melee, the tournament might not exist.

Beware the sheltered copses, the hidden ditches ... beyond the sight of the many. Gil shivered, his eyes on the dark forest. But it was from the sun-dappled willow that the charge came. Three knights burst from the green shadows. Two, in the lead, spread out to cut off Gil's escape. The third, helm and mail bright gold as the sun, lowered his lance with slow purpose and aimed it at Gil's heart. *There, vengeance is wrought. There, men are killed.* Gil looked wildly to either side, but there was no way out. Gathering the reins of his terrified pony, he faced the Golden Knight.

Guidbairn's lance cracked against his shield, splintering the rim and tearing the leather loop from the wood. The shield flew from his arm. Gil whirled his mount and again sought escape. But Guidbairn's two outriders blocked him, left and right. "Take him for ransom!" one shouted. "*His* father will pay with more than gold!"

But Guidbairn unhooked his ventaille, revealing his handsome, blond-bearded face, and shook his head. "It is early in the day to be burdened with a hostage, is it not, my friend?" He smiled at Gil. "It would spoil the game." He turned back to his knights. "Go," he said. "Leave us to our sport."

They nodded solemnly and backed their horses away. Turning them suddenly, they galloped for the distant lists. Guidbairn returned his vivid blue gaze to Gil. "There are rules. Courtesies. It appears as chaos, but it is well ordered. Still, the tournament is not welcome in the towns or near the churches. Only at the borders where law is a threadbare thing. It is, at its heart, an outlaw's game." He smiled again, as if his only interest in Gil was conversation. "Sometimes, I think I would see you reach your manhood. Why do you imagine that to be?"

"It would be fairer," Gil murmured. "I might win."

"Fairer!" Guidbairn threw back his head and laughed. "No, my friend. For every year that your body grows taller and stronger, your power against me diminishes. You will compromise. You will cheat and betray. You will become like all men, determined to live at any cost. Now, just now, you might yet defeat me. That is the glory of youth. Which is why I will kill you, now." He snapped the ventaille in place and settled his helm. "Do not regret your shield. Without it, you will die more readily. Which, I assure you, you will prefer."

He spun his great charger and galloped toward the forest and then spun it again and drew it to a halt. Horse and rider froze motionless, like statues of steel. "At your command," called the Golden Knight.

Gil turned his trembling pony once more. He thought of Janetta. He thought of his ship. He thought of the white sands of the Holy Isle, in the clean, cold North. Then he lowered his lance and shouted, "The Field!"

The charger and Lionheart leapt as one. Before Gil drew a breath, the distance between them halved. Guidbairn sat firm as a rock, his shield held close to his saddle. Gil's eyes sought some chink in the knight's defense, but every inch of his body was clad in mail, glittering with gold overlay. "It's heavy," Gil murmured. "Get him off his horse. He'll be slow."

With the charger a stride away, Gil ducked flat on Lionheart's mane. Steel flashed over his head as the big warhorse stormed past. Gil grinned triumphantly over his shoulder. But the charger spun, swift as a cat, and its rider again lowered his deadly lance. Gil swung upright and turned Lionheart. "Right, Floki," he muttered. "*That* didn't work. What now?"

The Knight lunged into his second charge, the air shaking with the thunder of hooves. Gil hunched low and aimed his lance for his opponent's thigh, where; between hauberk and chain chausses; might lie unguarded flesh. But the steel point never reached its target. Something struck Gil's right arm, like fire, and the lance fell, tumbling beneath Lionheart's feet.

Blood sullied Lionheart's buff neck. Gil reached forward in alarm, but the flash of pain in his arm, between hauberk and gauntlet, told him the blood was not the pony's, but his own.

The cuff of his linen undercoat turned red. Sickness ran up his throat. He forced it down and, swaying in his saddle, turned to the sound of charging hooves.

Lionheart squealed and reared. Pulling against Gil's weakening grip, he shimmied sideways. *Face him,* Gil cried, reaching for his sword. But then he saw what Lionheart saw and an instant later, Guidbairn's horse saw it too. A grey shadow streaked from the willow copse, shaggy as a bear and half the height of a horse. In three bounding strides, it reached the knight's panicking charger and leapt, slamming into its haunch and sinking gleaming teeth into the cantle of Guidbairn's saddle.

"The wolfhound!" Gil cried, exulting at the sight of the great grey dog he had seen, first, hunting in Caledon beside the Golden Knight, and last, at the Linn of the Rainbow Bridge, transformed into Lance'lot. "The Change-Thing. Dad's Change-Thing!"

Guidbairn turned to draw his sword, but the beast's jaws closed on his arm, dragging him from the saddle. Overbalanced by his heavy armor, he plunged to the ground. His foot, snagged in its stirrup, dragged the rearing charger down until it crashed to the ground beside him.

Soaring over the downed knight, the wolfhound bounded to Gil. Lionheart backed away, eyes wild. Gil slapped his neck with the reins. *He's on our side. Follow him!* For even as the Knight struggled with his panicked mount, the wolfhound was streaking toward the lists, leading Gil to the safety of the melee.

They crested a rise in the gently rolling ground and suddenly they were again in the midst of the tournament. Packs of knights pursued lone riders. Others fought chaotic skirmishes with friend as well as foe. A smiling lad led a string of captured chargers toward a recess. Then, out of a tall stand of marsh grass burst a determined young rider, with three more on his heels. "Turn him!" a voice shouted to Gil. "He's Sir Danane's nephew. A worthy hostage!"

"Garlon!" Gil cried happily.

"Where do you go?" Allein called. "Look, we find Briant!" Sir Brandel's blond son raised his lance and smiled.

"Join us," Garlon called. "We share the ransom. All four."

Gil turned in his saddle, seeking the wolfhound. Where the

grassy meadow joined the forest, he glimpsed a grey, shaggy back slipping into the trees. He looked down at his reddened sleeve and back to his smiling companions. Were it not for the pain, the whole terrifying encounter might have been a dream.

"You are hurt," Briant called. He rode closer and gestured to Gil's arm.

Gil grinned shakily. "Met someone who doesn't like me." Garlon gave the arm a brief glance and turned back to the pursuit of Sir Danane's nephew.

"I bind it for you," Briant reached to help.

Gil shrugged and twisted the bloody linen sleeve tight and tucked it under the mail. "Let's get him," he said. Briant grinned and together they rode back onto the field.

They caught the boy a hundred yards from the willow copse where Gil had fought the Golden Knight. His horse plunged down into the stream bed, and finding itself blocked by a steep sand bank, baulked and reared. The young rider turned it to face his pursuers and gave a sheepish shrug.

"You are hostage!" Allein cried. He galloped down into the water and caught the charger's reins. But Garlon held his own mount back, and sat, unmoving, on the grassy bank above. He nodded to Sir Danane's nephew and then to Allein.

"Let him go," he said.

Allein shook his head, but Garlon said, louder, "I tell you, let him go." With an uncertain glance at Gil, Allein released the reins. Sir Danane's nephew rode up out of the stream and turned his horse so that he and Garlon sat side by side. Garlon gestured with his chin for Allein to join them. Warily, Allein brought his horse into line. "And you," Garlon said to Gil.

"Why?" Gil gave Briant a bewildered glance. The blond boy sat on his tall, old charger with stoical calm. "What are we doing?" Gil said.

Garlon smiled. "Sir Danane," he said, "Is a mighty knight. But a poor one. But Sir Brandel," his eyes lit as he turned to Briant, "he is both mighty and rich." He looked back at Gil. "Who now will pay the higher ransom?"

"Brandel!" cried the captured boy. He grinned at Briant and drew a pretend sword across his throat.

"But he rode with us!" Gil protested. "And yesterday he helped me rescue Janetta. He's my friend!"

Over his shoulder, Briant said quietly, "There are no friends in tournament." He smiled at Gil with the same calm dignity. "You have won. It is fair."

Gil shook his head. "No! It is not fair and I won't do it." He nudged Lionheart closer to the tall charger.

Garlon shrugged. "A ransom divided by three is better than a ransom divided by four." He nodded to Allein. "Take him." Allein looked nervously at Gil but rode forward and took Briant's reins.

Take him. Suddenly Gil was on the deck of *Silver Dragon*, closing on the merchant's hapless knarr. *Take him.* Take what we want. Silver. Ransom. That was the whole point. Silver for Danni and Ismail. How else did he raise a ransom? He looked desperately from Briant to the line of eager young knights. There were three of them, now, and one of him. Briant would be a hostage anyhow. They weren't going to hurt him. It was just a game. And Gil had won.

He sent Lionheart forward and turned him to face the blond boy. The smile never left Briant's face and he gave Gil a courteous nod. But a small light of friendship faded from his eyes.

The herald met them at the recess and led them, with their hostage boxed in between them, behind the lists. Watchers turned from the field to jeer and the two women on the timber cart laughed and shouted, "Send him home to his mother. Too young and pretty to fight with men!"

"He fought well!" Gil cried angrily, but that only brought more laughter. He was glad when they reached the shelter of Sir Brandel's pavilion.

The grey-bearded knight rose to greet them as the herald led them within. The interior of the pavilion was hung with tapestries; its floor, carpeted, around a hearth of loose brick. Briant looked small and defeated, standing with bowed head amidst the grandeur. When he raised his gaze to meet his father's, Gil saw his cheeks streaked with tears. The old knight smiled gently. "Not every tournament can be a victory," he said. Then, as he looked past the boy, to Gil and his companions, a figure stepped from the shadows.

"Nor is there shame in defeat, when neither courage nor honor fails." The man smiled at the blond boy and nodded briefly to Gil.

"Dad," Gil whispered. His heart thudded and he felt suddenly that he, not Briant, was being judged.

A second figure, tall and dark-bearded, moved into the firelight. "I am sure that all rode with both, and only fortune stood between the victor and the vanquished." Palamedes bowed to Gil and to Briant, and then to the herald.

"Good sirs," the herald said, "It is my duty to warn you, you have enemies upon this field."

"They have retired early," Lance'lot answered. "One of their number has taken a hard fall."

"Ah," the herald said gravely. "Thus is tournament."

"Thus indeed." Lance'lot sounded equally grave, but the corners of his mouth twitched as he looked back at Gil.

The herald nodded. "There is the matter of ransom," he said then, as if in apology.

"Of course." Sir Brandel called out and two young esquires entered the pavilion, carrying a wooden treasure box. Then the four older men fell to discussing sums of silver, like merchants in Deer Bay.

It pained Gil to hear Briant's worth so callously weighed; his youth lowering the price, his lineage raising it, his qualities as horseman and swordsman debated and calculated in coins. And yet, as the silver was handed over and Gil himself given his quarter share, excitement rose in him, uninvited, at the cold weight of it in his hands.

The ransom completed, they left the pavilion, still escorted by the herald. Briant stood steadfastly beside his father, and with the old knight's comforting hand on his shoulder, bowed as Gil passed. Gil winced and shook his head, but when he turned to speak to the boy, his own father's hand closed on his good arm and hurried him from the tent.

"That is tournament," Lance'lot said. "It has its rules."

"I hate them!" Gil burst out.

Lance'lot smiled.

"We all hate rules until we meet a world with none." He reached for the reins of his charger, held by a patient esquire behind the pavilion. "Come. A wealthy man needs a guard. We will see you safely to your ship."

As Gil mounted Lionheart, Martin de Troye appeared suddenly, carrying both Gil's lost lance and his familiar Pouncing Cat shield. "Many a useful thing turns up on the tournament field," said Palamedes. "There is mending to be done, but a shipwright should manage in place of an armorer."

Startled and grateful, Gil slung the battered shield around his neck and set the lance again in its fewter. He turned at a shout and saw Garlon and Sir Danane's son displaying their full purses. "We meet again, one day!" Garlon called. "And win another ransom."

Allein held up his portion of the silver. "I thank you," he said fervently. Suddenly he smiled, "And I pray you, bid my farewell to the beautiful lady. I would carry her favor, were she not already pledged." He blushed as the others laughed, turned his horse, and galloped away.

With his purse of silver thudding against his thigh, Gil rode from the tournament ground, guarded by his father, Sir Palamedes, and Martin de Troye. Late sun was slanting through the trees and the tide was already running when they reached the path through the marshes. A white line of surf marked the outer bars. Nearer to shore, rivulets of encroaching sea glistened like cold snakes in the sand. Across the wide bay, Gil glimpsed the pale bluff of the ayre where the ships lay and prayed that Ciarnan and Ragi had finished his abandoned task.

His arm throbbed and his stomach ached with hunger. After the exertion of the day, exhaustion enveloped him like the mist already wrapping the sands. He barely heard Lance'lot's order to halt. Palamedes gripped Lionheart's bridle. "Stay, good sir," he warned, until we learn who goes there." Ahead, a man and a boy stood in the shelter of a last, wind-bent tree; the man dressed in a long cloak and leaning on a staff.

"Pilgrims," Martin de Troye said. "Look, there are others, beyond."

"They go on," Lance'lot studied the two figures. "Why do these remain?"

As if to answer his question, the man bent briefly over the boy, and then straightened, sending him toward the waiting knights. Palamedes drew his sword.

"He's just a little kid," Gil protested. The boy, a rosy-cheeked lad in Frankish dress, approached, smiling, with something clutched in his fist. Lance'lot turned from him and swept the marshlands with wary eyes. Gil watched the closed hand. But the boy opened it, innocently, revealing only a bright coin.

"The holy man gives me this," he said. "He asks that he may ride behind?" Lance'lot nodded and spurred his horse forward. "No, sir," the boy said. "Not you. Him." He pointed boldly at Palamedes. "The holy man says he is known for his courtesy."

"What?" Martin de Troye growled. "He begs and chooses, too? The devil take him. If he rides, he will ride with me."

But Palamedes waved him back. "He asks for me. Courtesy demands I accept. All must aid a pilgrim."

He rode forward, but Lance'lot followed. "Courtesy may be accompanied," he said drily. Martin de Troye brought his horse in at the other side, and Gil urged Lionheart after. The boy trotted happily back to his holy man, who stood calmly waiting, his face shaded by the cowl of his rough-woven robe.

"He might meet us halfway," de Troye grumbled. "These pilgrims. Beggars all."

But the man did not move, until Palamedes charger loomed over him. Then he bent again and spoke to the child. "You see, I am proved right. Sir Palamedes is a knight of true courtesy." He straightened up and lowered the cowl of his cloak, revealing his face, and shaking out his mane of blond hair.

"Floki!" Gil cried, with sinking heart.

"My noble friend!" Palamedes leapt down from his horse and enfolded the young Northman in his enormous embrace.

"A holy Viking?" muttered Martin de Troye.

Palamedes stood back, holding Floki's rough-clad shoulders at arm's length. "But why do you dress so? Surely you do not make pilgrimage?"

Floki smiled. "Surely I do not, indeed. I will tell. But first, I have business with this lad." He crouched down, then, before the Frankish child and gave him a second coin. "Our bargain is complete. Go home, now, the hour is late."

The boy admired his new coin. "I am not afraid of the dark," he said with a swagger.

"I am," Floki said. "It is full of beasts with fangs." The child blanched and, clutching his coins tightly, turned and ran back toward the tournament ground. Floki stood and watched until he was out of sight. Then he turned and surveyed his companions, his eyes drifting blandly over Gil to rest again on Palamedes' smiling face.

"I call upon a kinsman," he said, "But not wishing to trouble him, I do so without him knowing. So, too, I do not wish to trouble any here with preparing me a welcome. So, I pass among the crowds thus." He drew the cloak close over his bright tunic, "And so I admire the glories of the tournament unobserved." His eyes flicked to Gil, then returned to the Saracen knight. "I see the noble Lance'lot yet favors you with his company," he nodded briefly to Gil's father. "But these others are unknown to me."

Palamedes stepped back, puzzled. He gestured to Janetta's father, "This is Martin de Troye, whose young daughter you have steadfastly fostered," he said.

Floki bowed his head and then turned to Gil. "And this young knight?"

Palamedes shook his head. "What jest is this? Surely he is known to you."

Floki looked Gil up and down. "I know a Viking with a face like his. And a slave, as well. But not a knight."

"A slave?" Lance'lot looked curiously at Gil. Gil nodded slowly. Then he dropped the reins on Lionheart's neck and swung down from the saddle, grimacing as the pain shot through his arm.

"Yes," he said. "A slave." He undid the thong binding his purse to his belt and stepped forward and knelt before Floki. Jerking the purse open, he scattered its contents in the meadow grass at the Northman's feet. Then he raised his head and, unflinching, met his icy gaze. "And I bring my earl a slave's silver."

Floki stepped back slightly. "Well done," he murmured. "You are as clever as you are bold." He looked up to Lance'lot. "You raise this son well. Enough courage and almost enough sense." He rested his hand on his sword hilt. "Do you mock me, Warrior?" he said.

"I learn from you," said Gil.

Floki's fingers played lightly along the sword hilt. Then his eyes suddenly lit with mirth and he laughed delightedly. He dropped to his knees beside Gil, took the purse, and began gathering the spilled silver from the grass. Gil leaned forward to help, but Floki shook his head. "No. I grovel in the dirt for my slave, since he is cleverer than me." He finished collecting the silver, rose, and reached to help Gil to his feet. Gil winced and Floki studied his arm. "Who does this?"

"Not a friend."

"Good. For neither is he now a friend of mine. Come. I deal with that later. We must go now. The tide leaves us little time."

Palamedes mounted his horse and extended a hand. But Floki grasped the high cantle of the jousting saddle and pulled himself effortlessly to the charger's back. Sitting sideways, like a lady riding pillion, he rested his blond head on the Saracen's mail-clad shoulder. "Oh, Sir Palamedes," he whispered girlishly. "I swoon to ride with so mighty a knight."

Palamedes wrinkled his brow painfully. "Sit properly or you will fall."

"When do I fall from a horse?" Palamedes sent the charger into a canter, weaving in and out of clumps of marsh grass and jumping ditches, but Floki did not fall, and rode without handhold that way, all across the tide flats to the ships.

There, with the sea lapping closer, farewells were brief. Janetta came, with Percy, both chaperoned by Grimhildr, and bid her father a last farewell, as Gil did his own, and then the three knights of Arthur galloped away through the rushing tide, to the forest of their exile.

Janetta reached out hopefully to take Gil's hand, but Grimhildr stamped in between, and with a sigh, Janetta returned and stood obediently beside Rachel. The crews of both ships abandoned their board games and storytelling to stare at Floki in his pilgrim's garb and Gil, armed yet for the tournament. Gil caught Ragi's eye and got a wary shrug as Floki turned his attention to his ship.

He crossed the sands to the beached hull, laid a hand on a strake and trailed his fingers along its length, quietly admiring the well-scraped wood. Then suddenly he spun around. "And who has done this work, assigned to my erring helmsman?" Feet shuffled, thumbs were hooked apologetically in belts, rough-bearded chins stroked, as the eyes of all slid away from Ragi and Ciarnan. "I will have an answer," said Floki.

"Yes!" Grimhildr's voice rang with assurance. "While you are gone, great trolls come out of the forest!" She gestured inland and waved her arms, troll-like, in the air. "*They* do your slave work! Thank them, or they will send winds down to sink you!"

"Ah," Floki said. He turned slowly and looked at the forest. Then, with a nod to Grimhildr, he bowed to the distant trees. "I thank the trolls for their good work. For this slave has won his freedom and the freedom of others as well."

He grinned suddenly at Gil and then called Grimhildr to him. "Come," he said, gesturing that she should sit by the fire. Grimhildr lowered herself to the sand, smoothing her skirt modestly over her lap. Floki opened Gil's purse and up ended it. The silver rushed in a bright stream into her spread apron, winning shouts of admiration. "Silver for a ransom!" Floki said. "Guard it well, Troll-Maiden, lest your cousins from the forest seek payment. And now," he turned to Erling, "Bring me water and ale. And you, Pretty Hawk," he addressed Rachel, "Linen to bind a wound."

He sat Gil down on the other side of the fire and lifted off his chain hauberk, exposing the blood-soaked sleeve of his padded undercoat. Gil shook his head at the offered ale. "I'll just get sick. I haven't eaten."

"A little, Warrior. This will hurt." Floki drew his knife and carefully sliced the sleeve away. The arm flamed with pain as the cloth came off and Gil reached for the ale horn and gulped the contents down.

Grimhildr led Janetta, weeping, away, but Eirik wormed his

way in close, with a ghoulish grin. Percy watched with round eyes. "Does it hurt, Gil?" Gil nodded fiercely, tried to smile, and started to cry.

"You are a baby!" Eirik crowed. "Warriors do not weep!"

Floki swatted the top of his flaxen head. "Warriors do weep," he said. He finished cutting the cloth free and began washing away the crusted blood with hands as gentle as a girl's. When he was done, he ruffled Gil's hair as if he was a child and said, "Good. You will have a fine scar that, another day, will please you." He took the linen bandaging from Rachel and bound the wound, studying Gil's face as he did. "You do well this day, helmsman. But you are not pleased."

"I betrayed Briant." Floki nodded and continued wrapping the long bandage. "He was a friend. He helped me rescue Janetta. We rode with him, pretending we were after another knight. But he was really Garlon's friend. We all turned against Briant and took him."

"Clever," said Floki.

"But it was wrong."

"Men must live."

Gil shook his head fiercely and winced at the pain it caused him. "I don't want to live this way!"

Floki nodded again. Gently, he tied off the last of the bandage. Drawing his knife, he cut the linen free. Then he flipped the blade around in his hand and laid the cold steel against Gil's throat. "No? Are you certain? For that is easily solved."

Gil groaned and shook his head. Floki lifted the knife away and returned it to its sheath. "Men do wish to live," he said. He laughed and stood and helped Gil to his feet. "Now, food and sleep. For there is work to be done tomorrow."

"And you need me?" Gil said tiredly.

"No, Warrior. I need a cat."

CHAPTER TWENTY

They left the camp in the golden light of the next evening, riding swiftly across the treacherous sands. Floki chose a route that brought them ashore by a little forest, midway between the tournament ground and Mont Tombe. It was the closest Gil had been to the island since their approach from the sea. He stared up at the fortress, looming against the fading sky.

"What see you there?" Floki pointed to a low dark line running between the island and the shore.

Gil lowered his gaze. "It looks like stone. A road?"

Floki nodded. "It is a causeway. The highest tides will cover it, but it rises above all others. It leads to the landward gate. But it is for nobility on fine horses, not for Northmen on woolly ponies." He ruffled his mount's winter mane playfully. "We find a more humble road, Warrior. But first we leave the beasts here."

He swung down from his saddle and led the animal into a vine shrouded thicket. Gil followed with Lionheart, tethering him beside the Hrolf's Isle pony. "Leave your sword and shield," Floki said. Reluctantly, Gil unbuckled his sword belt and laid it down. He winced as he dragged the shield strap over his head.

"That pains you." Floki nodded to Gil's injured arm.

"A little."

"Too much to climb?"

"Climb?" Gil stared again at the rocky height of Mont Tombe. "Climb that?"

"Only a small part. I do most."

Gil shrugged and winced again. "I can climb."

Floki took off his own shield and laid it beside Gil's, but he kept his sword belt, carefully wrapping his cloak to conceal it.

Then he untied a sailcloth sack he had bound to his saddle and shook it out as he led Gil toward the beach. Before they left the wind battered scrub, he bent and pulled a clump of marsh grass and then another and stuffed them into the sack. Gil watched, baffled. Floki grinned and slung the sack over his shoulder.

"A man with a sword is a warrior. A man with nothing may be a warrior in disguise. But a man with a sack is a peasant gathering shellfish."

Gil looked out from the last shelter of the trees. "Are they watching?"

Floki shrugged as he strolled onto the open tide flats. "Perhaps. But I think not," he said mildly. "Their noble guest leaves them tomorrow and so they are feasting. I learn this yesterday, on my pilgrimage. I learn, too, something of this fortress. Come, I tell you as we walk."

He continued at the same leisurely pace, ambling from one weed-strewn rock outcrop to another, bending to tug free clusters of blue-black mussels. "You, too," he said to Gil. "This peasant has a very lazy son."

Gil pulled a bunch of mollusks free and looked up uneasily as the last sun left the high thatched roof of the fortress. "It's getting dark."

"That is my wish." Floki squinted at the setting sun. "I am a mighty peasant. Even the sun obeys me." He held out the sack for Gil's shellfish. "Besides, Grimhildr will welcome something for the pot."

"We're going to climb that in the dark?" Gil peered at the impregnable rock.

"Warrior, you trouble yourself for nothing. I climb it. You are in this sack. I tell you I need a cat. And, besides, do not cats see in the dark?"

"Cats do," Gil said. "What about you?"

Floki held his hand out a few inches from his face. "I only need to see this far. Any further, and I am falling."

"Great."

"That is well then?"

Gil nodded grimly.

"Good. A man with fear in his mind does not think. I need

you to think." He pointed to the stone and timber structure on the island's summit. "This chieftain builds his hall as an eagle builds its nest. It is not easily reached. There is a staircase running up from the causeway. It joins another from the sea gate, on the far side. We cannot use these.

"But there is a steep rock face behind the church and I think those holy men did climb it. I find there a few cut steps. Perhaps they sought birds' eggs. Or to pray. They like their aloneness, as Aidan does." He paused suddenly, his eyes drifting to the sea, as if his home in the North lay just beyond the mists. "Yesterday, I climb it, too." he said.

"Now," he stopped suddenly and caught Gil's good arm. "There. See there, high above the black cliff: a row of windows. And above, one more in the stone, lighted now." Gil's gaze followed Floki's pointing finger. A dim light glimmered from a narrow opening in the lofty wall. "You see? There are Ismail and Hakon."

"You saw them!" Gil cried joyfully.

Floki shook his head. "I hear them. There is another voice, also. Servant or jailer. I think it not wise to show my face."

"But they're there," Gil breathed. "And Danni?"

"Surely she would be held separate," Floki said, "with serving maids." He shook his head quickly. "It does not matter. You will find where." He pointed again at the flickering light. "That is where I take you. Just below. I put you on the window ledge and you go in. It is narrow, but you will fit. Cats are narrow."

"In with Ismail and Hakon," Gil cried happily.

"That is easy. But they are behind a locked door and you must go beyond. Everywhere beyond. I wish to know this man's hall as well as my father's house."

"But why?" Gil said, trotting, as Floki quickened his pace in the shadow of the island. "We have silver now. And the letter."

"And if he has no Latin to read the letter? Or if he holds a grudge against his brother in Deer Bay? He is my kinsman, Warrior! When he is a hundred ship lengths behind my back, then I trust him. For now, it is King's Table. Always another piece. Always another move." He paused. They had reached the rock foot of the island, rising precipitously from the sand. "The room in my longhouse, where I make my bed? How many doors has it?"

"Two," Gil grimaced, remembering the straw wall.

"Two doors. One for peace. One for war. We have silver and a letter of good faith from a liar. He has a fortress, an army, and the hostages. Find the rooms where he keeps them, Warrior. And find the doors."

Floki laid both hands on the dripping rock face and looked up. Then he reached for a handhold above his head and scrambled easily to a sandy hollow, a man's height above. Favoring his injured arm, Gil followed. "Just a short way, Warrior, then you may take your rest." Finding another handhold, Floki set the toes of his boots into a slanting crevice and edged out along the cliff. When they were clinging to bare rock, thirty feet above the sands, he grinned over his shoulder at Gil. "They say it is better not to look down."

Then he pulled himself up to a ferny ledge and lying flat, reached a hand down to Gil, dragging him up after. Gil wormed over the lip and lay clinging to the ledge, gasping for breath. Warily, he rolled over. A roof of rock shut out the sky. Floki stood, feeling his way along it. Then, with a nod of approval, he laid down the sack with its grass and shellfish, unbuckled his sword belt, and laid it, also, on the ground. "Now, Warrior," he made a circle of the belt and beckoned Gil, "Here, where even the most sharp-eyed will not see."

Gil got to his knees, crept to the circle, and then stood on shaking legs. Still clinging to the rock face, he stepped within the sword belt and murmured the blessing. "Have courage!" Floki grinned. "No cat fears high places." But, even as the world surged upward around Gil, rich with light, sound, and scent, he knew that one cat did.

Cat held up his sore paw, stretched his neck long, and peered all around. Then he sank into a crouch and yowled. Working back on his haunches he pressed himself against the cliff. "What do you fear?" Floki demanded. "Look, you cannot fall. You have claws!"

He got down on hands and knees beside Cat and pawed

at the ground with curled fingers. Cat crouched lower. Floki closed his hand on Cat's scruff and dragged him to the edge. "See! It is nothing for you. Use your claws!" Cat rolled over and wrapped all four paws around Floki's arm. "Not on me!" Floki shook his arm. Cat clung tighter.

Floki picked up the sack and held his arm over the opening. Cat looked down at the dark mouth of the sack and yowled in despair. "Cats do not fear sacks! Look, it is full of nice shells." Floki gave a final savage shake, breaking Cat's hold. Scrabbling with all four feet, Cat dropped onto a heap of mussels. The light vanished as the Northman drew the top tightly closed. Cat drew in his claws and hunched down in the darkness.

Then, almost at once, he liked the sack. The grass was soft. The mussels smelled intriguing and clinked pleasantly under his paws. He yowled once more when Floki slung the sack over his back and then he settled down. Snugged against the warmth of a human body, he stretched his paws in pleasure at the gentle swaying of the sack, stood up, and turned in a nesting circle. The sack swayed harder. Cat turned the other way.

"Be still," Floki muttered. Cat stretched and circled again, padding his paws up and down. "Warrior! This is not easy." Cat liked the rumbling sound of the Northman speaking and padded harder. Deep in his human mind, an image of Floki clinging to the sheer rock face of Mont Tombe lurched into view. But it wasn't Cat's problem. Kneading and purring, he went to sleep in his shellfishy night.

"Out!" Cat woke with a startled meow, as the sack thudded to the ground. Light flooded in, followed by a hand. Still pleasantly sleepy, he licked the hand. Then the fingers closed on his scruff, dragging him from his refuge and dropping him onto gravel. Cat's body went long and slinky and he sniffed the air.

He smelled new human scents and heard new human sounds and, looking up at the flicker of light and down at the glimmering sea, he saw he was again on a ledge. But already he was getting used to ledges. He crept curiously to the edge and was fetched back by the hand. "I do not do *that* twice, Warrior. Stay here." Cat sat down and washed the hand mark off his fur.

Then suddenly there were two hands holding him, one on his scruff, and one under his belly, and he was being hoisted into the air. "There," the hands set him on a new and tiny ledge, "That is where you go." Cat went rigid, stiff legs jammed against the rock. But as one hand released him, another shoved him firmly into the narrow space, until, with a screech, he skidded through, tumbling feet first into the light.

An instant later, his paws found cloth and hair and leather and he sank reassuring claws deep into each. "Odin curse you!" an outraged voice cried, and a hand, far rougher than Floki's, dragged him, spitting and hissing, from his paw holds and flung him to the stone floor. He landed neatly on his feet.

A boot swiped at him, but he eluded it with scornful ease, scuttling under a little low table. Then another voice cried, "No! It is only a cat. It means no harm."

Ismail! Cat meowed. He thrust a nervous head halfway out of his refuge. Two shadowy figures loomed above. Hakon's face, older and thinner, glowered down at him. He ignored it because Ismail was there, taller and older, too, but with a calm gentle light in his eyes.

"How comes it here?" Hakon demanded, rubbing his thick black beard.

"It climbs. It is a cat." Ismail's white grin spread across his thin brown face. "It is hungry and smells food." Cat became aware of a very nice scent of roasted meat drifting from the table above his head. Ismail's hand appeared, dangling a scrap of delicious fat in front of his nose. Cat nibbled it happily. Ismail smiled, and then as Cat stepped from under his shelter, Ismail's dark eyes widened. "It is not just a cat!" he cried.

"No! 'Tis a cursed Frankish demon! No cat climbs such a cliff." Hakon's boot lined up again.

Ismail laughed. "No demon. It is Gil! See! I know him anywhere!" Cat stepped proudly forward and hooked the end of his tail. Ismail crouched and stroked his back from ears to tail tip. Hakon leant closer.

"It is so? Truly? Warrior's Change-Thing?" He jumped to his feet, pulled the table to the window, and stood on it, craning his neck fruitlessly. "Surely my cousin is near." His dour face broke

into a smile and he slapped Ismail's back. "Soon we are free!"
he cried exultantly.

Cat jumped up on the table beside him, selected a piece of
roasted venison, and carried it away to a dark corner. Hakon
laughed. "You can have my dinner," he said. "Indeed, I will
feast you properly in my father's hall, when we are home." He
looked up suddenly at the sound of footsteps beyond the closed
door.

Cat crouched, ears flat. A key rattled in the lock. "Hide!"
Ismail whispered. But Cat slipped smoothly behind the opening
door, as a bulky figure plodded into the room.

"Good fortune is yours, this night," the man's voice rumbled
cheerfully. "In honor of his pilgrimage, our noble guest bids his
feast be shared, even with slaves." He bent and set a covered
dish on the table, removing its lid with a flourish. Cat's nose
twitched with delight.

No. Gil roused himself from feline gluttony. *We've got stuff
to do.* With a wistful sniff, Cat bolted from his hiding place,
whisked between the serving man's legs, and out the door.

"What goes there!" the man cried.

"A rat," Hakon murmured drily. "Your master's house holds
many. Though not all make pilgrimage."

Cat swished his tail gleefully. Then he sank into the shadows
thrown by the flickering wall sconces, as the jailer emerged from
the room. Locking the door after him, the man retreated down
a long stone corridor, disappearing around a corner at its end.
When his fading footsteps merged with the sounds of revelry
beyond, Cat sat down, washed his paws and face, and thought
about the food left behind. Then he stood and trotted easily
after the jailer, eyes and nose alert for what he might learn.

He knew at once that this was no Northern longhouse, where
chieftain and guests ate and slept in one great hall. Several
doors were set into the stone corridor wall, some standing
open to reveal bed chambers with furniture and tapestries. Cat
entered three, prowled around their corners and sniffed at their
bedclothes, before dismissing them.

The fourth room was larger, its bed draped in Cloth of Gold
and an oil lamp burning wastefully nearby. He sniffed the still

air and his hackles rose from his nape to the tip of his tail. On stiff legs, he stalked the room, making his scent mark in the corners. Then he jumped up on the bed and, overcome by an irresistible and unwise urge, squatted in the midst of its luxury. Leaving a warm puddle behind, he leapt down and shot out the door.

Trotting again toward the distant light, he passed a final room. A new sound reached his pricked ears and he stopped, holding his sore paw high. Behind the thick plank door, a girl was singing. *Danni*. He gave a little chirrup of pleasure. But he remained, paw up, thinking. The voice was sad, a prisoner's voice. But the language was not English. Suddenly, he remembered Danni singing in the Latin she could not speak: *Hosanna, hosanna, in Nomine Domine .... She does that. She likes the sound*. Cat meowed. There was no response from the singer and he meowed louder.

High up in the door a dim light showed through a tiny window. Cat leapt at the door, scrambling up it, meowing. Midway, he lost his hold, and slid down with a screech of claws. He tried again, bruising his sore paw. But the wood of the door was well-dressed and smooth. On the third try, he got a paw onto the window ledge before he slid, yowling, to the floor. The singing stopped. *Danni! Danni!* He mewed. *It's me."*

"Away with you!" an angry woman's voice shouted. A boot kicked at his haunches. Cat leapt out of the way with a hiss. The woman, big and broad, with a clanking spoon dangling from her belt and a face red from the cooking fires, dashed at him, kicking again, while balancing a dish of food. "Filthy cat!"

Cleaner than you, Cat snarled. Then he ran. It didn't matter. He knew where Danni was and Floki would get her out of there if he had to take down his kinsman's hall, stone by stone.

At the end of the corridor, he stopped and crept on stealthy paws around the corner. A flight of stone steps ran down toward the light. At the bottom, the way divided. To one side, more steps descended into smoky darkness. But from the other came music and voices. As he watched, two men clambered up from the darkness, bearing platters of food. Cat slipped into the shadows as they passed and then trotted quickly after them, through a tall stone archway, his nose raised to the scent of cooked meat.

Then, suddenly, he froze, every hair on his orange-striped back aloft. Before him lay a mighty feasting hall, crammed with people and clamorous with their voices. A steady beat of drums shook the floor beneath his paws. Boots thudded and skirts swished as men and women paraded by, dancing to the wailing of pipes and horns. Cat flattened himself against a wall, and then, spotting a dark refuge, dashed through the thunderous stamping feet to its shelter.

Shielded from the noise, he crouched and looked around. There were still feet, but at least these were lined up in a quiet row. Overhead was a wooden roof, muffling the voices and small clinking sounds that came down from above. The wooden floor beneath his feet was dotted with scraps of meat and bread. As he sniffed one, another tumbled down from above, landing right in front of his paws. He pounced and ate it before it went anywhere else. Then he looked up. *A table. I'm under a table.* He rose on hind legs and sniffed. More food smells drifted through a crack between planks. His nose twitched and he pounced on another scrap. This was better, even, than the sack.

When he'd browsed his way up the table and eaten his fill, he sat down, washed, and thought about the sack again. Then he remembered Floki's hand hauling him out and purpose hit him like a splash of cold rain. But the sensible feline order of food and then sleep resisted it. Particularly now, when the glow of the long hearth fire was beckoning him, just beyond the shelter of his roof.

Small sleep, he decided. *Cat nap.* Then he'd do all the human things that seemed so important until he was Cat. He stretched, head down, and then emerged, stretching his head up, from beneath the table.

Bright light squeezed his eyes shut and the din of the music flattened his ears. But over it he heard a high girlish squeal, "Oh! 'Tis delightful!" Cat waved his tail. *Of course he was delightful.* He looked up, blinking lazily, and then leapt back and hissed. His tail bushed, his claws shot out, and he gripped the warm hearthside with stiffened legs.

Before him, joining the ends of two long tables, was a third, as in Floki's hall. A row of richly costumed people sat facing him. In the center, enthroned on a pillared high seat, was a lean man with a warrior's scarred face and a ruddy beard reaching his waist. He rested back in the chair, surveying the hall with lordly good humor. Beside him, a woman, with a jeweled headband restraining ropes of brown hair, balanced a small child on her knee. Two other children, little girls in white linen dresses, clambered on hands and knees over the table in their eagerness to claim Cat.

" 'Tis mine!" the larger shouted. But the smaller pulled her sister's hair and scuttled past her, reaching eagerly for the furry prize. Cat's back arched and he hissed again, not at the squabbling sisters, but at the man who sat so quietly at the warrior-chieftain's side. Dressed in Cloth of Gold and flanked by two of his own fierce bodyguards, Jocelyn Guidbairn nodded and smiled at Cat.

He can't know me, Gil protested in his human mind. *He can't.* But the blue eyes locked with Cat's and Guidbairn nodded again, as if he knew more of both Cat and Gil than they knew of themselves. Then, at once, both boy and cat became aware of two other creatures at the table. Cradled in the Golden Knight's arms, as gently as the chieftain's lady held her baby, were two small, sleeping dogs. *Lapdogs,* Gil thought wonderingly. *Like Hakon's.*

Terriers, thought Cat. And both cat and boy were again in the Forest of Caledon, running, running, the yapping snarling terriers at their heels. Cat turned to dart under the table. But two small, fat hands gripped his flanks, squeezing the breath out of him, fingers kneading his fur. "Mine!" the child crowed.

Cat wriggled, brought in his claws, and patted her hand with the pads of both paws. *Not now!* he mewed desperately. But she only lifted him in her arms and turned to face her smiling parents. Hanging helplessly, Cat saw the Golden Knight quietly lean down and lower one and then the other of the sleek white dogs to the floor. "Go," he whispered, so only Cat heard. And only Cat heard their eager snuffling. But then they caught his scent and wild excited yipping filled the hall.

They burst from beneath the high table, five cat bounds

away. Cat wormed his sinewy body from the child's arms and hit the floor running, five cat bounds from death. He streaked beneath the long table and through the startled dancers' legs, with the hunters yowling at his heels. But through his feline terror, a human outrage rose, for the children who would see Cat's hideous end.

Not today! Boy and cat shared grim resolve. With a spine-chilling screech, he leapt from the floor, claws extended, and hurled himself at the face of a hurrying servant maid. Shrieking, she flung the tray down, showering Cat and his pursuers with honey cakes. The terriers fell upon them, squabbling and gobbling. As their master shouted impotently, Cat ran through the archway and out of the hall.

Scuttling down the stone staircase, he dashed through the darkness and smoke into the kitchen and skidded to a halt at the edge of the great fire pit. Around it, scurrying maids and servants cast enormous leaping shadows over the stone floor. Huge black pots bubbled on iron stands. A deer carcass sizzled and smoked on a turning spit. More carcasses hung like blackened ghosts from the soot-caked rafters. *A picture of hell,* Gil thought.

Heaven, thought Cat. All along the smoke-stained walls stood casks and kists and laden baskets. A hundred dark nooks and crannies beckoned between them. Cat dashed into the nearest, whirled, and became nothing but two glowing eyes as the first terrier, sated with cakes, came snarling through the door.

"Out!" The stout woman, who had accosted Cat in the corridor, hurled her clanging ladle at the terrier. "Filthy dog!" Sparks flew from the stone floor and the beast turned tail, yipping, and collided with its fellow. Cat snugged back into his crevice, as both dogs ran.

He stayed there, warm and safe, until the kitchen grew quiet. Moonlight filtered through a high window and he thought briefly about Floki, waiting at the foot of the cliff. Then he yawned and stretched and lazily washed a paw.

Creeping out from his refuge, he found the fire burning low and just two sleepy servants playing chess on the top of a cask. Still, he waited near his shelter in case the dogs returned. But only an occasional tired maid came into the kitchen for more food and drink, so he stretched and set out to explore.

He remembered he must find a door, and again the thought of Floki waiting came into his mind. But then he found the rat. Lured by fallen scraps, it had crept boldly to the edge of the fire pit. Cat pounced so fast that the tip of its hairy tail slipped through his teeth as it escaped. It scuttled behind a barley kist. He made himself thin and slipped after. It ducked under a stool. Cat flattened his back and followed. Through baskets of apples, over the carcass of a pig, between dusty flagons, the rat fled. And then it found the door.

It was dusty and low and only a whisker's measure ajar. But the rat scuttled through and so, thin as a snake, did Cat. Even in the darkness, his pounce was sure. His teeth sank into the rat's fur and met in the bloody sweetness of its throat. He shook it, dropped it; tossed it in the air. Then he crunched up its skull and devoured its warm twitching flesh until nothing remained but the dry, unpleasant tail and a thin smear of blood on the floor. With a final sniff, he abandoned it, climbed to the top of a cask, washed meticulously, and curled in the black warmth to sleep.

Twice, the door opened and a maid collected a flagon or a cheese. Sometime after, it was shut suddenly, with a clunk and the falling of a latch. But Cat only curled tighter, covered his nose with both paws, and slept, as chinks of moonlight measured out the night.

The moonlight was grey daylight when he awoke. *Floki*, Gil thought. And then, *The tide.* He had missed the tide. And if he didn't move fast, he'd miss another. But it was safe and quiet behind the closed door and Cat wasn't in any hurry at all. He stretched and washed and with leisurely grace, jumped from his cask to the floor. He sniffed the dried blood of the rat and then a sweeter smell reached his twitching nose.

Sniffing eagerly, he stood on hind legs against a damp pottery jug, and then scrambled up its side, tipping it easily. Frothy white milk rushed out over his paws. He shook each, lapped happily from the stone floor, and washed gratefully. Then he went to the door, sat, and waited, watching with infinite feline patience, until, with a creak and a flood of light, it opened at last.

"Locked in the dairy!" a sweet female voice exclaimed, "Poor Pusskins!" Cat thought of Janetta and his paws went melty.

It's not her! Gil cried. *Run!* Reluctantly, Cat ran. He'd liked the dairy even better than the table. Or the sack.

The kitchen fire again blazed brightly, surrounded by maids and cooks. But the room was filled with light and fresh air, for, at its end, a door stood open to sea and sky. Before it, the cook with the ladle fanned her red face. Cat darted for the door and she shrieked as he scooted between her booted feet. Unhooking the spoon from her belt, she swung it, swift as a Viking sword. The ladle clanged behind Cat, but he was running already, sun on his back and salt air in his nostrils, down the precarious stone stair to freedom.

His staircase joined another and wound lower around the foundations of the lofty fortress. Below lay the roof of the church and the landing, lined with ships. And the sea, sparkling in the sun, its outer bars white with incoming tide. With long lithe bounds, Cat crossed the steep hillside, finding cat paths where no man could walk, seeking the familiar amid the unknown. He came upon old mossy steps, leading to the church, a precipitous grassy bank, and then, the rock face Floki had climbed. With a last light leap, he landed, secure on the shell-strewn shore.

He mewed and sniffed the air, holding up one paw. But there was neither sight nor scent of the Northman. And the tide was plucking at his toes. He ran back and forth twice and then set out in his bounding run, across the glistening sand.

At first, it was no wetter than rain-soaked grass. But soon puddles appeared, splashing his fur with each bound. And then, suddenly, water was everywhere, up to his belly, drenching his tail. He lengthened his bounds, leaping from one sandbar to another. Then the sandbars were too far apart, and the water, shallow for a human, was nose high on a cat.

Find a circle, Gil's boy-mind cried. But there were no circles to be seen, and Cat kept running, into the water, and in the water; until there was no sand beneath his feet. Four paws paddling, small pink nose straining above the surface, he ran on.

Cat's swim! Gil exulted. *But how far?* His paws grew tired, his sodden fur, heavy. His nose dipped beneath the water and he sneezed. Then a huge splash beside him cast a wave over his head. Batting his ears, he re-surfaced. A new splash submerged him. His sore paw stopped working, so he swam, lopsidedly, with three. A third splash overwhelmed him. Under the water, his small paws swam on and his cat mind accepted the change of circumstances, resigning itself to not breathing.

Then something closed on his nape like a terrier's jaws, jerking him back and up, claws flailing. He broke surface, and the thing shook him until the water flew from his fur. He opened his eyes and glimpsed sky, sunlight, and a flash of red, before the thing released its grip and dropped him. Braced for water, he hit something rustling and dry. The light narrowed to a small circle over his head and then vanished.

The sack! he thought happily. Swinging and swaying, warmed by the sun outside, and snug in his grass, he shook himself, and settled down to wash. He was not surprised. Or even curious. Though he did wonder where the shellfish had gone.

Cat had finished his paws and started on a flank, when the sack suddenly jumped in the air, turned upside down, and opened wide. "Out!" Floki's voice growled. Claws scrabbling, Cat tumbled from the sack, twisted neatly, and landed on his three good feet. His grass bed just missed his ears. He sat down, holding the fourth paw in the air, and blinked. Floki flung the sack down beside him.

Still holding the paw up, Cat looked around. They were on the little forest-sheltered strand. A few feet away, Lionheart and the Hrolf's Isle pony grazed on marsh grass. "Ah," Floki said solicitously, "Your paw is hurt." Cat held it higher. "I am expected to be sorry?" Cat continued washing, where he had left off. "And you are wet," Floki murmured. "That is to grieve me also?" He leaned over suddenly and snapped the sack at Cat. "Well, I do not grieve!" he shouted.

"I wait in the cold and the dark beneath the fortress until the tide rises so I must swim. And, no, that is not a difficulty. But this," he waved furiously at the shore, "This is the difficulty.

Here, where I must sleep with no bedding but my cloak, no fire, and no supper but cold shellfish. And that animal," he pointed at the tethered ponies, "That animal complaining all the night! 'It is cold. It is dark. I hear a sound. A mouse ran over my hoof!'" He whirled and grabbed Lionheart's forelock, "Until I think to slay him with my sword and use his skin for a bed! And where are you?" Floki unbuckled his sword belt and glared at Cat.

Cat finished his flanks and began the tricky neck bend involved in washing his shoulder blades. "Where? Curled asleep in a heap of furs by a kitchen fire?" Cat stretched his long pink tongue and flicked water from his back. "Where?" Floki shouted. He whipped the sword belt into a circle and grabbed Cat's scruff. And suddenly Cat was flying through the circle and tumbling with boy-heavy clumsiness into the salty grass.

Gil sat up quickly and holding his aching arm, wriggled backward as the Northman strode closer. "Where were you?"

"Floki, I ...."

"Do not blame your Change-Thing, Warrior." Floki scooped up his sword belt with one hand and pointed the forefinger of the other at Gil. "I warn you."

"But I ...."

"Do not!" He slung the sword belt around his waist, buckling it angrily.

"I found Danni," Gil said, at last.

Floki's hands stilled on the buckle. "What say you?"

"I found her. And Hakon and Ismail. They know you're here."

"My lass," Floki whispered. "She is well?"

"I didn't see her. She was locked in a room. But I heard her singing."

"She sings?"

"She sounded sad," Gil said, with cautious honesty.

"But she sings! And soon she will never be sad again! I will guard her from sorrow all my days." Floki closed his eyes, his fierce, handsome face gentled by joy. "Warrior, I thank you."

"I tried to see her," Gil said. "I jumped, but I couldn't reach the window. And then a woman came with a ladle and chased me." He paused and shrugged. "I guess she was just a cook."

"But you were only a cat," Floki smiled. "And a cat is wise to fear a cook, guarding her butters and cheeses."

"I found the bedchambers and the hall. And Guidbairn set his terriers on me. But I found the kitchens then. And this morning," he ducked warily, "I found the kitchen door. It's around the back, above the church."

"Good! Now we have three ways to take our leave. But we will enter by the sea gate, as the noble kinsmen we are. Warrior, you do well!" Floki smiled again fondly. "And I reward you well!" He looked across at Mont Tombe, and then, reaching within his tunic, he drew out the leather pouch he wore always around his neck, and from it, the amber necklace he had pledged to Danni at Einar's Holm.

He held it out toward the fortress, as if offering it to the girl imprisoned there. "On my marriage day, Warrior, you sit at my right hand. And I give your lady a dowry for the one I take from her." He turned the necklace, so the golden links glimmered in the sun. "For this, you will have the best farm on Hrolf's Isle. You will be first to us, after our sons."

Gil stared. Slowly, he shook his head, even as he saw himself and Janetta reaping barley above the sea. "It can't happen," he whispered.

Floki slapped his shoulder. "Of course it happens. I make it happen!" Then he caught Gil's arm, before Gil could speak again. "Silence, now. Listen."

Across the flowing tide came the sound of the herald's horn. A great party of people poured out of the fortress and down onto the stone causeway leading ashore: mounted knights, men and women on foot, wagons stacked high with provisions. "Another tournament?" Gil asked, puzzled.

"No, Warrior." Floki bowed to the procession, "Behold! A king makes pilgrimage. And with the usual humility." He grinned wryly and handed Gil his sword and shield. "Come. We will watch."

Quickly, they saddled the ponies and rode into the forest. In sight of the roadway from Mont Tombe, Floki dismounted and again led the animals into thick undergrowth. Then, grasping a branch above his head, he swung up into an ancient beech tree.

Gil followed, scrambling up the smooth grey trunk and edging along broad branches after Floki, until they were both twenty feet above the ground, under a red-gold canopy of autumn leaves.

The road, white with a bedding of crushed shells, was deserted, but for a peasant child driving a flock of goats. Then the herald's horn sounded again and the first of the knights rode into view. Five abreast, they filled the narrow roadway. The child gathered his goats and hurried to the grassy verge, as ranks of knights followed, all bearing the golden pennants of Camelot's new king.

Behind them came ladies of the court, walking delicately barefoot. Men in penitents' cloaks followed, barefoot, too; though as they passed, Gil heard the familiar jingle of mail. "Well armed, these pilgrims," Floki said drily.

Seven wagons followed, and on one sat a sad-eyed boy and two women in grey woolen habits, their faces hidden by white veils. One was stooped and old; the other slender, her body beneath her modest clothing swaying with youthful grace. "He brings holy women to pray for his soul," Floki murmured, "Should death find him, before he finds Rome." Then he laughed suddenly. "See, Warrior! What lies beyond the bend!"

Out of sight of the procession, a man stood holding the reins of a magnificent white charger. Two others, clutching bundles, awaited the approaching pilgrims. "Why?" Gil whispered.

Floki touched his arm and pointed. "That is why."

Striding barefoot into view came the Golden Knight, dressed in a coarse brown cloak and holding his pilgrim's staff. Regal, even without his finery, he smiled graciously at the boy with his goats. Two armed men stepped to his side as he bent to give the child a coin.

Then he went on, passing below the branches of Gil's tree. There, the procession halted. The court ladies bowed and turned back, hobbling on tender feet. The penitents tossed back their cloaks, freeing their sword arms. The child and his goats were hurried away as the charger was led forward. A servant brought boots and sumptuous garments. Clad again in Cloth of Gold, Jocelyn Guidbairn swung up into the saddle of his mount.

He tossed his pilgrim staff to one of his men and his humble robe to another and took up the charger's reins. Then, at the sounding of the herald's horn, he set out on the penitent road.

Gil again heard Floki's soft laugh. "Holiness is a heavy cloak, Warrior. He flings it from his shoulders lest it drive him to his knees. Come." He slipped easily down to the branch below. "We go now. Our way lies clear."

Chapter Twenty-One

They set out the next morning at the first silky ripples of the incoming tide, slipping down the river channel to the sea. They crossed the bay to Mont Tombe under oars, but with masts raised and ready sails billowing around their lowered spars. The ponies stamped in their pen at the sound of flapping cloth and Lionheart snorted and reared. *It's the sail*, Gil kept his eyes on the channel, his hand firm on the tiller. *You've met it before.*

He glanced back at *Sea-Raven*, riding their wash. Erling's beard jutted forward suspiciously as he eyed the landing below the fortress. The Golden Knight's great longship rested far up the strand, its mast down and its gilded strakes shrouded for winter.

Floki loosed the steering oar and took the tiller from Gil. Deftly, he steered *Silver Dragon* through the shallows, with the raised rudder just brushing the sand. "We beach on the first flow of this tide, helmsman, and already before it turns, we are far out to sea. With empty purses, or bloody swords, however my kinsman wishes it."

The keel grounded with barely a shudder and the oarsmen shipped their oars. Beside them, *Sea-Raven's* prow thudded into the sand. "Lightly. Lightly," Floki called to Erling. "I would launch them with a feather. The most welcome guest," he said with a grin, "is he who is most ready to leave." He left Ulf at the helm, and six strong oarsmen seated at their places, and jumped down to the strand.

Bjorn followed, a bowline coiled over his shoulder. Landing with a ground-shaking thump, he strode off to secure the ship ahead of the tide. Floki stretched up and lifted Percy down, and with the boy close by his side, he beckoned Gil and Ragi to join him on the strand. "And you, Pretty Hawk," he called to Rachel. He reached to help her down from the beached prow, but Ragi was there before him.

"I do it!"

"Would you were so willing when it is water casks." Floki turned away, smiling. Then he ducked as Eirik flung himself, sword in hand, from the rail.

"I am ready!"

"You stay," Floki said. "Troll-Maiden!" he called up to Grimhildr, "I would have you and your treasure."

"But *he* comes!" Eirik pointed at Percy. "He is bigger, but I am more clever."

"And one of you is enough. Besides," Floki put an arm around the child, "I have a charge for you." He pointed to Bjorn. "Guard him. Let him not leave your sight, even for a moment, lest he be stolen away."

Eirik's small face lit with delight and he ran off to stand, sword at the ready, beside the towering, black-bearded Northman. Floki smiled again. "Erling," he called. "Come with us."

Erling finished securing his own bowline. Then he looked up at the fortress, high on the island's summit, and back to Floki and the small group clustered around Grimhildr and the casket of silver. "I would have more men."

"Any more is a raiding party," Floki said. "I would not alarm my kinsman." Then he laughed, lifting Rachel's chin with a teasing finger. "That my women are fiercer than my men, he need not know. Come." He turned and led the way, splendid in his red tunic and fur cloak; his braided hair bounding girlishly on his shoulders.

At the foot of the stone staircase from the sea gate, Erling stopped. He jerked his chin up toward the wooden stockade surmounting the outer wall. "They are watching."

"Of course," Floki said. He looked up suddenly, flashed his white grin, and waved. A head vanished down behind the parapet, and Gil laughed.

Floki smiled. "Enter any man's house as if it were your

own. A man is treated as he expects to be." Gil nodded, his eyes scanning the curving stone steps, over hung with rock faces. "But remember to look behind the door posts," Floki added with another smile.

When they reached the wall, a solid plank door, studded with iron bolts, barred the way. Floki nodded mildly, but before he approached the gateway, he sent Ragi and Rachel to a rock outcrop, shadowed by the overhanging parapet. "Watch the ships," he said to Ragi. "Should any approach them, send my hawk." He smiled at Rachel, "Come to me at once, Pretty One, wherever you find me."

He turned, then, back to the gate, and rapped politely on the weathered wood of the door. A flap was raised, revealing a surly young man behind an iron grill. "State your business," the youth growled. "Or be gone."

"Ah, the courtesy of the Southerner," Floki murmured to Gil. Then he smiled at the gatekeeper, through his grill. "Tell your master that his kinsman, Floki Magnusson, would drink to our fathers at his hearth."

The flap banged closed and after a mutter of voices behind it, keys rattled, the bolts were slipped and the gate swung open. Beyond was a sheltered courtyard, scented with herbs in the autumn sun. Fruit trees spread their branches along one wall and a small black goat nibbled at a grassy bank.

With a quick glance left and right, Floki entered, signaling the others to follow. The surly-faced man drew the gates closed and locked them with a key from an iron ring hanging from his belt. Then he backed off to a wary distance, with his hand on his sword hilt, while his companion left the courtyard through a door at the far end.

Floki looked around thoughtfully. "These tall windows, Warrior," he pointed high above their heads. "Where are they?"

Gil looked up. "It must be the hall," he said softly, with a glance at the distant guard. "Hakon and Ismail are around that side," he pointed left. "The kitchen is at the back. Landward. And the staircase from it runs beside this wall."

"Very good," Floki nodded. He smiled brightly at the guard and called, "Fine stonework. I commend your mason." The gatekeeper shrugged and said nothing.

Percy tugged at Floki's hand and pointed at the goat. Floki smiled again. "Yes. It is very pretty. Perhaps *that* is my kinsman. But you stay here. Or by Grimhildr." Percy slid under Floki's cloak and watched the goat from its shelter.

"He is in no hurry, your noble cousin," Erling growled. But Floki only admired the garden, as if they had nothing better to do. And when, after a longer time, still, the second guard re-appeared, he greeted the youth graciously.

"He will see you," the guard said. He turned curtly and strode back to the door, beckoning them to follow. As they passed the goat, Percy bolted from beneath Floki's cloak and ran to pat it. Floki caught him in a stride and then stopped and knelt beside the boy, while the guard watched impatiently.

"Do as I say, now," he said gently, "and when we return home, I will go raiding and bring you a goat of your own."

"My own goat!" Percy beamed wonderingly.

"Two!" Floki said. "Black ones, with big black horns." He made horn shapes with his hands and then stood, nodded to the guard, and followed him, looking quietly left and right as he crossed the threshold.

They found themselves in an empty, stone-floored ante room, as cold and grey as the courtyard had been sunny. Wooden benches lined the walls, and Gil imagined them filled with hopeful petitioners, awaiting the chieftain's pleasure. "Your kinsman reckons himself an emperor," Erling growled. "Perhaps we approach on our knees?" He stamped after Floki, but the guard held out an arm, barring his way, as they approached a further door.

"One only."

Floki shrugged and turned and smiled at Erling. "My kinsman is shy. I go alone."

"No. They will take you and kill you." Erling stepped forward. Floki gestured him back.

"Not until they have the silver," he said cheerfully. "And that stays with my Troll-Maiden." He bowed to Grimhildr. "And you stay there, too," he gave Percy a shove. "So close, you can pull the ribbons of her headdress. Though you do not do that," he added. Then he turned and followed the guard from the room.

The wait seemed even longer than in the courtyard. Erling paced the room. Grimhildr sat on one of the benches with the treasure chest on her knees, pretending not to see Percy snatching at her ribbons. Gil tried to picture the rooms he had seen as Cat, lying beyond the wall. He crossed once to the courtyard door and looked out through a slit in the planks. The gatekeeper was dozing in the sun. The goat, perched on a rock, scratched an ear with its hoof. Gil jumped back when the bolt of the inner door rattled.

But it was only their guard, returned alone. He crossed the room without speaking and went out to his post in the courtyard. Erling groaned. "If I know we spend the night here, I bring my sleeping fur."

"They must be talking," Gil said. "That's good!"

"Or Floki is creeping yet to the throne on his knees."

Gil grinned. "There wasn't any throne. Just a High Seat, like on Hrolf's Isle."

"On Hrolf's Isle," Grimhildr put in, "We leave no guest without ale or fire. Earl of a pigsty, this one." She snorted with derision and then looked up suddenly. "You! Back here," she shouted at Percy. Percy turned quickly from the slit in the door Gil had used to watch the courtyard and scurried obediently to her side.

Then, after another long while, the inner door opened again and Floki came in alone. Erling jumped up from his bench. "So? He lets them go?"

Floki held a finger to his lips. With a hand on Erling's shoulder he steered him and Gil to the bench where Grimhildr sat with Percy. "There is another guard outside the door," Floki murmured. "Soft voices." He sat, then, beside Grimhildr, setting Percy at her other side, and took the treasure chest onto his own knees, and opened it, studying its contents.

"He agrees?" Grimhildr said. "He will have the silver?"

Floki laughed quietly. "Oh, he will have silver. He sits there, like a merchant, with his scales, ready to weigh my people's worth. I show him, of course, the letter from his brother in Deer Bay. He pretends to read it, and then he hands it to his wife, who, practiced at her prayer book which rests on her knees, reads it for him. And then he bargains.

"Hakon, he says, is not truly kin, nor indeed am I, since our connection is out with the bonds of Holy Church."

"Because *he* is of the bastard line, you must pay more?" Erling's blue eyes narrowed to bright points of indignation.

"I also find it odd," Floki said mildly. He shrugged. "But the master of the house lays out the gaming board." He shrugged again. "For Ismail, he sets a lower price than I would, but I do not argue."

"And Danni?" Gil said eagerly.

Floki let the silver run through his fingers as he said evenly, "My great treasure he dismisses as so worthless that at first he will take no payment at all. He laughs and offers me, as in a jest, two of his maids instead. I do not accept. He offers three. Again I refuse. And then he sets a price so high that were it not for my helmsman's skill on the jousting field, I would be at a loss to pay. Which is, of course, his intention, as I see from the shock on his face when I agree to his price.

"He pretends to laugh. 'All this for a serving maid? A slave girl?' And then I see he must want her for himself. For all his pious wife and pretty children, he would beget another bastard line. For so honors he Holy Church." Floki grimaced. "And all the while, he laughs, unaware of his good fortune. For were not this silver sufficient, I would pay him handsomely in his own blood."

He flashed his white smile, returned the casket to Grimhildr, and jumped to his feet. "Come, Troll-Maiden, we will do business." Then he stopped and looked quickly around. "Where is the child?"

Gil whirled and saw the courtyard door ajar, sunlight flooding in. Floki was already running, sword in hand, when they heard Percy scream. Gil drew his own blade and raced after. He burst into the courtyard and stopped, caught between outrage and relief.

In the middle of the sunny garden, the two sullen young guards were laughing on either side of Percy, throwing something bright and glittering in lazy arcs over his head. At first Gil thought they were teasing him with a ball, but as the child leapt for it, stumbling and sobbing, he recognized the gold armband from Deer Bay.

"It's mine!" Percy cried. "It has my wolf!" The glittering bracelet clattered to the ground and Percy dove at it, but the gatekeeper snatched it at the last moment, from beneath his hand. He held it up, tantalizingly above the sobbing child's head. And then suddenly he froze.

Floki walked with soundless steps across the courtyard, his sword lowered at his side, his empty hand extended. "Come, now," he said. "It is my gift to the child. I ask you to return it." His voice was soft and he smiled slightly.

The guards fell silent. They seemed suddenly very young. Wordlessly, the gatekeeper held out the bracelet to Floki. Floki smiled again. "I thank you." He handed it to Gil without taking his eyes off the guards. "Take the child, Warrior."

"Floki," Gil whispered. "I think it was just a game."

"*Take the child.*"

Gil turned to put his arm around Percy. The guards' eyes fell on him, pleading. One reached out a hopeless hand as Gil led Percy away. Neither even thought to draw his sword.

Gil held his hands over Percy's ears as he crouched with the boy behind the closed door. But the door could not shut out the butcher's whack of steel on bone, or the strangled shrieks that ended in silence. It was so quick. And so quiet afterwards. Sweat poured down Gil's shivering back and nausea crept up his throat. He clutched Percy tighter as the door creaked open.

"Warrior." Gil looked up and flinched. Floki was standing quietly above him, his red tunic darkened with blood. Blood spattered his face and his yellow, be-ribboned braids. "The bracelet, Warrior?" he said softly.

"Are you hurt?" Gil whispered.

"Of course I am not hurt." Floki took the golden bracelet in his blood-stained fingers. Then he knelt, also, beside Percy. "Come, child." Percy looked up, and seeing him, released his grip on Gil's waist and flung himself into Floki's arms.

"They took it! And you gave it to me!" he sobbed hysterically, burying his face in Floki's fur cloak. Floki stroked his back, rocking him gently.

"But it is here now. You have it back. See, here is your wolf."
Smiling gently, he traced the fierce jaws of Fenrir. Then he
slipped the bracelet onto Percy's arm and gathered the sobbing
child close.

"Floki," Gil whispered, looking nervously at the door.
"What do we do now?"

"A moment!" Floki's eyes flashed fury. "He is frightened. Do
you not see?"

"We are all frightened," Erling said gruffly from across the
room. "You've shed enough blood here to float a ship. Do we do
business *now*?"

Slowly, Floki released Percy and looked up. His eyes clouded
with a dazed new awareness and when he spoke it was not to
Erling, but to Gil. "Warrior," he murmured, "I do something
very stupid."

"Yes!" Erling shouted. Floki ignored him. He stood, crossed
the room, lifted a heavy bench, and set it across the inner door.
With his arm around Percy again, he led them out into the
courtyard and covered the child's eyes with the folds of his cloak.

"Warrior," he nodded toward the two blood-sodden bundles
that had been the guards, "Get the keys."

Turning his face from the raw blood-stench, Gil knelt beside
the dead gatekeeper and hacked blindly at the youth's belt with
his knife until the iron key ring fell free. Gasping, he jumped to
his feet and ran with the clanking keys to open the gate. Outside,
he drank the fresh sea wind in great gulps. Rachel and Ragi
whirled in alarm from their watch. Floki hastened Grimhildr
and Percy toward them. "Man of the High Island," he called to
Ragi, "Take them aboard the ships. Release the lines. Turn the
prows to the sea."

He knelt again beside Percy. "Go with Grimhildr now. I
will come after." Reluctantly, Percy let go his hold on Floki's
cloak. Grimhildr hoisted the treasure casket onto one hip and
drew Percy under her other arm. Floki leaned closer to Ragi. "If
others come before us, do not wait." He turned then suddenly.
"Erling. Go with them."

"No!" Erling shook his head, outraged. "I do not leave you.
Stupid though you are!"

Floki smiled and looked heavenward. Then he drew his sword and rested its tip against Erling's chest, parting his voluminous beard. "I do not build *Sea-Raven* to see her wrecked on a Frankish shore. Go to your ship, Maiden-Face." He twirled the blade cheerfully, catching a curl of the beard, "Or I shave you, now, as my mother shaved you."

Erling balled a fist and shook it. But he turned and stamped off behind the others. Floki watched until they were halfway down the stone staircase and then he quickly clasped Gil's arm. "Helmsman," he said urgently, "The door for war."

Gil looked quickly left and right, remembering the landscape as Cat had seen it. "This way." He jumped from the steps onto the steep, grassy hillside. The ground fell away toward the sea in a sheer drop that, at cat-height, he had not seen. Legs shaking with fear, he worked his way around a buttress of rock, with Floki following, sure-footed, behind.

Ahead, he saw the rough, winding kitchen stairs and he struggled toward it eagerly. Floki caught his arm. "Look up, Warrior." Gil craned his neck and saw parapets and a small, high window that had meant nothing to a running cat. "Go above, where none can see." To Gil's dismay, Floki climbed up from the safety of the steps to the mossy cliff face. Clinging to the rock, they worked their way to the top of the stairs, and the door from which Gil had escaped. Again, it stood open to the sun. "What lies within, Warrior?"

Gil described the kitchen as he remembered it, leaving out the rat. "And there's another room, where I got shut in. A dairy. There was milk."

"I am sure," Floki grimaced. "But it locks?" Gil nodded. "Good." Floki drew his sword. "I go first. You follow. Women we lock in the dairy and men who do not argue. Kill any who draw a weapon. No matter how small."

Gil nodded again and felt his gut clench tight. He drew his own sword as Floki positioned himself at the side of the open door. With a quick glance to each side, he leapt through it, swinging the shining steel in an arc above his head. "Be still! I do no harm!"

Shrieks and shouts sounded in response. Gil dashed into the

kitchen behind Floki, his eyes sweeping the room. Three maids and two serving men cringed against the wall. The red-faced cook stood, eyes blazing, ladle in hand, before her cooking pots. Gil felt his cat hackles rise.

Floki swung his sword over the fire pit, slicing through a hanging ham. A clean-cut half fell sizzling into the flames. He held the blade up and smiled at the trembling kitchen staff. "Yes. Very sharp. Warrior," he inclined his head toward the dairy, and Gil ran to open the door. "In," Floki said. "And keep silence if you wish to live."

Maids and servants scurried to obey. Only the cook rebelled, shaking her ladle at Floki on behalf of her fallen ham. Deep within Gil, Cat snarled. But Floki laughed and with a gentle flick of his sword, tapped the ladle from her hand. She cried out in fury and crouched down to claim it, but Gil had it first. "In!" he shouted. And as she turned in belligerent obedience, he whacked the ladle across her broad rear. With a shriek, she ran into the dairy and Gil slammed and bolted the door.

Floki laughed gleefully. "Warrior! Where is your knightly courtesy? You are but a filthy Viking!" Still laughing, he ran from the room with Gil on his heels. At the foot of the steep smoky stairs, he stopped. "What lies ahead?"

"The hall to the left, and to the right, more stairs to the bedchambers." Floki ran lightly up and paused at the top. Stepping cautiously toward the hall, he paused again. "I hear no alarm," he whispered. "They still await my silver." He turned and stood midway between the Great Hall and the kitchen stairs. "I hold this place, Warrior. You go with the keys. Free the men first, that they may help you. And then my lass. Run. Before my kinsman's patience fails."

Keys in hand, Gil dashed up the stairs, ducking beneath wall sconces that had flared high above Cat. He forced himself past Danni's door, and then past the room, now open and empty, where the Golden Knight had slept. The sour reek of feline urine yet lingered. Grinning, Gil went on until the sound of soft voices led him to Hakon and Ismail.

Holding up the iron ring, he went through the clutch of keys, trying one and then another and then a third. Panic rose in his heart. Maybe the gate keeper had other keys. Maybe he missed them in his cowardly haste. Then, as his shaking fingers turned the second to last, the heavy bolt screeched and slid.

"Guard, you are clumsy, today," Hakon said, as the door swung in. Then he jumped to his feet in astonishment. But it was Ismail, poised wary and ready behind the door, who cried, "Gil! My friend! You come!"

He strode forward, half a head taller, leaner, more man than boy, and embraced Gil with arms of steel. Laughing, he drew back and shook his tangle of frizzy braids. "See, Hakon! It *is* right cat."

"My cousin?" Hakon cried eagerly.

"Downstairs," Gil gasped. "Holding off the household. We've had a change of plans." With a quick nod, Hakon hurried Ismail before him, and followed Gil out the door.

At Danni's room, Gil reached again for the iron key ring. But as he slid the first key in the lock, he felt the door lightly shiver beneath his fingers. He pushed harder and it swung effortlessly open onto a barren room.

"It is not locked?" Ismail said.

Gil looked hurriedly left and right as he ran through the doorway, but there was no need. The room was empty, even the bedding gone. Nothing remained to show the singing girl had ever been there.

"She's gone," he cried.

"Another room, surely," Hakon said. "You were wrong."

"It was this door. Look! There are my claw marks."

Hakon grimaced, uncomfortable with Change-Things. "Try the others. Perhaps they move her."

None of the other doors were even locked. Gil stared into the last bare bedchamber in disbelief. "She was here," he said dully. "I heard her."

Hakon shook his head. "Since Deer Bay she is kept apart from us. We neither see nor hear her, again."

With a last despairing look down the empty, silent corridor, Gil turned in defeat, shepherding Hakon and Ismail around the corner and down the stairs. "Cousin!" Hakon cried at the bottom. Leaping down the last steps, he enfolded Floki in a bear hug. Floki wrapped his free arm around his foster-brother and rested his head on his shoulder.

"A whole year I think you dead," he whispered. He stepped back then and grinned. "And all the while you take your ease with Northern kings and Southern brothers. Behold, you grow fat on Frankish food!"

"Fat indeed," Hakon glowered. "Unlike you, I learn to work for my dinners."

Floki laughed and released him and embraced Ismail. "Ah, little Saracen, you grow tall. Soon you tower over Palamedes." He looked up then and his eyes fell on Gil, standing miserably alone on the stairs. "Warrior," he said, "Where is my lass?" Gil shook his head, unable to make the words come out. "Warrior?" Floki's smile faded.

"She's gone," Gil whispered. "The room's empty. All the rooms." Floki stared at him in shocked silence. Then, with icy eyes, he turned toward the chieftain's hall.

"Cousin!" Hakon barred his way. "We are four. And they are forty and more." Floki shoved him aside. But then a sudden, surprised cry sounded from below. Gil drew his sword and raced down the stairs. Floki pushed past him and they burst into the kitchen a stride apart, with Ismail and Hakon just behind. Gil's eyes swept the room. Nothing had changed. The only sound was from the ham, spitting and sparking in the flames. Then a shadow moved at the door and Floki lunged.

"Have mercy!" A slim young girl, clutching two pails, shrank back against the wall. Floki bounded across the fire pit, cornering her beside the door. "Have mercy!" she cried again, flinging her hands across her face. The pails clattered to the floor, spilling torrents of milk across the stone. *Poor Pussikins.*

"Leave her, Floki," Gil shouted. "She's just the dairy maid."

Floki threw his sword down at her feet. "I do not harm you! I do not harm you!" He reached for her with shaking hands. She looked up for an instant, and glimpsing his blood-stained tunic and hair, shrieked again and slid sobbing down the wall.

"Child, please. The girl. The girl in chains. Where is she?" He crouched down beside her and lifted her chin with his fingers. "Please, child. I do not harm you, whatever you say."

Slowly, she slid her hands from her eyes and looked straight into his. "But, sir, all know that. She is gone. My master has sold her to the king from Alba. She is on the road to Rome." Floki slipped to his knees beside her and bowed his head. Startled, she leaned forward, her fear vanquished by compassion. "Is she yours, sir?"

He looked up and met her earnest gaze and whispered, "She is mine."

"She is very beautiful," the girl said shyly.

"Yes." He got slowly to his feet. "And she has a beautiful heart. As do you. Come, child," he reached a hand down to help her up and gently guided her toward Ismail and Hakon, watching in silence. "They will only lock you in your dairy. You will be safe and soon someone will come to free you." His eyes followed her until the door closed behind her. Then he slumped against the wall, like a wounded man with no strength left in him.

"Warrior," he murmured. "We saw her."

"*What?*" Gil stared.

"The holy women on the cart. One so young and slight and lovely in her body?" Gil nodded, remembering then the veiled women in the Golden Knight's entourage. "She passed a sword's reach from my hand," Floki said. "And I let her go."

He stayed there, leaning against the wall, staring into a nothingness over their heads. Gil and Ismail exchanged baffled looks. "Cousin," Hakon said softly.

"Yes, Sea-Friend," Floki said, still without moving. "I know. We must go." He straightened then, bent down, and lifted his sword wearily. Sheathing it, he turned to Gil. "Come, Warrior. We are done here, now." Suddenly, muffled shouts arose from the distant hall and the sound of running feet. "And they are not done with us!" Floki snapped awake and threw Gil and Ismail ahead of him, out the door. "Run for the ships! Go!"

They fled down the staircase, mindless of the dizzying drops beside the mossy stones, or the shouts from watchers on the parapets. In full view, they joined the path to the sea-gate. "Raise sail!" Floki called, from a hundred feet above. Sailcloth billowed in the rising wind as the rakkes rode up the masts.

Steadying oars splashed on either side.

They ducked through a narrow defile hacked into the cliff above the sands. A flicker of movement on the rock face caught Gil's eye. He shouted a warning, but Floki was already turning when a small, wiry shape crashed onto his shoulders from above. Gil saw the flash of steel and dashed forward, sword in hand.

"Let be!" Floki waved Gil away. "It is only Royalty." Laughing ruefully, he unpeeled Eirik's arm from around his neck and removed the large knife pressed against his throat.

"It is Bjorn's knife," Eirik protested. "Bjorn taught me!" Bjorn smiled happily, where he stood beside Erling, knee-deep in the rising tide.

"I thank you, Bjorn," Floki said drily. He returned the knife and with Eirik still riding piggy-back, signaled Gil to take the helm.

"Cousin," he faced Hakon solemnly, "I bring you a gift from Eyolf Grimsson." He extended a gracious arm toward *Sea-Raven*, raising her white wings. But Hakon was staring at the boy clinging to Floki's back.

"Eirik?"

"Hakon!" Eirik crowed happily. He waved a free arm.

Hakon shook his head. "Cousin," he pointed disbelievingly at the blond boy. "How is he here?"

Eirik gave a small, shamed shrug. "Floki holds me hostage. But when I am grown, I am allowed to bring warships and kill him."

"We have an arrangement," Floki said, attempting to swing the boy down to the sand.

"Hostage?" Hakon shook his head again.

"Until his father can be trusted to return your crew. Then I take him home. Let go, Royalty, you throttle me." He unpeeled Eirik's skinny arm. Eirik replaced it with the other.

"Him!" Hakon pointed. "You take *him* hostage!"

"Had I sense, I take his sister. Far less trouble. Enough!" He wrenched Eirik free and set him, giggling, down. "Go to Grimhildr."

"You touch his sister," Hakon cried, "And I kill you."

"You what?"

"I warn you, Cousin," Hakon pointed a shaking finger at Floki's chest. "She is ... we are pledged."

"Pledged? Pledged to wed? You?" Floki's eyes lit with delight. "In chains you win a king's daughter? I had not thought you such a lover!"

"And I had not thought you such a fool." Hakon swung his big fist, connected with Floki's cheekbone, and sent him stumbling into Gil. Floki found his footing in an instant and his hand gripped his sword hilt a moment later.

"Erling! Give him your sword."

"No!" Erling shouted. He cast an eye toward the fortress where shouts of alarm sounded all around. But Hakon strode to his side and snatched the weapon from its sheath.

"You take his son! His son! How can he give me his daughter now?" He swung wildly and steel rang on steel as Floki parried with ease.

Stepping back, he looked down his shining blade at Hakon. "He would have given her at the point of my sword, Cousin, had you not struck me. Now she will be a widow before she is a bride."

"Good!" Hakon panted. "Good! For I will not live without her. I will fight you to Valholl and fight you there."

Erling looked up again at the fortress and raised his hands in the air. "There are men coming who will assist you both there. And us as well. Put aside your swords and move these ships!"

Floki waved him away. Hakon lunged and swung viciously and again the blades clashed. "And what of my lass who you should have protected?" Floki demanded.

"I was in chains!" Hakon swung again and again steel clashed on steel. Then suddenly there was an explosion of light and sound, and both blades flew through the air and thudded into the sand. Floki and Hakon rubbed bruised hands and stared at each other. Then their eyes slid from the fallen swords to the two throwing axes buried in the sand beside them. Slowly, they looked up to Grimhildr, standing hands on hips, in the sea.

Skirts trailing in the water, she stamped up onto the beach and pointed a calloused finger at Hakon. "Your cousin builds a ship for you. He raises an army for you. He sails to Norway and to Deer Bay and to Francia for you. And this is how you repay him?"

Abruptly, her pointing finger swung to Floki. "And you. Are you a boy, yet, Floki Magnusson, to meet every slight with steel? No. You are a man and an earl. Behave like one."

She scooped up her axes with one hand, flung a protesting Eirik over her shoulder with the other, and splashed back through the sea to *Silver Dragon*. Thrusting the boy aboard, she clambered up after, shoved Ulf aside and took the helm. "And now," she shouted, signaling the ready oarsmen, "We sail!"

"Yes!" Erling bolted for his own ship, sheathing his reclaimed sword. He swung himself aboard and grasped the steering oar. The sheets tightened, the oars dipped deep, and both ships began to move. Gil and Ismail turned warily to Floki, standing side by side with Hakon, his eyes fixed in amazement on Grimhildr.

"Cousin," Hakon ventured. "Does she jest?"

Floki shook his head. "She knows not how." He spun around to a shout from behind. A dozen armed men ran down the stone staircase, brandishing weapons and bellowing threats. "Nor do they." He grasped Hakon's arm and shoved him toward *Sea-Raven*. "To sea, cousin. We talk there."

Ismail grinned happily at Gil and they raced for their ship, side by side, arrows splatting around them into the sea. Ciarnan hauled Gil up and Ragi let go his oar to rescue Ismail. But Grimhildr held her steadfast course, even as Floki fought the flowing water beside the moving ship, heeling already before the wind. Dragging himself over the rail, he flopped exhausted on the deck. "Ulf!" he gasped, laughing, "Find another bride. I marry the Troll-Maiden, myself."

Grimhildr ignored him. She checked her taut sail, called the order to ship oars, and handed the tiller to Gil. Then, with a shake of her wet skirt, she strode off, adjusting her headdress against the wind. Floki bowed to her departing back and joined Gil at the helm. Leaning against the rail, he looked out beyond the dragon's tail to the rapidly diminishing shore.

Gil glanced behind. Mont Tombe was a dark shadow, the sea

between bright blue, splashed with white. "Are they following?" he said.

"No. Nor shall they. It takes time to launch a warship. They would struggle to catch us."

"Won't they try?" Gil said.

"For the sake of two slaves, I think not. He has done well enough, now, from the markets of Deer Bay."

Gil flinched from the look in Floki's eyes, but said quietly, "What about the guards?"

"He will pay their fathers in silver and be done. Still, sail on, Warrior. Take us beyond sight of land." He left Gil, and though he sent Ciarnan up the mast three times, no sails were seen. At last, with the sea calming and the sun dipping toward the horizon, he bade Gil to head up and signaled *Sea-Raven* alongside.

They lowered the sails and lashed the hulls together and as both crews gathered aboard *Silver Dragon*, Floki sent Gil for the wine and silver goblets. Hakon, solemn and stern as his father, Ragnvald, embraced his cousin as if the battle on the strand had never happened. Then he raised his cup in a gracious toast to his new ship.

"She will not be *Storm Serpent*," Floki said gently, "A first ship is a first love."

Hakon smiled and shook his head. "Our grandmother, Sigrid, would say, 'a man marries his second love.'"

Floki laughed. "Then I hope you love another, before the lady in Norway. For she sends you this." From within the wooden box that held the goblets, he retrieved a small, cloth-wrapped parcel. "With this," he said, handing it to Hakon, "She pledges herself true to her word, whatever fathers or cousins may do."

He looked up as Hakon carefully unwrapped the cloth. "King's Son!" he shouted. Eirik waved proudly from the top of the thirty-foot mast. "Should you fall from there, you swim alone. I have had enough of the sea, this day." Eirik waved again, swaying perilously. *"Down."* Floki pointed to the deck.

"Gudrun's ring!" Hakon cried. He held up a glint of gold. His dark face softened with wonder. "Look, Ismail," he beckoned the African boy, "Have you not seen it often, on her hand?" Ismail smiled happily.

Floki lowered his voice and said, "I had little choice, Sea-Friend. I did not trust him."

Hakon nodded. "He is not his daughter."

"This I saw. Nor indeed, his son." Floki looked up again as Eirik slid down the last few feet of the mast and trotted to join them.

"Did you see me, Hakon? I climb as fast as Ciarnan, now." He grinned and wormed in beside Floki. Floki sipped his wine.

"Cousin," he said. "To right this wrong, I do this: I return the boy to his father's house, alone, and without arms. What debt our blood owes his, I pay."

Eirik looked up at him with wide, scared eyes. "He will kill you," he said.

Floki nodded thoughtfully. "He may do that. And with no regard for our arrangement. Such is the discourtesy of life, Royalty. But look, perhaps you raid Bjorn, instead. He has a nice farm." Bjorn grinned, drew his sword, and stamped his feet cheerfully at the boy.

"I cannot accept this!" Hakon cried.

Floki leaned back on the bench and raised his eyes to the dimming sky. "Hakon, there is no pleasing you."

Hakon balled a fist in frustration. "Why can you not be like other men, cousin, and at least *try* to see grey hairs?" He glowered, swallowed his wine with a gulp, and then, as Floki smilingly refilled his cup, said, "So be it. I will accept. You may do this on the day I bring back to you the girl I lost."

Floki's smile broadened. "Now who disdains grey hairs? This is a dangerous course, Sea-Friend. And besides," he said seriously, "There may be others here who would see their hearths this winter."

But when he turned calmly to let those others speak, not a man protested. He looked from one to another of their sea-weathered faces and then smiled and raised his wine-cup to them. Then suddenly the ranks of men parted and a slim figure stepped forward.

"It is wrong," Janetta said. "Neither Hakon, nor you, should go. He has taken your lady because you have taken his. I will go to him, if he pledges to release her."

Gil gripped the edge of his sea-kist, shaking his head. He rose to argue, but Floki waved him back, beckoning Janetta closer. She stood before him, small and fearless, twisting her windswept hair into a black rope. "Ah, Wildcat," he said, "No finer creature walks this earth. But do you think he would honor such a pledge, even were I to permit it? Which I do not." Gil sank, trembling with relief, onto his bench. Floki took Janetta's hand and said, "Go to your young love. The world is not made for such as you."

Then he poured wine again and nodded casually to his cousin. "How many days say you?"

"Sixty."

"Ah, you are timid as always. In these ships? Forty. With time to spare."

"Forty days?" Gil said. "But we are just offshore and they are only a day ahead. We saw them!"

Floki laughed. "A day inland, with an army surrounding him." He shook his head. "We are swans, Warrior. Like the sea-king."

Gil stared. "You're just letting him go?"

Floki's laughter stilled. His eyes turned as icy as his Northern sea. "Let him go? I will never let him go. He may flee to the Seats of the High Ones and climb the World-Tree of Odin. Even there, I will hack him down."

He stood up, emptied his goblet of wine and turned to his crew. "Set the *Dragon* free and let the *Raven* fly." He watched grimly as the hulls were released and the sails again raised. Then, turning to Gil, he smiled. "Helmsman, set course for Rome."

About the Author

A lison Scott, the daughter of two writers, Alexander Leslie Scott, master of the western detective novel, and artist turned short story writer, Lily Kay Scott, was born in Manhattan. Her brother, Justin Scott, is a master of thrillers, mysteries, and sea stories, including the Isaac Bell Adventures. A Junior Year Abroad from her American university took her to Scotland, where she met her future husband, Clement Skelton--an actor, playwright, film cameraman, Battle of Britain Spitfire pilot, and monster hunter. She had her first baby while living on the shores of Loch Ness.

From an apprenticeship in Gothic romances, she went on to publish her first hardcover novel, A World Full of Secrets, writing as Alison Scott, while her husband became C.L. Skelton, writing successful family sagas. After she was widowed, she continued writing while raising their two sons, Professor Alasdair Skelton, geologist researching in climate change, and actor and gardener Justin Skelton.

As Alison Scott Skelton, she has published several works of contemporary and historical fiction in the US and Britain; among them, *Different Families, A Murderous Innocence, Saving Grace, An Older Woman,* and *Family Story.*

The Warriors of Tir nan Og, the six-book series that opens with *The Underwater Bridge,* is her first work for a young adult audience.

Curious about other Crossroad Press books?
Stop by our site:
https://www.crossroadpress.com
We offer quality writing
in digital, audio, and print formats.

www.ingramcontent.com/pod-product-compliance
Lightning Source LLC
Chambersburg PA
CBHW020251200626
46816CB00001BA/239